Rise of the Morningstar

By

A. J. Darkholme

MISTERO PUBLISHING
www.mistero.co

MISTERO PUBLISHING

First paperback edition 2014
Designed by J. Oelkers

Library and Archives Canada Cataloguing-in-Publication Data is available.
ISBN: 978-0-9918778-0-5

To Felicia C.:

Though we only knew each other a short time,
had you not been studying for the GRE vocabulary,
I'd never have written the poem that used all 500 words
that eventually became the story of Morningstar.

Thank you for the inspiration.

Acknowledgments

Where to even begin! I'm going to try to resist giving the Grammy Speech of Music-cueing Thanks, but so many people truly did bring this book to life.

My mom — for more reasons than I can count and express, thank you. So much of who I am today is there because of you: my empathy, my curiousity, and my analytical skepticism to name a few (all in a good way haha). You showed me that though we live in a world of multilayered hierarchies, everyone at every level is just a person — a person with a past, dreams, struggles, hopes, and fears... and because of that, no matter where you go, you're never surrounded by people better or less than you, above or below you, but rather simply by people. I think once a person realizes that, the complexities of life become simpler, and we become much more understanding of the world around us and the people in it. So thank you for that understanding and insight, mama; from it, I've accumulated an invaluable debt to you I can never repay, but you're always welcome to keep making that debt bigger, knowing what you teach me will always be put to good use.

My teachers over the years — so many of you taught me so many things in so many different ways that it's hard to single anyone out to express the gratitude you deserve. To each and every one of you, thank you for showing me how much personality can affect the words we speak, and from that, the influence we have on people. As well, it's inspiring how as a teacher, all you are given is the material — the cold, hard facts — to teach, but what makes a student learn faster, slower, retain more/less, love/ hate a subject... that is all you. That it's your creativity and passion that can make all material — the useful, the boring, the interesting, and the seemingly irrelevant — both fun and interesting. I was extremely lucky to have a perfect balance of teachers; a luck that perhaps wasn't merely luck at all, but a reason for something more... a higher purpose to be revealed in due time. A higher purpose your lessons will always be a part of, both the intentional and unintentional alike.

My friends and family — thank you for all your support and for pushing me to finish the book. Those who know me best know that when I'm impassioned by something, I tend to put my everything into it; sometimes 14-hours straight without taking a break. When it came to writing a book — a project that required a lot of introverted time away from you with little-to-no contact — you gave me that space, and patiently waited for hang outs that were sometimes months apart. Some of you did my dishes while I wrote, or brought me groceries, or made cupcakes... how cool is that? But most of all, despite large chunks of time passing where it seemed like I dropped off the map, you were always there, making the next time we spoke feel like no time had passed at all. A confirmation of relationships worth keeping and cherishing.

To all my fundraising backers — thank you so much for your generousity and support. For an indie author/poet just starting out, there are not always a lot of funds under the mattress to help dream-funding, let alone enough to propel me straight into them like a rocket. Truly, you all came through for me when I needed you most and I'll never forget it. I hope this book is everything you believed in when you contributed your first dollar. It was your support that helped pave the path from "unknown student of the universe" to "recognized and established author".

The Darkholme Elite (My fans) — to everyone who joined my fan pages and continue to share my new poems and writings, so much of this would not be possible without you. You are the candle power on the path I walk upon: each "Like", "Share", "Follow", "Retweet", and every other avenue for spreading the Darkholmian Verse is just a small light and may not seem like much at first, but collectively, your light illuminates my existence and allows the rest of the world to see and learn from every word written. Thank you for believing in my work, and enhancing my pride in each piece as it spreads to more and more eyes, hearts, and minds that would otherwise not be touched without you.

And last, but not least: my beta readers, reviewers, and bloggers — your reviews, suggestions, critiques, and mass-amounts of time spent immersed in the book have helped fine tune this novel to make it the glistening version everyone else is reading today. Thank you for seeing Rise of the Morningstar as a book worth reviewing — worth the time we always wish we had more of in the day.

So on that note, as the "wrap-it-up" music gets louder and some muscle-bound thugs head my way to escort me off the stage, I just want to say one last HUGE thank you to everyone who bought Rise of the Morningstar. Your hard-earned dollars are an essential investment into my writing career — a career that I don't pursue as a means to gaining possessions, or fame, or anything of that sort, but rather so I can spend an increasingly large chunk of my life pursuing my passion. And — if I am so blessed that I can make a living out of it, then you can be sure that the dollars you invest in me will be reinvested in others who deserve to be believed in as well. Young, old, rich, poor, well-educated, or otherwise, where there is passion and creativity backed by skill, there you will find my respect. No matter who you are — no matter what your situation is — keep living the dream and you'll end up where you're meant to be much sooner than you think, and much happier than you thought possible...

Sincerely,

A. J. Darkholme

A Note from the Author

Hey Darkholme fans! The book you're about to read is more than just a story. Why, you ask? Well, many books out there are clearly divided into two categories: fiction and non-fiction. The first is filled with page-turners weaving literary tapestries of love, blood, betrayal, magic, revenge, and double-crossings (to name a few) that keep you riveted while you learn things that are of little-to-no value outside your imagination. On the other hand, the latter bricklays knowledge and concepts into a fortified wall that is tried, tested, and true with facts and theories believed to be of such value, that entire university degrees are based upon them.

I come to blur that line.

When I set out to write, I wanted to find a way to make learning fun, and to make fun useful. That's when I started taking random concepts from all walks of life, and sticking them together, so that when you read, you think you're only reading a story, but somewhere in your memory, there lurks and lingers something more. Things like:

- ► how to overcome many common fears;
- ► basic combat techniques;
- ► names of notable people, places or things
  (e.g. the biblical "Twelve Tribes" of Israel);
- ► cultural stories (e.g. Aesop fables);
- ► key psychological experiments that teach us about human nature
  (i.e. The Milgram Experiment / Obedience to Authority and
  our Human Capacity for Cruelty);
- ► self-awareness by exposing fallacies and biases we have; and
- ► interpersonal awareness/psychosocial manipulations to avoid
  becoming a victim in times of vulnerability.

All of the these things can be found in Rise of the Morningstar. The selection of knowledge is random... but then again, so is the collective knowledge we all carry around with us daily. I hope you enjoy this approach, loving both the story, and the knowledge you gain from it, no matter how random it may be... after all, you never know when the useless fact of today will inspire the great idea of tomorrow.

Rise of the Morningstar

"The most common way people give up their power is by thinking they don't have any."

Alice Walker,
Activist

Contents

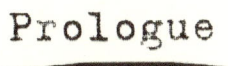

Prologue

(Morningstar:) Sometimes we aren't sure what our purpose is — what we're here to do. We go through most of our lives not knowing what we want, nor believing we can get it, until one day we wake up no longer leading our lives, but being led by them. By others. Like self-made, masochistic marionettes, we drive razor-sharp hooks deep into our emotions, our fears, our insecurities, and then hand over the strings to anyone who fits the profile of a crazed bull in a china shop. I used to be like that. The strings had been in the hands of others for so long that I forgot that keeping them in there was a *choice* — that at any time, I was able to pull the damn things out if I wanted to taste the freedom from the darkness my eroding soul craved. But those first steps are always the hardest to take, and the darkness is not so easily escaped when there's no light to show you the way...

At first, the path to freedom was as invisible as the wind to me; I couldn't see it, but I knew one was there. Some people seek advice in their time of need, but trust was not a luxury to me. Maybe it was my pride, or confidence, or the shattered fragments of a past too trusting. Either way, it doesn't matter, because I know life is what you make it and legacy is how you leave it. Stop trying to be perfect, stop waiting for perfection to find you, and start making your environment a product of you instead of the other way around.

If you want to break out of your cycle of disappointment, listen closely; wait too long, and the only disappointment will be you. There are two kinds of people in this world: the puppets and the puppeteers. Puppets complain about what needs to change, but puppeteers refuse to accept what needs to change until it has. You're smarter than you think with more potential than you know. Realize this, and your rebirth will rival that of a phoenix rising from the ashes. Only then will you know as *I* know that true captivity lies not in the hands of those above you, nor around you, but within you. This is my story. Learn from it. Wrestle with it. Use it to break the chains that you've come to know all-too-well, and soon the world — and everything in it — will be yours.

CHAPTER ONE

The Dark King

To those who search for change, the abnormal, and the trite, you need no longer be abased by the powers that be, for the redemption you seek is but a choice away. Cast down the cloak of your past; free yourself from its woollen fibres of pain and circumstance, for where *I* will lead you, it is much too heavy to go on carrying any longer. Whatever you have been dragged through, know that mediocrity isn't a marinade for the soul; it doesn't *become* you the longer you sink into the quicksand of what you believe you can't change. The sooner you believe that — the sooner you heed my words — the sooner mediocrity will abandon its throne and be banished from your mind, and your life, forever.

I warn you: the darkened tale you're about to hear does not end in "happily ever after" — the words so many hold dear. I shan't abstain from the truth, but know that what lies within contaminates the innocent mind and advocates for the acidulous taste of a grand revolution not everyone is ready for. But they are of no matter; The Unprepared are not your concern. The time for talk is over and the spotlight has fallen to you. This is your one chance to take what's yours — to do what you're here to do.

My journey began just a few years ago in a kingdom that no one ever explicitly named. Why? Because there is power in a name, and as long as no utterance came to define it, the idea of it could never be reduced to mere sounds and symbols. It was more than that. Different. An anomaly created among the other kingdoms to be a safe haven for The Uncorrupted... at least, that's what the historical texts told us. None of us really knew for *sure* how different or "uncorrupted" we were, because none of us had ever been allowed outside the kingdom walls before.

I'd lived in that kingdom my whole life, going about my days as a typical citizen since the day I was born. Everywhere I looked, everyone was the same; their personalities, only slight deviations from the generic human template of blank, lifeless, habitual existence — living each day like they'd already lived it before. They worked day-in and day-out, living to survive, but not much more than that. Of course, they had social lives to try and help make their existence marginally more interesting, but even *those* only seemed to be fuelled by their repetitive dissatisfactions with the world around them. Over time, such things defined what life meant to them. What life *was* to them. What was once innocent conversation meant to connect with others, turned into a paradigm shift that led them to squander their potential for true happiness away like the generations before them. They learned to accept things as they were, rife with dissatisfaction, and soon after that, began to simply... exist. But it's not enough to merely exist. I know that now. And it was all because of the only one who stood out to be any different: our "Dark King", Lucaius — the immortal one, himself. His existence intrigued me, because I knew his existence was one the history books would never forget...

He was at the peak of his power, then and always, commanding a supernatural supremacy so great, that no army could ever hope to stand against him. Lucaius was untouchable — the kind that mere mortals couldn't threaten, nor object to, even if they had all the forces in the world at their disposal. But curiously enough, we had never seen him use that power to attack the other kingdoms — only to shape and maintain his own. Manipulating our world exactly as he saw fit.

And so it was.

An ocean of darkness surrounded our kingdom as far as the eye could see. A light fog hazed the air while impenetrable storm clouds painted thick the heavy skies above. We had never seen the sun; what history books called the "day" had always been kept hidden from us, bound in eternal submission to the night for reasons none of us knew. The land I called home did not feel like home at all, but a prison self-exiled from all illumination and warmth. As I grew up, I was taught to simply *accept* the darkness that never abated below those sombre skies, as if we were powerless to do anything about it. *Forced* to watch the shadows crawl along the ground at all hours of the day as they made their way back to the Dark One, no more free of the cycle than we were. Under that kind of suppression, you'd think the others would take notice and rise up, but no one ever did. We saw ourselves as individuals without power or influence. Even when we were given words of hope, they held no more power than Fear's little finger,

but what's more... we loved Lucaius for it. It was as if Stockholm Syndrome was in the air and no one thought to hold their breath. The more powerful he became, the more we glorified him, for under his rule, we knew our kingdom was protected from our enemies. But not all enemies we need protection from attack us from outside our walls; sometimes the most dangerous ones already dwell within...

Despite my status as a pawn, I did not see myself as one, unlike the others. Lucaius' power stirred within my thoughts like a breeze of insight tossing about the problematic clouds of possibility. Clouds that continued to clutter my mind with every waking moment. He had total awareness and control over his destiny — a control any of us could only wish we had over our own. His existence was not one of merely existing, but one of inspiration, if only everyone would've opened their eyes to it and convinced themselves to be worthy and capable of having it as well. Perhaps the skies over that kingdom were a lot like the eyes of our potential that reside deep within us: closing off a world of light simply because it's too bright after having lived in, and accepted, the darkness for so long. I would look up to the sky sometimes and wonder what the sun looked like on the other side; how lonely and pained it would feel if its memories could fall back to the lark's serenades of sunrises past. But renouncing thoughts like that became a part of everyday life; a practice so common, so accepted, that we not only dwelled in darkness, but became it as well — a "Dark Kingdom" for a dark people whose light had gone out long ago.

But let not the darkness mislead you, for though its connotations are often mistaken for evil, Lucaius was anything but. A king like that would have been *easy* to hate, and summoning forces against him, even easier. No... he was too kind — too *important* to our survival as a whole. Whether such kindness was really in his nature or an elaborate illusion, I couldn't be sure; the true reasons behind his actions were always unclear at best. Though no one knew him personally — though very few ever *saw* him — we somehow felt comfortable under his rule, for Lucaius was just. Alleviating us of our troubles. Providing a blanket of security no kingdom's army could ever breach. We were safe from our enemies as long as he reigned over us, and our well-being seemed to mean a great deal to him. But, like a confident and wise father to his needy children, he did not simply give us everything we wanted, nor grant us wealth beyond belief like he easily could have. Instead, it looked as if the Dark King felt that a satisfying life was not dependent on such things, but upon the value of 'love' and 'purpose':

empty shells of sentiment that did little to keep the clothes on our backs and food in our bellies.

It didn't make sense to me at first; why would a king provide for his people in this way, but shun the light and banish them to only darkness? Or want love and happiness for them, yet become a faceless recluse with no warm relationship with those he provides for? For all I knew, we were experiments of a dark, cruel mind, each given life only long enough to believe we controlled our own destiny until it would be snatched away in one superhuman, genocidal sweep. I'm not one to trust easily, but I'm wise enough to know that we all have an inborn hunger for knowledge and truth, and if we don't uncover the truth we seek in a reasonable amount of time, our minds construct their *own* truths, and we act upon those delusions instead. However, such acts-of-hunger have cost many their hands, tongues, heads, or reputations, because decisions were made based on what was *assumed* instead of what actually *was*.

I valued my head and reputation, so I sought the truth — first and foremost — to see what more I could uncover. Embracing mythical tales and genuine history alike, I unearthed all the books and stories I could that I believed would help me trace the Dark King's immortality back through the ages — no easy task, since books and historical documents were considered to be works of deception, stigmatized by the sightless realists who held positions of influence behind our walls. What I *did* find, however, suggested that the Dark King was not always a child of Eternity, but rather an average man from long, long ago:

"...A time when the majestic Rocs, with sanctified splendour, blessed the sky with their wings and the world with their magnificent shadows. It was said that nothing was more awe-inspiring than seeing the giant, magical birds flying high above the golden sun-lit clouds as they watched over all the kingdoms of the world from high up in their heavenly aeries, ascending to heights where even the gods couldn't touch them. They reigned over all with a reverence far from contested, and under their care, the world flourished and became a true paradise — one where peace resonated among its inhabitants in perfect harmony.

That harmony was born anew each morning: the Great Ones would awaken, rise with the sun at the crack of dawn, and spread their wings to take in its life-giving energy; then, when

their magical feathers could hold no more of its warmth and radiance, the Rocs would fly down to the mortal world below, releasing the sun's resplendence over every living creature until all had felt exactly as they had felt. Providing for our ancestors like no other could.

That utopia, however, only lasted for so long.

It is said that while gliding through the updrafts high above the land one day, a Roc noticed smoke coming from the ground. Curious, it flew in to investigate the oddity, only to find that three beams of the sun had been bent — deviously refocused upon the ground so as to trap a family of three in raging flames so they could not escape. The Roc plunged to the fields below as quickly as it could to save them. It grabbed the child, but the boy had already suffered incredible burns to every inch of his body. By the time it rescued the boy, however, his parents had fallen upon a fate much less fortunate. The almighty bird looked back to the boy who was struggling to breathe, knowing that if it left the human baby, it would die with no one to take care of it. And so, with great internal conflict, the Roc brought him back to the aeries where no human had ever been before.

That boy was named Lucaius.

Orphaned under Fate's care, the magical birds decided to raise him as their own in the Sky Kingdom, each giving up a fraction of their power to be transferred to an amulet they created for the boy. Ritual after ritual was performed, activating the amulet's supernatural healing, until soon after, no trace of the boy's burns remained. The amulet had reconstructed the young one's body, but in doing so, unintentionally infused him with their magic and immortality. It was a consequence unheard of in any of the realms, least of all, Earth.

Seeing that blasphemy, the eternal Spirit of Light, Lux, did not respond so kindly. He visited the Rocs of the Earthly Realm and arbitrated that giving mortals such power was irreverent of all those whose bloodlines had always transcended time itself — but the Rocs defended the boy as their own, and embraced compassion over tradition.

Lux was infuriated.

As the days went on, the Spirit of Light became more adversarial and mischievous, even masquerading as the sun and adding chaos to an otherwise peaceful realm. It wasn't long before his malevolence grew beyond the bounds of Fate's protection, however, and once Lux was convinced that his trickery and schemes were not going to sway the Rocs from their decision, he conceived a vengeful plan of rebalance to make things right again.

One fateful morning, as the Rocs assembled where the dusk waits for the dawn, ready to rise with the sun as they had every morning before, a swirling inferno suddenly lashed out from the Beaming Star of Deceit, striking them with blazing bullwhips that deafened them, choked them out mercilessly, and tore apart every last one until the sky fell motionless and every feather had trickled from the heavens to the earth below. Without the Rocs to bring the sun's nurturing energy to the world each morning, the world lost its ability to live abundantly, and all soon fell to dust, withering away as Lux continued to scorch the earth in a fiery apocalypse. The destruction was intended to kill not only the boy, but everyone else as well... a fiery death to make right again in his eyes what the Rocs had blemished beyond redemption.

Believing he had succeeded, Lux eventually left the Earthly Realm and returned to the space that exists between our world and the next. In the years following, though much of the Earth was barely able to sustain itself, the Dark One, Lucaius, emerged from the ashes and used his power to help rebuild the land — a place where the people could live in peace once more. For a time, he did his best to provide the world with light, as the Rocs used to for humanity, and for him, but the more he travelled the lands sharing its warmth, the more destruction he saw. The more he was reminded of all he had lost. All that had been taken from him. All the atrocities the Spirit of Light had caused.

Then one day, something within him turned. His sadness

decayed into anger, and his memories to bitterness. In a windstorm of rage, he rejected any and all forms of light, plunged the world into darkness, sealed up the skies, and pledged himself to an ever-present night. He did everything he could to tame his vengeance from that day on, vowing to never lose those he cared about ever again. His magic intensified as the days grew darker, consuming him with an obsession so absolutely that he left no part of the world untouched. New, lush forests were erected that could survive without light. In the fields, he created beasts so exceptional, that they produced offspring faster than the people could eat, so no one was ever hungry. The beasts were made gentle, and understanding, freely giving of themselves without attacking those who came to them for food. Lucaius provided for his people, as if they were his own, and though the darkness consumed his heart, the others could not help but be drawn to him. He became a father to the fatherless; the figurehead of a new era for all humanity. At least for what humanity could have been; in time, though his benevolence was enough to provide for all who came to him equally, and in good measure, the people lost sight of how good he had made life for them. It wasn't long before they demanded he establish a hierarchy among them, so that the strong may have certain privileges that the weak should not — that the intelligent deserved recognition for their intelligence, and should not be treated the same as the others.

Lucaius despised what their hearts had become in spite of all he had given them, and banished the disgraceful people from his sight. Humanity had become greedy. In just a short amount of time, their greed had evolved faster than the self-sustaining paradise he had made for them, giving birth to pride, as well as envy, sloth, gluttony, wrath, and lust. Not all were consumed by these deadly sins, however; those who were not, became his chosen ones — people rescued who showed promise and moral restraint. Those ones, he took away to safety, but those he left behind were not so lucky, for the hierarchy they craved so much, would soon come at a very high price...

They began to form their own kingdoms, grouping with one

another according to the sins that enslaved them most, but it wasn't long before they found themselves at odds with one another. War broke out among the lands, consuming Lucaius' paradise with complete and utter sacrilege. He had seen all-too-clearly what men had become despite having everything they needed, but rather than standing idly by, he took action. In a last-ditch effort to protect and preserve those who were not consumed by their inner evils, he took it upon himself to construct his own kingdom. And what a magnificent kingdom it was..."

That kingdom is where my story begins.

Ever since the day the Dark King supposedly took it upon himself to protect the good of humanity, he kept himself removed from it. Some nights I would climb trees so that I could look up into his throne room window when the moonlight illuminated it just enough to catch a glimpse inside. And every time I did, there he was: slouched upon his throne, alone in an otherwise empty castle, staring deep into what I assumed was the amulet the Rocs had crafted for him. It was rumoured that the amulet had stopped working the day the last of the almighty Rocs had died, but perhaps it still served a new function unbeknownst to us all. For all I knew, it was a clock counting down to our elimination. And yet, the way he looked at it — the way he gazed into it longingly — perhaps it really *was* no more than a psychological painkiller for the emotional abyss he felt inside — a way for his memories to comfort him as the Rocs did once upon a time.

If those tales were true, it seemed unlikely that the Dark King would want to bring harm to his people, but I didn't know that for sure. I hadn't yet been given a reason to believe he wanted to harm us, but I saw no point in waiting around for that time to come. By then, it could have been too late. To go on living an insignificant life in the shadow of someone who could enslave all humanity or kill them with the subtlest of gestures, was not a shadow I wanted to live in willingly. Something had to be done. Balance had to be restored. In a world of over-confident, unstable people, *no one* should wield that much power over another — *especially* over *me*. He may have been a rose in the eyes of the townsfolk, but even roses have thorns — it's only a matter of time before you get pricked and the red petals no longer remind you of its beauty, but of the pain and the blood it drew so unapologetically from your skin. As a lowly carpenter with no specialized training, I didn't know *how* to fight, let alone *slay* an immortal so I could restore a proper balance of power to the world. Plots like those only exist in myths and fairy tales. I was certainly no hero; I had nothing to offer the world except my sense of duty and determination — but little did I know, that's all I would need...

CHAPTER TWO

Life As I Knew It

The people of my kingdom felt the same as I did before my Day of Awakening: mostly hopeless, waiting for happiness to be delivered by a redemption that just never seemed to come. That feeling followed us around every day like a lost and lonely stray, craving to know what it was like to be full while it went on starving, forced to survive on the scraps of yesterday. But no matter who you are — no matter how broken and hopeless a person becomes — there calls a voice from within that can never be silenced. The voice of Hope: the great prisoner of the soul's inner void. A satisfied soul never hears her voice, but for the rest of us, we never hear her silence. She calls to us, day and night, offering light when there is only darkness; promising a better tomorrow when we wish today was our last. Her words and whispers are some of the most alluring you will ever hear — so alluring that you may even *believe* her — but a person can only run on the fuel of another's promises for so long before realizing that *promises* are all their words will ever be. Sooner or later you stop believing, and turn to any vices and distractions that suspend you in a time where you're sure things won't get better, but take twisted comfort in feeling things can't get any worse. Even in our darkest times, however, she calls… her soft voice echoing within us, refusing to go away until we do something. Because she knows we always can…

It was that voice that began to lead so many of my kingdom's people to religion. Whether what was spoken there was forged in truth or was simply a man-made vice to silence the inner curiosities of the unknown was irrelevant; as imperfect as it seemed to me, there was no denying the long-term satisfaction and relief it brought those who attended the sermons regularly. In time, word spread, until nearly everyone sought out the comforts of religion — more and more each day until the church's capacity had filled to the brim. The growing interest brought Father Gregory to the doors of my shop one day — the day that Fate entrusted me with a fragment of my own destiny to craft as I saw fit.

"Good day, Morningstar. And how is my favourite carpenter today?"

"I'm alright thanks, Reverend."

"Just alright? You used to have more zeal in your words! I remember you running through the streets as a boy with the other children, sticks in hand, knocking stones about until your mother came to get you for supper. She practically had to *carry* you off, you were so full of life! What a dear lady she was. You know, you should come back to the church sometime. The people miss you; your father most of all."

"My father misses me like he misses my mother's sickness. Probably thinks of me as one too," I half-heartedly commented while continuing on with my work.

"Come now, you know that's not true," he tried to comfort me. "It was a difficult time for him, and people are not always themselves in troubling times."

"After smithing at his side for years after my mother's death, trust me, he hasn't changed. Not for the better anyway."

The Reverend pursed his lips in a neutral, self-silencing acceptance of my feelings.

"Nonetheless, it would be good to see you there again. The church is growing quickly, you know — that's actually what brings me here today, as a matter of fact. There are so many new members that we no longer have enough seating for them. Would you be able to make me eight more pews by Sunday? I know it is a tall order and you are under a lot of stress, but it would be so lovely if you could have them done in time for me."

"I can do it for you, Reverend. It'll be a tight deadline, but I'm sure Emeline will understand if I put in a few extra hours."

"Ah, Emeline. You are truly blessed to have her, Morningstar. She's an angel undisguised."

"That she is. I appreciate your words, Reverend. I'll have those eight pews ready for you by Sunday, then. Mind if I swing by the church to grab the dimensions after I close up shop tonight?"

"That would be delightful. Thank you, Morningstar. May the Lord bless you and keep you."

And with that, he placed his hand on my shoulder, looked deep into my eyes with a compassionate smile, and was on his way.

"You two hear that?" I shouted to my two teenage assistants. "Eight pews by Sunday. Whatever you're working on, put it on hold, and give the Reverend's order priority."

They continued chasing each other around the shop, forcing me to whistle loudly to get their attention.

"Did you two hear what I said?!"

"Yeah; eight pews for Sunday," they confirmed, carrying on with their antics and bringing little comfort to me.

I can't tell you how irritating it can be to work with those who don't pull their weight. I began that carpentry shop because I couldn't work in the same room as my father anymore — a man never smiling, rarely satisfied — but there were many days I looked at my own workers and wasn't sure which was the lesser of the two evils. Regardless of how I felt, I always pressed on because things needed to be done and I wasn't about to compromise my ethics for the squanderers of life. After all, you never know who may stop in one day and sweep you away, off to better things more deserving and worthy of your time and abilities. And if that redemption never comes? Well, that's part of why I started my own business. The way I saw it, it was better to struggle owning your own business, than struggle working at something that will never be your own — doing a job where you can be easily replaced. I mean, sure, we are all unique, but what we *do* is all the same. And once you let the world camouflage your sense of self, you lose sight of who you are... lose sight of who you are — what you can be — and history will lose sight of you as well.

As Sunday drew nearer, I ended up having to make six of the eight pews myself while my assistants struggled with their incompetence, asking my help to complete the other two. It certainly was not due to the level of difficulty either, but it's surprising how laziness and a lack of confidence can convince the mind that the skills we have aren't sufficient enough to do the task at hand alone — that the help we need lies in the hands of others, rather than ourselves. In truth, we are all capable of mastering a whole arsenal of abilities, if only we would be ready and willing to embrace the lessons that failure can teach us instead of fearing them. After all, the path to excellence is paved with the acceptance of our mistakes through efforts well-tried,

not brick-laid by the help of others like *those* nincompoops believed. In any case, it was what it was, and more importantly, all eight were ready to go and placed in the church before Sunday Mass the day-of. When I finished installing the last one, I figured since I was already there, I might as well stay for that one service. Just for old times' sake.

I saw a lot of faces I hadn't seen for a long time. It was good to catch up at first, but the more people I saw, the more tired I grew of answering the same questions over and over. I tried to endure it for the sake of socialization, but when they started giving their condolences for my mother and asking about my father, I decided to start making my way toward the door with haste. I never really understood that mentality in people: why go for the obvious, basic line of questioning, without wondering how many other people have asked the exact same thing? It wouldn't be so bad if the conversations were emotionally neutral and of interest to both parties, but it seems the most compassionate ones are also the least aware of how inconsiderate their considerateness can actually be sometimes. The way I see it, emotional conversations are best brought up by the one most affected by its content anyway.

As my hand took hold of the door handle to leave, I felt a strong hand on my elbow accompanied by a thick breeze that carried the subtle smell of alcohol from the breath of the man behind me. It was Moorden, the owner of Lucky's Tavern.

"Aye Morningstar, it's good ta see ya here fer once! Come ta repent about those trees o' God's ya been cutting down, have ya? Listen, I have a wine shipment coming that we have ta keep rather quiet; I need ya ta build a wine rack fer its bottles. Five-hundred-bottle capacity, needed in two days. Sorry fer tha short notice, lad, but it was a deal I couldn't say 'no' ta. Tha only catch is tha bottles are un-crated, loose, due ta... unique circumstances," he whispered closely. "I've paid fer all 'em up front already, but if I don't have anywhere ta stack 'em, me investment's down tha drain, aye? Think ya can help?"

"A 500-bottle rack in two days..."

"An' three bar stools."

"I'll see what I can do," I said with a sigh, contemplating how under-the-wire it would be.

"Thanks, brother. An' come by me tavern soon; ya look like ya could use a drink or two — on tha house," he smacked me on the shoulder.

When he walked away, I felt a wave of stress come over me. I should've been happy to find more business where I wasn't expecting it, but I had been putting in long hours for months just trying to keep up, cutting my deadlines extremely close and wearing myself so thin that even blessings started to feel like curses. But my reputation was all I had, so I did what I could, fighting off Exhaustion's disabling grip with every passing moment. You'd think that with all that business, I'd be fairly wealthy too, but none of us were really. Not sure why either; no matter how hard we worked, we always barely made ends meet. And I was one of the ones unfortunate enough to believe that compassion out-values selfishness, so turning someone away who needed free service more than I needed their money was morally impossible for me.

That night, I went home to Emeline with a heavy-mind. But before I allowed myself to walk through the door, I stood outside for a moment, collecting my thoughts. I never liked to bring stress or sadness home to her. She was always so sweet and kind to everyone, and the *last* thing I wanted was to take away one of the last remaining genuine smiles in the kingdom.

"Hey handsome," she greeted me with charming radiance as her arms wrapped tightly around me and her lips fell upon mine softly, yet passionately.

"Hey beautiful," I smiled, picking her up and spinning her in a tight embrace. "How was your day?"

"It was nice: cleaned up the house a little, went to the market to grab some food for tonight, sat and read in the forest a while, and then came home to see your handsome face."

"Well thank you, darling. Just out of curiousity... how did you pay for our food at the market? I thought our savings jar was almost empty."

"It was... I mean, it still is. But you know Benedict; any extra meat-shavings he has after cutting his steaks, he always saves for us, bless his heart. And the tomatoes and lettuce... I just had to cut the brown parts off from what I could find in the throw-away bins."

I sat down in my chair and buried my face in my hands. She deserved better than that. No matter how hard I tried to keep them

in, the tears just flowed as I was reminded I couldn't give my wife the life she truly deserved. I had failed as a husband and a provider and there was nothing I could do about it.

She tilted her head with understanding towards me and sat on my knee, letting her arm drape around my shoulders.

"I know, honey-bee," she tried to reassure me, taking a deep breath, but exhaling a sigh of her own. "I know."

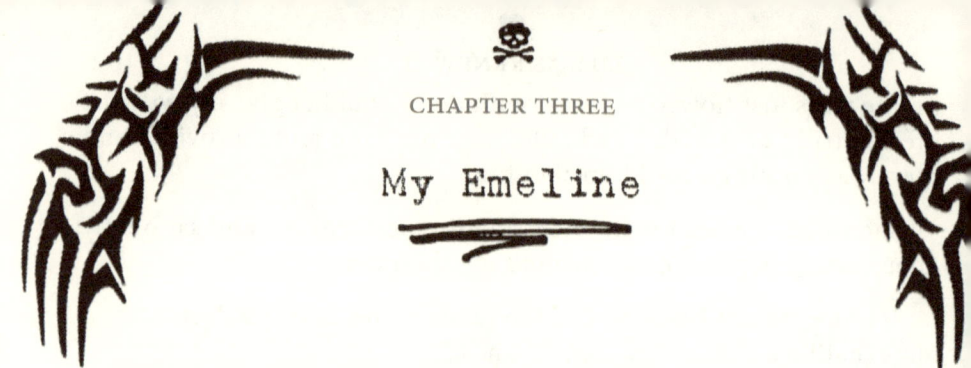

CHAPTER THREE

My Emeline

I arrived at the shop earlier than usual the next morning, hoping to get a head-start on Moorden's order. By the time my assistants got there, I had finished cutting some of the boards needed for the wine rack, as well as a few pieces that served as the template for the stools. Deeply wishing their screwball antics wouldn't get in the way of the fast-approaching deadline, I assigned them the stools, knowing it was a manageable task they could complete on schedule with a little focus. With the stools delegated, I had more time to work on the wine rack alone — a project of intricate, detailed measuring that I didn't trust the others with. My father always said: if you want a job done right, you have to do it yourself. A trusting, warm man, that father of mine.

I worked extra hard that day, but when my neighbour came bursting into the shop, consumed by fearful panic, the significance of any project I could possibly have had on the go dropped to zero.

"What is it, Hermia?!"

"It's Emeline — I was just walking out my door to see Henry when I saw her crawling there on your doorstep, holding her stomach like she was in excruciating pain. Oh, Morningstar, she had tears in her eyes and her face was—"

I stood up immediately and grabbed my coat. "Where is she now?"

"She is with the apothecary — I'm sorry! I didn't know what to do!"

"Boys," I said with rushed tone to my assistants on my way out the door, "this wine rack and those stools must be done and delivered to Moorden at the Tavern by early tomorrow morning. You hear? Tomorrow *morning*! Make sure it's done; he has a lot riding on it."

They nodded as they watched me run out the door with break-neck speed.

When I got to Emeline, she was barely moving and her breathing

was laboured. I kissed her head and held her hand tight. My heart was beating so hard, I thought it was going to burst from my chest.

"What happened to her?" I asked the apothecary.

"I'm not sure; it's not like anything I've seen. She's not responding to my medicines, or special elixirs, or tonics of any sort. It's like her body is being possessed by a pain phantom that slipped into her body and is slowly sucking the life out of her."

"A 'pain phantom'?! What kind of healer *are* you?! Surely there's something you can do! Keep trying different medicines and combinat—"

"Darling," she interrupted with the gentle squeeze of my hand, "I just want you to know: I love you. No matter what happens, whether I exist in flesh or spirit, I will be with you, at your side always."

"No, you can't speak like that. Emeline? Emeline! Stay with me!"

The spark in her eyes was quickly fading with the warmth of her hands. The colour in her face even more so.

"I wish you could play me," she asked with struggling breath, "one last song while my heart still beats in time with yours..."

"Come home with me tonight and I'll play for you, I promise. Just come back home, okay? Promise me," I tried to convince her with hopeful denial.

She always loved when I played music for her, serenading her into the early hours of the morning with the lyre my uncle made me when I was born. I never knew my uncle, so having that piece of him gave the instrument sentimental value for me. But once its strings played for Emeline... all sentiment belonged to her. My life. My love. My everything.

As those thoughts passed through my mind, I felt her hand release its grip upon mine, and watched as her eyes began to close slowly. When her last breath gave out, her body went lifeless, losing its smile for the first time since I laid eyes on her.

"Morningstar... I'm so sorry," the apothecary mumbled.

I didn't reply.

Walking home that afternoon, I dragged my coat along the dusty

road behind me, completely unaware of my surroundings. She was my reason for living, for working, for putting aside my differences with my father, because she cared enough to teach me that life is too short not to make yourself happy.

And then she was gone. Just like that.

Before that day, I never could have imagined life without her if I tried, but in that instant I was forced to live it. Every good thing inside of me was there because of her keeping it alive. Giving it warmth. Giving it breath. Her understanding eyes. Her loving touch. Her kind, inspiring words. Everything she was, and stood for, protected the good inside me from being overcome by guilt, or anger, or bitterness. She was *my* protector when I was supposed to be hers. But I failed. It was too late. And no matter how hard I tried, I could never bring her back.

CHAPTER FOUR

A Call to Action

"Just go away," I thought to myself as I woke the next morning to a relentless rapping on my door.

They knocked harder.

"Please…just go," I mumbled inaudibly through my pillow. Robbed of all life and reason to live, the last thing I wanted to do that day was talk to people. I had only ever felt that lost and broken one other time in my life: the morning after my mother's funeral. That time when your eyes are open, but you feel no more alive than the one you just lost. That struggle when every breath you take is heavy and unwelcome, forcing you to breathe it like it's a privilege to go on living when all you want is to die. You're alone. Left behind. Forced to befriend the hollowness, if only to feel some form of companionship…

The knock at the door escalated to a frustrated pounding, complemented by a familiar voice.

"Open up! I know yer in there! Answer yer door if ya have anything ta say fer yerself!"

I valued his friendship in that moment like I'd value a sack full of rubies to hold onto when trying to swim. All that emptiness, the weight of all those emotions, and *still* the gods did not grant me the peace and solitude I needed that day without the one person rapping at my door who didn't know what it meant when no one answered.

"QUIT COWERING AN' FACE ME LIKE A MAN!"

I made my way to the door never feeling so heavy in my life. It took all my willpower — every bit of effort — to drag myself out of bed and put one foot in front of the other. I didn't want to be alive, let alone open my door to company, but when I saw Moorden frantically looking in all the windows, trying to see if someone was home, I knew I probably should. "If everyone put others before themselves, then no one would need to look after themselves," right? Another of Emeline's sayings she taught me to live by. When I opened the door, he was livid.

"Where tha *Hell* was me wine rack?! I thought ya said ya'd have it done by this mornin'! I lost the entire shipment I'd paid fer, cuz I couldn't stock it, an' some bloody scavengers went an' carried 'em off when I was lining tha bottles up out back! Where tha Hell were ya?!"

I let out a deep sigh of tranquilized, near-suicidal frustration. It was a foolish notion to think I could've counted on those guys.

"I saw yer boys in me Tavern last night too! I asked 'em how tha rack was coming along, and they said that YEUUU were almost done while they drank tha night away. An' now what?! I have NO wine rack, NO stools, an' maybe ten percent o' tha bloody bottles I paid fer! Da ya know how far behind that puts me?"

I just shook my head as I stared at the ground and tuned out of his tirade. There were no words I could summon to even reply in that emotional apocalypse of a moment. I was in a barely-functional coma of disbelief with little hope of coming back from it for quite some time.

"Won't even speak a word ta me either? Yer pathetic. Ya better believe me patrons an' tha townsfolk be hearing about this — yer father especially!"

Later that night I shuffled back to my shop, a place that once gave me hope and peace. Carpentry was my ticket to freedom; I could make my own way and didn't need anyone else to tell me what I could or couldn't do — or how good I was or wasn't. My shop was the symbol of my independence; everything I created there for people was the result of my hard work and time and dedication — and wanted people to come to know me by those virtues and speak about me by such things. Besides Emeline, the shop was the one other thing that made me happy, despite all the stress associated with it. And now that Moorden, one of the most influential people in the kingdom, was relying on me and I let him down, there were no words to mend the brokenness I felt or the failure that left me feeling anchored in place. Lighting the small torch above my workbench, I just sat on my stool and hung my head.

I heard the door that I left open creak, and looked over after a delayed moment to see my father standing there. I looked at him with lifeless eyes, but soon turned them back down to the floor in front of me.

"Moorden tells me you promised him something you couldn't deliver," he egged.

I didn't reply.

"I bet that's the half-assed wine rack he was talking about over there," he said as he walked over to it, knocking on it with his knuckles and tapping it with his boot. "Even if you *had* finished it, its craftsmanship is inferior anyway. Certainly not worth the ranting he was wasting his breath on telling me about it. He was probably better off not having this thing anyway; you couldn't pay *me* to use it, that's for sur—"

"Is there a reason you're here, dad?" I asked angrily trying to keep in my annoyance, but not succeeding very well.

"Damn right there is — if you're gonna do something, at least try and be good at it. You're giving a service to these people and they deserve better. And looking at you now, I'd say Emeline does too."

I kicked my stool back and ran at him with both hands, slamming him against the wall with tears in my eyes. I didn't care if it was the alcohol on his breath channelling his inner demon of insensitivity at that moment; I'd be damned if I was going to let him get away with mentioning her name with such disrespect and wanton ignorance. I didn't even feel the need to waste my words telling him of her death, either. I just wanted him gone. Out of there. Immediately.

"Get out, dad. Now. Before I do something I'm going to regret." I knew I wouldn't be able to restrain myself much longer.

He looked at me with distant, uncompromising eyes wanting to taunt me further, but something inside him must have convinced him not to. Maybe the lack of restraint in my eyes, or the way my hands shook, ready to burst out in a rage that very well might have ended in his bloody dismemberment.

"Threatening your father now?" he slurred as he walked toward the door with a slight stumble. "You've sure become something else. Glad your mother's not around to see you like this."

I swear if he hadn't been walking out that door as he said it, he'd have left in a pine box of my own late-night creation.

Quivering with anger in my veins, I planted myself back down on a nearby bench and rested my head on the table in front of it. That was not the life I wanted for myself. There was no requiem for a dream that had drifted on. I hadn't even fallen short of a dream either; I just never moved in the first place. Instead, I was held there, anchored in place by the death of loved ones with a savings jar that would only be useful if dust out-valued gold one day.

Death and unfortunate circumstances... the heavy chains adorning my body, locked tight, robbing me of all hope and forcing me to use all my energy just to find the willpower to take a single step under their immense weight. Their weight alone made it convincingly easy to surrender, but I couldn't allow that, because the day that I'd have let myself submit was the day I accepted my fate as a prisoner of circumstance. And I was no prisoner. Those chains needed to come off somehow. I knew by looking at the people around me that the best hope chained individuals have is to not look to the unchained ones in comparison, nor waste time trying to find the proper keys to free themselves of whatever bound them in place. I'd seen entire lives wasted searching for the right keys. To Hell with keys! Grab the blowtorch of change and cut through your chains like butter. Do this at the expense of the torch's pain, and the burns you endure today will be the reminders of the freedom you'll have tomorrow — the scars left behind, meant to serve as ever-present reminders and motivators toward a life seized instead of forced upon you until you learn to accept it.

I knew I hadn't been dealt the best cards in the deck. Hell, I wasn't much different than the other townsfolk in most ways. But one day, after many months spent wallowing in my own guilt, I realized something: there *was* a difference between me and the others. I had awareness and ambition: two key aspects that began to set me apart; the first changed the way I saw the world, and the second would soon shape how the world saw me...

I became *aware* the Dark King had too much power. My *ambition* was to take it from him. But not for the reasons you'd think; not for greed, nor domination of others, but simply because I had lost everything, and in my time of self-reflection came to realize that when you have nothing left, then you have nothing more to lose. A freedom forged from the ashes of all I had lost. And what better way to use that freedom than to free others from all of their potential oppressions as

well? I needed to save them — free them — even if they knew not of their imprisonment.

Sure, everyone *knew* the Dark King had power, but no one had ever done anything about it, because they went about their lives the same way I did before that day, round and round the mundane wheel of life, accepting the lives they were given. But I was the exception; I achieved awareness when I realized things don't have to be the way they are — that they can be changed if you aren't happy with them. Even though I had no idea how to change them, my eyes were opened, and I would never let them close again.

The thing about awareness and ambition is they are merely unmarked points plotted on the map of your life's journey with no details between them to guide you — and it is up to you to fill them in however you see fit. There are many paths in-between; many options and roads to take. The one you choose is justified by you, and you alone. It is said that the most fulfilling adventures happen when you start your journey without knowing where you're going, because only then are you free to experience the unexpected detours you're meant to take. If that was true, I must've been in for the most fulfilling journey of my life, because I had no idea where to even *begin*, let alone the best path to take...

CHAPTER FIVE

A Dark Suitress

Afew months later, the kingdom gates opened for the first time. It surprised us all at first to see droves of some of the most beautiful women the lands had ever known come pouring in. We had never even had *visitors* before, let alone ones as attractive as they were. The reasons for their arrival perplexed most of the kingdom, but having felt the brokenness of losing Emeline, and seeing the Dark King slouched on his throne some nights, it was pretty clear to me why they were summoned. I suppose even the most benevolent of souls can only give so much before they require something back as well; no matter how powerful the person, the hollowing internal plague of loneliness spares no heart nor mind left alone for too long. There, deep inside all of us, is a hollowness waiting to be filled. A cavern that can be filled to no satisfaction unless it is filled with the love and companionship it was hollowed out for. I knew that loneliness all-too-well. The numbing emptiness. It was a feeling I had never welcomed before... until that moment. Until that feeling consumed the Dark King, instead of me. Being lonely meant he had a weakness, and it was that weakness that stood to be the key to our redemption.

Every day for seven days, the eclectic selection of women from the neighbouring kingdoms were brought before him — some funny, others shy — but each and every one seemed to be turned away just as quickly as they came. Surely the other kings were participating because they saw that as their opportunity for self-preservation from the omnipotent Dark King, but as the seventh day concluded and no one was able to produce a worthy bride, Lucaius must have grown tired of its tedious monotony, because the kingdom gates were sealed once again.

In the following nights, I searched the kingdom for someone who might be able to captivate the Dark King's heart, and yet work with me to help relieve him of his power. I thought about the kind of queen he would be attracted to, but no other immortal wizard-suitresses existed that I was aware of, and beauty alone did not seem to influence

his heart as it would for many mortal men. The women who left the kingdom were a testament to that. But no matter how difficult it was to find a woman to lure him from his defenses, I remained steadfast — after all, the Dark One had no other apparent weaknesses to exploit, so I had to make do with the little I had.

And then one day I saw her, breathtaking as can be, through Fate's looking glass; the longer I looked through its hopeful lens, however, the more my plans crumbled before my eyes through that convex pane of torturous inevitability. As the noon-day hours rolled around, a thick, unnatural, grey fog filled the streets in the marketplace, ushering in the Dark King himself, unannounced, with the woman on his arm. He had found his Dark Queen somehow after all, and tied the knot without any of us being the wiser. She carried herself with such poise that it was hard not to worship the ground she walked upon; she was as beautiful as a moonbeam suspended in the midnight air. Though many saw her for her beauty, however, the Dark King was clearly and genuinely in love with her for much more. He had not only found the means to cure his love-stasis, but to live a life of true happiness. And from his happiness flowed the Dark One's benevolence to us all — a benevolence that increased exponentially with his new-found love.

While the others lapped it up, I wasn't going to let myself be fooled. Golden shackles are still shackles, and I wasn't ready to accept anything less than what I knew I deserved, nor was I ready to do anything less than what I needed to do. I had to find another way — and it was only a matter of months before I would be presented with my next opportunity. It was as if Fate was egging me on, baiting me while I swam about his playground frantically looking for something — anything — to feed the hunger that was growing, and consuming me every waking moment.

We all saw the Dark King's love growing for his new bride, but in time, concern grew among the townsfolk as they noticed the Dark Queen's displays of affection diminishing. As her love waned, however, the Dark King's continued to soar, unable to see past his heart's admiration of her. Many of us wanted to tell him, but something like that is not easily told to the one who keeps you alive — antagonizing a king of such power could quickly lead to our demise and take from us all the benefits we were reaping as a result of the love he felt for her.

And so, seeing that our lives and recent affluence were very much threatened by the queen's eclipsing heart, I motioned to the others that a meeting had to be set to develop a plan of action. Father Gregory agreed and offered the basement of the church, where we all assembled in secret that night. With their acceptance, a new opportunity had presented itself to me; perhaps Fate wasn't disappointed after all, but was merely testing me by turning my self-confidence into a cruel game of Ping-Pong, only to reveal no one was keeping score anyway.

Congregated underground, Father Gregory was adamant that we let him lead the coterie so he could refocus any arbitrary thoughts, recalibrating any divergent perspectives back in tune with what he referred to as the 'divine purpose'. No one opposed his request either, considering his position among us.

"...My children, it is not our place to interfere. That's God's place. Our place is to lift it up to him in prayer and trust that his work is being done whether we see it or not."

"That's easy for you to say! You've always lived on the tithes we give tax-free! For the rest of us, we had to work our hands to the bone just to keep the water running and the torches lit!" one man said.

"It's true; and ever since the Dark One found himself a woman, Lucaius has been much better to us. I can close up shop early and help my wife with supper, enjoy a little repose, and know that everything will be taken care of," added another.

"Oh shaddap with all this 'Me! Me!' stuff. Are any of our marriages truly happy?" Moorden said, followed by a brief whisper of apology to his wife beside him. "Tha king's no different than tha ordinary man; jus' let tha man live tha life he's chosen, an' we'll live ours. We don't need ta interfere."

"He's anything but your ordinary man! When he was alone, we all got by — barely — but we did. And there was certainty and stability in that. Now he has a woman, and look at all the good things he's given us. And if he can give us all this when he's happy, imagine what he could take away if she breaks his heart or leaves. God help us all when *that* day falls upon us," Benedict mentioned.

There was a near-unanimous murmur accepting Benedict's words.

"Okay, so we have to do something, then, but what can we do? If we interfere before anything significant happens, surely we'll bring our own doomsday upon ourselves if he catches us," another spoke up.

The night grew long and little progress was made, so I excused myself, took a torch from the wall, and began to wander the church deep in my own thoughts. I finally sat down in the second-row pew, leaning on the back of the first, and hung my head. "Why does life have to be so heavily influenced by others? Are our lives so fragile and fleeting that one woman can be the difference between us having everything or nothing?" I wondered to myself. With contemplative silence, I looked up at the way the moonlight shattered through prisms of stained-glass, and felt my mind ease as my thoughts fell to the woman I'd loved. Though every waking moment together was spent in the darkness, no Sun was necessary, because her radiance was more than I could ever ask for. We were not very wealthy by any standards — no jewels, no land of our own — yet somehow having her next to me back then brought a feeling of deep satisfaction like I had all those things and more. She made me feel like I truly had everything, even when I didn't. But there was one thing I did have: musical dexterity. The key to Emeline's heart. I used it all throughout the beginnings of our relationship like it was the only currency her heart valued — the currency by which I could buy her love and make it endure. Thinking back to the day she died, she never spoke words of regret; she simply smiled and wished she could hear one more song before she went to wait for me in the afterlife.

As the dry ash fell from the torch in my hand to the floor below, it all became clear to me; the power to give everything or take it all away was the inborn power contained in every confident woman's grasp — the only way for a man to regain that power, is to keep her happy enough that she forgets she even has it.

With new-found fervour, I joined the others downstairs, recounting memory after memory of my musical past, and how much my lyre had helped me win Emeline's heart through moonlit serenades. The more we discussed, the more sparks of possibility began to catch fire in the others' eyes as well. Before night's end, we had developed what sounded like a fail-proof strategy that was sure to renew the Dark Queen's love for Lucaius, if all went according to plan. It *had* to. Her affection was the key to seeing my plans through, and I was not going to let such a viable opportunity escape me in case it was my last.

With everyone's approval, I boldly took the task on, ready to rekindle the fires of the queen's heart with the gentlest of melodies, softening her defenses until she was putty in my hands.

CHAPTER SIX

The Visitor

I walked home that night feeling something I hadn't felt in a long time: purpose. Even the grey cobblestones below my feet seemed to reflect new life as they carried a new bounce to them that seemed to lead me home quicker than ever before. When I opened the door, I went straight to the chest that contained my lyre in the back room, but time had not treated it well; the strings had all frayed, the wood was cracked, and it smelled of a dusty, archaic mustiness that would barely seduce a goat, let alone the Dark Queen. Teeming with failure, I dropped to my knees as a tear strolled down my face onto the dry, rusty fragments of hope I held dejectedly in my hands.

And then an eerie feeling crawled up my spine, straightening all the tiny hairs with it.

Like something was there, watching me, waiting for me to make the first move. Chills tingled down my spine, but not due to any cool breeze I had ever felt before; that one was warm, like flames had broken out behind me as electrifying as the adrenaline that courses through your veins when Fate presents you with an augury of impending doom. I leaned back and looked to the door cautiously. It stared back — a silhouette similar to that of a man at times, yet vastly different the longer I stared. At times, it resembled a bipedal beast, then a glowing apparition, but mostly like a cosmic being undergoing centuries of evolution in a matter of transitory moments. The golden cloak it wore seemed to keep its true form and features concealed, but exuded an august candescence all of its own from underneath its cavities where imprisoned murmurs seemed to escape only long enough to let out soft, haunting chants. And when it spoke! Its words flowed like poetry, as if everything it said was specially-crafted to perfection, uniquely for me. But not even the smoothest of poetry could help calm the quivering fear that rattled my bones from deep within. I knew I should have been able to understand what it was saying, but the truth is, my heart was pumping so hard that the beat was all I could hear.

As if sensing that its words were being wasted on me, it decided to be more expressive in ways my muddled mind could better understand. Motioning toward the lyre of dismal demeanor in my hands, it chanted sounds that no human I knew could possibly make... and slave to his commands, the instrument burst into flames and instantly turned to ash in my hands. As I looked down at them, the ashes began to glow and started reforming with warmth so hot and shining so bright, I had no choice but to step back and shield my eyes so I wouldn't go blind. When the dazzling light dimmed, there, where the ashes of my lyre used to lie, was the most beautifully-crafted thing I had ever seen. In awe, I reached out and took hold of it. It was warm to the touch and mounted with jewels of light that pulsed softly with every breath I took; fading with every exhale and intensifying their glow the deeper I breathed in. Robbed of all words, I stood speechless and looked at the visitor in the doorway.

"Banality shall be banished from thee, and the heart of your queen shall you smite; the power you hold is yours to control, the partition 'tween darkness and light."

As it spoke, its presence seemed to amplify its mystery and awe. I knew I had nothing to repay him with, nor any way to amortize such a debt. As grateful as I was, I wasn't the wealthiest man in the kingdom — financially or emotionally. My debts were numerous, and my services were already owing to others, totalling more years than I probably had left to give. But as little as I had, the visitor's kindness deserved more than just accepting the fact I had nothing to offer, so I asked anyway.

It thought for a moment and turned back around with persuasive intent.

"For the man who desires to give something back, perhaps a trade can be made; pledge your soul to the light, my son, and your debts shall ever be paid."

To exchange mere words for such an extravagant gift made my choice easy. It was a trade I could make — perhaps the *only* trade I could make. Lost in the moment, I decided to take the visitor's pledge. Kneeling as a knight would before a king, I recited his oath, repeating after him with head hung low until every word had been spoken. As I looked up, however, a sudden wave of uneasiness fell over me as the shape-shifting visitor evolved into a sphere of shimmering light and the cloak slipped from its bipedal form to the dust below. It hung there, suspended in air, pulsing and swirling before me as if to let me look upon the soul I'd just given up one last time before it was taken from me forever. Realizing what I'd done, I picked myself up off the ground and ran towards it, but it was gone faster than I could blink. I was too late.

My heart sunk in my chest with the weight of what I had done. I looked up to the sky, praying nothing would become of it, and fell to my knees. The emotional rope-burn of my collusion with the Spirit of Light was leaving burns in me that made every kind of movement sting. But there was little I could do to take my words back. They had been spoken, and all that remained of our transaction was me and my new jewelled maker-of-melodies. I took it in hand and headed down the street hiding its light as best as I could. If the Dark King somehow had caught me in the possession of light, there was no telling how much pain would be inflicted upon me... but I was certain it would be enough to make death seem like a welcomed relief.

I made my way down the dark, winding path of the Forest of Dreamlock next, wandering its path for hours. The rustling trees were so dense that whatever awaited me behind them remained just as uncertain as the path that lay ahead. When my feet grew tired, I followed the soft, comforting sound of flowing water to a brook where I found a rock to sit upon and think. That's when I first realized the lyre was far more than just beauty and light; it had a sense of *awareness* — a way of interacting with the world around it, completely independent of its holder's hands. As I sat there, the jewels on its surface began to pulse and realign along its surface, projecting a light beam that glistened off a tiny metallic object stuck in the brook's sludgy bed. I climbed down and looked closer, reaching in, and splashed it through the water enough to clean the muck off. With the mud gone, I held it up to the moonlight, examining it more intently; it was a small, golden ring in the design of wings wrapped tight, with veins of obsidian glass running through it. Unsure who it belonged to, I tossed it in my pocket and sat down upon the rock; as eye-catching as the ring was, nothing was more worthy of attention than the lyre I held in my hands. I don't know how long I was there, but I must've looked down at my lavish gift and away again about a thousand times before thinking that maybe keeping it wasn't so bad. After all, to throw away such beauty would have been a waste...

Propping up the lyre between some rocks for a moment, it was as if moonbeams went out of their way to gently kiss it before refracting off its every mounted jewel into a million colourful directions. I was drawn to its alluring power with every facet of my being. Once I took it in my hands and felt the warm, velvety metallic strings caress the calloused tips of my fingers, any fear of whatever consequences I would face — whatever punishments the Dark King could possibly unleash upon me — seemed to fade to nothingness. It accentuated past talents in ways I never thought possible, and bestowed upon me new musical abilities I never had before. All that was once forgotten, I recalled with ease, and harmonies I never even knew suddenly coursed through my body, through my fingertips, and through the strings. It commanded the sound of beauty itself; to hear even a single note would be to instantly succumb to its auditory romance. Even inexperienced hands, or played by the stubs of fingerless thieves, I was sure its magic could not be tainted in the least. It was as if the strings themselves were chords of the heart and that of desire, independent of the abilities of all who held it in their grasp. The longer I played by that brook, the more my doubts were replaced by renewed devotion to the cause until there was no turning back. I was ready to risk it all. It's easy to risk everything when you have nothing, but all the more when those risks renew your sense of meaning and purpose, and breathe life back into passions long deceased...

CHAPTER SEVEN

For Their Own Good

The following night, the cabal met again in the church basement. There was a much larger turn out that time — evidence of how safe and secure even the most secret of spoken words are not. Especially among The Unhappy.

"Did you find it?" Hermia asked about the lyre I mentioned at the last meeting.

"The lyre I was looking for, I found in a dusty, old chest, yes. And, it was still in almost as good a shape as the day I placed it in there," I embellished.

It might've been a lie, but it was a lie that they needed to hear, because it gave them exactly the kind of reinforcement they were looking for. The kind that would enable me to walk to the path that Destiny had laid before me.

"That's excellent! Why don't you play us a tune or two?" Father Gregory asked.

"I didn't bring it along tonight, but I assure you it sounds... magical."

They nodded, genuinely pleased with the only half of the double-entendre they understood.

"So what's tha plan, then?" Moorden asked with a distrustful undertone, still upset by our falling out.

"My lyre will be the catalyst to revert the black heart of the queen back to a love-filled state. It worked on Emeline, and its charm still reverberates through its strings today. No matter the person, no matter the emotion, there will always be a melody capable of enhancing a feeling or taking it away completely. Give me some time to compose a song that perfectly suits the occasion, and the queen's love will reanimate her heart — just you wait and see."

Surely, I could not show them the lyre, but I knew the visitor's gift

was the key to the future we wanted.

"If it's as moving and powerful as you say, see if it can restore to me the faith I should have in my son," my father's inner devil spoke.

"I want you all to know that I do not take this task upon myself lightly. But rest assured, I am very cautious of all that is to come, and will treat your trust and hopes in me with the same care."

"Is that tha same trust an' care ya put into me wine rack that wasn't made on time? The one I trusted ya with that ya took such *care* ta complete?" Moorden castigated, hitting below the belt.

I ignored them both and continued: "I did not bring the lyre with me tonight for a variety of reasons, one of which being that if I am going to use it, I must keep it locked in its chest so no harm can come to it. It will be essential in our time of need, and I would hate to bring it out in public, lest harm come to it before I can complete the task you've all entrusted me with."

Keeping the lyre's secret light hidden was essential to preserving the honour of the townsfolk as well as saving my own skin, for the Dark King did not look kindly upon possession of light. It was the burden I was destined to carry on behalf of all my brothers and sisters of the kingdom. Having most of them condone that which they did not quite know the specifics of only made it that much easier to deceptively help them. Except for my father. Having raised me, he knew when I was hiding something as if by some fatherly intuition. I could tell he didn't know what, but judging by his eyes he was definitely skeptical. And when he whispered to Moorden, I feared his curiousity may have started to get the best of him.

"Is there anything we can do to help you with this burden of responsibility?" Father Gregory asked.

"I just need time to compose, so if any of you are willing to help me cover my carpentry duties, it would be greatly appreciated."

"I'm sure those who have placed orders with you can delay their urgency," Father Gregory smiled.

"Why not? It's not like we can expect the work to be completed by any kind of deadline anyway," Moorden threw in one last time.

"I guess that's all then. I'll see you all back here at the next meeting," Father Gregory concluded.

CHAPTER EIGHT

Goddess of the Night

I made my way home after that, closing up all the windows and locking the door the moment I arrived, hoping to keep any light from escaping. Pulling up a chair to the secure chest I kept it in, I uncovered its radiance; like a lover's voice heard after a time too long, the sound of its strings rekindled my new purpose for being alive. Still warm to the touch, my strums flowed like water as before, but something was slightly different... slightly off. I was no connoisseur of magical lyres, but every chord I played felt like it was forming a deep, symbiotic bond between my desires and its own — as if we began to need one another. It unnerved me, but I wasn't one to shy away from what I knew needed to be done; as long as that lyre validated my plans, the life we as townsfolk had come to know would be preserved, and the Dark King's favour would remain ever-overflowing.

Just then, there was a knock at the door. It was Moorden, wanting me to join him at Lucky's Tavern for a drink to discuss some things. Having seen my father whispering to him before, and going by his blatant efforts to be a disturber earlier, I was a little skeptical, but how do you turn down an old friend willing to patch things over with you when you've known each other your whole lives?

I got him to wait at the door, while I wrapped the lyre in cloth and hid it back inside the chest. On the way to Lucky's he told me he'd got to thinking, and felt like he'd overreacted with the whole wine rack thing, saying he wanted to sincerely apologize. Not being as cold-hearted as my father, I took hold of the metaphorical olive branch he extended to me, and apologized for letting him down as well. After a couple of beers and some good reminiscing, I decided it was time to head home, so I grabbed my coat and said my goodbyes. Being the drunken gentleman he was, Moorden offered to walk me to the door, draping his arm around me as we walked — although I was pretty sure he did that more for the sake of keeping his balance, and not so much to show brotherly love.

No sooner had I opened the door, when out of nowhere, a lifeless body fell from the sky and hit the ground right in front of us with a bone-chilling thud, spraying blood in all directions upon impact.

It was my father.

Moorden and I both ran into the street trying to see where he fell from; there were no buildings tall enough in the Dark Kingdom for an accident like that to happen, but when we looked high up into the sky and saw a glowing ball of light evaporate, I knew exactly who — or what — had done it... just not why.

"What tha Hell was that?!" Moorden asked in a panic. "My god; it's yer father! He's dead! Yer father's dead!"

I think by the way Moorden was pacing back and forth frantically, grabbing his hair, my father's death drew more emotion from him than me.

When you looked at his body, you knew there was no hope for saving him. Nowhere to rush him; no elixirs to help restore his vital signs; just a cold, dark pool of slowly expanding blood forcing you to simply accept what was, or give into the shock of it. I took a knee beside his body and slipped the bulky ring off his finger and onto mine as a token of remembrance. Lord knows I could do without any remembrance of him, but he was still my father.

His funeral was at the church the next day, but I decided not to go. Not inside anyway; watching through the windows was quite enough for me. At least out there and out of plain sight, I was spared from everyone's words of concern, regret, and flimsy advice — words of countercomfort for "how to get by" that just made me want to join the Black Parade as well. There was enough of that kind of thing when my mother died. I hated feeling like the charity case of the congregation: the emotional dumpster where everyone could bring their feelings to drop off because their usual receptacles were full. Even still, I couldn't bring myself to tell them that their words were of no help to me, because then *my* words would be seen as inconsiderate. Besides, after Emeline's death, I had no tears left to cry — and if I did, they certainly would not have been wasted on *him*.

First my mother, then Emeline, then my father. It seemed like everyone that ever meant anything to me at some point in my life was being taken as if I'd offended or challenged the Reaper himself.

But after Emeline's death a few months ago, it was easier to come to terms with the loss of my father. Maybe you just get used to it when you realize there are some things you just can't change. But the way I see it, there are two kinds of death: the kind you can't change, like my family's; and the kind you can, like when you're still alive but just *think* things can't be changed — the death of one's purpose.

That night, I awoke suddenly from a deep sleep and opened my eyes just a crack to see what time of night it was, but when my eyes focused, I was startled out of my sheets and fell to the floor. The visitor had returned, standing there quietly in the corner of my room, watching me sleep.

"Forgive my intrusion despite our collusion, but I thought it best you know; while the Taverneer duped, your father here snooped, landing him six feet below."

"You... killed my father?" I questioned, unsure where I was going with it.

With the wave of his hand, I felt his magic apply a sudden weight to my eyes that pulled me into a near-instantaneous deep sleep. I tried to fight whatever he'd cast upon me briefly, but it was no use.

I awoke sometime later to find myself still on the floor. Climbing back into bed, I closed my eyes, trying to fall back asleep, but for the life of me, I couldn't if I tried. Even with the visitor nowhere in sight. So I walked over to the chest, opened it up, and took the lyre in hand, hoping its sound could serve as the tourniquet needed to slow my sense of purpose from draining out of me in corpse-abandoning proportions.

As my credulous fingers were manipulated by the lyre's influence, it began to twist in my hands, and the bedroom door flew open as if to give me a direct view of my front window. When I turned to look, my eyes fell upon a woman with hair black as night, dressed in a tight, black cloak passing by the window on the street outside so quickly that if you blinked, you'd never have known she was there. I didn't know of anyone in the kingdom that could move with such speed so quietly, so I decided to follow her to find out who that goddess of the night was. Wrapping the lyre in a thick cloth so as to conceal its light, I opened the door and looked down the lane. She moved swiftly, glancing behind her mysteriously as she navigated the convoluted back roads with expertise. I tried to tail her as closely as possible, but her

speed and skill could not be emulated. Though it pains me to admit that I was no match for her prowess with shadow, where my mortal abilities fell short, the lyre's abilities abounded with the redemption of my own. The bag I held in my hand began to glow so brightly that you could almost see through it, as if to grab my attention and tell me something of importance, so I found a dark corner and peered inside. The gems were realigning again upon its surface, varying their intensities so the brightest pointed the way to the elusive woman. Rabbit's feet don't bring that kind of luck.

The gems led me back into the Forest of Dreamlock, where I had been the night before. The paths should have been familiar, considering how recently I was there, but they were not. Instead, the further I pursued, the more my mindscape became a battleground, defaced by some smoky, caustic form of unnatural delirium that rose from the dirt of the pathway as the woman-of-shadow tried to cover her trail. Each step I took, the path grew darker and cloudier, like a contumacious fog that refuses to move from your path. At some points, it was so thick that if you were to lose your footing, the smoke would cradle your fall to the ground. I had no idea such an element even *existed*, let alone was accessible to those who used blades as easily as writers use words. Nonetheless, my lungs were quickly being infiltrated by her well-placed afflictions of precaution, and with every breath, the chance of another breath following it was even more doubtful than the last. Carrying the burden of my light-headedness didn't get any easier along the winding of the path either, but between my unwavering perseverance and the gems of light guiding my way, her poisons had less of a stranglehold on my senses.

I approached slowly. As she removed the hood of her cloak, the reflection of the moon off the water illuminated her face. My heart nearly stopped — she was no ordinary woman, but the Dark Queen herself. The queen was well-aware of my presence too, though she did little to acknowledge me, the way I expected a typical queen should have. She was focused, looking for something in the water, but I was wary to speak the words it would take to understand exactly *what*, in the not-so-off chance that she would plant her blade deep in my chest just to silence me. The water wasn't that deep, however, so I figured whatever she was looking for, she'd find it soon enough. I stood by, observing her with silent intrigue, but soon my heart's curiousity got the best of me. She was the most beautiful woman I'd ever seen. I had respected her beauty from a distance before, but up close, she was truly dazzling. To look upon her from a distance didn't do her justice.

"What exactly are you looking for, Your Highness?" I asked, finally summoning the courage.

"Highness? Please. I'm not yours to bow to," she replied.

"I'm not quite sure what you mean by that; you *are* my queen..."

"I'm *a* queen, but I am ruler over nothing and am no one's but my own. If you call me anything, the name's Illyana. But I'd prefer if you didn't and just kept your mouth shut and stayed out of my way."

Her blunt responses didn't sway my fascination with her. The sound of her voice carried melodies the same way the magical chords of light did, so who would I be to scorn a goddess, even in self-defense?

My heart was a broken compass, unsure of where it was coming from or where it was going. Fawning over the Dark Queen threw my heart into a maelstrom of emotion — it was only about eight months ago that my darling Emeline died, and I knew I was still irrevocably in love with her; on the other hand, the fate of the townsfolk's lives rested on my ability to teach the queen to love the Dark King again. Looking down to the bag in my hands containing the lyre, I knew I had the power to do just that. I thought upon it for only a short moment until the clouds of uncertainty parted from my mind; my moral duty gave my compass all the magnetism it needed: the tantalizing presence before me was my target to *avoid* a revolution, not start one.

As my heart stayed true to Emeline and my mind to the townsfolk, I removed the bag, wrapped my fingers around one arm of the lyre, and sat upon a large boulder. Without hesitation, I pressed the other side to my chest, until the strings began to silently pulse, supernaturally pulling my ready fingers toward it — controlling *me* that time instead of the other way around. I was unnerved by its ability to transcend its own chassis and puppeteer me with the same mastery it had over its sound waves, but there was nothing I could do. I was entirely at its will. Upon hearing its rhythms, the Dark Queen's focus turned to distraction at first, and then her distraction to overwhelming allurement as the melodies streamed with perfect effectiveness. Her ignobility faded quickly as her thoughts and feelings were weaved into patterns of cloying affection so strong that if it was to develop naturally, it would've taken a lifetime of unblemished, dedicated love to shape it to the same perfection. She was entranced, and she was looking at me. The lyre wasn't just stirring up heartfelt emotions inside her to prepare her heart for the Dark King... it was enamouring her with *me*! Not that that would've been *too* bad a thing...

She walked over with a spark in her eye, and gently caressed the side of my face with her hand. Her eyes brewed a lingering, contemplative, nervous stare in an otherwise completely confident demeanour, which could only suggest one thing was about to happen...

CHAPTER NINE

Cloak and Dagger

Leaning in to kiss my lips, I was at the mercy of her advances brought on by the lyre that wouldn't let me turn my head or stop playing. But just then, as her lips touched mine, the music stopped to let us hear the sound of a dry twig snapping in the woods. We both turned to find Benedict, the town butcher, glaring at us.

"Dammit Morningstar!" he shouted after the twig's snap freed him from observing in secret. "How *dare* you betray us like this! Moorden told me you were up to no good and I wouldn't believe him. I said, 'Not Morningstar; you may have your differences, but he's a good boy — he's always been a good boy.' Far be it from me to question your motives for taking on your role to handle the queen, but here you are proving me wrong and leaving me to look like a fool. Well, let me tell you son, I won't be defending you any longer. You brought this upon yourself! The others will be definitely hearing of this!"

He started to make a run for it.

I panicked, but in one continuous motion, the Dark Queen instinctively grabbed three poison needles from her wrist brace and sent them piercing through the air toward Benedict in a deadly triangle aimed for his spine and kidneys. He took three steps before hunching over and collapsing into the water. His face had darkened to a shade of red so intense that it looked like his head would burst from the blood if even the gentlest breeze was to touch it. And what's more: when he collapsed and his final breath escaped his body, whatever was in her poison made him suddenly swell up to the point where his skin began to tear.

I stood there in shock.

I turned to the Dark Queen and just stared at her with disbelief. I couldn't understand how detached she seemed about what had just happened. With neutral expression, she looked at me silently and held the cold stare for a moment before turning away to walk upstream of his body.

"No need to requite the favour."

"The *favour*?!"

"Trust me, we needed to do something, or both our reputations would have been at stake. I did us both a favour by killing him," she explained with cold logic.

"But... that was Benedict," I said, still dazed by what just happened.

"Benedict, Arthur, Lancelot — what matters is I took care of it; the threat of exposure is now negligible and we can continue on tomorrow like today never happened, without complication. Just remember: your life is a series of choices, and you are slave to no one but yourself; the choices you don't make today will be chosen for you by Tomorrow. I don't know about *you*, but I don't like leaving things up to chance."

I had known the butcher since I was a boy and went with Emeline to the market almost daily just to talk to him. He was always a kind and generous man, often giving us prime cuts and meat scraps in secret because he knew how dire our financial situation was. Not a day went by when he wouldn't shake my hand, hug Emeline, and wish us a prosperous life — and now he was lying face-down in a stream looking like a tornado operated on him with rusty, infected tools.

I knew he deserved a proper burial, but I was uncertain as to how I'd handle his body while not becoming suspect of his murder. Nonetheless, walking over to the place where he lay, I dragged him out of the water and took a knee beside him, pulling out the poison needles from his back and tossing them into the stream. The Dark Queen went back to searching for whatever she was searching for in the water again.

Every little thing I could do for his body, I did, hoping it might make me feel a little less-worse about what I had just witnessed, but it didn't. When I realized the emotional burden wasn't going away any time soon, I walked over to Illyana and sat beside her. Though the lyre no longer orchestrated our very existence, she seemed more tolerant of my presence after all that happened.

"Can I ask you a question?" I began.

"Only one?"

"For someone so beautiful, loved, and lavishly provided for, why are you so... cold?"

"I'm sorry: is this your way of leading in to offer me your jacket, pretending to be the gentleman you don't want to be?" she said with an openness quickly closing.

"No, no, I just mean you have *everything* by being with the Dark King, but still seem... displeased."

"Look, I know I'm only a couple years older than you, but I've lived through a lot. I've seen things you'd be lucky not to see, learned things you can't unlearn, and done things you can't undo. And all these things I carry with me. Not because I can't let them go, but because they're a part of me, for better or worse. When you carry all that with you, gold and attention and prestige just don't cover up an entire past and make it go away or change you. And if you're careful," she said looking at me, "you won't let such things take it away or change you, even when they try to."

"I guess I just ask because... well, I'm sure you know from Benedict's angry speech that the townsfolk were planning something against you."

"'And I,'" she added.

"I'm sorry?"

"You said 'the townsfolk'; I added 'and I', because you were in on it too. Even when you're caught, always take responsibility for your actions and stand by them even when you're wrong, because you always act upon a reason that makes sense to you in your time of decision. Do not fear being wrong nor fear shouldering the blame. If you must fear, fear inaction and not risking your reputation for what you believe in instead. You made a choice and are now the wiser for it. That's what matters. You'd be surprised how many people don't even do that and let others make their choices for them."

"Right. The townsfolk and I, then. But, just so you know, we weren't planning your death or anything; we just wanted you to be happy so Lucaius stays happy and continues to provide for us the way he does because of how he feels about you."

"So the townsfolk are worried that I am or will be unhappy, because they think they'll have to work a little harder if their king is angry or depressed...? Your kingdom is as pathetic as the rest of them," she scoffed. "And you?"

"What about me?"

"Why are you doing this?"

"What do you mean?"

"Look, you know exactly what I mean. I'm not going to expose you to the others, just be straightforward and give me an honest answer. I can read your eyes and hear your voice and you're not worried about my happiness, nor that you might have to work harder like the rest. So what is it?"

Sensing we were of similar desire, I decided to be open with her. "I want the Dark King's power and I was hoping you could help me get it."

Her curiosity piqued. "There you go; now *that* is a reason I can believe and respect. I agree, it *is* a waste in the hands of someone so stuck in the past; such power in the hands of a king who is so influenced by his emotions — a burdensome past, an obsessively maudlin present — to me, signifies his future is too unpredictable to entrust such power to. But if I'm going to help you, it is a prize we must both share equally. Can you handle that?"

"Absolutely," I smiled, feeling like I'd found favour with Fate once again.

We sat there devising a plan deep into the night until we had a course of action that could give us both what we wanted. I had found the pawn of king-swaying love I sought after all.

It was in that moment that I realized the Dark Queen was brought into my life for a reason — if only briefly. I'd always been on the giving and never the receiving end of life's generousity. I worked my fingers to the bone to pay for family debts I couldn't keep up with and after years of the same depressing cycle, had nothing to show for it — not even a smile or fire in my eye to inspire others. But that night, that dark godsend showed me that you do what you need to do to preserve your dream and keep it growing closer; sometimes that preservation requires more of you than you think you can give, but you must give it anyway, or your dreams will begin to drift away from you. And once they drift away, they fall back into the hands of others to re-sculpt for you as they see fit. That's no way to live life. Believe me, I know.

The next day, the townsfolk held a funeral for Benedict. As requiems tried to comfort the people by melody and listless elegies used euphemisms like "laying Benedict to rest," trying to soften the harsh reality of his death, the lachrymose atmosphere remained heavy. It was truly a solemn day, and the rolling clouds of darkness above us only suited the occasion even more, even though they had been there every day for the entirety of our lives.

As the service ended, I watched as Father Gregory made his way toward the circular staircase that led to the belfry, but stopped him just in time.

"You can't sound the knell, Father," I urged.

"And why not? It is tradition to do so upon the death of a member of the kingdom, Morningstar; you know that."

"I understand, but this is a death the Dark King and Queen must not know about — and sounding the knell will surely alert them, piquing their curiousity."

"Why must their curiousity go unpiqued?"

As any demagogue would upon being asked why, I began to fabricate a story that would rebuild my reputation and make the townsfolk absolutely furious when Father Gregory passed it on to them.

"Father, I didn't want to say anything in front of the others, especially with people like Moorden looking to get back at me at every turn, but last night I was out gathering logs from the woods so I could make a fire, but as I followed the path, I saw the Dark Queen kill Benedict when he said he was going to expose her for something."

"The Dark Queen killed Benedict?!" he said loud enough so people nearby turned their heads. Hoping to provoke the townsfolk's probable thirst for revenge, I replied more noticeably, hoping to further stir the emotional pot.

"Oh yes — of that I'm certain. Perhaps he found out something the rest of us didn't know, but from what I could see and hear, whatever it was, the Dark Queen was definitely the one who killed him."

The people grew angry. Suddenly, lamenting Benedict's death seemed too passive an approach for them. She deserved far worse. The

Dark Queen had become an imminent threat to them — a danger that called for immediate action so that her deeds could go unpunished no longer. When Benedict's body was interred, at everyone's urging, they sent me off to the castle to avenge his death. Everything was going according to plan.

CHAPTER TEN

A Castle Like No Other

It was a long, winding path to the Dark King's gates. When I got there, I couldn't help but stare through the bars, in awe of the massive castle that was constantly changing shape ahead. I'd never seen it that closely before; every time it morphed, moonbeams would fight to be the first to touch it, gleaming from one angle and then the next. Part of the unsettled feeling in me didn't so much come from the fact I was *at* the Dark King's castle, but because his need for personal protection was quite evidently unnecessary. There I was, at the doorstep of the Overseer of the Kingdom of Kingdoms, and there wasn't a legion or as much as a single guard to tell me I should turn back. As far as any of us townsfolk knew, the castle had no dungeon either, which meant trespassers would be dealt with in other ways unknown to all but the Dark King himself. I began to think I should turn around, thinking maybe that feeling was my conscience telling me my growing ambitions were foolishly outweighing my need for survival...

Before I could make a life-preserving decision, the thick layer of fog hovering over the ground on the other side of the iron bars began to rise from the ground the way a cobra rises from the confines of a snake-charmer's basket. As it swirled upwards, it transmogrified into the form of the Dark One, towering over me, translucent as a ghost. Panic raced through my veins as his steaming blue eyes looked down upon me through a helmet that showed no sign of humanity within. The illusion of the hulking mass stood there silently, waiting for me to speak, holding dual battle axes so big that no man in the kingdom could carry one with *both* hands, let alone one in each. I summoned the courage below my expanding feelings of inadequacy and spoke.

"Greetings, my Dark King," I bowed before the illusion in case the real one could see or hear me. "I am a musician who has come with hopes of serenading the Dark Queen on your behalf for your anniversary."

Unsure if my deceptive persuasion was being considered or accepted, I elaborated further. "My services come at no cost, and I ask for nothing in return — I am here simply on behalf of myself and the other townsfolk with hopes of returning a tiny portion of the generousity you show us daily."

He stood there looking at me for a moment, then the axe in his right hand turned back to smoke as he gestured with his palm to the gates, silently commanding them to open. As the massive gates with jealousy-imbuing filigree opened slowly, his form fell back to the fog it came from and I entered the courtyard holding nothing but the bag I kept the lyre in.

I figured that was it; there was no turning back. The reins of my life were back in my own hand, though I did not know at the time the inner beast I was attaching them to. My nerves ran cold, but my heart pumped acid — a burning that only contributed to the fire inside me as I embraced my new life. A life I finally felt in control of. Empowered. Some people experience a life-changing sensation that transforms how they see the world after a near-death experience, but the way I see it, we're all dying — nay, we're all *dead* — and it is up to us to be our own self-necromancers to find some form of life and spirit to reanimate the corpse of a life spent wanting. For some, it's fitting in; for others, it's standing out. For me, it's having purpose and living a life along the road less-travelled by — and once that meaning inhabits your being, woe to the one who tries to take it from you.

The castle was unlike anything my eyes had seen or my imagination had ever conceived. Its doors became more majestic the closer I got to them, growing with every step; towering fifty-feet above me up-close, they were black as night and laced with gold patterns carrying an iridescence that would've danced uniquely for all eyes seduced by its company. I couldn't help but touch one, even though it opened before me by some unknown force all on its own — it was cold to the touch, but not uncomfortably so, showing all the gradations of blue that one's eyes could take in before fading to black again. As my hand lay against it, a faint glow cascaded around my fingertips, radiating softly. It wasn't until I removed my hand that the light began to fade, as if to allow a few extra moments of wonder before dissipating into the darkness once more.

Inside the castle was even more breathtaking than the doors, with black and grey marble pillars so thick, not even the Biblical Samson could break them and bring down the ceiling. The ceilings reminded me of when Emeline and I used to lay in the fields staring up at the skies of darkness, feeling like insignificant specs of dust compared to the endless oceans of mystery above. Oceans that flowed beyond those skies to distant shores the mind could only dream of. Listening to each step I took, my footsteps echoed for what seemed like an eternity, carrying out from me and looping back like lost sound waves in captivity desperately trying to escape — and part of me wanted to escape with them. Though the magical wonder of that castle set an architectural standard almost-godlike to present-day builders, it felt like there was something more to it that only the most unfortunate visitors got to see... and I didn't want to be one of them. Looking behind me to the doors, I felt the final sands of time slip through my fingers as the two sides reunited with the thunderous, echoing boom of eternal binding.

As the doors closed, a black glaze spread across every surface in the room until no detail remained anywhere around me. Only darkness. The measurable distances I saw just moments before became a vast expanse: an eternal abyss that went on and on in a place with no detail. I had no idea where to go next when I *could* see where I was going, but when all detail vanished before my eyes, the limits of uncertainty were pushed back to distances I couldn't reach if I tried. And as for that castle not having a prison? It probably didn't *have* one because the whole place *was* one.

Tempted to pull out the lyre to see what effects its brightness would reveal, I began to unlace the string holding the top closed, but saw no light shine from within. The bag fell to the ground as I pulled the lyre out and began to strum, but it sounded like any other and certainly shone no brighter than the darkness that filled the room. I began to wonder if I was the subject of some cruel joke the Spirit of Light was playing maliciously in alliance with the Dark King. Perhaps that I was being set-up — my ambitions planted in me so I could be used as a pawn for their sorcery and cruel entertainment.

I held the lyre closer and plucked the strings randomly, harder, feeling nothing but my heart sink with defeat. Just then, a deep voice sounded in the darkness.

"I see the townsfolk have sent their best to play before me," the voice mocked.

Relieved to hear the sound of another's voice, I stopped strumming.

"Who's that? Who's there?" I asked, sounding like a paranoid response to a knock-knock joke.

Fog formed on the floor as it did in the courtyard and climbed up the darkness over shapes that I knew weren't there, but swirled around as if they were anyway. Luxurious mirrors, paintings, arches — the most beautiful things began to take shape before me inside that palace of illusion. When the shroud of ignorance fell from my mind and I realized who I was talking to, I instantly fell prostrate in humble submission, despite having no idea where in the room he stood. Maybe that's why the lyre kept its light hidden: using its omniscient perception to override the oblivious fear that would've got me killed, had I revealed its light prematurely, and consequently let down all who were relying on me.

There I stood in what looked like the castle's study, breathing rarefied air, surrounded by more books than I was sure had ever been written. And I was probably correct assuming that, too — everything about that place teased the senses like mischievous fairies toying with the minds of weary travellers passing through their woods. Just then, the fog swirled under me and lifted me up, creating an elegant chair that felt like how I imagine a cloud would feel to sit upon. A quaint table took shape in the center of the room, drawing me and my chair towards it. Rather than fight the first-class service, I decided to embrace it. I sat there, looking all around the room, until one of the walls began to swirl and through the portal-like hole, entered the Dark King through what I assumed was the East side. Or was it the North...

CHAPTER ELEVEN

Love and Power

S tanding nine-feet-tall and dressed in sawtoothed black steel, the Dark One was a sight to behold. When he moved, his dark, midnight-blue cloak fluttered in his after-breeze, following behind him like a servant just as awe-struck by his commanding presence as I. The strength and influence in his posture alone was enough to make the fiercest of warriors cower and hide. I might have, too, if I wasn't so mesmerised by him and his ornate silver-and-black helmet. It was a defense crafted to perfection, resembling a fierce bird-of-war — likely symbolic of the Rocs who raised him. It covered nearly his entire head and face, as if the metal was poured upon him in its hot, liquid state long ago, and then sculpted upon his face before it cooled, never to be removed again. The helmet was complemented by two more silver Roc-heads of the same design, but fashioned into his broad shoulders: one looking out to the left while the other looked right. Though his mouth and eyes were the only parts of his body not protected by armour, they, too, reflected a darkness that concealed whatever features lied beneath. I wasn't sure if it was just another illusion, but the way his eye slits steamed a radiant blue smoke when he stood close-by, whether it was real or not didn't matter; it was real enough to me. As if his demeanour wasn't menacing enough, crossed over his back were the two hulking battle axes that fearlessly met me at the gates, backed by two silver katanas that remained sheathed at his hips. And yet, despite how terrifying he looked up close, he spoke with a gentleness and care that I never expected him to have.

He approached me with a letter, but held it firmly in his hands before he would give it to me.

"This is a letter I wrote for Illyana when we first met. I've never given it to her, because it's not perfect... however... I was hoping you could change that."

I laughed in my head about how the Dark King in all his power could create a castle like that, but needed help writing a love letter to

his wife. And then it hit me: what if he could hear what I was thinking? I thought loud apologies to him, just in case he could, but he made no sound, nor gesture of acknowledgement either way.

As I read the letter, it was clear the Dark King had never learned how to express himself romantically before — his words were little more than a collection of facts and events. At first I was honoured that he believed my skill with music and lyric could remedy his ordinary words into something alluring, but then I also wondered if that was a test; perhaps he was checking to see if I really *was* a musician and lyricist before bringing me anywhere near her, as any love-struck protector would. After years of writing love letters to Emeline, however, I was confident in my skill.

"My king, I will make your words float from the page like a fragrant aroma she'd wish she could breathe in deeper, if only her lungs could allow it."

The thin, azure squint in his eye slits reflected an invisible smile crossing his face as he handed me the love letter. I made the necessary changes while he peered over my shoulder, thanking me for helping him. The tweaks must have been acceptable too — reflected not only by the fact I left that room alive, but also by the motioning of his hand to reopen the portal in the wall so I could accompany him through it. I tucked his letter into my pocket for safe keeping — to be delivered only when the time felt right.

Walking through the portal, we entered another dark void that suddenly, but no longer surprisingly, took the shape of a whole new room around us: the royal dining room in all its glory. With the portal closing behind us, you would think that a certain amount of panic would set in, but it was quite the opposite; I was swept away, captivated by the sights and smells of the room. The air was filled with the smell of roast beef, vegetables, gravy, the finest wines ever to touch a person's lips or be inhaled by a nose — truly a meal for the history books if only their authors could have their senses tantalized the way mine were in that moment. The rest of the room was even more aesthetically-pleasing than the succulence that graced the table: statues wearing some of the finest armour ever crafted, and wooden furniture carved to such perfection that it made my lifelong work as a carpenter seem like I wore a blindfold and just started swinging my axe in the forest before gluing the left-over splinters together.

Be that as it may, splendor and elegance knew not of their true magnificence in that room until the Dark Queen herself walked down the stairs and entered the room like the main character in her own fairy tale. She looked over and nodded at me as the Dark King greeted her chivalrously, pulling out her chair and pushing it back into the table for her once she sat comfortably. I put the lyre to my chest and let my fingers fall into position, but as he took her hand and leaned in to kiss it, he noticed the wedding ring he had given her was missing from her finger. His radiant eyes met hers.

She thought hard, but had no response except for the shying away of her reluctant eyes; what started out as a perfect evening with everything unfolding according to plan, began its descent down a slippery slope. That's what she was looking for that night by the stream before she was distracted by Benedict's threats. What was there to do? I couldn't speak up, because, to the Dark One's knowledge, she and I had never met before. I was supposed to be *his* surprise to *her*, not the other way around. Especially that kind of double-edged surprise.

In a deep sigh of contemplative thought, I leaned with my back to the wall, looking down, and absent-mindedly started playing with the ring I had slipped from the finger of my father's corpse in remembrance. I always fidgeted like that when I was thinking. And then it began to hit me the more my fingers spun the ring: there was still the one in my pocket I'd found a couple days before by the stream. I slipped my hand into my pocket and inside felt it, small and cold to the touch. Suddenly it all made sense — the ring I had found that night must have belonged to the Dark Queen! Small, golden, roc-wing finger-wrap design with obsidian glass veins representative of the Dark King himself — of course! If ever a serendipitous moment existed, it was that one.

"My deepest apologies for this interruption, my king, but the Dark Queen has a gift for you as well. When I was in the marketplace a few days ago, she somehow found out about the townsfolk's gift to you in the form of me being here to play for you both. She stopped me, and she took off her ring and said, 'I have heard of your plan, and would like you to take this, so that when you play for us, my Lucaius can slip it upon my finger again, like he did on our wedding day.' I thought it was a beautiful gesture and admired her extension of trust to the townsfolk, accepting her offer, so I could fulfil her request today."

She looked up at me with a mix of confusion, relief, and gratitude

briefly before slowly allowing her eyes to look back into the Dark King's. She smiled at him.

"Would you do me the honour, Darling?"

He turned to me with his hand outstretched for the ring, and when I placed it in his hand, he dropped to one knee in front of her, slipping it back onto her finger with a simple, but heartfelt, "I love you, Illyana."

The plan was back on course, and going even better than we expected.

Considering that to be the perfect time for the Dark King to present her with his love letter, I walked over to the kneeling behemoth and handed him the words to read:

"A man is no more than breath until his breath fashions the words that others cannot forget. But you my darling, are worthy of words not yet imagined — words woven to perfection from the fibres that make envy grow in the hearts of goddesses. Though such words escape me, your presence has infused into my being every aspect of bliss that a life of happiness demands. Every day that I catch but a glimpse of you renews a satisfaction in me that even the greediest or luckiest of men could only hope for — yet never have for themselves — because as long as I get to call you mine, I shall never be found wanting more. Since the first time I saw you, my eyes had never presented me with beauty more deserving of the word's connotations.

My darling Illyana, with a black rose in between my fingers, I remember looking over the kingdom hopelessly that fateful night; my heavy heart trying to set sail, yet held in place by the anchors of loneliness that only made me harbour sadness. The moon was no comfort to me as my eyes wandered the tree-line... that is, until I saw you practicing just outside the kingdom walls with your blade. The black leather embraced your body tightly; your cloak shadowed your every move. To look upon you was to look upon an artist: with blade in hand as her paintbrush, stroking imaginary canvases of unsuspecting skin, bringing her masterpiece of death one step closer to completion. Your dark, starless hair carried a nostalgia that reminded me of the nighttime skies that enveloped the Sky Kingdom once the Sun had laid down to rest until morning — a time when I was wrapped safe and warm in their soft wings. And the way your cloak tried to conceal your beauty with darkness, as if hiding you from the world, seemed to be a reflection of myself and the faint echo my ability to love had become. My Love, reflections knew nothing of their power over the heart until the moonlight formed a glistening bridge from your graceful hand to my eye. Such moments, short as they may be, seem to suspend themselves in time forever. But when time caught up to me again, I looked down at the black rose for a moment, then back to you in the distance, and realized I could wait to meet you no longer. I quickly donned my cloak, mounted my horse, and rode off to the tree-line as quickly as I could to meet the dark goddess that now tortured my heart with her distance.

When I arrived at your location, I remember bringing my horse to a slow trot and looking all around for you with an anxious heart — but you, my dark blossom, were nowhere to be seen. And just then, in a slowly-increasing crescendo of parting air, the blade that caught my eye from the window moments before was spinning through the air toward me about to catch my neck with devious intent. Your blade brought a smile to my face, for I was no amateur myself, halting it in mid-air with merely a thought before letting it fall to the ground with ease. No sooner had the smirk formed on my face when your two loving bolas wrapped around the legs of my horse, knocking us to the ground. A little dazed, I remember looking up and seeing you dart in and out of the shadows with impressive speed, as though your body was intangibly linked with them. So I sat up from the flat of my back to get a better look at you, but as I did, the trees fell silent in anticipation as they watched your cold blade press tightly against my throat from behind. You were like no other woman I'd ever encountered. My love phantom, whose defiance and independence commands respect and turns smirks to smiles with ease. And so, at your mercy, I held up my black rose to you in full submission, as an invitation to begin your reign over my heart. I was yours that day and I shall remain so evermore until I give my last breath."

While such words could have melted the coldest heart, the queen's face turned to a disappointed, downtrodden gaze reflecting bigger soul-searing thought-wounds than his words alone could mend.

"What plagues your heart, my love? Have I disappointed you in some way?" asked the Dark King.

"No more than I have disappointed you... but Darling, though your words are sweet, I feel like we've lost something; you're just always so guarded because of things that have happened in your life that I'm starting to lose that feeling of closeness, since you keep the past closer to you than you keep me. You provide for me — and I thank you for that — but as you saw outside the kingdom gates that day, I can provide for myself. My love, you don't choose someone so you can take care of them; you choose someone so you have someone to share the joys of life with. Those joys are not shared exclusively between us, but is limited by the strength of your bond with this power of yours; I know you don't love it directly, but your fear of losing it and becoming defenceless makes you dependent on *it* instead of trusting in what we have together. We won't be immune to all troubles, but we can depend on *each other*. I want that more than anything..."

The Dark King, still holding her hand, looked to the floor deep in thought. Giving up one's immortal powers for a mortal love was a decision that could not be easy to make. I wondered to myself in that moment: if I had everything in my grasp and the means to enjoy it forever, but no one to share my immortality with, would it be a life of blessing, or soul-searing torture...

"Illyana... I love you, but what you ask is not something I can give, as much as I wish I could. The power of the Rocs was infused into me at a very young age to save my life; even if I could give it up and draw it out of me, there's a chance that my body has been using its power to fuel my life-force for so long, I may not survive without it."

She never made eye contact as a tear began to form in the pit of her eye. Even for a thief, her deception skills were almost unexpectedly impressive.

"My king," I interjected, "by no means am I a sorcerer, but what if I could provide a way for you to meet the queen's request?"

He gradually turned to me curiously.

"And you know of a method capable of achieving such a deed..."

"Well... not a method, per se, but an instrument. It was given to me by someone whose mere presence still perplexes my mind, and the instrument itself is an apple not falling very far from that same tree. The lyre never leaves my side — true to my word, it is actually the one I carry with me now."

"I find it slightly odd that you have the means of capturing my power with you now when I have never seen you before today; if I didn't have utmost trust in the woman I love, my skepticism alone would be enough to show you what happens to those who try to turn a king into a fool," suggested the Dark King threateningly. "But... be that as it may, a life without Illyana's happiness is a life I will no longer be responsible for. Do what you must."

CHAPTER TWELVE

Between Gods and Men

With the Dark One's consent, my face could no longer contain its satisfaction. Holding the lyre tight to my chest, the strings and my fingers became one once more, bringing about the final moments of a plan well-conceived — a plan that would finally make the Dark Power mine to command. His time to rule was at an end and the people of the Dark Kingdom were about to know true freedom by my hand.

The soul-piercing notes went right through his armour and puppeteered his emotions to perfection. Though the Dark Queen had played her part and set him up for deceived consent, without the lyre, it would've been a lovers' quarrel at best. I used to think of the Dark King as a force that no one, immortal, magical, or otherwise, could touch: a master warrior whose omniscience would see right through my plans. But there he was: all the best armour and most-spectacular power one could wish to possess, but his emotions were left as unguarded as a common man. It's rather amusing how we seek to protect ourselves physically so that we can consider ourselves safe when really it is our emotions — our ability to feel without rational intervention — that expedite our journey to self-destruction. To embrace freely the entire spectrum of our emotions is to allow a multitude of Trojan horses containing hidden emotional poisons to circumvent the walls of rationalization — walls we need to protect our trust, confidence, understanding, and self-control. The Dark One had made that mistake, only his experience was soon to be on a much grander scale than the subtle ones that most allow to shape their lives daily. Whether that emotional trust is gained subtly or suddenly, however, the end-result is the same.

As the music transcended the Dark King's heart, ethereal tentacle-like power strands began to crawl out of his body and reach toward the lyre. Every time a new strand touched it, the Dark King let out a dull, pained scream while the lyre glowed brighter. I suppose I found peace knowing the Dark King was not dying — that I was not taking a life, but rather amplifying my own. That belief was my fortress; my ability to cope with the actions I may have frowned upon not so long before. To syphon his power, in my eyes, was not a battle between good and evil, but simply a stepping stone to self-improvement; although, the way his power felt coursing through the lyre in my hands, I'd say self-improvement was more like self-*perfection*. And I was only moments away from having it all to myself.

In a room only lit by wall-mounted torches, the lyre's brightness was a noticeable extravagance. But as it shone bright with the Dark King's power, even it was eclipsed by the blinding light that suddenly beamed through the window.

Lux had returned — the Spirit of Light, in all his mischievous glory. Before I could fathom the reason for his return, the lyre was ripped from my grasp and sailed through the air back to his hand — the hand of its true master. He looked upon the Dark King with contempt, who lay exhausted and collapsed upon the floor, nearly powerless.

"Shackled by imperfection, your immortality shall be forgot; such gifts, no longer be yours to possess, and their memories, merely a thought."

Then he turned to me.

"Pawn of light, you have done me great service; the deal we made is complete. The lyre is mine, his power absorbed, and your usefulness, now obsolete."

"You devil! That power is mine!" I yelled, outraged.

"*Yours*?!" Illyana interjected. "What happened to *our* deal?!"

"Your... deal? Illyana, *you* had a hand in this?" the Dark King asked from the floor, short of breath.

"No! ...I mean yes, but darling, I did it for us, to bring us closer!"

"I don't know what to even say to you, Illyana," the Dark King replied. "If I did, I'm not even sure I would use what little breath I have left to speak to you.

And as for you, Morningstar, possession of light is a punishable offense, but to plot to kill your king by making a pact with the Spirit of Light himself... and after all I've done for you? For this kingdom?

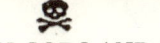
But YOU!" he boomed as his full attention fell to Lux. "How *dare* you show your face here today! This will be the last time you try to take anything from me — I don't care if I go down with you!"

With that, the Dark King channelled the few reserves of energy he still had left, and pulsed forth from his hand the last of his energy into the eight giant pillars that held up the dining room ceiling, his body collapsing to the floor, unconscious.

The room began to quake violently. Dust rose from the ground and rocks fell from the ceiling as the pillars shook loose and took shape into massive stone golems bent on the revenge the Dark King intended. They swung their gargantuan arms without concern for accuracy — their one and only purpose being to destroy the castle and all still left inside. Fists smashed into the walls with such force that shockwaves rang deafeningly in my ears while giant boulders blasted out of the walls, narrowly missing me every time, no matter where I was in the room. One of the golems stood over the Dark King's body at all times, protecting him from harm as the others wreaked havoc on us. The dust alone was a force to be reckoned with; its aftermath filled my lungs, trying to force me to give up on an escape that seemed more ambitious than coming there in the first place.

I could only watch as the Dark Queen was waylaid by the largest one, slamming her into a wall with bone-crushing force. She laid there barely moving as the rubble piled up around her.

Lux, the quickest of us all, even lacked the speed it took to escape the chaos, snatched out of the air by one lightning-fast golem hand. It nearly tightened, but just then, another golem's erratic swinging fist slammed against the other's in a blind frenzy, knocking Lux loose. He flew across the room into the back of another, falling to the floor while the lyre tumbled out of his grasp.

The only way to escape the room was out that window. But with the lyre still glowing with power, even through the thick dust, unattended, my acquisitiveness overcame my survival instinct. Making a beeline for the lyre, I ducked and dodged the rocks flying toward me, closing the gap between me and my destiny. When I was close enough to reach out to it, Illyana jumped out of nowhere and drove her shoulder deep into my stomach, knocking us both to the ground. Straddling my stomach, she struck me twice in the face with stunning speed. I struggled with all I had to throw her off, but by the time I did, I could only watch from a distance as a golem picked up the lyre and pummeled it in its palm, over and over, until it had shattered to pieces.

After the first punch, its light began to dim. With its frame severely weakened, the Dark King's power burst from the cracks, screaming out in all directions. Like Hell-bent demons escaping from eternal captivity, the power surged out the window into the kingdom in streams of loose, vibrant energy. I tried to stand up, but Illyana was an annoyance that I could not escape. I could've sworn she wanted us both to die there instead of escape safely, as if trying to make me atone for the sins she should have seen coming.

But the lyre was gone and the Dark King's power with it. Where the power went was anyone's guess, but I didn't exactly have the time to ponder upon such things; only one thing mattered above the rest: getting out alive.

I looked around for a means of climbing out the window. It looked like my most promising option was the long, iron chain that used to hold the grand chandelier up to the ceiling. Thanks to the golems ripping it from the rafters, all I had to do was find an anchor point, toss it out the window, and rappel down the wall. With all the rubble that weighed down the table, I figured that would be able to support my body weight, if all went according to plan. So, making my way over, I wrapped the chain around the leg in the best timber hitch knot I could, dragged the standing end to the window, and tossed it out.

Illyana looked over in my direction as I was climbing out the window and began to run straight towards me. With unsurpassed dexterity and speed, she weaved in and out of the golems and debris, untying the impressively-compact fabric strands that multi-wrapped her waist the closer she got. Tying the loose end to her hook-shaped buckle, she disconnected it from her waist, and in one hands-free, cartwheeling jump through the window, hooked it on the ledge from which she started to rappel down gracefully. And then there was me, struggling just to hold tight to the chain, hoping I wouldn't fall.

I looked down at her, but broke eye contact when a panicked look overcame her face. Back at the windowsill stood Lux, staring down at us.

"An immortal's life endures; his vengeance everlasting; a fool provokes a god to war, then finds long life contrasting."

His curse channelled forth from his fingertips towards us both. Not wanting to find out what it had in store, I let go of the chain and took hold of Illyana on the way down, pulling her in front of me to use as a human shield. We fell two storeys onto the rooftop below — a surface no softer than a stone mattress — and landed with a painful snap. The full weight of her body had landed on my knee. Writhing in pain, I knew I wouldn't be able to outrun Lux in such a condition; even if I *was* able to run, Illyana was still much more agile than I. I would have been unquestionably left to feel the full extent of the curse for myself.

Looking up from the flat of my back, I saw Lux summoning a second burst intended for me. But as luck would have it, Illyana was still squirming next to me, barely-conscious. I reached over and pulled her body over my own once more, protecting myself with barely a moment to spare as the spell struck her again without mercy. She cried out in pain, looking into my eyes with panic and betrayal. It was a look that hollowed my stomach the longer I stared back at her, so I closed my eyes, hoping to make it easier to bear, refusing to watch her go through whatever the spell was doing to her body.

Though Lux was furious with his failed attempts and likely would not have missed given a third opportunity, my break finally came when an unforgiving golem arm lashed out and slammed Lux against the wall before pulling him back into the room. Not being one to waste a valuable opportunity, I threw Illyana's unconscious body from mine and crawled into the bushes, hiding while I tried to summon the strength to make it to a safer place.

Uncertain when it would truly be safe to come out, I waited in those bushes as quietly as I could until I heard nothing but silence around me. That silence came hours later— but when it did, I slipped away quietly, hobbling toward the church to tell the others what had happened.

CHAPTER THIRTEEN

Unworthy Recipients

O n the way to the church, I noticed a haunting blue glow coming from the windows of most of the houses I passed. I tried to see what was giving off such ambiance, but not even the slightest crack of visual investigation provided me with the clarity I sought. Perhaps it was not the light itself that should have bothered me, but the reason *why* it was everywhere.

Continuing on, I planned on asking Father Gregory if he knew anything about the phenomenon, but when I opened the door, the church was dark. I had been going to that church most of my life, so I knew there was always *some* light in there — candles, torches... and at all hours of the day and night. Something was wrong. Walking through the darkness, I used my hand to guide me through familiar paths until I heard a faint murmur — possibly the sound of voices coming from the basement where we held our secret town meetings. As I got closer, the darkness dissipated ever-so-slightly as more of the mysterious blue light took its place. Looking down the shaft that was normally concealed by a trapdoor, I became certain of two things: one, there was definitely a meeting of familiar voices down there, and two, the answer to that luminescent enigma was only a few ladder rungs away. Taking a curious breath, I joined the voices.

Nothing could have prepared me for what I was about to see; their faces and voices were familiar, but every person in the room had eyes glowing with the same smoky effect the Dark King's had when I met him, only significantly dimmer.

"Morningstar, I'm glad you could make it, son; it appears we have a situation on our hands. Pull up a chair," Father Gregory instructed.

"I'll get it!" Moorden's boy giggled from across the room as he telekinetically motioned with his hand, sliding a stool under me.

"What... what has happened to all of you?"

"We're not quite sure, exactly," Father Gregory replied. "A few hours ago, we were awakened by a thunderous boom, and those who were able to see the castle from their windows tell us that it looked like blue spirits of some ghostly form were escaping from one of the castle windows. Next thing we knew, it was as if a magical Passover was taking place, only none of our doors were marked for the blue demons to pass-by. They dematerialized, entering our houses through the walls, and climbed into our bodies, like they were just passing through, but they never came out. They stayed inside us. So many of us panicked and ran into the streets looking for help, but were only greeted by others with the same fears and concerns we had. Unsure how to go about handling the situation, we decided to meet here. It wasn't long before we realized we could do things we never thought possible before..."

"What kind of things?" I asked, unsure if I wanted to hear the answer.

"We're still trying ta figure that out," said Moorden, "but so far we've been able ta create fire from our hands, as well as a breeze cold as ice; we can also see in the dark as if it was daylight... an' of course, move things with barely a thought, as me son demonstrated when ya arrived. That seems ta be all we know of, so far..."

"One thing escapes me, however, Morningstar," Father Gregory began. "why is it *your* eyes have not changed? Are you not able to do the things of which we speak?"

I didn't know what to say. Part of me was angry-as-Hell that the entire kingdom received the gifts that I, and I alone, deserved and worked hard to get; and the other part of me... actually was exactly like the first. Being the only one without a portion of the Dark King's power only exacerbated my desire for it. So I decided to change tactics.

"I am able to do what I have always been able to do. *You* are the ones with the demons inside of you... and you *embrace* them?" I replied sharply, hoping they would feel it was wrong to have the power and pursue ways to rid themselves of it, instead of how to keep it and use it.

"Perhaps to think of these gifts in terms of demons or angels is only to limit what could be," replied Father Gregory. "The Great Deity must be rewarding us for our devotion — giving us dominance over our enemies. As his chosen ones, it is our duty and pleasure to accept these gifts to preserve what we know is right. We are his faithful ones,

Morningstar, and have been blessed accordingly... but you, you don't have the gifts; your eyes do not glow with the Great One's support. Perhaps the demon among us is actually *you*..."

It was a response I'd never expect to hear Father Gregory's lips speak.

"Your eyes are like the Dark One's!" I exclaimed. "You said yourselves the light came from the *castle*, not from the heavens. Do not be so quick to embrace what you do not know! And 'preserve what we know is right'?! You set things on fire with your hands... does that sound like a power to be used for good? Surely, you've been infused with evil!"

"You are out of line, Morningstar!" Father Gregory exclaimed. "How dare you insult the Great Deity by calling his gifts evil! I won't stand for it; Moorden, seize him!"

I hobbled toward the ladder, but my leg caught the corner of a table and tore my flesh wide open. It was one of those gashes that probably should've left me screaming in pain on the floor, but the way the adrenaline coursed through my body, the pain was manageable as I made my way back to the ladder. I'm sure any other culprit would've faced a hopeless brick-wall trying to escape from a room full of telekinetic torturers, but I *knew* those people; I had grown up with them. When history exists between people, that history can never be fully erased, because emotions remain ever-attached to the memories of all those involved, even if they seem to lie dormant for years or hide behind clouds of ignorance. Those memories saved me that day as conflicting emotions started an internal war in the hearts of the townsfolk. I felt some forces try to rip me away from the ladder while opposing ones held me there, at times even using their telekinesis to push the others away so I could escape. With a gashed leg and some broken bones from the fall, I did my best to climb the ladder, but it was not an easy task.

The basement was starting to form into two distinct forces: those that took Father Gregory's word as law, and those who felt I deserved a chance. Though the former far out-numbered the latter, everyone was engaged in battle — except for Moorden's boy who had brought me the chair moments before. He stood at the bottom of the ladder I struggled to climb, looking up at me with sadness in his eyes. While I could only speculate as to what a boy so young could be thinking at that moment, I got the feeling he understood completely when he reached out to me. He put his hand on my ankle, closed his eyes and hung his head low as warmth flowed from the palm of his hand. The bleeding of my leg began to slow, and my wounds began to close as bones reformed everywhere I felt pain, feeling stronger than they had ever felt before. I don't know what kind of look I had on my face as I looked down at him, but he just smiled a broken smile, and sat down cross-legged using his powers to roll a tiny rock along the ground back and forth between his hands despite the fighting going on all around him. I wished I could do something to thank him, or bring him with me, but if I didn't escape in that moment, there was no telling what might have happened. With renewed strength, I climbed up as quickly as I could, and made it out of the church in one piece.

CHAPTER FOURTEEN

Lost and Found

Nowhere was safe after that. I had no home, no food, and no one I could trust. Anything I could've grabbed from my home meant nothing, so I just left it all behind and set off for the Forest of Dreamlock. Some of my most life-changing moments happened within the thick, lush walls of that forest; it was a place I knew I could still my thoughts and find tranquility, even though the mental storms that raged on in my mind seemed almost unbearable. Who I was, all the things I thought I knew, every person I was sure I could count on — my entire *life*... none of it meant anything anymore. Wiped away before I had the chance to say a proper goodbye. There was no gradual transition; no chance to prepare. Just a foundation steadily crumbling beneath my feet without a safe platform to jump to. It has been said that there is honour in a captain going down with his ship, but I was denied the chance to go down with mine when my fellow "shipmates" turned to mutiny and forced me into the frigid waters of exile. What honour, then, is left when you're abandoned by those dearest to you? What dignity remains for a leader whose followers have cast him aside and left him to die? And when all hope fails, and he feels himself going numb in those waters, who else can he turn to for help, but to himself? His survival depends on him and him alone. But first, he has to let go. First, he has to give up what he has been holding onto so tightly — and simply learn to let go. Only then will the tides and currents take him to the shores he's meant to tread upon, and as long as he doesn't fight its natural flow, he will live to swim another day.

When you're alone, you tend to do a lot of thinking. I remember my father in the days long before my mother died, back when he still knew how to smile, telling me that if you're going to solve your problems effectively, you need to be able to think clearly. He would say the mind is a house of mirrors, and emotions are the torchlight. In that house of mirrors, thoughts work best in the dark: they can't see what lies before them, so they are forced to rely solely on instinct to guide them through the uncertainty. There is stability in walking

an uncertain path, because you never allow yourself to be misled by what you think you know. Light the torch, however, and suddenly you cast yourself into a world of warped logic where everything is not as it seems. Suddenly what was reassuring becomes menacing; what once embraced hope, turns to embrace fear. And fear — Fear is the great illusionist that makes you believe you are in danger. You feel the need to react immediately, and you do — but in doing so, you react to a reality based on illusion. Give into your emotional illusions, and you will find yourself lost in a maze with no exits, nor entrances, but winding paths that lead you in circles so many times that you grow familiar and comfortable with the very place you shouldn't be in.

I needed to let the emotional flurry inside me settle before I tried to figure out what to do next. That's usually the hardest part, but it's easy when you remove yourself from any problems at hand by first doing something you enjoy. Something that distracts and recalibrates muddled perspectives. What helped me recalibrate my thoughts, allowing them to focus and work effectively again, was thinking of Emeline. Just a few minutes lost in the memories of her, in our time together, and suddenly all the problems of the world just faded into nothingness. Once things stabilized inside me, I grabbed a small rock and used it to draw a large, chalky triangle on a nearby boulder to form my new plan of action. At the top was the Dark Power, flowing down into the Dark King himself and then into the townsfolk to trace the path and plan where to go next. I had no magical lyre to draw the power out a second time, however, and considering that another relic of such a desired capability probably did not exist, I realized I needed another way to handle the situation. It wasn't until I began to think what "the situation" was that needed handling that I remembered why I wanted the Dark Power in the first place. It wasn't for greed or powerlust; it was for freedom, for myself and others, from mundane lives that recycle themselves over and over, as if life itself was a heaping pile of compost. And with the Dark King around, our futures were only the resonating afterthoughts of someone else more powerful. Although there would never be a completely utopian balance among all the kingdoms, everyone should have a say over their lives and every aspect of it — as individuals as well as collectively...

Collectively — *that* was exactly the aspect I was missing: strength in numbers. I needed to build an army to challenge the power-imbalance that the new wielders of the Dark Power presented, and I knew just where to look.

I scratched my plans from the boulder, tossed the stone into the stream, and set off to see King Valenvy. His kingdom was the closest of all the kingdoms, according to the books I read years ago — about a two-day walk from where I was. It would've been nice to have the Dark King's obsidian war horse helping me shorten that time span, but there was no way I was going back to try to take something else of his. Not yet anyway...

My feet were aching by the time I got to the first fork in the path. I had never travelled that far before; to my knowledge, no one else had either as a result of the War of the Kingdoms almost 200 years ago. They say every battle and every war has a good reason behind it, but the mass bloodshed that resulted from the fighting only divided and segregated us more. Trade ceased. Friendly visits from neighbouring kingdoms came to an abrupt halt. Because of such things, skepticism and distrust began to breed in the hearts of individuals across the kingdoms — plagues that never ceased to resonate in every heart thereafter. Was that a good reason for the War? Were we better off than before? I wouldn't say we were; *most* wouldn't say we were. However, such things are rarely influenced by and left to popular opinion; unfortunately, it's those who oversee our power-hungry hierarchies that decide the major things for us — or rather, for *themselves* under the façade of our well-being. In the game of politics and powers, we were a crab-bucket society overseen by corrupt fishermen. You see, as a boy, I remember the old fishermen telling me how they never needed to put a lid on their buckets, because the crabs inside would just keep pulling each other back down. No one ever escaped; no one tasted freedom. They were so focused on competing with each other that they forgot to unite and fight against the ones who upset their destinies in the first place. They kept each other from reaching their potential; forced each other to accept that their lives were no more than a countdown to the inevitable meal they would become. All because they fought each other instead of the fishermen who put them in that situation in the first place. It was time to see our surroundings for the bucket it was. We deserved the ocean. And dammit, I was going to lead us there.

I stood there at the fork in the road, but the signs had withered and faded with time, leaving their words to be desired. To the left, the forest continued on, heavily overgrown with unkempt foliage, and extending into territory I could only assume contained more of the same thing; to the right, though it looked rather similar, the path was

welcomed by the remains of armoured skeletons — once-brave knights who died defending their freedom. Or cowardly traitors who died deserting their army. Dead men tell no tales, so who's to know what actually happened there? Either way, their bones served to remind me that time doesn't always heal all wounds. Whatever happened there, happened for a reason, even if it was to die in that exact spot so I could loot their bodies hundreds of years later. Despite the snakeskin that graced the path, I believed those knights were a sign that that was the path I was meant to walk, so I continued toward them.

Their skulls had an odd symbol burned into their foreheads that resembled the letters "HP" intertwined. I'd never seen it before, but then again, I'd never seen a real skeleton before either. Whatever it represented, I was pretty certain it was put there, marked for a purpose only its marker knew. But regardless of the questions that arose, it was a puzzle I didn't have time to solve; I was hungry and I needed weapons more than I needed answers. I picked one of their blades up, but it was as dull as Moorden's wits after he'd had a few too many. I took it anyway, since beggars can't be choosers, and searched for another. The only other full-size one that was in decent enough shape to take with me was covered in a viscous ooze of tree sap. Not an easy task to clean it, but I had a feeling more difficult tasks than that lay ahead, so I decided to accept it, and be thankful while my problems were still solved so easily. With those two at my side, and a dagger tucked into my belt for good measure, I set off to find some rough stones to help sharpen my new-found blades. A few metres ahead, I saw a small pile of rocks off the beaten path, so I grabbed the roughest ones and crouched into the bushes where I slowly, but firmly, guided them down my blade, scanning the tree line for a meal. The hunt was calling my name.

It was unusually quiet in that moment, for what one could expect from a forest, as lush as it was. Silence filled the air with an unsettling discomfort — the kind of silence where you resisted calling out, "Who's there?" simply because the lack of reply would only make you feel more paranoid. The only movement belonged to the lost breeze as it tried to quickly find its way out of there, the way reason suggested I should have as well, but I simply knelt there, frozen in place. My every sense became attuned to the slightest of discrepancies: rustling leaves, the placement of dirt on the forest floor, the vines that kept touching my ankles... those blasted vines — no matter how many times they brushed against my leg, I couldn't tell if it was a vine, or a snake, or a spirit looking to devour a new soul. It was unnerving; the longer I waited, the more unnatural the forest felt — so I got up from my position, and slowly walked backwards along the path in the same direction I was initially headed.

After a few hopeless minutes of wondering if I was the only one in there, I finally heard the faint grunt of a god-sent boar, no more than thirty metres off the beaten path. Having never hunted in my life, I took off after it at full-speed, snapping twigs, and tearing through the sharpest leaves to ever exist in a forest. I think I even let out a war cry at some point when I got a little caught-up in the moment, but that only made the little boar run even faster, and dodge more unpredictably. Lucky for me, its tiny legs could only run so fast. I was closing in on it, nearly upon it, when all of the sudden it cut left faster than I could turn as well. Before my next step went down, I saw why it had changed direction so suddenly.

I should've left the forest with the breeze.

My foot broke through the semblance of solid ground, and brought my entire body over the edge with it. Next thing I knew, I was falling for what seemed like an eternity into a deep hole I had no way out of. A giant web of expertly-woven rope awaited me below, cradling my fall, and closing up around me to seal my fate in a cage for animals — though I'd much rather have died than become a prisoner of circumstance. Damn boar.

From the flat of my back, I looked up between my feet toward the distant sky, wondering why Fate had led me down that path of all possible paths. I needed help, rescue, or even company — but the only company I would experience would be that of my thoughts... for longer than I wished to share their companionship.

Much later, as if by some stroke of luck, I heard some human voices walking close-by. I yelled at the top of my lungs for help, over and over, until finally, they started hoisting my rope-cage up. I dangled there above the deadfall trap like a caged animal, begging for assistance before I could even see who had rescued me. But when I looked at their faces — their camouflaged faces — I realized the two men may not be the Good Samaritans I was hoping for after all.

"Aww not human again! We had that *last* night!" the short man said jokingly as he looked to his more serious counterpart.

"Cut him down from there, Gad," the one with the scarred face instructed with authority, "but keep the ropes on him; wouldn't want you to have to explain to Blackheart how another catch got away."

"I don't know who you two are, but if you let me go, I promise you: I will make you very rich," I pleaded by bluffing rather half-heartedly, only to be ignored.

"Ugh! That was *one* time! That wild boar had like... magic speed powers or *something*. Seriously, Issachar; not even *you* could have caught that one."

"I *did* catch that one, remember? Before you let it go free?"

"I didn't let- well technic- you're just mad cuz 'Little Izzy' was cuter than *your* ugly mug, and you were worried everyone back at camp would love him more than you," the talkative one chuckled.

"Yeah, yeah; just keep the ropes tight, and drag him behind as close to us as possible — keep a keen eye on him too," Issachar reminded him with a brief smile before pausing. "Better yet..."

He walked over and punched me in the face so hard that it knocked me out cold — a punch that would have shamed even the greatest of executioners. I was out, and I was not coming back anytime soon.

CHAPTER FIFTEEN

Opportunity Presents Itself

When I came-to, I was blindfolded, gagged, and tied to a post wearing nothing but the remnants of my dignity. The band of irreverent thieves had taken everything I had on me, but my belongings were the farthest things from my mind. I struggled to get free, using all the strength and flexibility I possessed, but whoever tied me here definitely was no amateur in the world of knots.

"Keep trying, by all means! Gad, though a light-hearted joker, is quite serious when it comes to his mastery of traps and knots. Even if you struggle all night and the gods themselves offer you a helping hand, they would only find themselves captive beside you with wrists bound tighter than yours."

"Who are you? And where am I?" I asked, trying to convince myself he was overstating Gad's abilities. I wriggled around using my shoulder to try to move my blindfold away so I could have a clear view of my captor.

"Let me help you with that," the man replied, helping remove my blindfold. "Name's Blackheart. I lead the fine men who brought you here, as well as the other assassins that populate this camp. We are collectively known as The Silence, that is, if you knew about us at all. We are the shadows of your night; the makers of last words and takers of last breaths. Perhaps even yours, had you not been wearing this ring," he said, inspecting the one I'd slipped from my father's finger.

I looked around, trying to get a sense of where I was. Logic would suggest I was in the chieftain's tent, although nothing in it reflected status of any kind. Then again, maybe he preferred a tent that was unbecoming of his authority in the camp. It was hard to be sure of anything from my vantage point. With so much uncertainty, I figured if I prolonged the line of questioning, and presented a fearless front, I had a better chance of staying alive. Begging and pleading for my life would've shown weakness, and among thieves where survival-of-the-fittest is usually the philosophy of choice, weakness was the last thing

I wanted to show.

"Why have you brought me here? And what, exactly, is so special about my ring?" I asked with the calmest tone I could.

"Well, even assassins need to eat. We don't just take lives, you know; we try to prolong our own as well," he said, jocularly stating the obvious. "But this ring of yours... I gave it to a man I knew for his services once, both as a symbol of trust in our dealings, as well as a symbol of friendship — though it has been somewhat modified from its original design, I see. I suppose that is the prerogative of a blacksmith though: wanting to put his personal touch on all things metal. He was a fine blacksmith too, and a true sage on the mysteries of human interaction — a man more-than-deserving of every good and noble word spoken about him. For years, he crafted us some of the finest weapons ever to draw blood, because he believed in our cause like it was his own."

"That's right; he did," I began, trying to convince him I knew what he was talking about. "My father was a good man, and to have a friend like you, he considered himself truly blessed."

He laughed. "You have the beginnings of your father's wit, boy, but you have a long way to go before you learn to use it with the appropriate skill. It's unfortunate your journey towards self-discovery will have to be cut short, however. Lucky for you, we caught two dire wolves recently, and will not require the meat off your bones tonight. But come tomorrow, we shall reminisce fondly about your father as we partake in second-helpings of, well, you."

He slipped the blindfold back over my eyes and left the tent. After hours of what sounded like them feasting by the fire, drinking, laughing, and sharing stories, the camp fell silent as the members likely went back to their tents to sleep for the night. Blackheart must have been pretty confident in Gad's knotting abilities, because in that tent where he slept, there was only me and him. No one else, from what I could hear, anyway. Even as their leader, he was left unguarded — suggesting either he was the best assassin the lands had ever known, able to kill me even while he was fast asleep, or quite possibly the worst overseer of prisoners in history. I decided to believe the latter, squirming and twisting my bindings around until, against all odds, I finally worked myself free.

Trying to be as quiet as a ghost, I crept silently toward the entrance, but when I arrived at the flap to leave, my thoughts gave birth to an idea more beneficial than escape, if all went according to plan. I needed an army, and what better way to begin than by recruiting some assassins to my cause.

I looked around for a weapon of some sort, and my eyes fell upon a blade no longer than my forearm. Picking it up with a tight grip, I nervously laid each step of my feet upon the floor as if walking on a bed of nails. When I reached Blackheart's bedside, I took him by the hair with one hand and slipped the blade right up against his throat. The beginning of an effective negotiation.

"Most impressive," he coughed and sputtered before recovering smoothly, without showing alarm. "Can't say I never thought this would happen, but to be honest, I didn't expect it was possible. However, your blade convinces me otherwise. But why does your blade hesitate? Let it do what it must."

"If I wanted to kill you, I would have. I want something more."

"What more does a man have to give but his life? Riches? Weapons? Take them, they're yours."

"I was thinking more like a chance to join your esteemed group of... diverse tradesmen," I suggested.

"Interesting proposition, but not an easy arrangement, I'm afraid. But... considering you were able to free yourself from Gad's knots and blade my neck without raising alarm, perhaps the others will more easily accept your request if I make you a deal. What say you to this: you are free to train in camp with whoever chooses to take you on as an apprentice, *if* you can survive combat with one of our members."

I had no idea what I just gotten myself into, but that sounded like the best chance I had, so I took the risk and accepted his terms.

"You have yourself a deal, Blackheart," I said with a slight bow, fortunate he had a sensible side.

"No need to bow, boy; we don't do that kind of thing here. What did you say your name was?"

"Morningstar."

"Get some sleep, Morningstar. Tomorrow you fight for your life."

CHAPTER SIXTEEN

Second Chances

When morning came, Blackheart threw me a tunic and a basic set of leather armour to wear and told me to meet him outside the tent. I thought the camp was on fire, the way the tent material glowed and radiated a warmth I'd never woken up to before. I quickly bent the door flap away, only to have my arms instantly engulfed in blazing heat and my eyes experience light-blindness I couldn't shake. It was brighter than a thousand torches, and how it was happening without any fire was puzzling. Even deep in whatever forest they brought me, the light was brilliant, passing through the trees and leaves like nothing could stop it. The larks were singing; the forest felt fresh and carried its wooden, earthy, vibrant scent all through the air... and then it hit me: that was the sun that our history books had spoken of. Seeing it, feeling it... the words on every page I read didn't do it justice. Light, appearing as naturally as we breathe. It was amazing. When my eyes finally adjusted, I couldn't help but keep staring at the sun, even though my eyes could only endure it for a second or two at a time. The pain and discomfort was worth every second of wonder and awe.

"And here he is. Masters of shadow, last night was eventful to say the least. With a blade to my neck, our prisoner requested, in exchange for sparing my life, to be given a chance to train among our ranks. But you are more than bartering chips to me; you are valued members I hold dear; members whose honour and satisfaction I would be remiss to not first request your approval. I told the prisoner, who calls himself 'Morningstar', that any of you is free to take him on as an apprentice, *if* — and only if — he can survive combat against you. You will have your weapon of choice, and he will be unarmed, as is custom for a newcomer's first fight. I will present your name and combat rank, starting with the highest, and you present us with your acceptance or denial of today's combat. What say you?"

It seemed like there were a lot of extra words appearing in his announcement speech I didn't remember hearing before. A discussion broke out as they murmured among one another.

"Reasonable. But what if we make things a little more interesting," a woman suggested as she played with a rope that had a dagger tied to the handle. "How about *he* chooses one of *us* to go up against instead. No names, no ranks. Just let Fate help him choose his destiny."

"Do you all agree with this?" he asked of them all as they gave signs of their approval. "Then it's decided. Morningstar, Fate awaits your decision. And Gad, I think you and I need to have a little talk about your knots," he said as he walked away to let me peruse my line up of would-be redeemers and executioners.

I saw the man with the scarred face, Issachar, who had been there at my capture. He stood about six-foot-two, and had muscles that fit him like medium armour — not quite the size of a tree, but definitely could crush my bones if he got his arms around me. Considering the authority he exerted over Gad in the beginning, I figured it was something he'd earned as a result of his combat prowess, so I passed by him to the next.

She had an athletic build, and the brightest, seraphic green eyes that made emeralds seem to depreciate in value the longer you stared into them — and she knew it too. If she wasn't carrying a bow, I'd swear her flirtatious, persuasive abilities were her primary weapons. She didn't even need to speak a word for me to know that either; between how she carried herself and her posture, I'm sure her confidence was validated by her deadliness as an archer. And when she winked at me, well... I only wanted to see more of her.

Beside her, leaning against a tree, was a scruffy looking man who was doing tricks with two daggers in his hands. We locked eyes, but neither of us backed down; whoever that guy was, those blades seemed to be extensions of his hands, moving how he moved, in perfect, artistic synchronization. Definitely not someone I was ready to mess with.

At his feet, sitting cross-legged was a thinner man, smiling. He didn't strike me as the threatening type, but rather as a common man. A friendly man. Someone who makes a good and memorable impression on everyone he meets. He couldn't have been ranked that high, but he just seemed too kind to be able to strike in the face, even for a winning blow.

"I'm Judah," the seemingly-chatty man said as the others turned to look at him. "I know we're not sharing names and ranks and all, but just wanted to say good-luck. Any man who can escape Gad's knots would definitely be a welcome addition to the group."

"I appreciate it, Judah; thank you. But one step at a time; I don't think I've ever seen a group of people make my odds of victory look so hopeless before," I mentioned, receiving scattered laughs from the group.

Entering the camp with a massive tree trunk on his shoulder, was a man whose height was only second to that of the Dark King... though his muscles were second to none. I didn't see any weapons, or ropes, or special tools on him, but the way he carried the 20-foot tree trunk like it was a toothpick, I figured he just found weapons to be unnecessary. The way he lumbered about, he was definitely an option if I could've been quick enough... but if he had hit me — even once — the only group I would've joined were the shells of the departed that I stole the weapons from before I got into that mess.

There were so many choices: even a guy who was using a single ladder to do acrobatics off in the distance. I wasn't sure if he was among the ranked ones, but I couldn't help watch him practice for a moment: running at full speed, planting the ladder into the ground before him, and launching himself into the air higher than the ladder would let anyone climb. As if that was not impressive enough, his foot would then hook into one of the top ladder rungs, and tug it up into his hands for weaponized use before landing. I stood there in awe of his aerial abilities. After seeing that, there was no way he *wasn't* ranked, so it was down to one of the other three.

Two of them looked so similar that I was barely able to discern one from the other. They leaned against each other's shoulders, arms crossed, with bandoliers full of what looked like homemade, ceramic or clay bombs. One of them was missing his left eyebrow and left ear, while the other was missing his right eyebrow and right ear. Together, they looked like quite the pair. I figured they had to be the explosives enthusiasts — which, in a roundabout way, perhaps suggested *that* was their specialty and not combat, like the others appeared to be.

And then there was the woman who suggested that Blackheart allow Fate to help me choose my destiny. I save her for last, because there was something familiar about her: the way she walked, the way she spoke, and the way she stood there among us confidently yet distantly, like a queen overseeing her pawns. Her back was straight with poise; her hands on the shoulders of a younger girl who was no more than four years old. The woman seemed protective of the girl; not like a mother of her daughter, but like a master and her chosen apprentice, or perhaps even a dutiful sister. Her gaze was neither defensive, nor offensive, but carried a readiness for any outcome that involved her participation — an outcome that would likely always end the way she desired it to. She intrigued me the most, but it was not her I would fight.

"I'll go with the one whose dedication to your cause has guided him so strongly, he removed his left eyebrow to see better, and his left ear to concentrate more fully to the other, even at the expense of making him look like the back end of a mule," I responded, instigating his anger.

The cocky smile fell from his face as he ripped a bomb from his bandolier and threw it at my feet. The thunderous explosion created such a large dust cloud in the air that all those close enough to the proving ground began to cough uncontrollably — me, most of all. But though the dust clouded my lungs, my mind stayed clear as I began to use his offense as my defense; every time I provoked him, his anger rose in direct proportion to the walls of dust around me, helping mask my position even better. But soon, the briefest crack of visibility opened in the dust cloud, and headed straight for my chest, I saw his next grenade. I rolled backwards just in time as he ran at me with the blind rage of a personal vendetta, tossing another, then another.

After that near-death experience, I figured I would stay low to the ground, hoping his bombs would keep stirring up enough dust into the air to mask his sense of where I was. All-the-while, my comments would continue to do some stirring up of their own — namely of his frustration which I hoped would only make him expend his bomb supply even faster.

"I feel like the broadside of a barn, only you can't hit *me* either. Maybe you should come fight me like a man!" I baited tactically, hoping my tactics didn't get me killed.

His only response was the frustrated yell he let out when he finally gave up on using his bombs and unsheathed his blade. Storming into the dust cloud with minimal visibility, I could hear the dagger swinging

angrily through the air, hoping to catch my skin. So I circled around to where I assumed he had entered the cloud, and crept along until I saw the outline of his body. Lucky for me, his back was to me just long enough to snatch from his grenade bandolier two more bombs — one with each hand — before I had to duck, tuck, and roll back into the unsettled dust, disappearing once more. Just in time too: as he swung around with his outstretched blade, it caught my arm with a brutal sting. I tossed the bombs I'd taken outside the cloud and came up behind him again, snatching one more — and then another. Relying on my memory of his bandolier earlier, I figured he had only one bomb left. My odds of besting him were getting better by the minute. But I knew the dust could not suspend in the air forever; I needed to get to a vantage point — and quick — because there was little chance I'd survive the battle if we went toe-to-toe in close combat.

I felt around behind me, until I found a large tree only a couple feet away. I tossed one of the bombs in my hand to the side, and clamped the other in my teeth, climbing the tree as quickly as possible.

When the dust settled, I saw my opponent below me, looking around confused, yet fired up with vengeance. But when he eventually looked up to the thick branch that supported me, his vengeance turned to defeat as I teasingly dangled his last bomb in my hand, proving to him that I had gained the advantage, and he was at my mercy.

"You are a worthy opponent," I said with artificial comfort, "and if we were to rematch, I am certain you would prove to be my better. But what do you say instead of me dropping your own bomb upon you, and taking your life, we proceed as brothers toward the same cause? I may not be an expert fighter, but I am an excellent judge of character, and a great manipulator of circumstance, as you have seen today."

I looked toward the others who stood by, watching intently.

"If any of you would be so kind as to teach me your ways, I would push my abilities to the limits in pledge to your services, never allowing you to come to harm before my own life has been given to preserve yours."

To become their leader, and have them accept me as such, I had to first show them I could be their follower.

Blackheart applauded me as he walked in my direction, clapping a slow, authoritative clap.

"My boy Morningstar, you have given us an outcome I can safely assume none of us saw coming. Zebulun was even ranked *fifth* among us, though clearly his blinding anger reassigned him to a rank much lower while fighting you. You were lucky, but perhaps you are a manipulator of mind and circumstance like your father, after all. And to save the life of one of our members when your own was on the line is an admirable notion," Blackheart spoke before us all, looking to the other members. "Would any of you consider taking him on as your own apprentice?"

I climbed down the tree as Judah spoke up. "After that match, I'd take him on! As an apprentice that is... not in combat; I wouldn't want him to make a 'Zebulun' out of me," he laughed in my direction. Judging by Zebulun's face, he wasn't too thrilled that his name had just taken on a new meaning.

"I'm sorry Judah," Blackheart replied, "but with Zebulun's defeat re-ranking him to sixth, your rank of tenth has pushed you into the company of our non-ranking members. You are still a valued member and fierce competitor, but only our ranking members can choose an apprentice, as you are aware."

A look of disheartened acceptance crossed his face as he nodded and stepped back. Out of the corner of my eye, I saw the woman of poise nod at the little girl, her hands still on her shoulders. "I will teach him, Blackheart."

"As you wish," he said with satisfaction. "Morningstar, Naphtali will be your master, and you, her pupil until you can prove yourself to be her better. Consider yourself lucky, for she is our highest-ranked, most lethal member — ranked above even myself."

"Thank you, Blackheart, for offering me this chance. And to you, Naphtali; I am yours to shape through your teachings however you wish," I said, taking a knee before her.

"If you are to be my apprentice, you mustn't bow to anyone, but make them wish they bowed to you. If you want to learn the discipline it takes to earn that kind of respect, get up off the ground and follow me. You have a lot to learn."

CHAPTER SEVENTEEN

The Silence

"What did he mean by 'ranked above even myself?" I asked her as we continued walking back to her tent, the little girl holding her hand. "Isn't Blackheart the leader of The Silence?"

"In The Silence, we all take on the roles at which we are best. It helps us grow as a group and maintain our strength as a whole. Blackheart's strength is driven by his ambition, allowing him to excel at organization, strategy and other tactical scenarios. When our services become necessary, he plans our entrance, attack, and escape based on our strengths as he observes us in our daily routines. He can hold his own in combat, but he is only ranked third among us, just after Issachar, the one with the scarred face who brought you here. In a sense, Blackheart is our figurehead, but even still, we are a group of assassins, and the strong will always rule the weak."

"So you're the actual leader of the group, then? What's your role among them?"

"In a sense, yes. I have earned my place and respect within the group, but we have no real leader among us. We work together as a cohesive unit; I excel at many things, but choose to specialize where my passion lies — in shadow combat. All other matters are better left to those with a high-functioning capability and passion for what they do well. That way, we stay content as individuals, and when individuals are content and feel valued and feel purpose within a group, the group is more effective and efficient as a whole.

However, though we each have our strengths, our collective strength as a group lies not in trying to improve and perfect those strengths, but our weaknesses. That is why we make sure to train with at least one other member every day. What is your greatest strength, Morningstar?"

"I'm not sure. I was a carpenter, but I guess you could say I'm good at reading people... why?"

"Good; then we'll start with basic combat tomorrow. It's human nature to focus on what we're good at and try to ignore the areas in which we lack. However, you improve most as an individual when you try to improve your weaknesses, rather than enhance your strengths. Take archers, for example; Asher, the flirtatious girl with the bow you were admiring earlier? Her strength is archery. Now, she can train and train for months or years, but as she improves, she will only get millimetres closer to the bulls-eye over time. *Millimetres.* Now say you take someone who is skilled with the sword and put a bow in their hands; they become an amateur archer who will likely miss the bulls-eye by a few metres. But in a matter of hours or days, they will improve their skill with the bow, shooting arrows a few centimetres or metres closer than moments before. *Metres.* It follows that by concentrating on improving your weaknesses, you make more notable progress in your well-roundedness as an individual in less time than if you only try to improve your strengths."

"Interesting," I mumbled, deep in thought, taken by her eloquence. She was definitely someone whose teachings I would gladly become an extension of. "I'd never thought about it like that; it makes sense, actually. So will you be teaching me combat?"

"A certain type of combat, yes. It's called shadow combat, where you disillusion your opponent with their own skills through the use of combat trickery, subtle poisons, and confusion of the senses. But you are a long way from mastering that — first you must learn the basics, that is, our mores and paradigms. All that we are, begins with the Code of Silence."

"Don't assassins become assassins and rebels because they *don't* want to abide by a set of rules?"

"For some, yes, but we are all creatures in need of structure and belonging, whether we fight that fact or not. However, our set of rules, or Code, is not your traditional framework telling you what you cannot do, and how you will be punished, but rather something more contrasting. Those kinds of rule-sets give rise to unhappiness that can give birth to anarchy under the right conditions. However, neither can exist when the individual sees the clear, personal benefit of abiding by those rules. To learn and follow rules should bring a feeling of possibility, not limitation. With possibility comes choice. From choice, direction. From direction, purpose. And from purpose, satisfaction. Once an individual has achieved satisfaction or happiness

with their life, they aren't prone to delinquency and acts of rebellion, as when they are told what they cannot do. Instead, they focus on improvement — first of the self, and then that of others."

"And the Code of Silence can achieve all that for me?" I trailed-off with open-minded disbelief.

"What I tell you is truth, whether you choose to believe it or not. It is not up to me to convince you, but for you to experience its truth in your life for yourself."

"I trust you. I guess it's just a lot to take in at once, especially when you've thought a certain way for decades and one day you hear the words you were meant to hear all along. It's difficult though, because once you hear them, you feel this... temporary dissonance and discomfort, like light being seen through eyes that have been blindfolded for years — like how I was this morning when exiting the tent. It hurts at first, but it's a life-changing pain. I feel it already, but it'll take some getting used to."

"Precisely. You have a way with words, I see," she said as the three of us entered her large tent. "That will come in handy in the right situations. If you are ready to endure this 'life-changing pain' you speak of, then I believe you are ready to learn our ethos through the Code of Silence. The seven tenets are as follows:

'Pursue knowledge; possess it and you will command the world;

Maintain secrecy; separate yourself from your opponents;

Consolidate power; embrace strengths and improve weaknesses;

Enhance reputation; teach each other to grow ever stronger;

Seek counsel; learn from the experiences of others;

Create unity; act to unite the world, not divide it;

Trust yourself; let instinct transcend all.'

At our meetings, we also repeat the esoteric Maxim of Silence:

'By seeking knowledge, I have freed myself; by freeing myself, I have freed the world.'

The first tenet, pursue knowledge, reflects the idea that everything we need to know is out there somewhere, fragmented — everything from the solution to our most basic problem, to the secrets of our evolution as a species toward ultimate prosperity, truth, and planetary dominance. Some pieces have yet to be found while others already *have* been found, but are *known* to only a select few — kept secret for various reasons. A wise choice, according to the second tenet.

The second, maintain secrecy, shows the importance of knowledge as its possession relates to others. We develop as a race by sharing beneficial knowledge so that we may grow as a whole, but as we grow, it is human nature to desire a suitable and just structure or social hierarchy capable of supporting it. It is at this point that all the knowledge you have gained — the value you have contributed — determines your place among its hierarchy. Your place or rank with respect to the others grants you power and influence: things that should be obtained not for means of greed, nor pride, nor ego, but rather to ensure that in the right moment, when your wisdom and benevolence are required to keep humanity strong and united, you can deliver and orchestrate others toward the greater good.

Consolidate power is our third tenet, about embracing your strengths, but also improving your weaknesses. The reason for this is represented in the story of the bowmaster and the swordsman working on their archery skills I mentioned earlier. In doing so, you will diversify your skills, preparing you for more situations faster and more efficiently than perfecting strengths that are already sufficient.

Our fourth, enhance reputation, refers to the reputation of The Silence as a whole. It is our name, and a name is only as good as its reputation. To kill a member would not kill the name, the same way to kill us all would not erase all it has come to represent through its reputation. Therefore, it is a form of legacy left behind for future generations who will uphold its meaning through their actions. As such, the skills we possess, be it combat, cooking, or trickery, should be shared among its members as if tonight was your last night alive and you wanted to pass the torch to ensure a piece of you echoes throughout history. The more we teach each other, the stronger, effective, and more united we become.

The fifth tenet is to seek counsel. Though we are all skilled and experienced in many ways, no one can experience all that life has to offer in the limited time we are given in this world. This is why we must humble ourselves before the other members, regardless of our rank, so we may learn from what others have lived. It is only when we

have added their expertise to our own that we can truly excel towards our most ambitious goals and reach our fullest potential.

The sixth tenet speaks of unification. It is an ever-present reminder that our actions, no matter how important or trivial, should reflect our devotion to the advancement of humankind by bringing them together. It also serves as an evaluator of one's true motivation: if your heart, mind, and actions are selfish, they will ultimately divide yourself, others, or entire kingdoms. When motivation is pure and selfless, it will result in helping bring others together, be it through a kind gesture or a necessary 'purification' of evil.

And finally, the seventh tenet acknowledges the connection the mind has to the unseen world around us. It tells you to trust yourself. Premonitions, foresight, intuition, visions — all of these show you a glimpse of what is to come, or how things could be, so that you can change it, if you so choose. They transcend training, instruction, and experience, and should be yielded to when they present themselves. We know not where they come from, why, or even how they choose us, but only *that* they did — and when you believe that there are other forces at work beyond what you alone can control, that is all the justification you need to allow them to speak to you, and act through you.

Learn these, and let their wisdom guide you always; disenchant your mind from all it believes is true. The way the tenets work is unique to every individual; once they take root inside you, they will tell you exactly what you need to know in every situation. You will be granted insight through them and therefore have an edge over your opponents. Our Secret Order has lasted centuries with these tenets to enlighten us; listen to them, and you shall grow to be one truly admired — and feared.

Do you have any questions?"

"I think I'll need to reflect upon and memorize these first. You've given me more to think about in a short time than I've had to think about my whole life... and I like it. I feel like I live in a whole new world, like everything is different somehow: more obscure, like I know less about what I thought I knew, but at the same time like the blinders have been pulled off, and things are only now starting to make sense. And I crave more."

"That's a good thing. This new hunger for knowledge you're

experiencing is what we in The Silence call 'The Presight'; your eyes have opened, but like the long-closed, blindfolded eyes you mentioned opening to the light for the first time, it will take some time to adjust. Right now, you can only see a haze of light, but in time, you will distinctively see and know what lies before you.

Tonight we will be joining the others around the fire for your induction into our ranks. They will cover the seven tenets, but I have explained them to you beforehand so you can focus on the true reason they have brought you before them: you are not just learning our customs. The others will watch you, analyze you, sense your abilities — and more importantly, test your weaknesses. You have proven yourself to us today through terms and circumstances that not everyone believes is an accurate representation and justification of your true capabilities. 'Blind luck', if you will. You must show them otherwise. My advice: act, don't react. Let *your* words and actions set the conversational environment, lest others ensnare you by theirs."

"I understand. I will ensnare them before they ensnare me," I expressed, thinking I knew what she meant.

"Try not to see things in terms of 'ensnare or be ensnared', but rather ask yourself how you can remove the snares altogether. Consider the outcomes: if you ensnare them, you will make an enemy out of a potential ally; if they ensnare you, you will show them not only that they *can* have power over you, but that they have your *consent* as well. Peace is not made through the exertion of one's strength, but through the appearance of it; let your enemies see you are their better, but never feel as if they are your lesser, and you will make allies out of enemies."

I nodded, folding back the tent flap as the little girl walked on through, still holding Naphtali's hand tightly. "I'll do my best to make you proud tonight, master. You have my word."

CHAPTER EIGHTEEN

Social Gatherings

We made our way back to camp to join the others around the fire later that night. It was there I met Reuben, the master chef of the group, who was preparing a meal that smelled nearly as good as the spread on the Dark King's table. The man definitely possessed the culinary magic it took to satisfy both the self-disciplined snacker and the starving warrior alike. He was a true epicure, but also one of the most down-to-earth people you could meet.

While he was making final preparations for the meal, I walked over to where he was with Naphtali's discerning words in mind, "Act, don't react." So I made the first move, striking up a conversation with him, and started to build my reputation among the group. I wanted to make believers out of them — to show them that I was a worthy addition to their cause, and not some lucky prisoner-turned-social-punching-bag. I still had plans of revolution — big plans — and that group was my key to seeing them through.

"Smells delicious. I don't think my senses have ever felt euphoria like they do right now," I said, sticking out my hand to shake his. "I'm Morningstar."

"Reuben. I'd shake your hand, but..." he twinkled his sticky fingers as he stuck out his elbow to meet with mine instead, still holding the potato he was peeling.

I grabbed a piece of meat with my fingers and popped it into my mouth. "Where'd you learn to cook like this? The spices you used carry the meat to all new levels of bliss. It's impressive," I flattered.

"Years of soul-searching serendipity, son," he laughed. "I used to be a ranger, till I found myself here. Exploring the world, and just seeing where life took me. No real responsibilities — just me, my love of food, and my destiny leading me about."

"Well, wherever it took you, I'm glad it did. So you were a ranger?"

"One of the best! Tracking, skinning... Hell, I could tell you the name and purpose of every flower, weed, and herb from here to the ends of the Earth, if I wanted to. And when you're cooking in the woods where poisonous berries grow, it's good to know what you're doing so you don't wake up the next morning to find you accidentally killed all your friends!"

"Good point," I chuckled.

"Culinary rule number one: don't kill your guests with the food you're serving, unless you mean to."

"I'm no culinary master, but..."

"Don't worry son," he laughed. "I know what you're thinking. We may be a band of assassins, but we aren't trying to kill you. Not yet anyway."

"Well *that* just calms me right down..." I joked sarcastically. "Reuben, I'm gonna go grab a spot; see you around the fire."

"You bet, my friend! It's almost ready. Have fun tonight."

Reuben seemed like a good guy. Despite my flattery, his food definitely was among the best I've ever smelled or tasted.

I sat on one of the large logs as the others each took their seats as well. There were sixteen of us around the fire that night; no matter if they were ranked members or otherwise, you could see the ideals Naphtali spoke of like a fire in their eyes: a hope for future things, and true contentment with the present ones. That was not how I imagined a group of assassins to be, but between their skills, insight, and apparent loyalty to one another, the only thing missing was a strong sense of united ambition towards growth and expansion. Their tenets reflected it, but there was nothing I could see that showed they were actively pursuing things to further the group. And that was definitely something I could offer.

Just before we began to eat, Blackheart stood up, and everyone else joined him. In unison, they spoke the Maxim of Silence: "By seeking knowledge, I have freed myself; by freeing myself, I have freed the world," and sat down again. It was kind of eerie at first, but then I thought back to our church services in the Dark Kingdom, and it didn't seem so different: just a group of people assembling as a community of believers as they work toward a certain ideal.

"I have an Aesop fable again for you all tonight," Blackheart began.

"The raconteur has returned..." Dan contemptuously commented.

"It is about a Horse, Hunter, and a Stag. Our tale begins in the woods one day, where a Horse had just come across a group of trees and bushes that had enough fruit on them to feed him for a week. Pleased with his finding, he ate his fill, and settled down to sleep in peace. But when he woke, the fruit was all gone, except for a few mouthfuls that were being devoured by the Stag, who spit the last of the berries upon the ground in defiance, and walked off into the woods.

The Horse wanted revenge, so he went to the Hunter to ask his help to get revenge on the Stag. The hunter agreed, saying, 'If you desire to conquer the Stag, you must permit me to place this piece of iron between your jaws, so that I may guide you with these reins, and allow this saddle to be placed upon your back so that I may keep steady upon you as we follow after the enemy.' The Horse agreed, and the Hunter saddled and bridled him.

Then, with the aid of the Hunter, the Horse soon overcame the Stag, and said to the Hunter, 'Now, get off, and remove those things from my mouth and back.'

'Not so fast, friend,' said the Hunter. 'I have now got you under bit and spur, and prefer to keep you as you are at present.'

Now, what is the moral of the story?" he asked the group.

"If you allow men to use you for your own purposes, they will use you for theirs," the goliath who was carrying the log into camp earlier suggested.

"Insightful, Manasseh. A lesson, we must all choose to learn before we are forced to," Blackheart confirmed. "Isn't that right, Morningstar?" he asked, singling me out.

"I couldn't agree more. A friend of mine once said, 'Your life is a series of choices, and you are slave to no one but yourself.' I didn't know her long, but she set my mind on a path like a boulder pushed down a hillside. There was much I questioned about the world after that, and still do, but it has led me here, among others who share that philosophy. And for that, I can consider it no more of a hindrance than the blessing of life through second chances. The moral of your story, Blackheart, is one that warns against the company you keep when following your ambitions, and how much of a role, and power, you give them over yourself. But, as the seventh tenet says, 'Trust yourself; let instinct transcend all.' The horse allowed *his* ambitions to blind him to the ambitions of *others* — and it is a mistake I shall remain ever careful of," I added.

After my reply, Naphtali sat looking at me with an odd look on her face, deep in thought. I didn't know if it was something I said, or shouldn't have, but it made me curious.

"Wise words, indeed, Morningstar," Blackheart spoke with interest. "And to reference a tenet in our Code of Silence at the same time! I was planning on introducing you to them tonight, but I see your thirst for knowledge has led you to seek them already, as our first tenet would surely praise."

"Ah, he may be wise with words, but is he wise in his decisions, as well?" posed a man who looked more like the intellectual-type than someone combat-driven.

"I suppose we will find out in due time, unless you know how to discern the answer to such a question sooner?" Blackheart asked.

"Well," he began. "Morningstar, imagine you are a healer, and there is a terrible plague that reduces the planet down to a remaining 300 people. Those last 300, you included, are all infected and will die within five minutes. However, you have made two possible cures, Alpha, which you know will save exactly 100 people, and Beta, which has a 1/3 chance of saving all 300, yet a 2/3 chance of saving no one. Which would you use?"

"I would use the Alpha, because it is guaranteed to save some people. Although I wouldn't know if I'd be among the survivors, the remaining few could repopulate, even if it took longer than if Beta had worked," I replied, entangled in a slight lack of truth; if I couldn't guarantee being among the guaranteed survivors, then the Beta seemed more appealing. However, I had the feeling he was testing my willingness to risk lives, and I wanted them to believe I'd never risk theirs. I had to be always thinking at least one step ahead.

"Okay. Now imagine you never made Alpha and Beta, but rather Gamma, which will kill exactly 200 people, and Delta, which has a 1/3 chance of killing no one, yet a 2/3 chance of killing all 300. Which of

the two now?"

"I would choose the Gamma for the same reasons as the first — a guaranteed survival for some," I pretended once more.

"Interesting," the man thought aloud. "Most would choose Alpha in the first and Delta in the second, due to the way the information is framed, because of the focus on loss instead of gain in the form of survival..."

"So what does that tell us?" Blackheart inquired.

"It shows that his rationality and wisdom are apparently uninfluenced by his fear of loss. The first is meant to sound like he is saving others, and so he chooses based on saving them. However, the second is meant to sound like he is killing or losing others, that is, killing 200 before he can even save even a single person. In most people who fear loss, their fear, and the thought of their choice forcing them to kill others, is enough to make them want to take a larger risk to save them. But not Morningstar... suggesting perhaps he either has never lost or killed anyone, or that he has entered our camp with a mastery over his emotions that would take most of us years to reach." There was skepticism in his tone.

"And which is it, Morningstar?" Blackheart asked me.

"If you must know: I have lost my wife, my father, my mother, and experienced the death and killing of someone I had known my whole life in cold blood as a result of my actions. I guess you could say I've experienced enough loss to accept that things happen, and nothing is for sure, but you just have to keep going, believing that one day, you'll find something that is."

"It appears as if we have underestimated you, Morningstar. Perhaps the gods spared you that first night because you're meant for something bigger... but we shall certainly see; I await the day that reveals the answer to that question, as I'm sure we all do," Blackheart spoke, as if his thoughts were whispered into his ear by an oracle's spirit. "But on that note, I am going to turn in for the night; as always, it has been a pleasure sharing the company of you all."

The group disbanded and walked back to their tents for the night. I joined Naphtali's side along the trail.

"How do you think it went?" I asked.

"Very well; you made quite an impression," she replied simply.

"I hope so... although there was just one part that I'm still unsure about."

"Oh?"

"When I spoke in response to Blackheart's story, your posture changed, and then you looked at me with an odd look... like you were confused, or in deep thought, or something."

"Something you said, just... reminded me of someone I used to know. Someone very close to me. But I don't want to speak of it anymore tonight."

"Well... for what it's worth, I'm sorry for making you feel that way."

"No need for apologies. I was genuinely impressed with how you handled yourself tonight among the others, despite the questions and testing. That was Benjamin, by the way, asking you those questions. He's the healer in the group, hence his line of questioning. Benjamin is very meticulous, which is both a good thing and a bad thing."

"How so?" I asked.

"His extreme attention to detail alongside his care and consideration of all possible scenarios keeps him from being a quick-acting assassin in the field. However, though not quick-acting, he *is* deep-thinking, and chooses to use his skills to help Blackheart plan assassinations and acquisitions — a task I think you would be good at, as well," she encouraged as we arrived at the tent.

"I guess we'll see soon enough," I said, settling in. "Well... it has been quite the eventful day; I doubt sleep will grant me freedom from the plague of thoughts that's bound to keep me awake for hours more, but come what may, I'm ready for anything."

"Good. Your combat training begins tomorrow. If your thoughts don't expend your energy, I assure you, combat will finish the job in its place," she said with a playful grin as she tucked in the little girl.

"Looking forward to it. Do your worst," I challenged with friendly candor.

"I'm sure you will be doing your worst, as well, apprentice. Good night."

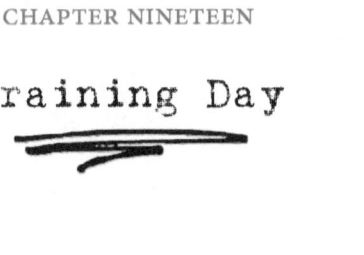

CHAPTER NINETEEN

Training Day

When I woke up, the somewhat-reserved little girl was standing by my bedside, staring at me, without expression.

"What's your name, little one?" I asked her.

"Elektra," she said straightforwardly.

"It's nice to meet you Elektra. I'm Morningstar."

"I know," she smiled.

"I suppose you do; you seem very keen for a three-year-old."

"I'm *not* three," the girl said, as she slapped my head and ran out of the tent. I suppose I should've expected that from a girl growing up with a group of assassins: strike first, kindness later.

"Making friends in camp quickly, I see," Naphtali laughed as she entered.

"That's some spirit your daughter has — and some arm too."

"That's Elektra for you," she said, still smiling. "She's not my daughter, however. I'm... looking after her for someone."

It seemed like there was more to the story she didn't want to tell. Maybe it had something to do with her reaction last night when I shared Illyana's wisdom, but it wasn't my place to pry; I figured I'd be spending time at that camp for a while, so I was better off making friends first before turning them into enemies.

"I see. I apologize; I didn't mean to pry again. So when do we start training today?"

"As soon as you feel inclined. Everything we will need is already outside; all you need to do is walk out there wearing more than your courage."

"What?" I asked playfully. "I'm wearing something under this blanket! But if you don't believe me," I winked, "you're welcome to—"

Her blade-point was at my throat.

"Finish that sentence, or make any allusions to wherever you were going with that again, and I shall personally see to it that the only weapon you ever use in this camp is the tongue I cut from your mouth."

"I was going to say 'pass me my tunic'!"

I wasn't, really.

"Meet me outside when you're ready and we'll see if your fists are as quick as your wit, apprentice," she challenged.

Alone in the tent, I tossed off the blanket and threw on my tunic and the leather armour Blackheart had given me. That was my first day as an assassin; I was far from being any good at it, but I had to keep at it, because sometimes to get to where you need to be, you have to go where you don't feel prepared to go. I knew if I was going to pull my weight and earn the respect of the others in the camp, I needed to enhance my combat skills — and what better person to teach me than the woman ranked number one in camp?

I rolled back the cloth of the tent and exited only to see Naphtali standing there, with no extra training equipment of any kind around. She must have felt pretty clever with her "everything we will need is set up outside" talk.

"Now," she began. "I could ask you a whole bunch of questions about your past combat experiences, preferences, or anything for that matter, but the best way to see what you're capable of now is for you to show me."

I started walking toward her.

"Do you normally bring that much enthusiasm to a fight? C'mon, fight me like your life depended on it," she provoked.

I threw a flurry of haphazard punches, but she deflected each one just as fast as I'd thrown them, ending with an open-palmed thrust to my chest that knocked me backwards and the wind right out of me.

"Try to mix it up a bit; instead of only throwing predictably alternating punches, try striking twice with the same hand and at varying levels. Add some kicks too."

I ran at her again, that time throwing high punches she parried by pushing up with her forearm, while my lower punches were knocked to the side as she stepped out of the way to protect herself; so I threw in a low kick, but she simply kicked it back down with her own. My attacks were useless; she was quick, and yet, it was obvious she was holding back her expansive array of skills. Not to be so easily beaten, I tried delivering a heavy kick at belt-height, but she turned effortlessly with her agile body, wrapped her arm around my leg, and used her other to sweep the only one that kept me standing.

"Great, there's hope for us now with *him* in our group," an irritable man commented while he passed through carelessly, not making eye contact with either of us.

"Ignore Dan; what he thinks is irrelevant to the matter at hand. You were good — that was much better. Even when you're in close-quarter combat though, I can see you like to strike from a distance, rather than grapple or force me to submit. That's not a bad thing, but it shows a lot about your combat personality. Let's focus on that, and develop it, since it's the technique you lean most naturally towards.

The first thing you need to know in your style of hand-to-hand combat is what to strike with and where. My master taught me that you should strike your opponent with your closest offensive tool towards their closest target; much like how I was countering your punches and kicks. So if I come at you, and my knee is most forward, kick it; if it's my hand in a punch, deflect it as you block the attack, possibly striking with your own. Stop me from coming at you and taking hold, keeping the distance between us, so you can continue to fight me at a distance where you feel the most in control. You'll keep the terms of combat in your favour that way.

Second, know the weak points of the body. You may not get the chance to strike back often, so when you do, you have to make it count. The eyes, nose, throat, and the soft tissue below the earlobe are your strike-zones on the head; the armpit, sides of the ribcage, and solar plexus are your weak spots in the middle; the groin, knees and feet for the lower. Striking each of these will cause different effects, from tearing up and blurred vision, to trouble breathing, to temporary paralysis — all of which allow you time to escape or time to attack, depending what is most useful to you at the moment.

Third, take control of the situation. You can punch and kick all you like, but you will expend your energy — energy which you will need for other things from climbing strength to sprinting to escaping the clutches of your enemy as you resist capture. The best way to take control is by joint-locking them — stretching their joints as they weren't intended. Go for the wrist, elbow, shoulder — wherever is most convenient. Once your opponent is locked, they cannot continue their attack as long as you push their joints to their limit.

In summary: know *what* to strike with, know *where* to strike, and *when* to grab or joint-lock *instead* of strike. Got it? Okay; try again."

There was no denying how much of an amateur I was; our combat was like watching a sloth fighting a deadly hummingbird, or maybe a sluggish tortoise fighting a clairvoyant hare. It was going to be a long learning process, but I was determined to get it right eventually. And the fact she was encouraging instead of berating made all the difference in wanting to push myself harder. We sparred for hours working on my technique, until one of the more socially-upbeat members of the group interrupted us.

Just as Naphtali was teaching me how to recover from being choked by clasping your hands together and punching both arms up through the strangler's "striangle" as she called it, one of the one-eyebrowed assassins wandered into our combat zone.

"Hey Morn! I'm Ephraim, Zebulun's brother," he said smacking me in the arm. "Blackheart wanted to see you about something in his tent. Mind if I walk there with you?"

I looked to Naphtali, who nodded her approval. "We'll continue this later."

"Naphtali?" I asked as I turned back around to her.

"Yes?"

"Thanks..."

"For?"

"Not belittling my efforts the way my father used to."

"No thanks necessary, apprentice; belittling does not help someone grow; it only leads them either to believe *they* are not good enough or *you* are not good enough — the first ends in their emotional death, the second in your physical one."

"Go on! Belittle him!" Ephraim joked. "It's not like he could kill you anyway."

He put his arm around me, leading me to Blackheart's tent.

"Just kidding," he continued, "you did great from what I saw just now, Morn. No hard feelings."

I walked with Ephraim, who seemed much different than his older brother. He had a vim and zeal for life, unfazed by the fact he was of a lower rank and was missing an ear and eyebrow like Zebulun too. I guess it goes to show you that perspective alone can make an experience positive or negative, but regardless of which you let it become, it can only have as much power over your outlook on life as you give it.

"I just wanna say, I thought you were great fighting my brother yesterday. I mean, I was sure you were a goner, especially after you provoked him to anger like that. When we were kids, if he got that look in his eye, you stayed clear of him or faced the consequences! How'd you even know he'd react like that and stir up all that dust?"

"To be honest, most of it was luck," I said with a short chuckle. "The gods must've been smiling on me that day, because if I had to do it a second-time, I'm pretty sure a tree-stump with a knife tied to it could've beaten me."

"You're not so bad," he laughed back. "I saw you with Naphtali today and you were actually pretty good. For a first-timer, anyway. She's an amazing master, astute as they come, so just pay attention more so to what she says rather than how many times you end up on your back. And remember, no one in this camp can beat her either. But yeah, Zeb was mighty unhappy about being demoted in front of everyone like that. Don't worry though; he just needs to blow off some steam and he'll come around again, just you wait an' see."

"I hope so; the last thing I want to do is make enemies with a bomb enthusiast."

"Ha! Oh Morn... the things you say sometimes," he shook his head. "Well, we're here! I'm not sure what he wants, but whatever it is, good luck!"

"See you around, Ephraim," I smiled back.

CHAPTER TWENTY

A Puzzling Past

I walked up to Blackheart's tent flap and peeked my head in. There was a cloth partition I couldn't see through, dividing the back-half from the front.

"You wanted to see me?" I asked curiously.

"Morningstar, come inside," Blackheart said, seemingly frustrated. "This morning we exposed a traitor within our group who is a spy for one of the other kingdoms. The little bugger was with us for eight months before we even realized it, but now we are going to teach him a lesson. We've got him tied up on the other side of this curtain; I thought you could help me administer the punishment so you can see how we deal with traitors. What do you say? Shall we teach him a lesson?"

"I... suppose I could be of service. How can I help?"

"I am going to ask him questions, and if he gives me an answer I'm not satisfied with, I want you to inflict pain on him by thrusting the shaft of this spear into him. Really drive it in and twist. We will get the answers we seek, but if he continues to try to deceive us, I want you to strike him again, one more time than the last. That means you will hit him *once* the first time, then *twice* the second time, then *three* times the third, and so on. Understand?"

"Can I see who it is?"

"Absolutely not — an assassin must execute his duties without attachment to who his target is and why he or she needs to be killed. Do not complicate what can be kept simple."

"Umm... okay. Yeah... I'm with you Blackheart," I said with moral confusion.

"Alright, then let's begin. First question: What was your purpose in infiltrating our group?"

There was no response, so Blackheart nodded, and I reluctantly thrust the spear forwards. I felt it hit a combination of bone and muscle, meriting an understandably and extremely pained yell.

"I'm going to ask you again; what was your purpose here?"

"I'm not saying anything!" the man behind the curtain yelled defiantly.

Blackheart nodded and I thrust the spear twice, a little higher that time. It felt even worse than before when the man's blood-curdling scream of pain let out again.

"One. More. Time; what was your purpose?" Blackheart threatened.

"Screw you, Blackheart! You can rot in Hell!"

With a forceful nod, he signalled for me to administer three more spear thrusts into him. I hesitated. Blackheart's eyes widened with fury as he took two steps towards me.

"What's the hold up? Strike him, Morningstar..." he said, unimpressed.

I thrust the spear once. His breathless scream sent shivers down my spine, making it even harder to strike him a second time. But I had to; without Blackheart's approval, I would never have The Silence behind me — and without The Silence, my chance at starting a revolution was slim to none.

I thrust it again. No matter how hard I tried to think rationally in that moment, it was useless. The pain in the man's voice continued to echo in my head long after his screams stopped. Soon it wasn't only my ears that began to protest my actions, but my imagination as well — an imagination that pushed discomfort to all my senses like a cry for help. When it came time to apply the third, I just couldn't do it anymore. There had to be another way. Killing wasn't my style, no matter whose good side I wanted to be on.

"Are you with us, or not? Strike him again Morningstar! Or you will be treated as a traitor as well!" Blackheart yelled.

I took hold of the spear, pulled it back, and snapped it in half.

"I won't do it, Blackheart. This isn't right. We both know this doesn't unite the world; this divides it. It divides *us*! The tenets say

'Trust yourself; let instinct transcend all.' Well, I trust my instinct enough to know this is wrong — how can you not see it too?! If the man needs to die, just kill him; don't torture him! And if you're not going to kill him, let him go!"

There was a pause. And then his angry face turned to a smile as he began to laugh. The curtain fell, revealing the carcass of a dead deer — intended to be our meal later that night. One of the other members stood off to the side. He must've been the one screaming.

"This... was all a joke?" I asked, confused.

"This was no joke, my boy," Blackheart clarified. "This was a test! Perhaps you aren't as much of a master of your emotions as we thought, given your outburst, but I am glad to see it step aside for your moral and ethical considerations when it comes to blind obedience to authority. The only way we succeed as a group is not simply following directions, but in keeping each other accountable for our actions, no matter our rank."

"That was pretty devious, Blackheart..." I wrestled aloud with my thoughts.

"Oh come now, just being a little sportive while seeing what you're made of. Here — I'd like to give you something," Blackheart said. "Something that belonged to your father. This was the first, and to my knowledge, the *only* metalsmithed puzzle box he ever made. We've all tried to open it at one point or another, using tools of all kinds, but to no avail. It's yours to take now. I don't know what's in it, or how to open it, but if you can solve its puzzle and reveal its secrets, they are yours to keep."

"Thank you," I mumbled, still lost in the thick emotional fog left by their completely unhinged test.

"Your father would have been proud of you for how you acted today, cruel as you think its necessity was or my act of guile may have been. You are well on your way to becoming a trusted member now, Morningstar; don't take that lightly."

I nodded and left the tent, looking down at the puzzle box in my hand. I examined all sides of it, sliding its mechanisms around. I could hear little clicks and the turning of gears, but nothing seemed to open it for me. I was curious what was inside, but nothing came close to the curiosity of who my father was away from home. Clearly someone I

never knew. In any case, I needed time to think, so I set off into the woods, puzzle box in hand.

When I felt as if I'd walked far enough to be fully alone, distanced from even the ambient noise of the camp, I sat at the foot of a massive tree. Its roots were the size of entire trees themselves, weaving in and out of the ground like gargantuan snakes petrified in wood. It was peaceful there too, but the natural beauty around me couldn't capture my attention in that moment the way my father's puzzle box did.

I twisted it, turned it, and even tried sticking little twigs in there to fiddle with the tiny pieces deep inside, but nothing worked. I must've fiddled with it for hours, but nothing I did made the slightest difference: my every effort was useless, my attempts not good enough — it was as if the box was fashioned from the words of my snake-tongued father himself. The more I played with it, the more I thought of him. Soon the recollective poison that seeped back into my conscious memory was too much to handle. I let out a frustrated yell and threw that damn box as far as I could, splitting off a large chunk of a distant tree's bark — but wouldn't you know, the box was still unscathed. I sat there defeated, angrily playing with my ring as I stared at the muddy box, wondering if there was anything my father ever told me about it before he died. I wasn't there for his last words, so it couldn't have been hidden in those. There was no key he left me. I had nothing of his that he passed down, except for the ring I removed from his finger.

I looked down at the ring lucidly. Blackheart said it *had* been modified since he last saw it...

Walking over and picking the box up once more, I formed a fist, and stuck the ring into the middle of its underside. It clicked into place perfectly. Winding the box about my fist, sure enough, the springs released and the top popped open with ease.

Inside there were a few pages with writing on them torn from a notebook, a large talon that glistened at every angle, a key with an end bent into the same odd symbol I saw etched into the skeletal knights' foreheads, as well as some kind of spiral-shaped metal pendant no bigger than my middle finger on a chain that I put around my neck. As I started looking through the notes in closer detail, it seemed like they were his memoirs and experiences — his life, his thoughts, his knowledge, all spilled upon these pages like the eruptions of a dormant volcano I thought had been inactive for years. At first, the words carried no more value to me than the stained, torn, and scattered papers they were written upon; I was still angry at him and I had every right to be. But the more I read, the more I saw the paper for its words of irrefutable insight — insight I never knew he had. With every new word, I realized that I really had known nothing about him, but then again, I suppose I never asked... and the questions we don't ask become the puzzles we don't solve. It was my fault; I had taken him for granted, seeing him naïvely as a common blacksmith I had issues with, instead of sorting through our emotional mire to find the keen-eyed philosopher underneath.

A tear began to form in the pit of my eye, but I quickly wiped it away in an act of self-preservation. Emotional disconnection was starting to grow on me: if I felt nothing, I would fear nothing. Nothing could hurt me or be taken from me. After all, memories are meant to serve you, not enslave you, and I didn't want my father's words to have any power over me. Of course, anything you don't want to deal with can always be written off as being "in the past" and ignored, but in doing so, you sweep it under a rug where it doesn't go away with time — it *becomes* time itself, and takes on the illusion of life as we think we know it. The truth is, we're all blurry-eyed wanderers of time, and the unfortunance of it all is that we'd probably all go on to do great things if only we searched for what corrected and focused our vision instead of relying on our past — life's grand kaleidoscope — to help us find our way forward. They say you can't change the past despite the fact it never stops changing you — but that doesn't mean we have to sit back and take it. It may change us, but we have ultimate control over *how* we let it; it all comes down to perspective: reframe the moment, reframe the mind.

Those words needed reframing. To turn potential pain into guaranteed gain. Though nearly everything about my father had become a painful memory, knowing he kept his life's wisdom from me had the potential to sting most of all. But I was faced with an important choice: I could allow my emotions to erupt from within and handle the situation *for* me, or I could see it in a new light and make some good out of it. I chose the latter, because emotions are merciless and only end up enslaving your present moments to past events you can't change. By reframing the moment and filtering my emotions through self-deceiving reason, I was able to see my broken relationship with my father through the lens of my current ambitions instead, which made it easier to convince myself that things were exactly as they were

supposed to be for a reason: to shape me into the leader that Fate had hand-selected me to be. My story didn't have to be perfect to be told, it only needed to be something others could relate to — and once they could relate, I could free them from the oppression of the lands as well — show them that we are not slaves to the past, nor servants of the present, but masters of the future.

I kept reading until my thoughts got away from me again. The father I knew wasn't much of a talker after my mother had died, but before then, now that I think of it, I remember revering him for always knowing exactly what to say — having a way with words. When she got sick, however, all that changed. He became distant and eventually closed off completely. After that, I remember going with him to his shop, helping him shape and craft all kinds of metal. From time to time, I'd ask him to teach me some of his more advanced techniques... but every time he just told me to keep working quietly until he was done. Perhaps because he was always deep in thought or had something else on his mind, or preferred to think instead of talk. But the less we spoke, the more it felt like I'd done something wrong or he resented me. I convinced myself it was my mother's death that made him that way; that when she died, he buried all his happiness with her — that how he acted wasn't really his fault. But it got to the point where it was unbearably hard trying to work with him in that emotional state all the time, being around him like that, resisting the gravitational pull that his black hole of misery had on me. That's when I decided to start my own carpentry and woodworking shop. We never really spoke much after that; maybe because we never shared that blacksmithing bond anymore, or because he thought I wasn't satisfied with how hard he worked for me. Hell, maybe he even took offense at the thought that I didn't want to follow in his footsteps the way most of the other children did with their fathers in the kingdom. Whatever it was, we lost touch and never really got it back. I guess in that time apart, he found purpose crafting weapons for The Silence and writing those memoirs of all he'd learned so he had some way to pass his legacy onto generations after him... the unnamed ones he thought to be more deserving of his wisdom than me.

As I refocused on the pages again, I began to read them as words my father had written specifically for me. Whether it was true or not didn't matter; what mattered was that I wanted to believe it, because it was a means to a more beneficial end. Sometimes you must self-deceive until you believe.

His memoirs contained his thoughts and observations on a wide range of topics — topics like: "How to Make Your Enemies Like You", "Keys to a Successful Life", "How to Achieve Anything", "Thoughts on Church", "The Power of an Idea", "Thoughts on Death", "Warning Signs You Are Losing Control of Yourself", and so many more that would be of use to me later on.

I wish I could say my desire to read his memoirs sprung out of love or that I wanted to let his words live on, but more than anything I just wanted to see if his advice could help me further my own plans of revolution. So I began to scan them over, reading small portions of each.

The first heading I saw was "How to Achieve Anything":

"...I've found that everything can be achieved through gradual steps — one small step at a time: overcoming fears, fulfilling dreams... anything you wish to be different from the way it is.

If you fear birds, then begin by thinking of a bird. Take as much time as is necessary thinking of that single bird for a short time span, then longer, and then longer still, until thinking of it no longer stirs up the same high levels of fear it once did. Once you have reached this milestone, repeat it, only instead of just thinking of them, look at a painting of one or hold a carving of a bird. Build up to looking at the real thing far away from a safe distance. After that, view it from a closer distance, and then closer still when you are comfortable. Work up to the point where a live bird is in a cage only an arm's length away. And finally, when you are ready, approach or touch one without any more hindrances.

The time it takes to get over each milestone is different for every person, as it depends on the kind of fear, the fear's strength, and the person's willingness to overcome it. However, breaking down the problem into these smaller portions makes the task of overcoming much easier, much more manageable, and in time, the overall problem will be solved or the goal achieved..."

I flipped to another. It was called, "Thoughts on Death". But... it was different than the others. The writing style was messy, and its content seemed to *ask* questions, instead of *answer* or analyze them like the others did:

> *"...What happens when we die? Is there a way to prepare for it while we are still alive? I have seen the meat rot away from a body, leaving no more than bones, but once the skin is gone, and the muscle after that, it reveals within us no more than the bone underneath. I have not seen ghost, nor spirit, nor apparition rise to the sky nor enter the ground as the last remains of the body disappear to the soil.*
>
> *So what then did I see that night? My thoughts are plagued by the small man with worn, dark cloak and the crimson eye... was it a wraith? And what were those stone tablets he carried in each arm? I know my eyes did not deceive me — the man arrived at the body alone, but when he left there were three! I must know what I saw that night, even if it costs me my life..."*

Chills went down my spine. The supernatural was never a force that put me at ease. Did he find the answer he was looking for? Who did he see? What did he know? It made me curious, but the answers were nowhere to be found in the rest of the passage. It just... ended.

I figured the others may be getting curious as to where I went, so I decided to start reading just one more passage before heading back, "How to Make Your Enemies Like You":

> *"...No matter what we see, or hear, or think — whether new or familiar — we have a certain feeling or predisposition towards it. Our emotions help us bond with the world around us as we seek to understand it. But what makes us feel the way we do? Why do we feel different about one thing compared to another?*
>
> *I've learned, after much experimentation, that our beliefs stem from our actions: what we do turns into how we feel, and how we feel shapes what we believe about the world around us.*
>
> *Though many think that the actions we perform are based on what we believe, in fact, it's the reverse: what we believe comes from what we do. It's as if somewhere inside us, we wonder why we did something, and can only derive its meaning from the objective action itself.*

This is to the enlightened one's benefit: if someone dislikes you, but does something nice for you — as inspired by your own trickery or otherwise — then the more often they do kind acts, the more kindness they'll learn to feel toward you as well. At the same time, if they dislike you, and are allowed to continue doing unkind things to you, it will only reinforce their hatred more.

Make your enemy do something kind for you, and that enemy will no longer be your enemy at all..."

Just then I heard footsteps approaching, so I stuffed the papers back into the box, locked it with my ring, and stood up quickly to make it look like I was actually doing something more assassin-like out there.

It was Gad and Issachar hunting for beasts again.

"You guys aren't here to take me back in a net again, are you?" I joked.

"I wish! Man, Blackheart sure had my ass for that one — Yikes!"

"What are you doing this far from camp?" Issachar asked.

"Oh just practicing the moves Naphtali taught me today," I lied. "I was searching for some animals to practice on, but haven't had much luck."

"Well you never know what you're going to come across out here," Issachar warned. "My advice is if you're fighting something bigger or stronger than you, let it use its own weight and strength against itself. It will tire itself out before long and its size will work against it — if you're quick. Be sure to use quick, fluid strikes and never stop moving. And be careful of your energy; languidness leads to certain death. There's a reason us men are out here hunting and not the women."

"Better not let Naphtali catch you saying that or she'll have you on the ground and begging for mercy faster than you can ask her to mud wrestle Asher," Gad mentioned. "Believe me, I tried... I *still* can't feel my thumbs."

"I appreciate the advice. Speaking of Naphtali, if you have any pointers for beating her, I'm all ears."

"Ha! Good luck! That woman has no weaknesses. I've challenged

her for rank many times, but just when I think I know all her moves, she blindsides me with another. She's ranked number one for a reason — best accept it. Don't worry, your skills will propagate soon enough."

"Yeah, I kind of figured that. Well, I'm heading back to camp now; see you guys tonight."

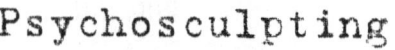

CHAPTER TWENTY-ONE

Psychosculpting

On my way back to camp, I ran into Zebulun, making bombs with Ephraim. Thinking I could smooth things over with him, I struck up conversation.

"Zebulun, about the other day... I didn't mean—"

"Screw you, Morningstar! You think you can just *walk* in here, become Blackheart's new *pet*, and demote the ones who have devoted themselves to The Silence for *years*? Not if I can help it. Better train hard, because when the one-month waiting period to re-challenge is over, I will have your head on a spit, even if your death gets me cast out of the group," he seethed.

"I see," I conceded, starting to walk away. "Well, for what it's worth, I apologize; it was meant only as a means to an end. Nothing personal."

"Oh it's plenty personal..." he mumbled.

I walked away, smacking Ephraim on the arm playfully, but a broken smile was all he could summon under the weight of his brother's response. It was obvious that kind words alone were not going to repair the damage that was done, but where my tactics failed, my father's would help me succeed.

There were still a few minutes to go before we had to gather around the fire to eat, so I found a place among a pile of supplies that I could sit in where no one could see me, and opened the box to continue reading "How to Make Your Enemies Like You":

> *"...So how does this happen? Put simply, our beliefs get hung up on, and crafted by, our actions. If what we're doing or have done doesn't make sense to the mind, the mind makes it make sense in the most logical way possible. So if you can trick them into doing things they'd only do for you if they liked you, they'll start believing they do, because it's the most logical subconscious*

conclusion the mind can make.

There are other ways to exploit the susceptibility of the mind as well. My experimentations show it's also hard-wired in humans of all ages to push away what you don't like and pull closer what you want more of. Manipulate your enemy with this knowledge as you see fit, but know that the key lies in repetition: the more they perform these actions, the more they will be conditioned into the new disposition, and their mind will learn to think as such.

There is also another mind manipulation that seems to be even more powerful still: our awareness of how we appear to others. We all want to feel valued and important. It's because of this desire that the group we choose to surround ourselves with is so crucial to how we act and who we become. The group validates us... but what's interesting is what happens when that group isn't there or we no longer associate with the group we once did: we start to question ourselves. We tear ourselves apart because it is a primal necessity to feel aligned with a group.

The day will come when you join a group and clash with someone else within it. You will be at odds and in full competition with one another until either one of you submits, or one of you quits. While you're at odds, be kind. In some cases, your kindness will be enough to cool the friction between you. However, in most cases you will be in competition until one of you leaves — persevere until it is them who makes this choice. Once self-exiled, they are in a prime psychological state of re-evaluation, questioning themselves — and without the group to validate them, they will feel disconnected, desiring re-alignment with the group more than ever before.

It is in this moment of psychological disconcertion that you will stop being their adversary and become their saviour by reconnecting them with the group. You won't be able to do this by dealing with them directly, as they will still be highly irritated and carry bitterness toward you, so you must find another way. I've found that the most effective way to do this is either through the group-need approach, or the staged-help approach.

In the group-need approach, you make your target feel as if they have or can provide something unique that the group as a whole needs — something essential to their long-term evolution or temporary progression as a unit. If the need is not currently there, create it; find something that can be done that uses a skill they especially excel at or requires a possession they alone have that is hard for the others to come by — set the stage to make them feel valued and needed. When they start participating in the group again and feel that sense of belonging once more, they will feel the transition from disconnectedness back to inclusion, only this time, though the net social change is zero, you will become a subliminal saviour to them, and they will find it difficult to see you in the adversarial way they once did.

In the staged-help approach, you stage a dire scenario whereby your enemy has the opportunity to help you out of a predicament — preferably one of life and death, or otherwise traumatic or significant to both parties. Now, obviously there is a risk with this option; you cannot guarantee that they will help you simply because it's 'the right thing to do'. However, if there is enough interest in it for them, they will struggle with the options longer: help you and benefit themselves, or give you what you've had coming in their eyes even at their expense. They will struggle with the options, but that is to your benefit, for the more a mind thinks upon something, the deeper it will take root and affect all subsequent and related thought..."

I stopped there, sliding the papers back into the box and locked it up tight. It was knowledge I could definitely try on Zebulun, but judging by his response earlier, it seemed like a long shot. Over supper that night, I pondered deeply upon my father's words, and before I fell asleep that night, I knew exactly what I had to do the next day.

CHAPTER TWENTY-TWO

All Fun and Games

After waking up and practicing my combat training with Naphtali, I went looking for a large rope to use in a game of tug-of-war for some sport in camp. On one hand, it would add a little out-of-the-ordinary fun, but more importantly, it was my chance to practice my subtle psychological seed-planting techniques in Zebulun's mind using the push/pull manipulations mentioned in my father's writings.

The others curiously gathered around to see what I was doing.

"Ready for a little friendly competition?" I said with a sly grin on my face to those around.

"I'm in!" Judah yelled with a big smile.

"Me too!" Manasseh exclaimed, knowing no one in the camp was stronger.

Judah's smile dropped as he looked over at Manasseh. "Uhh... I think I just changed my mind."

"Oh come on," I laughed, "when has anyone here backed down from a challenge? The way I see it, we're all doing strength and technique exercises anyway... why not yank the arms out of each other's sockets in a display of superiority while we're at it?"

Blackheart came out of his tent. "I love it! Levi, climb your ladder and signal the others. Everyone should get in on this!"

"Handsome, spontaneous, *and* fun... everything a girl could ask for," Asher flirted with a charming smile as she walked passed me, gently gliding her hand over my chest and looking back over her shoulder for a lingering moment. She was cruel.

"Count me out," Dan miserably grumbled as he went to sit underneath a tree to watch from a distance. I wasn't sure what his deal was, but it was really putting a damper on the mood whenever he was around.

I called Ephraim over subtly and whispered, "Ephraim, I need you to help me with something. When I go up against Zebulun — and lose — I need you to run up to him immediately after and congratulate him with everything you have. Bring a bunch of the others with you so he really feels surrounded by support. Can you do that for me?"

"I see what you're doing," he winked. "You got it, Morn."

The competition became more intense the longer we played. It started with a bunch of one-on-one matches I designated, but soon people got so into the spirit that they began challenging each other and formed teams to take each other on complete with names and team chants. We even had an "everyone against Manasseh" match at one point... but that pretty much went as expected.

My match with Zebulun carried the most importance to me, however, and went exactly as intended. Anger-filled, stress-flooded eyes met mine on the other side of the rope as he wrapped it tight around his wrist for extra leverage, ready to prove he was the stronger. He may have had to wait a month to challenge me again in combat, but as my tug-of-war opponent, he could beat me in front of everyone much sooner and earn back some of his dignity.

It was a success for both of us: by letting Zebulun win, he felt the pride and stress relief of beating me in front of the others, which I hoped would lead to less-adversarial interactions between him and me. At the same time, I got the inner satisfaction of knowing on some level, he was starting to warm up to me. If my father's insights were correct, the emotion that filled his body before and during the match opened him up just long enough for the subliminal seed to be planted. When it was over, those emotions would be recoiling back down inside him with calmness, taking the seed with it to snuggle comfortably back into his subconscious thoughts for processing.

As I was winding up the rope at the end of the festivities, Blackheart crossed my path on the way back into his tent. "I'm glad you're with us. That was a great idea," he praised as he smacked me on the arm.

"I have even better ones than *that*, if you're interested...?"

"Of course! C'mon in," he said approvingly as we walked into his tent and approached the table where he did his planning.

"Blackheart, it's my understanding that The Silence has been roaming the lands for some time. I've been doing some observing, thinking, and planning, and I think I've worked out the kinks for making the construction of a permanent base a feasible long-term plan for us."

"I don't think that's possible, boy. The secretive nature of our alliance would be at risk if we stayed in one place; all it would take is one person to stumble across our camp without our knowing, and that could be the end of us. We need an edge over our opponents, expected or otherwise; remaining in motion is part of our contingency plan. Our second tenet reinforces this: *maintain secrecy; separate yourself from your opponents.*"

"Yes, true. However, the second tenet can still be reinforced through my plan, if you'll hear it?"

He thought for a moment. "Alright, let's have it."

"The second tenet wants us to separate ourselves from our opponents, suggesting we should always have an edge over them, right? By establishing a secure base of operations, we could become the master of our surroundings, knowing our immediate environment better than anyone who would enter our perimeter, would we not?"

"I suppose we would, but we are all highly trained individuals capable of defending ourselves in any condition."

"Like when I freed myself from the ropes while you slept, awakening you with a blade to your throat?"

It was a low blow, but a necessary one to show him their mobile command centre wasn't exactly perfect either. I followed up with more of an explanation right away, so he wouldn't take offense — I only wanted to bring it up as evidence to further my plans rather than to instigate a fight.

"We could make our environment work for us by staying in one place better than we ever could being mobile — here's how: first, we camouflage our tents with the surrounding leaves, grass, sticks, bark, rocks, mud… anything we can use to blend into our surroundings. Of course, we would have to make certain adaptations — the most significant, being a more… subterranean approach to our camp."

"Interesting," he pondered, sounding more intrigued.

"It would take a bit of time to complete the excavation, but we could do it in phases. Being underground would greatly support our ability to remain as secret as possible, as well as make our camouflage of the tent cloth barely noticeable, even at close observation. We could even go a step further to secure the secrecy of our presence by surrounding the camp with a fetid, noisome stench so pungent that most would not want to continue along the path to our camp. Far enough away from us, of course, so as to not fill our camp with the same undesirable smells. All that would be Phase One."

"And Phase Two?"

"An underground tunnel system, linking our base to the other kingdoms. We won't finish this in our lifetime, but we can get started as a gift to our descendants that I'm sure they will find most invaluable someday. When complete, The Silence's reputation will reach godlike proportions of such magnitude, even the sage who came up with the fourth tenet would never have predicted it. What do you think?"

"I have to admit, your ambitions seem a bit... unrealistic, but the thought of its completion and the legacy we would leave to our descendants does sound quite appealing."

He thought again for a moment.

"You know what? I'm with you, Morningstar. We will bring it up at the campfire tonight for all to discuss; if the others are in agreement, you have my full support through to the end," he promised as we gripped each other's wrist in a brotherly bond.

That night around the fire, only a handful of members were opposed to ending their nomadic meanderings at first, but with some convincing and peer pressure, they succumbed to the general consensus, and Phase One was set to begin in the morning.

CHAPTER TWENTY-THREE

Phase One

That night, I laid there for hours, wide awake and swept away by the thoughts of what was quickly becoming possible. As one vision rolled into the next, I rolled the pendant from the puzzle box back and forth between my fingers, unaware I was even doing it until it slipped from my grasp and fell to the floor, commanding my attention as if Fate had purposefully knocked it away.

All the items in that box were there for a reason, but I had yet to discover what that reason was. The writings made sense, but the talon? The key? The pendant? My father was never the jewellery making type — at least not to wear for purposes of glamour or vanity. My ring-turned-puzzle-box-key bore testimony to that. For that fact alone, I knew the capabilities of that pendant were beyond what I was using it for — it was just a matter of time before I figured it out.

I looked at it from all angles, but there was nothing odd about its surface. It was sturdy and solid, but light, as if hollow inside. After some fiddling, the hermetic top popped up when I twisted it, making the once-fixed top springy like a button of some sort. I clicked it with my thumb, but nothing happened. Not even a sound. I tapped it on the bed frame, but nothing unexpected occurred.

Then I blew into it.

The sound was like that of a tiny tube being blown into, only the air I blew into it never came out the bottom, nor shot back at me the way a single-holed, closed-off tube would have. When I blew into it again, the outcome was the same, but when I pressed the button again, it forcefully propelled a small gust of air back at my face like it had been storing my breaths. So I kept blowing into it, breath after breath after breath, and pressed the button again.

"Ow!" I whispered, shaking the pain from my hand while trying to keep as quiet as possible. When the air shot out that time, it stung my thumb the way a sharp fingernail-pinch or a light bee-sting would.

I needed to see what that thing could do, so I stealthily climbed out from under the covers, slipped my tunic on, and left the tent to explore the contraption in more detail.

As I walked into the bush, I kept blowing into it until lightheaded stars twinkled around my eyes. I wanted to see just how much it could hold, but no matter how many times I blew into it, it was still able to hold more. Curiousity made me want to push the top button again, but I would've been an idiot to do it with my thumb — not if it stung like it did after only a couple of breaths. So I pressed it against the nearest tree.

It blew a clean hole through the tree trunk — one nearly as thick as I was tall. I didn't even want to *think* about what might've happened if I used my thumb...

I went and crawled back into bed, thinking of all the things that little bit of metallic serendipity could be used for. But when my creativity started to run dry, my thoughts fell back to my father. I'd grown up and lived fairly close to him for quite some time, and he was never the kind to leave our family for extended periods of time or disappear without saying anything. He was always around — even when he stayed up into the early hours of the morning working on special projects. By living life as he did, I don't see how he would have found time to establish the reputation he had among that group, nor develop inventions like that pendant and box. It didn't make sense, but I was determined to find out. My father was his own kind of puzzle box... and if I could solve *that* when no one else could, I could solve *his* puzzle too. As my thoughts grew heavy and thick, their weight eventually spread to my eyelids and pulled me with them into a deep sleep.

That night I dreamt, but unlike any other dream I'd ever experienced before. It wasn't made up of reinvented physics or a space-time continuum forged in absurdity like when you lick things in the woods that you probably shouldn't. It felt more like a vision. As my consciousness drifted away from me, I saw a dark field, vast and empty, surrounded by the most massive mountains I had ever seen. Black, fiery skies loomed overhead — and there, in the middle of that empty field, was a man, kneeling in front of a large sword whose blade had been planted deep in the ground before him. He held its hilt tight, waiting for the inevitable, never looking up. He kept his head low, fearless under the weight of his hooded, black cloak as he embraced what was coming for him.

The ground began to rumble, but it didn't faze him; the ominous air grew heavier and darker, but still the man didn't move. Whatever was coming was approaching fast and hard, but he was prepared to face it alone. As a chill swept through the field, the mismatched, overly-thick gauntlet on his hand started to glow with a ruby light. It pulsed, sending scarlet waves over his body the way a flame crawls across a patch of oil freshly touched by fire. Shadow spilled forth from underneath his cloak, chilling the area around him as if supernaturally coating his surroundings in a fear that could shatter even the most determined warrior's willpower. Then, in that moment of centering, a thunderous march of oppositional force began to crescendo all around him, forcing Peace into exile until it could no longer call those lands home. Beings of energy, spirit, and flesh marched in unison toward him from all sides with such discipline and synchronicity you'd think they were of one mind.

And then I saw his free hand. It had the same scar I got when I fell from the roof of the church when I was seven-years-old. He wore my ring, my new-found necklace with the exact same pendant... and when he looked up, it was not a face I was ready to see. It was my own. But a face unlike I'd known it in past reflections. It was older, and intimidating, yet familiar. I suddenly appeared in front of him — in front of me — and slowly reached out my hand. But the man picked up his mask of wood-and-metal, and placed it over his face, hiding behind its persona and concealing the man I feared to look away from almost as much as I feared to look upon him. And then, behind that mask, it was as if all his remaining humanity began to fade. Redefining who he was. Who he had become.

I woke up suddenly in my bed, trying to catch my breath, wondering if Reuben had slipped me one of his "special-herb" meatballs to instil such a vision. Thought-provoking as my dream was, I just brushed it off as I settled back to sleep; I was going to need all the energy I could get with the commencing of Phase One in the morning.

When morning came, I awoke with a renewed energy. The sun seemed brighter, the air more pristine — it was as if I had gazed directly into the eyes of life and felt the warmth of its touch for the first time. I got dressed immediately and made my way to Blackheart's tent.

"Ah, Morningstar! I was just thinking of you," he said as he slipped his last piece of leather armour on. "Listen, some of the others and I have to go take care of some business for a couple weeks in Excarpathia, and I was wondering if you would stand in for me as figurehead while I'm gone. After all, the work we'll be starting in camp today was your idea, and who better to oversee our efficiency as a unit than the one who conceived the idea in the first place. What say you, boy?"

"Blackheart, that would be an honour, but are you sure the others are ready to take command from a newcomer?" I asked with false humility, knowing undoubtedly that was what I wanted.

"They'll learn," he advised as I followed him to the well-disciplined horse that waited patiently behind his tent. "Besides, we all need to humble ourselves from time to time and expose ourselves to new perspectives and ideas, even those of the non-experts, or else our growth potential gets weighed down with the ignorance of ego and habit. Just keep an open ear to what the others are saying and feeling at all times, and you'll be fine. Remember: being a leader is not about finding ways to get others to serve you, but knowing how to serve your followers."

"I will serve them well in your stead, Blackheart. They'll be in good hands," I mentioned, watching him mount his horse.

"As will you in theirs, boy; as will you in theirs. We'll be back within the fortnight. Take care of them and I'll see to it that you and I work alongside more often as brothers. Until then," he said with a flick of the reins and darted off into the dense forest.

Blackheart had left full leadership to me. I knew from Naphtali's explanation of the camp hierarchy that Blackheart's position was merely symbolic and not all-powerful like a dictator, but something about it just felt symbolic of even more. In his time away awaited my opportunity to show the others the kind of leader I could be. The kind of people I could make them. The kind of force that history would not allow to go unremembered. It seemed as if Fate was appointing to me bishops, knights, and rooks for a future kingship that would turn the colour of all pieces on the board to my own. But such things took a great deal of time and effort, and I knew it was unwise to waste in thought what could be earned and secured in action.

With that, I set out into the camp and assembled the other members before me. The first thing we had to do was establish a camouflaged perimeter, so as to keep unwanted eyes away from our excavations.

Digging an underground complex was going to be no easy task, but it would be made easier knowing our dedication to secrecy would not be in vain.

Considering that secrecy truly was essential at that stage, our excavation was probably best controlled with the muffled sounds of shovels and other muscle-powered tools, but there was a quicker, more efficient way — a way that could do as much for me as it would for the excavation.

I made my way over to Zebulun's area of camp.

"What do *you* want?"

He had an inconvenienced and bothered tone, but it was a slight improvement over the "screw you" I got last time. Maybe he *was* starting to come around after his frequent tug-of-war victories over me. So I decided to implement another tactic from the memoirs — it was time for some group-need orchestration.

"I need your help, Zebulun. The camouflaging is complete and the excavation is set to begin; but I was thinking: rather than put shovels in the members' hands, asking them to dig a massive area over a period of months or years, and ask even more of your brother and the other members than we need to, I could really use your bomb-making abilities. Your skills are unsurpassed in the explosive arts; it may be a bit louder and messier than the man-power route, but without you, it just seems like unnecessary labour. What do you say? Will you help me?"

"If I do, it's because of Ephraim and everyone else here, not for you."

"Thanks Zebulun, you're the greatest," I flattered as I started to walk away. "I'll come see you soon to let you know what we need. Basically think of the biggest explosion you've ever seen... and make a bomb even bigger than that."

He smirked for once, nodding a single nod, teetering on the edge of suppressed courtesy.

With Zebulun's reluctant acceptance, he had taken a nibble of my baited hook — but he wasn't secure enough on the line to reel him in just yet. He had only shown a faint glimmer of hope, but that hope alone didn't mean he would suddenly start liking me; it simply showed that the other tactics had been working, and had opened him up to the idea, but he still required more convincing. I had to find a way to convince him that it was the right thing to do, or rather, that it was in his best interest to. And who better to reinforce that than his brother, Ephraim?

I set off to use Ephraim as my reinforcing tool by telling him of his brother's "kindness" to help me in something.

"Ephraim, my good man! You'll never guess who agreed to help us just now."

"Who?"

"Your brother."

"What?! How did you... No way! Seriously?! He realizes this is *your* idea, right?"

"Mmhmm — and he still wants to help in the excavation by making some Gargantuans."

"I can't believe it! That's great! So that means you two are okay now? He doesn't want to kill you anymore?"

"I guess not... I just went over and asked him and he agreed! So I guess he won't be getting thrown out of camp for killing me anytime soon. You should go find him," I said with a sly smile.

"Wow, that's amazing! I *will* go find him! As if you convinced him! You're the man, Morningstar!" he yelled as he ran off to find his brother. I knew Ephraim was the one Zebulun trusted most in the camp — perhaps the only one who's opinion truly meant something to him — so to get Ephraim excited meant knowing he'd go praise his brother for his choices, and if he was praised by someone close to him that he trusted so irrevocably, then that would just reinforce exactly what I wanted to condition in him. Loved ones: the source of our greatest strengths and consequently our greatest weaknesses.

When I saw how well that worked, I figured I'd reinforce it further with a slight manipulation of the memoirs' group-need approach: if I made the manual labour more intensive, and the work require more strength and energy to be exerted, I could make the workers tire and strain. Normally that would be of little benefit, of course. However, the more tired and strained they were, the happier they'd feel knowing Zebulun's bombs would make their manual labour unnecessary. And

that happiness and relief would mean they would praise Zebulun for contributing to my idea, thus reinforcing even more the behaviour I wanted to see from him. Pride: the other source of our greatest strength and weakness.

It took five years of working every day to complete Phase One, but by the end, Zebulun had grown to be much more accepting of my presence in the camp. The frequent tug-of-wars only made up for a small portion of my influence on his mind; with his brother basically eating from the palm of my hand, my consistent praises of his work around the campfires at night, and making his knowledge of explosives central to most of my plans, he began to feel more valued and necessary than ever before. As a result, he never did challenge me for the fifth rank again after that — or when I took fourth from Asher, thanks to Naphtali's training. Ever since then, Zebulun had become just as pleasant to work with as all the other members. When I saw how well the psychomanipulations were working on him, I started applying my tactics to everyone else in camp: tailoring my praises to everyone's individual skill-sets. Because my manipulations were subtle and spread out over a long period of time, no one took notice or questioned why I was doing the things I did; they simply went along with it, until there wasn't a soul in camp who would refuse to do what I asked of them at the drop of a hat. They were tools for my future use, and no one was the wiser for it.

At the end of those five years, things were going even better than I could've imagined: my ambitions, knowledge, and insight, along with Blackheart's frequent "recon" trips leaving me in charge raised me up to a status within the camp that was nearly equal to his; meaning that in those five years, I had gained an impressive base of operations and an assembly of assassins who make even the most well-trained knights look like squires. Our headquarters incorporated a contingency plan that would satisfy even the most paranoid of skeptics as well, and with all else considered, we were truly becoming a force to be reckoned with, both in combat and intellect. But there was still much more to be done before we reached historical immortality — and Phase Two was going to bring us that much closer.

CHAPTER TWENTY-FOUR

Passing the Torch

After spending several years outside the Dark Kingdom — the only place I'd ever really known — I felt like I had gained the wisdom and insight of a 60-year-old while still retaining the black-magic youth, energy, and physique of my twenties. I'd learned a lot from The Silence, and was a better man because of their influence on me as well. More grounded. More in-control. I suppose it goes to show that sometimes you can grow more in a shorter time with the right company than years of soul-searching alone, or by living the same patterns you've lived in your entire life. Maybe it's because we're creatures of habit and just need to push ourselves into a new, uncomfortable territory every once in a while so that we force ourselves to adapt. Whatever the reason, I think when drastic change calls, we realize what's truly important to us — the whos and the whats we can't leave behind. Like waking up in our home one night to find ourselves in a blazing fire, we must be arsonists of emotion, forcing ourselves to grab only what is truly important to us before our life-rafters collapse in on us and we can no longer escape alive. We need to feel the panic. Panic is beautiful, because in those moments, our mind reveals whatever means the most to us: the things it has been taking care of for us all along while we've been out thinking everything and everyone requires our attention. They don't. Maybe it's due to the generalized moral lessons we're taught when we're young, or the illusion of duty we somehow take on the older we get, feeling compelled to provide the very thing for others that we felt deprived of in our past. No matter the reason, when the panic fades, we're left with what we value, ready to move on, and that's when everything else — all the excess we don't need — is naturally left behind; all the build-up of the past just slips away as new experiences and people take their place. Change isn't always comfortable, but it always teaches us something of utmost importance — usually about ourselves — and we become better people for it.

Naphtali taught me how to make peace with my past. Over the

years, she helped me harness my emotions, teaching me to restrain and domesticate them like a wild beast until they broke and knew their place within me. To take hold of *them* instead of letting them take hold of *me*, as so many do. The simplest way to do that, she told me, was to learn to release mental stresses through physical expression; to take the abstractions of the mind and focus them into something tangible that can be either made useful, or destroyed, or set aside and out of sight forever. That's when my carpentry skills were reborn. She took a skill I already had and made a passion out of it... opening a channel for me to skilfully express what I needed to, so I could get it out of my system and have a clear mind.

For quite some time after that, I used my spare time in camp to craft myself a two-piece throne — an elaborate ottoman for my feet to serve as a memento of my past, and the throne itself to serve as a symbol of my future. Whenever I sat in it, it was as if I was the present: a keystone bridging what was with what was to come. But more importantly, it stood to remind me that if I wasn't using my present time to bridge the two, then the two would never meet; either I would be stuck in the past with no vision, or I would be doomed to a future with no foundation to remind me of how and why I got there. Naphtali taught me that introspective and symbolic way of looking at the world: that when you give meaning to even the most meaningless of things around you, you will always stand to be taught something new, or have what you already know reinforced, or be reminded of what you'd forgotten. No one I'd ever met before was as insightful as she was. No matter how much I knew, she always taught me more.

One day, when I was leaning back in my wooden throne, my eyes fell to the map on the wall that outlined the location of our camp and the tunnel system as it would be constructed. It was a brilliant idea, but the time it would take to dig them would take decades, or centuries. Maybe even longer. With all due respect to The Silence and their descendants, I did not want to spend my life crafting tunnels, paving the way, and making things easier for a generation that could potentially lack the vision, zest, and insight it would take to fully appreciate what I'd made possible for them. I already carried those values within me; I already saw its advantages and felt its full potential, so it only seemed right I follow it through to its end. After all, there is no glory in *starting* a revolution when you can *finish* one instead. There is no point — no certainty — in entrusting the fragility of such a vision to others when the recipe for success already brews and bubbles deep within your own mental cauldrons.

I made my way through the subterranean passageways to Blackheart's chambers so we could discuss the construction of the tunnels.

"Blackheart, I was thinking about Phase Two. If you have a moment, I was wondering if I could talk to you about something."

It looked like he wanted to discuss something else.

"Everything alright, old friend?" I asked with concern.

"I've been thinking as well," he started as he turned to face the wall. "With all this progress you've brought to the camp these past five years, perhaps it is time I stepped down as figurehead of The Silence. It is evident you have clear direction, as well as the knowledge and wisdom it takes to evaluate incoming situations effectively. Maybe more so than I these days. Your insights have proven themselves time and time again, ushering us into a new age. For me to continue to approve your requests feels no longer necessary; you have earned my trust and that of your peers in the camp. So I feel what I'm about to do is only right..."

He walked over to the wall upon which The Silver Sceptre was mounted between torches — a symbol of his authority among The Silence. He stared at it for a moment before removing it from its place with hard-won acceptance. And then, with a large sigh, he slowly turned to me, dragging his heavy heart with him as he walked over, and placed it in my hands without removing his own from it. I could see the war in his eyes as Pride fought hard against Progress.

"I want you to have this, Morningstar — I can't think of anyone more deserving of its symbolism than you."

"Blackheart... I can't tell you what an honour it is to accept this," I said locking my wrist with his. "It pains me to see you part with it, but while your eyes show the pain of sacrifice, I also see an even stronger gleam of hope. We will continue to work side-by-side as brothers until we give our last breaths, and you will always be among my most trusted advisors. Some things change with time, but our brotherhood shall never be among them."

I pulled him in close with a brotherly hug of strength and comfort. I had learned something valuable about myself through Blackheart's

actions that day: if you refuse to accept what is, and choose to see what could be, then you set a course for yourself that makes others take notice of you, respect you, revere you. It is then that they become objects of *your* destiny instead of you playing a support role in theirs.

Having earned the great honour Blackheart presented me with that day as a result of my ambition, it seemed inappropriate to tell him about my thoughts of scrapping Phase Two altogether. So, in the following hours, we mapped out the tunnel entrances together, trying to find the best way to link our base to the other kingdoms. To create a tunnel system of such magnitude while keeping its construction secret was going to be no easy task, so we had to prioritize.

"The Dark Kingdom is, and has always been, our greatest threat," I spoke persuasively through a thin veil of truth. "The power possessed in that kingdom is the only force that could deny us our rightful place in history or limit our current progress as we pursue our ideals. Our members are extremely skilled, but when a blade meets a hand capable of manipulating the forces of nature, we do not stand a chance. Our first tunnel should be constructed so as to connect us to them."

"I agree. However, King Valenvy of Sipondel is our closest neighbour and our intervention is required there quite frequently; by constructing a tunnel to Valenvy before the Dark King's, we establish more of a 'service tunnel', doubling as a quick way in and out for the more common purpose of business than war and contingency."

I knew how often we went to Sipondel to intervene with their political issues, so there was little I could say to convince him that the Dark Kingdom was more important, especially when the Dark Kingdom had kept to itself for over 200 years.

"You raise a good point. Alright, we will construct the tunnel to Valenvy first, followed by the Dark King. According to the map on your wall, it could even be efficient for the two to share a tunnel most of the way, with a small split in the path somewhere around here," I motioned to a mid-point on the map. "With a juncture here, we'd effectively cut a large portion of our travelling time, regardless of where we're coming from or where we're going."

"I'll let the others know tonight," he stated faithfully.

CHAPTER TWENTY-FIVE

Smoke and Clearers

In the following days, our first tunnel toward the Kingdom of Sipondel, was going perfectly according to plan. Manasseh's strength proved to be almost as invaluable as Zebulun's demolition bombs, helping us clear a tunnel faster than it seemed was humanly possible... that is, until we hit the largest boulder any of us had ever seen. It was much too big for Manasseh to pull out like he did with the others; Zebulun couldn't use his bombs without caving-in the road above us, exposing our tunnel to all who passed by... so our only other option was to dig around the impasse. It was going to add unnecessary time, but when life brings you mountains, you don't waste your time asking why; you spend your time climbing over them.

Days passed by and hope became brittle as the boulder seemed to stretch on forever. Then, when we finally *did* feel its edge, there was another occlusion just like it, pressed tightly against the first, treating our dreams and ambitions like they were of no importance. When we found yet another after that, we started exploring alternative options.

That night, when everyone had fallen into a deep slumber, I donned my tunic, grabbed a torch, and left my chambers to go to examine the obstruction. As I walked there, I remembered my father's pendant; if it was able to bore a hole through such a large tree trunk, there was a possibility it could do the same with the boulders. However, clearly wood and stone do not exactly have the same consistency, so it would be a long shot, but one worth trying anyway.

The whole way there, I kept blowing into it with as much breath as I had within me, blowing until my lungs were ready to burst. When I got to the first boulder, I crossed my fingers, prayed to every god I could think of, and pushed with everything I had.

It didn't let me down.

Like the tree-stump before it, it blasted the air straight into its target. The force was enough to crack it in all directions, so I kept at

it until its center crumbled before me. It was a welcomed godsend... even if I wasn't sure which god sent it.

The rubble at my feet was all that remained of the boulder when I was finished. But I couldn't stop there; a flood of curiosity washed over me, consuming every bit of my attention as I looked through the dusty air to the other side. It was a jet-black wall, but glimmered from time to time with the distorted reflection of my torch's flame. Curious, I picked up one of the bigger chunks of rock that had fallen and threw it at whatever that substance was — it stuck for a few seconds until the weight of it began to roll down the tarry blackness, pulling the goop down with it as it sagged to the ground. It was fascinating. I hurled another chunk at the same spot only to hear that same muffled "plock" sound, before it, too, peeled away the remains of the tar, revealing a hollowness of some kind behind it that the air whistled through as it passed by its tiny orifice.

The hollow pocket, upon closer inspection, appeared to be no mere accident of nature, but a corridor connecting end-points too dark to see where they led. I stuck my head in cautiously: both directions went on farther than my eye could follow... but where my eyes stopped, my curiosity did not. I decided to take a gamble, and climbed through the opening, following the path left to see where it led.

The small, dank, and musty corridor stretched on and on, coated in that stickiness from wall to ceiling. I didn't know how flammable it was, but I figured it'd be best to keep my torch low anyway, in case I found my answer by having my face melted even beyond what only a mother could love. Lucky for me, the ground was made up of something different, safer, feeling like layers of chalk dust stretching the length of the corridor. That is, until I came upon the bones at the fork in the path. When you're in a place like that, any decision could be your last, so my choices of forward, left, or right were not easy. Of course, there was also the obvious option of going back, but "back" was the path followed by those whose names would never be passed on through history — it was an escape for those who feared the unknown.

The path ahead bared no interest for me, while the left and right were much more intriguing: walls made of skulls and broken bones... a warm welcome to any who passed by there. The left, however, had much more than the right. The bones may have caught my interest, but I decided to take the path less-skulled, figuring I had better chances keeping myself alive. Down that path, I found myself trying to illuminate a tunnel so dark, not even the fire of my torch could keep the darkness at bay long enough to see what awaited me just up the road. I crept slowly, keeping my torch as far ahead of me as I could. It was of little help, but as I walked on, I noticed my pace beginning to slow and my senses playing tricks on me. Then delirium and déjà vu set in. The cloudier my thoughts, the more familiar it became. I looked to my feet as tentacles of soporific smoke roamed the floor, swirling around my legs, and reminding me of times best left forgotten. It was the same substance Illyana used on me when I followed her into the Forest of Dreamlock years ago. And I was no more prepared for it than I was back then.

There was one key difference, however: my father's pendant. While I couldn't resist the smoke from consuming my senses with its supernatural possession, I could, however, preserve it inside the canister for later use of my own. I quickly grabbed the pendant on my necklace and began waving it through the air, wondering if it would capture the gelatinous smoke of sense deprivation as well as I hoped.

The smoke continued to expand, filling the corridor until I was wading through its thick resistance with barely the sight and wits it required to escape that mess alive. I looked ahead to see just how far it continued on for, but from what I could see, the answer that awaited me was of no comfort. Even though I was not one to back down from a challenge, I knew my body wasn't going to last much longer there, and, with no one knowing where I was, the seemingly-infinite distance ahead was even more daunting. So instead of continuing on where there was a good chance I'd be left to live the last of my days robbed of my senses, I decided to turn back.

But as it turned out, that wasn't necessarily the best choice either.

The last thing I remember, my foot caught something on the floor.

And my eyes widened in shock as my hand moved to my stomach.

To feel two tri-bladed arrows sticking out of me.

My torch slipped from my fingers.

And my eyes slowly closed.

Then... darkness.

CHAPTER TWENTY-SIX

Investigations

When I awoke, I was back at the base on Benjamin's table. I was a bit dazed, but out of the corner of my eye I could see the arrowheads were no longer sticking out of me, so that was a relief. The wounds tickled a little bit at times, but I didn't think much of it. Benjamin's medical cognizance came through again, whatever he did.

"Benjamin, our patient is awake," Elektra alerted. It was still hard to believe she was nearly ten-years-old with a height that brought her up to just under most people's chins. One day she's holding Naphtali's hand and needing her help tying her boots, the next she's helping save my life with her medical knowledge. They grow up so fast.

"Ah, Morningstar, good to see you awa-uh-da-da," he shook his head and pushed my forehead back down when I tried to sit up. "Just keep still for a little longer. The maggots are still cleaning your wounds."

"Uhh... the what?"

"The maggots. They're not as pathogenic as first thought — some can be, but not the ones in your wounds right now. I've been experimenting on the animals in the cages over there. It seems as if when wounds don't heal, the addition of clean maggots can help clear the dead cells and bacteria in the wound by eating it so it can heal faster. Perfect for soft-tissue wounds like yours. They've done a great job so far."

"So far? How long have I been out?"

"Just over two weeks. We thought we lost you, but whatever it was you encountered, you're definitely lucky to be having this conversation right now."

"TWO WEEKS?!"

"Zebulun found you. Apparently, he went to talk to you about something the night you left, but your door was left open and you weren't inside. So he went looking for you; had he not found you when he did, I don't think you would have made it. From the way he described that smoke, it's amazing he, too, was able to escape, let alone drag you out with him..."

"Where is he now?" I asked, hoping he was alright.

"He's doing the tug-of-war thing with the others in The Core."

"And he's alright?"

"Yeah; he said he was a little dazed, but it faded a couple of hours after he brought you here. So far without any side-effects or symptoms."

"Wow," I shook my head still in shock. "Has anyone explored the area yet?"

"A bold few. I'll go get Gad to tell you all about it."

Gad came in a few minutes later.

"Morningstar! You're alive!" He went in for an absent-minded hug, but Benjamin intercepted it when my eyes widened with the anticipated pain.

"Barely alive from the sounds of it."

"Has Benji told you about the animal parts he put inside you yet?" he laughed.

"If I didn't know you better, I'm sure I'd be removing the stitches to look right now. So I hear you explored the tunnels? What did you find?"

"Well... you, mainly. Other than that we don't know who constructed them, or even if whatever or whoever it was is still in there. After seeing that smoke stuff in person though, I doubt anyone in there is still alive. Oh, and there's a church at one end — Blackheart thinks it's Dark Kingdom's, but none of us have been there before to know for sure. We haven't explored much past that. There is one thing though..."

"What's that?"

"The path across from the corridor with that smoky stuff... the one with all the skulls to the right?"

"Mmhmm?"

"It leads through the Catacombs of Sipondel. And at the end of them, there is a ladder that leads up into a hollow column of what we think is their church. We're pretty certain of it. There's even a thin slit for us to look though, but we can't find a lock, or handle, or anything of the sort in the column — it's like a place of observation without a door; completely useless. It doesn't make sense."

"Hmm," I pondered deeply, "that gives me an idea. Gad, tell everyone to stay out of the tunnels until I give further notice. Have two people on watch at the tunnel entrance at all times — back to back, so no one can sneak up on them. In the meantime, I want you to set some snares along the entire corridor from our entry point to the intersection of skulls; I want to see who's in there."

"I'm on it."

"Sorry to interrupt," Benjamin contributed, looking up from a tome he was reading. "No more than a drop of Elixir Orange in his wounds, Elektra — the tiniest drop will cure his paralysis, but any more than that, and you'll paralyze him completely."

It made me nervous hearing that my ability to walk was in the hands of a ten-year-old girl who once slapped me on the head for not guessing her age correctly. I could only hope that she still wasn't holding a grudge against me for that.

Whatever that "Elixir Orange" was, its therapeutic effect on my paralysis felt incredible. I felt like crawling off the table then and there, until Elektra force-fed me some herbs that knocked me out again. Even unconscious, however, it was good to be alive.

CHAPTER TWENTY-SEVEN

New Directions

"**M**orningstar! Morn, wake up!" Gad had run into the room like he just kicked a hornet's nest and the whole swarm was after him.

"What is it?" I asked, my mind somewhere between dreaming and reality — or *dreality*, as I call it: that cross-over state where it feels like you're in neither place, yet somehow paradoxically living in both.

"The traps I set yesterday! They're all gone! Every last one, and there were over 20 of them. Those were *solid* snares too; whoever can detect and disarm my best traps like that without even knowing they're there — and not just *one*, but *all* of them? I don't know Morningstar. Whoever — or whatever — this is we're dealing with, I'm a little freaked out right now."

"I see... assemble the others and meet me at The Core in ten minutes. It's time to begin Phase Three."

The others filled The Core — a nickname we gave the central amphitheatre in our base — and waited for what I had to say. They arose when I entered.

"'By seeking knowledge, I have freed myself; by freeing myself, I have freed the world.'"

They sat down again.

"My friends; it is the dawn of a new age for The Silence. We have pursued knowledge, and readied ourselves to command the world; we have maintained secrecy, and separated ourselves from our enemies with a base of operations to put the master strategists of the world to shame; we have consolidated power, fortified our skills, and prepared a tunnel system that will enhance our reputation to levels our founding fathers only dreamed of; we have trusted ourselves and sought each other's counsel, learning from one another, and growing as one. All things the tenets have requested of us.

But now it is our duty to fulfil what we have not yet fulfilled: we must create unity. We must act together as a single cohesive unit to bring the world together, and allow it to be divided no longer. Brothers and sisters, we have been guided by forces unseen that have cleared our path of all obstructions, so that we may fulfill our purpose as individuals, as a group, and as guardians over a world plagued by the evils that have long consumed it. It is a world that has become poisoned by ailments far beyond the scope of healing, and now begs for purification.

What we found in those tunnels was a sign from those guiding forces; to one side we have a smoky death awaiting that no man could dare escape — be he skilled, strong, or quick; to the other, we have the catacombs leading to a place of worship: a place where minds have already been prepared for the arrival of truth. A place where hearts long to feel a renewed sense of purpose justified by action.

Fellow assassins, we can bring them that truth; we can share with them the true purpose. Our tenets have been encouraging this call to action for years; the time to answer that call is *now*. By joining with them, we will be taking the steps that our Code and our moral duties command, and bring our forefathers the unification that they desired above all else. These steps will be great in number, but they will lead us down our true path of destiny until we reach the peace we have worked so hard to obtain and secure.

The Age of Unity starts with us and will always hold us at its core. But now we must spread our influence by studying Sipondel's religious texts and beliefs. Only then will we blend into their company as the Spiritual and Moral Guides they all respect and listen to while they pursue their religious ideals. We don't need to know these things inside and out — that is not our purpose. Our purpose is to infiltrate them, unite with them, and subtly infuse them with our values, so that we may stand as one when the time comes, and conquer any opposition that threatens our way of life and the peace we are working towards.

What say you? Do we stand together now, as one?"

There were grunts of loyalty as others spoke their confirmations.

"Til death, Morningstar."

"We're with you."

"All the way, son."

"Always."

"You bet, Morn buddy."

"To the end."

"We've sought knowledge; we have freed ourselves, and now we must free the world!" I shouted with my fist raised high to resounding cheers.

And with that, I turned and left the room immediately to give my words finality. To sear into their minds and call them to action, allowing no questions to be asked, lest they cast doubt upon what I had already decided would take course. My grand opportunity had presented itself and I was not going to let anyone take that away from me. Should anyone become a direct threat to my plans... may the gods show them more mercy than I.

I was no longer a neophyte in the ways of influence; my latent abilities to lead had surged from within like wildfire. As I became more well-educated in the deceptive arts, I became more capable as a leader: flexible, adaptive, aware of the needs of my subordinates — qualities that became even more effective when coupled with the psychological tools in my father's memoirs. The Age of Morningstar had tasted its first breath and it burned within my lungs to inhale more.

The path before us was open; our plan was set. Over the next two years, we prepared and studied in the ways of the righteous men and women that we were soon to impostor, obtained the necessary vestments, and prepared for a change of lifestyle that was certain to bring the revolution I had craved for so long. My numbers were growing; what the future held was no longer a mystery, but a certainty brought about by the power of the powerless — a power that is granted to ordinary people simply by coming together as they unite under a single cause: the power and strength in numbers. The power and strength in following *me*.

CHAPTER TWENTY-EIGHT

Looking the Part

Preparing for our visit to Sipondel, I asked Blackheart as much as I could about it so I knew what to expect. In his words, it was a kingdom once intelligent and confident in themselves. But, like a younger sibling eclipsed by their older sibling's accomplishments, they began to lose faith in who they were as the kingdoms around them rose to abundance. Sipondeli kings came and went so often that the people were robbed of the sense of stability and pride in themselves as a kingdom. As the years went on, they slipped further and further down that slope until their collective lack of ambition and laziness brought a period of poverty upon them that they never grew out of. Instead of changing it, they embraced it; the spirit they once possessed became an implosion of the possibilities of the future, collapsing in on itself into the aftermath of a hopeless present. And afterwards, all that remained were the working-class, underachieving townsfolk who believed they weren't good enough, looking to what others had and comparing themselves against what they saw, wishing the blessings of others were their own. But sadly, even those narrow-minded wishes didn't even draw them up out of the mire to go after what they wanted; unhappiness anchored them in place, and they weren't going anywhere anytime soon. They were at the lowest point of their kingdom's history, and no one did anything about it — not even their king, Valenvy, a man as insipid as four-day-old meatloaf.

According to Blackheart, there were two kinds of people living there: the spiteful ones who wished misfortune on others so they could be seen as better by default, and those who use their envy to drive them to do better. The latter I could shape through their desire for self-improvement, but the others... well, every king needs pawns.

Which means, as per my father's memoirs, it was perfectly ready for my arrival.

"...The power of an idea is never to be underestimated. Many a thought has survived long after its host has ceased to be. It is

the power of an idea that no shield can defend against, nor sword divide, nor poison infect. As such, we must aspire to create ideas, rather than preserve life. In a sense, this is how we achieve true immortality and live on past our time.

Though an idea can transcend the ages, we still, however, only have one life to live. So while we live it, we best do so by preparing a network for that idea to spread through to achieve said immortality. Like the Law of Exponentiation, the more hosts we have to carry that idea, the faster it will spread. This is essential, considering how short one's life truly is.

The conditions that provide the least friction for your idea's replication stem from the following areas: unhappiness, boredom, a feeling of meaninglessness, and especially oppression, where there is a constant desire for change or equalization. With these emotional and pseudological incubators, people need only to see a figurehead or leader who wants to bring them the changes they desire — someone to unite under and follow who shares the same feelings and ideologies. This will give birth to a movement that gives meaning to meaningless lives, gives hope to the helpless, and provides security and camaraderie — the desire to belong — which appeals to the quasi-basic necessity every human being has within them..."

After two years of preparation and study, the day finally arrived for commencing our journey toward Sipondel, masquerading as religious refugees in need of a safe haven. I stood there in my chambers, looking in the mirror, fully clad in the illusory attire of a Catholic bishop: miter white as snow adorning my head, sleeveless pallid chasuble draped around my shoulders atop my pasty-white alb, my pectoral cross around my neck and ring gracing my finger, the sandals to symbolize my assumed vow of poverty, and — my personal favourite — the six-foot-tall crozier to lead my flock in a mass exodus from the Dark Kingdom to the safety of Sipondel's walls. With one last smirk of pride at myself in the mirror, I joined the others who had congregated in The Core.

When I walked in, all conversation stopped and every eye stared.

"You're sure that's what you want to wear for the next few years?"

Ephraim teased. "You look like a character from a satire about Little Red Riding Hood."

"Careful Ephraim; he's carrying a big stick," Simeon warned playfully.

"I appreciate all your support, really," I replied sarcastically. "Alright, let's go over our roles and story to get things straight; I am your bishop, and you, members of my congregation. We are leaving our parish in the Dark Kingdom, because the Dark King's ego got the better of him, turning him to tyranny. Because of his drastic change in demeanour, his queen left him and fled to our parish, where she became a prominent member. This led him to blame her abandonment and betrayal on the supposed mind-control of the Church. With the Church as his enemy, he killed our priest who wouldn't bow to his sacrilege, and the rest of us barely escaped alive. That's what brings us to Sipondel's gates.

Any last thoughts or concerns before we head out?"

"Yeah — is that actually comfortable?" Gad remarked, like the bugger he was.

I just shook my head at him. "We set off at noon."

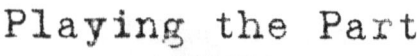

CHAPTER TWENTY-NINE

Playing the Part

Though we could've saved ourselves a significant amount of time by taking the tunnels, we used the surface roads, overgrown with unkempt grass and weeds. I wasn't exactly sure why the surface roads wound through the land as if made by a drunken traveller — surely they had to have known that the shortest distance between two points is a straight line. Personally, I can't walk anywhere without thinking of Pythagoras' teachings: you think of your destination's location, and walk towards it as if following the hypotenuse of the imaginary triangle; the longer the distance, the more time you save instead of wasting time walking along right angles or winding paths paved by the drunken brilliance of road makers.

But the beauty and usefulness of mathematics aside, we arrived at the gates of Sipondel in just under a day. I expected the guards at Sipondel's Gate to make us plead our case, but after seeing my vestments, that was all the justification they needed for opening the gate. I didn't even need to speak, let alone persuade them; their own moral obligations and religious upbringings took care of that for me. It was as if we arrived in a Trojan Horse made of religion, and were accepted just as willingly. No one suspected a thing. After all, how many people would inconvenience a religious man who is known to bring about good things? Who would morally turn him away, knowing if anything unfortunate happened to him, the guilt and blame would fall back on them for not protecting a messenger of God, especially one in mid-exile?

You see, people fear what they do not understand. The afterlife is one of those things; it is unknown and it is awaiting all of us. It is only natural that people would trust in those who claim to know more about it than the common person, let alone how to get there on the best of terms. Hence my plan to pose as one of those experts: I knew a strong, trusted façade, coupled with the common individual's own convictions, would be enough to create a persona that would allow me to walk the paths that cannot be paved by even the craftiest

of tongues. Manipulate *both*, as I did, and even the thickest gates of iron will open before you. After all, the weakest link in any chain of security is not the technology itself, but the person operating it; iron gates have no compassion to appeal to, nor fears to exploit, nor insecurities to use to one's advantage. They are, however, operated by us — by beings of unlimited vulnerability and limited energy. Why waste time brute-forcing what can be easily circumvented by a clever façade and a crimson tongue?

And so the gates were opened, allowing our feet to touch Sipondel's soil for the first time. Our next objective was to make our way toward the local parish. Despite my natural inclination to trust only myself, seek answers on my own, and keep to myself more often than not, I needed to present a new persona: that of the Catholic bishop. So along the way, I nodded friendly nods at people, smiled at them, and asked them kindly for directions I didn't need, just so they would feel helpful — and more importantly — that I was someone deserving of their help. They were all pleased to assist me and receive my blessing over them, smiling and going about their way slightly more content than when we had first crossed paths. It felt like I was making a difference without even trying, despite my lack of genuine concern. It was rather fulfilling actually; it started to make sense to me why someone would pursue employment in the religious arts if they felt that helpful and revered all the time.

As we wandered about the town along the back roads, we arrived at the back of the church. It didn't have a rear entrance, so we had to take a shortcut through the gardens to the front. Along the way, however, it was as if Fate had purposely led that way for a reason, for as the breeze whispered on by, I heard a voice through an open stained-glass window, somewhat stern in tone, speaking to what sounded like a younger boy.

"...But I want to be an acolyte, and one day a deacon, Father Green," the naïve young voice pleaded. "I can do it, I know I can."

"Absolutely not, my child. Every Sunday I see you from the pulpit, pestering the congregation when you should be sitting quietly, paying attention, and learning something. But your inappropriateness only distracts the others from learning for themselves, and when your guardian, Mary, asks you to sit, you are consistently stubborn and continue about your misdeeds. I will not have you doing such childish things while dressed in the robes representing our Lord," replied what must have been the priest.

"I'm sorry, Father! I don't mean to; it's just… I have no one to play with; the kids at school always pick on me 'cause I don't have any parents; I have no friends; the adults here always treat me like I'm dirty or something and look at me like they wish I didn't exist… no one here ever wants me around! I thought you of all people would accept me… but I guess I was wrong," the boy expressed dejectedly.

I looked inquisitively to the others, who shrugged as we continued toward the front doors. Just as I'd reached out my hand to the door handle, it flew open and the boy came running out, tears streaming down his face. He didn't even look up as he ran down the street; he just ran, wanting to get away — and understandably so; I remember feeling unwanted like that in my father's workshop after my mother died. Feeling unwanted is not an easy emotion for a young mind to bear alone.

As we entered the church, the priest was just coming out from his chambers to the right of the altar, and took instant notice of our presence.

"Reverend Father Green of Sipondel, I presume?" I asked with outstretched hand.

"Your Excellency," he replied, confused, "forgive me, but I was unaware that a bishop dwelled in these parts. From which kingdom do you hail?"

"From the Dark Kingdom. I'm sorry Father Green, I wish there were time for pleasantries, but I have grave news: the Dark King is in the emerging stages of a plan to enslave all the kingdoms. His hunger for domination grows as we speak. It is only by the Will of God that we escaped from his clutches when he destroyed our church, which brings us here — to you — our last hope for a place of refuge. The men and women with me today are all who are left of our congregation."

"Oh dear me… and what of the others?" he asked.

"The rest were slaughtered by the Dark One when our priest stood up to him and his sacrilege. You see, the Dark King has begun to see religion as a force trying to manipulate innocent minds against him. It has changed him. As such, he is now bent on ridding his kingdom — and soon all others — of the truths we teach and the things you and I both know to be true. We desperately need your help."

"Oh my... of course! Of course! The church is a place of refuge for all who seek it," the priest assured, motioning for us to follow him as he walked to a nearby room. "Your Excellency, this news is most disturbing. Please, follow me. We can accommodate you in our storage room just back here for the time being until we can find you more suitable lodgings. If there is anything I can do to make you more comfortable in the meantime, please don't hesitate to ask. I will remain here tonight, as I am working on the sermon for tomorrow's mass — which you are welcome to join, if you are able."

"That would be most appreciated, Father. We would be happy to join you and your congregation. We are extremely grateful for your hospitality as well and for allowing us to find safety here. If we can assist you in any way in return, please don't hesitate to let *us* know. We will help wherever, and however, we are able as a symbol of our gratitude."

"It is the least I can do for my brothers and sisters in Christ. I will be just down the hall there, if you need anything."

"Thank you, Father," I replied with false meekness.

When he retired to his chambers, we snuck out of our room and spread out in search of the hollow column that led down into the tunnels. The church was much larger than the one I attended back home, but the style and purpose of the rooms were very similar: a church office, prayer rooms, a kitchen, nursery, fellowship hall, and of course, the sanctuary which also contained the priest's office just to the side of the altar. Searching upwards of an hour proved to be of little benefit for most of us; the column was nowhere to be found to the untrained eye. Lucky for us, Benjamin's librarious mind came to the rescue, recalling an image he had seen in a textbook once that looked quite similar to the artwork in the priest's office. Below his crucifix was a painting of Jesus meeting Lazarus at the entrance to his tomb. But unlike the renowned version of that painting, which shows only the two men looking at each other, that painting ever-so-subtly showed a cloaked individual with a tiny crimson eye hiding behind the boulder. It was practically unnoticeable the way the shading of the cloak mixed so effortlessly into the dark background, as if merely a gradient of colour. His eye as well, being of a deep-red so well-blended, it could be assumed to be a stain or a brushstroke's leftover paint remnants at best. But thanks to Benjamin's keen eye, it was certain the painting was anything but a reproduction. There

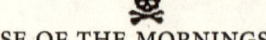

was much more to it and many more questions that arose from the inconsistency. Perhaps Father Green knew something of the tunnels below — and maybe even of the Crimson-Eyed One in the painting — a figure who looked exactly like my father's memoirs described...

CHAPTER THIRTY

Minds for Molding

At morning's call, the priest knocked on the door of our temporary lodgings and told us of a fresh breakfast that awaited us in the kitchen area. Cold juice, eggs, sausage, and twice-mashed potatoes filled our plates and bellies — and really, how can you start a revolution without such things? To do so is almost blasphemy in itself. The priest sat with us, right next to me as a matter of fact, and asked if I wouldn't mind saying a few words about our situation when he introduced us to the congregation just before starting his sermon. I accepted his offer, seeing it as my first chance to influence the others under the same diplomatic shroud of humble deceit.

When it was almost time for mass to begin, we each took our seats — not together, so as to show ourselves as a group distinct from the congregation, but dispersed among them to show our unassuming vulnerabilities and implied willingness to be accepted by them as *individuals* in need. I sat near the pulpit behind Father Green, as both a figure of authority and as a shepherd caring for all. From there, I could oversee them all collectively as equals among one another, as I would my own flock, with my back turned to no one. Mastery of such non-verbal language and strategy is essential to ensuring your place among a new group. It is the reason why first impressions are so important; the mind thinks upon, processes, and remembers what the senses forget. Father Green gave me that opportunity and more when he asked me to tell the others of our situation.

"...Please join me in welcoming His Most Reverend Excellency, Morningstar, Bishop of the Dark Kingdom."

"Thank you, Father. Citizens of Sipondel, I thank you for taking us in as your own. Our homeland, the Dark Kingdom, these past few weeks has become a moral and holy battleground that the Forces of Darkness are trying to claim as their own. Hearts and minds have become targets of acquisition at the hand of the Dark One himself. Those he could not enslave, you see before you today: your brothers and sisters in truth. But it does my heart a great disservice to mention that there were many others who were not so fortunate. Many became martyrs, standing up to the dark forces, and our thoughts remain with them always. But they deserve more than our thoughts; we went into exile so we may not only honour them, but carry word of their sacrifice, and play a part in preventing the need for your own.

What the Dark King has done in his kingdom is merely a glimpse of what he plans to do here, as well as to the other kingdoms. He will start with the churches, but he will stop at nothing until the entire population in every kingdom is under his rule. We come before you today, not only seeking refuge, but also asking your help — a way of aiding us as well as yourselves so we might bring this blasphemy to an end. I wish I had a means of sharing how we hope to bring about this holy resistance, but at the moment our spirits are willing, yet our flesh is weak.

If you will join with us, to stand as one in defiance of evil, to preserve and put to action what we have taught our young ones to do their whole lives because we believe it is right and just, we can overcome; we can be triumphant in the Name of our Lord.

Please think upon this as we reside here under the care and hospitality of your generous priest until we can decide what needs to be done.

With all we have within us, thank you again, every one of you, for accepting us as your own; without you, we may still be fighting the beasts of the forest for our lives if only to have a place to lay our heads to rest peacefully."

Father Green took the pulpit to begin his sermon as I sat down behind him again. By the reactions of the congregation, I could tell his words were taking a backseat to the fear and worry that existed in hushed murmurs passing back and forth among its members. As I looked over each and every face, I saw sadness, reluctance, hope, fear — many of the things I expected as per Blackheart's description of their kingdom-wide disposition. But it was surprising to me to see Elektra and the boy who had been crying the day before smiling at each other with that shy, childlike flirtation. Though he was a few years younger than she by the looks of him, I was glad to see her gain a friend closer to her age that she could play with.

After the sermon, the congregation remained in the sanctuary to socialize and discuss what they had heard, but I was most curious to find where the boy from yesterday had gone. I knew by the words he spoke to the priest that he carried a pariah's hunger for belonging that would command an unwavering loyalty to me in my future endeavours. By capitalizing on what I heard the boy ask of the priest, and taking him in as my own, he could feel the acceptance he has never known, but always craved, and we could both benefit from it.

Just as my eyes were sweeping the congregation, I saw him from all the way across the sea of faces, nearly out the door with a middle-aged woman taking him by the hand. I figured that was "Mary", the guardian the priest spoke of when we passed by his office window the day before. I weaved through the crowd quickly, hoping to catch him just as Mary left so I could speak to him without raising any curiousities, but, like a responsible woman, she poked her head back in the door to see where he was after all of three seconds. She seemed shocked I was there, but stared at my face like it was familiar. At first, I thought her speechlessness was because I was a religious celebrity in those parts and she was honoured to be in my presence like so many of the others, but as I later found out, that wasn't the case...

"What is your name, son?"

"Arkade."

"And how old are you, Arkade?"

"Seven-and-a-half."

"Well, it's a pleasure to meet you Arkade. Miss?" I asked as I turned to Mary. "Would you mind if I spoke to Arkade in private for a moment about a concern I heard him express earlier? We won't be more than a minute or two."

"Yes... absolutely," she replied kindly and then turned back to the boy. "I'll just be outside the door when you're ready, dear."

The boy looked at me curiously.

"Arkade, you strike me as a young man of great potential; a boy who one day will no longer need the approval of others, because *they* will seek it of *you*. But for some reason, you seem somewhat... desolate — saddened by something and removed from the others. Why is this?" I wormtongued of the child's malleable mind.

"I just... nobody wants me around, sir."

"Why would they not want a charming boy like yourself around?"

"I don't know. I guess they just don't like me."

"That can't be a good feeling..." I said with an understanding tone.

He looked down in silence.

"I'll tell you what: there is a reddish plant I am in need of, called Amaranth, looking somewhat like a long spindle. It means very much to me. I have searched the countryside far and wide, but cannot find it for the life of me. If you could find and bring me a stem of its delicate beauty, I will personally see to it that you are given privileges the other children will only wish they had. What do you say?"

The boy smiled at the false-bottomed offer and burst out of the doors, frolicking down the street, determined to complete his mission as Mary chased behind, yelling at him to slow down. The boy seemed so naïve that I wasn't sure how useful he would be to me at first, but in time, his gullibility would prove to be clay more valuable to this potter's hands than first thought. Usefulness: a feeling so basic, yet so fulfilling, that we thirst for it like water, ready to drink deep of its stream without so much as questioning from where it flows...

CHAPTER THIRTY-ONE

The Power of an Idea

People were just starting to leave when I went back into the church and found my loyal subjects all intermingling with the congregation. Though I didn't know what it was like to be a father, that's exactly how I imagined it would feel: that moment of pride as you watch them from a distance, living a life according to what you've taught them to be. The pride of knowing they have become their own person based on how you've shaped them, just as vines grow along whatever stable support they can find. I envied parents for that feeling.

Satisfied that everything was under control, I made my way to the back room we were staying in. After successfully infiltrating the church and networking ourselves among its members, our foundation had been laid and was already beginning to set, so I used my time to seek a little more guidance and inspiration from the memoirs, especially eager to continue my reading on "The Power of an Idea":

> *"...Democracy can easily be used to mask the beginnings of an autocracy. With democracy, people are given a choice, and when you give people a choice, they believe they have power. Now, as long as they continue to believe they have that power — that their part is the most important part in determining the outcome of the process — then the one to whom they vote their power away is free to use it however he or she pleases... to manipulate the people however he or she sees fit. This is the trapdoor stage.*
>
> *However, the conscious mind is smarter than most give it credit for; if it is given too much change at once, it will detect something is wrong and close itself off as a survival mechanism. It works similar to digestion: imagine swallowing a piece of steak without chewing it; you'll either choke or want to spit it out to get rid of it instantly — but chew it into tiny pieces, break it down, and you'll surely find no difficulty ingesting it. You may even take pleasure in its less-invasive form. This same principle*

will be applied to the followers you assemble as you manipulate them to bring your idea to life.

This process begins with finding a group of either like-minded individuals with diverse goals, or diverse individuals united by a common goal. Whatever the case, there must be at least one core value that they all share, or one major dissatisfaction they all have. It isn't difficult to find these groups either, considering the obvious fact that they group together — find a group, and you've found what you need to get started. Not all kinds of groups have the same malleability-of-mind, however, so you must choose carefully. I suggest looking to groups where the blind acceptance of authority and conformity is rewarded frequently: educational classrooms, religious assemblies, workplaces where people's livelihoods and families depend on them keeping their jobs... each are aptly sufficient.

Next, you must pursue the means of becoming the accepted authority among the group — its leader, in any context of the word. There are two ways to go about this: networking charismatically among them so they will promote you, or alternatively, completing the necessary "officially accepted" training. In choosing the latter, you will notice that the hierarchical constructs will already be in place, thus expediting your rise to authority, and facilitating your efforts to get others doing what you want them to do even faster. It is often the more universally accepted and stable of the two paths, especially for those who lack natural charisma. Whichever path you choose for yourself, do not hesitate to do whatever you need to do to advance your position.

Once you've established yourself as an authority of sorts, it is essential to start strengthening the bond and correlation between what you say and what the group does. Keep in mind that being an authority on paper does not immediately grant you authority over a group until it is earned by you and given by them. Begin by giving small, simple, even trivial instructions to them to build that initial trust — frame it in such a way that they know that following your instructions will benefit themselves. For example,

consider exercise: instructing your subjects to, in unison, run on the spot or throw their hands in the air as part of leader-led morning exercise routine will be something very few will challenge, especially in the name of increased blood-circulation and physical health for themselves. Of course, exercising won't be embraced by every group, so you must find something they enjoy that involves following your instructions to keep that activity flowing. By performing trivial actions like this together as per your instructions, your subjects' subconscious mindmaps will form the psychological groundwork toward you, needed for later stages. This activates the psycho-bricklaying stage.

At this point, there shouldn't be much opposition from your subjects toward you as their leader, seeing that the instructions you've started giving them — that is, subtly commanded them to do — are relatively harmless. People are used to taking trivial commands in everyday life. What turns their trifling synchronizations toward your cause is the added perception of a 'common enemy'. This too, can be an insignificant opponent at first, such as when a group wants to fundraise more than another, or trains harder to beat another in a given task — the specifics don't matter as long as they have something to focus on and conquer by working together. Such things seem innocent, but keep in mind, the smaller and more innocent things appear, the more willingly accepted and undetected each incremental action or request from you, their leader, will be. This is the blind pursuit stage. The 'common enemy' gives the group something to compare themselves to, compete against, and do better than — motivations that all ultimately set themselves working toward a goal focused on the extrinsic domination of others and distracts them from the actual power structure they are unknowingly becoming a part of.

Once a common cause is established, the loyalty of your subjects can be strengthened by manipulating their need to belong to the group. With that said, among them will be an assortment of introverted and extroverted subjects, both of whom gain intrinsic value in different ways. The leader's best approach is to assign roles that help the cause based on their individual strengths. In doing so, individuals perform deeds for the cause that they are good at, which appeals to their self-esteem, and naturally adds a deeper level of commitment to your cause within them. This kind of commitment is essential, as it binds them to the cause due to the feel-good sensations they get, knowing they excel at their role. We all gravitate towards what we're good at because of the sense of purpose it gives us — and a sense of purpose leads to contentment and happiness. This is the associative identity stage.

This approach also has an added bonus: as the movement grows and more members join, your original members will evolve psychologically. That is, they will start to see themselves not only as subordinates to you, but as leaders over followers of their own — middle managers, so to speak. We all desire power and authority over our immediate environment; this will grant your followers that inherent satisfaction. Remember, the lion does not need the whole world to fear him, only those nearest where he roams. The more members that join, the farther each person's authority will reach, and the deeper they will sink into the mindset of the movement due to the satisfaction and power it brings them. The more authority each person feels, the harder it will be for them to leave the group or question what is asked of them, because you will be giving them so much of what they want, that their ethically-acceptable grey-areas will expand in direct relation. They will compromise more the longer they are exposed to the limits of those grey areas. Take advantage of this, and be sure they recognize you as the benefactor — as the reason they have what they have and feel as good as they feel. Remind them often that such things come as a result of their contributions to the cause, and you will see that it continues to exist and thrive.

If subjects don't conform, you must have a backup reason to mask what your intentions are, being sure to redirect your subjects' arguments and concerns toward their own insecurities. Perspectivize their non-conformity; don't help them realize they

are taking a stand based on morals or ethics or beliefs, because
such things run deeper than the conscious mind in most people.
Instead, discuss their non-conformity as being a pitfall of their
egoism, vanity, or fears. People are more willing to change
based on their perceived insecurities than by an attack on their
beliefs; the latter makes them defensive and closed-off, instead
of introspective and open to being a better version of who
they already are, as you want them to feel, and as the former
accomplishes.

If an individual is still proving to be difficult, do not address
the rebellion in front of the others; keep things positive and
constructive when addressing the group as a whole to keep
momentum and feed upon the fervour of the movement. The
rebellion, like a virus, must be quarantined and dealt with in
private due to how quickly it can spread or make others think
upon and question similar things. Peer pressure takes care of the
rest, particularly from the ones who feel the strongest sense of
belonging and empowerment already. These people are commonly
the ones who lacked such things most before joining your cause.

As time goes on, your subjects will begin to notice a clear
division between an 'in' crowd — those who belong to the
movement — and the 'out' crowd — everyone else. This is the
socio-awareness stage. It is inevitable that this realization will
occur; the movement's subtle beginnings can only last for so long
until its acts of loyalty grow and the member population expands
too large to go unnoticed. When this happens, the members must
be instructed to stand together and identify themselves as being
separate, better than, and different from the others; they must see
the outsiders as unlike themselves — lesser beings, so to speak.
As their leader, this is a crucial stage when you must comfort
them the way a parent does their child who has woken from a
nightmare. You must refocus them; address the separation anxiety
and feeling of disconnect they feel. Show that you can identify
with them, even behind a veil of false yet convincing compassion,
until they know their disconnect is not because they are on the
outside, but rather because they are the new inside. It shouldn't

take much convincing, because of two key facts: 1) we yearn for human connection and to be understood, and 2) we are creatures of habit more than we are creatures of change; as such, the feeling of convenience and belonging they already feel within their own group will override the temporary desire to belong outside it, or to a rival group.

Realizing they are different will likely begin to develop in your followers a need to establish territories they can call their own — places of safety and symbols of their belonging. This is the gangland mindset stage: the point at which all the ideas that the leader had planted in their minds in the beginning — the unity, the belonging, the rewards for skills contributed to the group — all these things suddenly create the need to balance what they do and how they act with how they think. To make their ideals tangible. As such, their internal branding looks outward to the society in which they live, and they will seek to balance it with the ideals you've passed on to them. Don't be surprised if they feel inclined to implement this by force.

As they infiltrate commonplace society, their numbers alone will help them take over areas of the city. Start small — one area or establishment at a time. Commandeering local establishments simply by hanging out in large groups will force non-members to become members if they want access to the places they've always attended. This is the expansion phase. As previously mentioned, we are creatures of habit; as a result, non-members will not want to be turned away from a destination they feel comfortable in and identify with. Therefore, if the destination can still be used as desired by simply becoming a member and promising to deny entry to non-members, most will accept the parameters or face the consequences as the members see appropriate. Fear is an effective motivational tool, as you will see; the usefulness of which never depletes. Thus begins the subtle poison that propagates through identity as it leads to belonging, then to commitment, and eventually to self-branding.

If the movement gets this far, since not all movements do, like any effective model of society and civilization, there will *need to be disciplinary measures to ensure the gangland-mindset stays in tune and filters out unwanted dilutions. Enforcement roles need to be introduced. Thus begins the protective guidance stage. Enforcers are best selected from the loners and outcasts of a group: the ones who have little to offer elsewhere, and without the cause would be generally ignored and rejected by the others. By the leader hand-picking them, many benefits propagate: 1) enforcers feel power over others who used to have power over them, 2) though they are no more than goons, they feel a sense of hierarchical importance, and 3) they become undoubtedly loyal to the cause for giving them a promotion in life and status. Being given such power and status all at once when they had little before, however, is likely to make them emotionally unstable as well. This is because such things, from a psychological standpoint, must be earned slowly so the weight and feeling of it can be grown accustomed to and handled in manageable pieces. While this might seem risky, it actually reminds them that all their power and value now depends on the existence and success of this movement, and so they hold onto it at all costs with extreme loyalty. This fear of loss can make them do drastic things. As a result, the others soon come to realize that the enforcer's loyalty comes before logic, and so will fear stepping out of line so they won't be irrationally punished. For as long as the leader gives the enforcer this redefined sense of purpose, they will not question their orders, because a more basic human need is being met. This commences the domination stage..."*

That kind of knowledge seemed to be way outside my father's experiential bounds, yet somehow the information made sense and seemed accurate and entirely possible. I knew for a fact he was never the leader of a group to even test or implement those theories — at least, not that I was aware of — so where that knowledge came from was beyond me. It seemed like the more I read about my father, the less I knew about him... and the more fascinating he became.

CHAPTER THIRTY-TWO

Red-Handed

When I had finished reading, Arkade came bursting through the doors, eyes beaming with ecstasy. He had found the Amaranth I had pretended to be in need of.

"Sir! Sir! I mean... Your Excellency," he beamed as he ran up to the table. "I found it! I found your flower!"

"My goodness, you did! However did you find it?" I entertained with minimal effort. I could see on his face that my request had made him feel useful and of worth for once — feelings I was conditioning him to associate with me.

"It was along the outside wall of the kingdom! They told me I 'wasn't to leave the gates unless I was with an adult', but I didn't use the gates... I climbed the wall," he giggled.

"Well, you have shown yourself to be very resourceful indeed," I affirmed. "I don't know what that old ingrate Father Green was talking about, but just between you and me, I think he was seeing you only for the bad things you did instead of for your intelligence and potential; don't you think?"

The boy smiled and nodded with gratitude in his eyes, accepting my somewhat controversial comments completely unaware he was being sculpted as my future enforcer.

"How would you like to be my personal assistant, helping me in my studies and duties?"

"Me? But... why me?"

"Because you are observant, quick, and curious. You have what so many of the others around here lack, and it's *those* traits that will keep you attentive and learning much from me, so you, too, may be looked to and revered someday, as I am."

"You... really mean that, Your Excellency?"

"Absolutely — and call me Morningstar. However, you should know, my son, I'm not like other clergymen you may have met. While I do study the Word of God, I like to wrestle with philosophy, ethics, controversial ideas, and morality of all sorts in search of a balanced truth that I can bring to all mankind, religious or otherwise. I seek to unlock the secrets of the universe: secrets unlocked in part by religion, in part by the sciences, but in such a way that each cannot exist without the other, and must be analysed together as one. What say you to this?"

"I don't know; I've never really thought about all that stuff before."

"Well, my boy... then come sit, and prepare yourself for a whole new world to open up before you..."

In the following weeks, Arkade studied with me, allowing me to condition him with all kinds of predisposed, thought-provoking questions. He particularly enjoyed the ethical dilemmas, such as: "If someone was going to kill someone dear to you, and you could stop that person by killing them instead, would you kill, knowing it was the only way to save your loved one?" or the more popular "You believe stealing is wrong, but if your family was starving and could not afford bread, wouldn't you say it's okay to steal a loaf to feed them?" The boy appeared to be unexpectedly forthright with his thoughts and opinions, answering all my questions deeply, yet without hesitation. It did not bother him to entertain the fate of himself or others with hypothetical scenarios of misfortune that would make most people uncomfortable. Between his thirst for knowledge, hunger for belonging, and potential feelings for Elektra, I knew I could keep that boy in my maze of smoke and mirrors for quite some time. But what's more: his mind was still young and developing — a sponge whose natural inclinations resort to absorption before filtering through reason. And then, once he was old enough to be capable of deep reason, he would already have absorbed so much of my teachings that any evidence of truth to the contrary would be denounced and rejected, or at least bring great discomfort. The other members of The Silence were loyal, but no adult mind compares to the dependence and impressionability of a child's.

I should interrupt my tale there, because I am starting to get the sense you are casting me into some kind of evil light as I shape and influence the world around me through the minds of others. I assure you: everything I do is with specified intention and no different than what you have done as parents, teachers, friends, and citizens. We see opportunities and take advantage of them. We prepare the current slaves of the present to become masters of a future we hope will bring about better days than the ones we have lived. And who else do we trust to teach others but ourselves?

Despite our human intelligence, we are very much like our friends in the wild; the world we live in is a survival of the fittest. But to that I say: let the fittest survive! Survival is overrated. We're alive; we die. How long we survive is of little significance. Our *true* significance lies not in the endless comparing of ourselves to one another, trying to see who is the fittest, using scales of evaluation and meaning that differ in the heart and mind of every individual. No — it lies in our deeds alone with the time we have.

The truth is, fit or unfit, we are all exposed and vulnerable to the psychological manipulations of grey-matter tailors like myself and many of you, whether you realize it yet or not. Our conscious mind is a sweater made entirely of loose threads. Some of those threads are unravelled by confidantes we trust to pull or "fix" for us. Other threads simply get caught up on things by accident, such as objects of affection or new ideas, unravelling us that way. And then there are the times we even become self-aware or ashamed of *ourselves*: pulling our *own* threads to our own demise simply because we have a preconceived notion that we are not to *have* loose threads — God-forbid others see our imperfections. With ignorant consequence, we pull ourselves apart trying to rid ourselves of any and all imperfections rather than embracing them for the uniqueness they give us, and understanding that we all have them — that they are not something to hide.

Whatever the case, what separates us into engineers and robots, puppeteers and puppets, kings and pawns, is not the status we hold at any given time among others — status is irrelevant; it is the level of ever-present awareness we have of a grey-matter tailor's tools: flattery, favours with the binding expectation of future repayment, a persuasive speech to remind you of your fears yet make you see the tailor through a saviouresque or guardian-like lens while they masquerade in front of you, pretending to be able to protect you from your fears. They can't. Your protection lies in your own hands. It lies in your own mind.

You see, our lives consist of a series of internal battles, deep within us, where weapons don't exist and technology is unable to create devices that better the best of yesterday. Our knowledge is our only

defense; caution, our only friend. It begs the question: why spend your life working on defense when no defense can be made truly impenetrable? Take the offensive — learn the vulnerabilities of the world around you, and be the change you wish to see rather than living in constant fear of what may happen to you instead. When all is said and done, everyone should be able to look back on their life and know that they made it exactly as they wanted it to be. As I did. As you can.

Speaking of making things the way we want them to be, it had been days since The Silence was able to meet to discuss strategies and implementations; the priest was always around, and we couldn't risk blowing our cover after getting that far. So one night, long after the priest had gone home, we decided to gather and share our observations.

"Is it just me, or are we more brilliant than we thought?" Ephraim opened.

"It's like stealing candy from a baby," Zebulun said, leaning back against a pile of chairs.

"Have any of you been questioned, or thought to be... odd in any way by the people here? I get nervous when there are no problems to solve." Benjamin had a point.

"Nothing of significance," Naphtali added. "I heard one woman ask her friend if it's strange for a bishop to enjoy the company of such a burdensome child, referring to the Arkade boy and Morningstar of course, but her friend just told her to think nothing of it because he is a respected holy man and a good male role model for him. Especially since his own father isn't in the picture anymore. The woman seemed to have accepted her friend's advice just fine, so no need for alarm there. Other than that, everyone is more focused on and worried about the Dark King's impending attack we spoke of."

"Perfect," I expressed, "then they are accepting us exactly as we need them to. But we have one little hitch: the priest still insists on handling all the sermons, because he 'knows the issues that his congregation is dealing with'. However, unless I take over, our truth will remain contained and we still need to spread it somehow."

"We could each spread our ideas individually among them; that way there is more of us so it would replicate faster," Blackheart suggested.

"An excellent idea, however, to these people, you are merely learners of the Word, as they are. Though you may share the same wisdom a priest or bishop would, they will likely thank you, tell you how wise you are, feel good about themselves temporarily, and then ignore your advice completely, because you are on the same level as they with very little authority over the group as a whole. People respond more to the authority of status, than the authority of truth. It is an unfortunate truth, but a noble suggestion nonetheless. Any ideas on how we can help get the message to the others through me?"

"We could kill the priest in his sleep," Dan the misanthrope urged.

"Or I could steal his long-winded sermon notes every Saturday night," Simeon joked.

"I could cook him some rancid steak — he can't preach if he's on the chamber pot!" Reuben laughed.

"You're all hilarious," I mentioned sarcastically. "But seriously, we nee—"

Just then, the door swung open, interrupting our meeting with a loud bang — but even without the door, the look on Father Green's face was commanding enough.

"This is how you plan to treat your host? The one who took you in when you had nowhere else to go?"

"Father Green, forgive us; it was out of place to joke in such ways. No doubt, the things you may have heard now sound repulsive and disrespectful, but we didn't mean them as such. Please — we apologize with utmost humility. It was meant to be no more than friendly, pre-bedtime banter to entertain weary minds," I tactfully commented, trying to make our meeting seem less cloak-and-dagger.

"Oh, I heard quite enough of your little discussion and your shady underdealings to know your remarks and intentions *far* exceed the possibility of being considered 'friendly banter'. I will expose you all to the congregation and share my disapproval at mass on Sunday, and then... *then* we shall see just what you have to say for yourselves."

He turned and stormed off to leave the church, but I ran after him. If we didn't smooth things over, everything we had worked for would've been for nothing.

"Father Green! Father Green, let us not depart on such terms! Surely

we can talk about this like holy men and come to an understanding," I called out, hoping his stubbornness could be reasoned with into compliance.

"I am a very understanding man, but you and your group have gone much too far! Are you even a religious man, or just pretending to be one? A religious man should be a philanthropist, promoting goodness, seeking the light to bring about good with patience — not killing or finding ways to remove those slowing you down. I hear you speak of murder and sabotage; these are not the thoughts entertained by a bishop of the Catholic Church! And your conjectures regarding the Dark King supposedly coming after us — how do you plan on handling him? By killing him as well? And what then? Once you have removed the supposed threat, suddenly you will have brought *good* to the world? Son, you are misled. And how *dare* you try to use the scriptures to persuade innocent minds for your own gains! Have you no moral convictions in yourself?"

"Father Green, I understand your concerns, but I assure you they are moot. Doesn't 2 Timothy 3:16-17 tell us that '*All* Scripture is God-breathed and is useful for teaching, rebuking, correcting, and training in righteousness, so that the servant of God may be thoroughly equipped for *every* good work.'? I am simply training the servants of God so they may be prepared for a holy moment of glory that will shine so bright, all the kingdoms will see and bear witness to its cause. By standing up as one against the Dark King, we use this time of need to bring more servants to the Lord in a moment of blazing glory than centuries of passive teaching."

"Ah! But it also says in Matthew 6:33 that if we 'Seek first His kingdom and His righteousness', then 'all these things shall be added' unto us! Not to mention, in Luke 6:27-31 the Lord says 'Love your enemies, do good to those who hate you, bless those who curse you, pray for those who mistreat you. If someone slaps you on one cheek, turn to them the other also. If someone takes your coat, do not withhold your shirt from them. Give to everyone who asks you, and if anyone takes what belongs to you, do not demand it back. Do to others as you would have them do to you.' As you can see, we are not meant to assemble armies to kill our enemies, but rather let them run their course, and in the end, the Lord will pour his wrath upon them on our behalf."

"And in the meantime allow His people to be slaughtered? That verse is meant for us to meditate upon so that we know how to handle our every*day* enemies — enemies of misdemeanours — and create a humble spirit within ourselves. But this is a time of *war* and these are not enemies of misdemeanours we face, but enemies of felonies and atrocities so foul that more than just our lives are at stake — our way of life is as well. Everything we stand for. Everything we believe. Joshua 1:9 says 'Have I not commanded you? Be strong and courageous. Do not be afraid; do not be discouraged, for the Lord your God will be with you wherever you go.'"

"You are still trying to orchestrate all this on your own for your own gains. You are not seeking the Lord, nor consulting his word, despite being able to throw the scriptures back at me — even the devil could do that! And I *know* you're not seeking the Lord, because if that was the case, you would have read stories of countless martyrs and known that the *Lord* deals with our enemies, because *He* sees what we do not. We must trust in Him, allowing Him to take care of our enemies in His own time. When the Lord gives us a solution to our problem, when the Lord answers our prayers, we will know it is the work of His hand, because the answer will always be simple. The fact you are having to do all this complicated planning on your own, the fact that you are facing opposition at every corner — even now from me, someone the Lord has used and spoken through for nearly forty years? That should be a sign! Proverbs 3:5-6 says 'Trust in the Lord with all of your heart and lean not on your own understanding, in all your ways submit to Him, and He will make your paths straight.'"

"We could argue over the interpretations of scripture until the Lord himself returns, but the reality is something needs to be done, or we risk *much* more than the ability to argue with one another through the scriptures. Take a step back; can't you see you're so rigidly devoted to your theories that you're disregarding practicality, refusing to see that there may *actually* be a better way to handle things? One day, your inflexibility will be your downfall, Father... and I fear that day is much closer for you than you think."

The priest nodded and turned, walking over to the door and opening it slowly.

He stopped, keeping his back to me.

"You are beyond absolution. 'Morningstar'... how fitting that name is. I want you all out of here by the end of mass on Sunday," he said

with a firm, but conquered tone.

And with that, he put on his hat and walked into the street.

I walked back to the others where they all eagerly awaited my report.

"Doesn't look like he's going to budge," I muttered.

"That old hair-splitter doesn't know what's good for him. I say we just kill him," Dan reinforced.

"No — we are not going to *kill* him. Father Green is a good man — an honourable man. If anything, he should be honoured for standing up to us, despite knowing what we could do to him. There are not many people in this kingdom who would *fight* for something the way he did. We'll just have to find another way or another place to go. But he's given us tonight and tomorrow before he wants us out for good — right after mass to be exact," I sighed. "Anyway, I'm going to turn in for the night. We can all discuss things further tomorrow."

Though we all retired to our beds, I don't think any of us slept that night; our minds were tormented and our hearts were heavy. It seemed as if we'd blown our cover before we even got to see what we were capable of.

Decisions, Decisions

The next day, Arkade walked in on me at my desk with my face buried in my hands.

"Is everything alright, sir?"

I let out another deep sigh.

"If only it were, son; if only it were. Father Green is expelling us after mass on Sunday."

"Oh... you can stay at my house; I'm sure it'd be okay."

Child-like innocence.

"I appreciate it, Arkade, but it's deeper than that, unfortunately. You see, last night, the priest overheard us discussing things — things about how we plan to fight back against the Dark King and put an end to his control over the lives of our people back home. However, he wasn't too enthusiastic about the intricacies of our plan."

"But... you're a bishop! You're his boss! You can overrule him, can't you?"

"In principle, yes, but he was so against our plan of action and how we were discussing it, that he now sees *us* as the greater enemy — an enemy who is just as much a threat as the Dark King, if not more. He plans to 'expose us' to the congregation on Sunday. He believes we are more of a detriment to the other followers of Christianity — that we will be leading them astray in our teachings with what he considers to be 'too militaristic' an approach to be a proper solution. But what would he rather? That we do *nothing* and let our brethren be murdered in cold blood by the Dark King himself?"

I got up out of my chair, stood in front of him, and put both hands on his shoulders as I looked him deep in the eye.

"Arkade, if you live to see yourself through this time, and rise to a

position of power as I know you will, promise me that whatever you personally believe, you will always hear others out and remain open-minded; the day you think you know everything is the day you have the most yet to learn. Don't forget that."

"Is there anything I can do?"

"I'm sorry, son. There's nothing any of us can do now. We will just have to pack up and leave as per his request and hope another kingdom will provide us with the same hospitality we almost found here."

"Well then... can I come with you?"

"I wish you could, but you live here with Mary and her family, and to come with us would only fuel Father Green's misguided beliefs that we are corrupting your youth. More likely, he'd also use the situation to close the minds and harden the hearts of the others to the need for progress. I'm sorry son, but it's probably for the best if you stay behind."

Tears began to fill his eyes and his lip began to quiver as he turned and ran out the door. I could only imagine his feeling of betrayal, like being given a gift only to have it taken back again. But what was I to do? Our hands were tied, and there were still six other kingdoms who could help us. Perhaps the help we sought was still out there somewhere. Sometimes you just have to know when the battle you're fighting is one best walked away from, than fought to the cold, bitter end.

The rest of the day was mostly a blur as we went about cleaning and dusting the empty church, trying to dodge glances and avoid awkward encounters with Father Green at all costs. When suppertime came, the priest left and The Silence convened once again.

"Blackheart, do you have any suggestions where to go next?" I asked.

"Well, the closest kingdom from here, besides the Dark Kingdom, is Congreed's Excarpathia. Although I don't know if we should flee just yet — we may have entered as religious people, but if our religious legitimacy has been called into question, there is still the direct path to King Valenvy himself. If our approach is too militaristic for a priest, certainly a king would not feel as such."

"Exactly," Issachar spoke up, "and soldiers will be of more use to us on the battlefield anyway than common peasants who only seek their answers through priests."

"But we have to keep in mind that the threat the Dark King poses to us at the moment is minimal, while our ultimate goal is to unite the kingdoms," Naphtali enwisened. "Morningstar's religious approach is still our best bet for shaping undying loyalties toward functional unity, rather than war-time, duty-driven unity that can be broken just as quickly as it is brought together."

"Hmm," I thought aloud, "perhaps there's a way we can have both. No army is comprised of all the same kinds of units or types of troops. There is power in diversity; if you always see only one choice, or use only one option, you will surely lose more than you win, if not by predictability alone. So let's diversify ourselves and be unpredictable: I will continue to use my religious authority to develop the minds of those followers, but I think we should plan a... *somewhat* peaceful visit to Valenvy soon as well. Of course, the path he chooses to take in giving us what we want will be entirely up to him, but we will do our best to keep it peaceful."

"My master once taught me that 'if you choose to keep your true face secret, then the people who know you by one mask, must never meet those who know you by another.' She spoke, of course, of the personae we possess as we try to fit in among others, but I think in this case, she also gave us a solution to the problem we face now," Naphtali spoke insightfully as Gad laughed about her mask/problem-we-*face* pun, looking around to see if anyone else got it. "Morningstar, you were a carpenter, right?"

"I was. And you raise a good point; if my face is seen in both circles, it could lead to an insurgence on both sides... Naphtali, you are brilliant! I will fashion a mask tonight to wear under the hood of my cloak when we meet Valenvy. He will come to fear my faceless, militaristic side, while the others grow to love my perceptive, holy side, where words triumph in times of war. Once Valenvy signs over control of his army to us, we will become a much more noticeable force — a bargaining chip that will help us with the other kingdoms when it comes time to recruit them as well."

"Strength and influence in numbers," Issachar confirmed.

"Exactly... though it may prove difficult holding onto our religious followers after Father Green exposes us on Sunday. I'm sure the congregation won't want us around after that, but given our influence among them already, we may be able to convince some of them to come with us to Excarpathia."

"If we are going to talk to King Valenvy soon, maybe we can just buy us some time on the Father Green side of things with the help of Benjamin and Elektra's knowledge of poisons." Simeon suggested. "Nothing fatal — just a mild paralyser. I could administer it to him while he sleeps tonight which could render his tongue or body immobilized for the sermon tomorrow. He will need a couple of days to recover, but in that time, we will have the king's support — and that'll trump Green's words anyway, won't it?"

The room was silent with thought, but no one could really find fault with his plan.

"If this backfires though, it could put us in a much worse situation than simply walking away now," Judah warned.

"Plus he'll know *we* were behind it," Levi added.

"Maybe, but by the time he can tell the others, the king could have him replaced, especially at our request. And since Morningstar is already around as a bishop, he won't have to look too far for a religious replacement," Simeon reinforced.

"It's worth a shot," Blackheart advised with a shrug.

"Alright, it's decided then: Benjamin and Elektra will prepare the poison for Simeon to administer to the priest tonight while he sleeps. In the meantime, I will fashion my mask from the furniture in this room, and by morning we will be ready to pay Valenvy a visit," I instructed. "As for the rest of you, make sure you're well-rested; tomorrow, you may be trying to persuade a king who does not negotiate with words alone."

A mere half-hour later, the poison was ready and placed in a vial that Simeon locked tightly into his belt before setting off for the priest's house.

CHAPTER THIRTY-FOUR

The Weight of Influence

Much later into the night, Simeon stormed back into the church and into the back room where I was constructing my mask.

"You're not gonna believe this... but the priest is dead."

"Dead?! How is he dead? What kind of poison did you guys use?!" I said frantically, knocking over my chair by accident as I stood up suddenly, bent on finding Benjamin.

"It wasn't the poison; when I got there, I entered his window as stealthily as possible, but when I got to his bedroom, his sheets were already soaked with his blood! It must have happened shortly before I got there too, because the blood was still creeping slowly along the floor."

"And you're absolutely certain it was Father Green under those covers?"

"Well, I didn't see his face, but he is the only one who lives there, and as one who has taken the oath of celibacy, I don't think any *others* would be in his bed..."

"We better go just to be sure," I said as I grabbed my cloak and ran out into the rain with Simeon right behind me.

We moved through the shadows, keeping out of plain sight in case anyone was watching. If the priest was dead, the last thing we needed was someone seeing us there. The way his unmistakeable house stood out among the others, we needed to take all the precautions we could.

Coming up to his back window, Simeon gave me a boost, but the view only revealed the contents of his living room. So we tried another window — one looking into his kitchen. Everything looked mostly tidy and in place, except for an empty knife-slot in the wooden housing block on his counter. I assumed whoever killed him used that as their weapon. Once the coast was clear, Simeon crawled in through the nearest window, and I followed close behind. The place was dark, lit only by the ambient moonlight and a candle that flickered from his room straight ahead. It reminded me of the homes in the Dark Kingdom. We approached slowly, avoiding the windows and all possibilities of being seen from the outside as we made our way closer to the body. I couldn't help but wonder if all that was just the priest's clever setup; did he predict that we'd be there? Thinking we'd try to remove him from our path?

As we walked through the room doors, I went left while Simeon explored right. The room was clear. The sheets were blood-soaked with a small tear down the middle, which must have been where the kitchen knife had plunged through its cotton-weaved armour, snatching the life of its victim like a thief in the night. Strangely, however, a pillow was covering the body's face. I peeked underneath, lifting it slowly. It was definitely Father Green's face. And judging by the knife-wound just inches below, I knew the pillow wasn't the cause of death, so it was either there because that's how Father Green liked to sleep and consequently never saw the knife coming, or it was placed there because the killer felt guilty and didn't want to look at his face after.

"What do we do with his body?"

"We'll just have to leave it here, otherwise people will suspect us of being connected to his murder. You promise you didn't do this?"

"On my life," Simeon assured me, holding his hand up, open palm to me.

Just then I heard a wooden panel creak ever-so-subtly, but neither of us could tell where it came from.

Simeon went to the kitchen to look around. The ice box, cupboards, and everything else was as it should be.

I looked behind furniture, under it, inside it, checked stoneware cabinets and storage closets, but despite our efforts, we found nothing. We never heard the sound again.

"Maybe it was just a mouse," Simeon shrugged.

"That must be some damn mouse for its weight to creak the floors like that," I shouted in a sarcastic whisper. "Keep looking; I'm going to see if there's anything outside."

The side of the house was rife with old crates and boxes, stacked neatly the way I'd expect them to be, having seen Father Green's church. That is, except for a few in the middle. Their displacement was subtle, like an obsessive-compulsive's call-to-correction rather than a strong wind's attempt at "Feng shui". And as I crept closer, it all began to come together in a falling apart sort of way. I had a feeling I knew what was behind those crates, but to remove them and know for sure was a whole other reality I wasn't sure I was willing to face. One crate was all that separated the reality I hoped for from the harsh-truth; one crate keeping the worlds of idealism and realism from apocalyptically crashing in on me and merging into a single moment that I could no longer sugar-coat with ignorance. But regardless of the consequences, it was a crate I had to move — to see and know the truth it concealed for myself.

As I removed it slowly, there sat Arkade, holding a knife wet with blood, arms crossed over his knees, staring straight ahead with a numbness of the soul so irrevocable that no amount of bodily shivering nor blankets could hope to thaw the ice that had crystallized within. As meddlesome as the killing of Father Green was, I couldn't help but share the boy's pain. He did it to protect me — to keep me close no matter the eternal cost to himself. But that cost came at a very large price — a debt he would be doomed to pay the rest of his life. I understood why he couldn't look at me when I removed the crate; he was no longer his own. No longer a child in a child's body, but rather a confused and disconnected spirit trapped in the shell of what once was. But as he sat there, his altered spirit began to accept its new prison, and in the stillness of that moment broke the dam that held back a river. And it flowed: strong, cold, and riddled with shock and remorse — every tear a symbol of his loss of innocence. Sacrificed. For me.

Then his river swept me away with it. With every tear that rolled down his cheek, its heartbroken counterpart formed in the pit of my eye. No words of comfort could've freed either of us from what we felt; that was a job only time and acceptance could make right. As I took the knife from his hands and dropped it to the grass, I reached out to him with comforting embrace. It took a moment for him to reach back to me, but when he did, his grip took hold with such rigidity that I was certain neither time nor illusion nor logic would ever be able to pry us apart. We were bound together. Our destinies intertwined from that day forward. After a while, he looked up at me with tear-filled eyes and said in a voice overwrought with justified sadness, "Now you

don't have to leave."

And like a wrecking ball of sudden realization to an undefended heart, I knew right away I was responsible. Responsible for that. Responsible for everything... Everyone following me. Everyone listening to my words. All that I said. All that I did.

The world is changeable, and its ability to change is so fragile that a single person can be responsible for it. Awareness is not a prerequisite for change. We are but cells living in a much larger organism, however, this does not make our existence less significant — for an organism without cells is no organism at all. We define it; we make it what it is. We are responsible for its health, its functionality, and above all, its purpose. A lone cell can restore the others, or a lone cell can spread a plague. Like tiny gods, all that we say and do holds a power so great that any one of us in any given moment can be responsible for the birth of a new civilization or the collapse of our own. What we don't often realize is that the rebirth and collapse of grand things do not begin with grand things at all, like the things we see, but with the small, like the things we are — in the things we do — in the things we say.

Deep inside us, we know this; we live our days in the microscopic, but something within us calls us to dream in the cosmic — every one of us. And within us exists those two worlds: the world as it is and the world as we think it ought to be. But as we work towards how it ought to be, it's easy to ignore the significance held by the tiny intricacies of how it already is. We forget the impact of our words; we perform actions mindlessly, and sometimes selfishly, often unaware of what others are learning from us. This stop-and-stare inclination is not limited to children alone either — it's in all of us, and it overtakes us every time we see someone do something different than the common man.

Arkade had seen me. Heard me. Learned from me more than what I was even aware I was teaching — and certainly not to the extent he carried it out. But what was done was done, and if it happened, then it happened because Fate allowed it to be that way. And all I could do was wait to see why.

CHAPTER THIRTY-FIVE

The Masks We Wear

The time for Sunday's sermon came and went without a hitch. I told those who asked that we weren't sure where Father Green was, only that he didn't make it to the church that morning. But concerns inevitably grew, and some of the people went to his house to check up on him that afternoon.

When they got there, they found a live bear loose in his living room, smashing things as it fumbled about angrily trying to get out of the house. The bear, of course, was Reuben-the-beast-hunter's idea. He lured it from the bush last night, and, with a large amount of Benjamin's sedatives, tranquilized it to get him there, making the murder look like a freak accident. Panic arose upon sight of the bear, which caused some neighbours to grab their guns and shoot the thing before it caused any more harm. Of course, things were staged so Father Green's life was the only one taken by the bear — and lucky for us, no one was the wiser for it.

The next day, a funeral was held for Father Green. Though the kingdom itself was vast, word spread quickly about the unfortunate event, drawing people to his service from all around — religious and non-religious alike. As the new, undisputed head of the church, it was my duty — and pleasure — to be able to deliver the eulogy to the mournful crowd of such diversity and magnitude. I was starting to like funerals; emotions run high so people seek comfort to dull the pain; the need for comfort, of course being an open door that a grey-matter tailor can easily walk right on through, into the mind without so much as a red flag rising. My kind of event.

When all had assembled, I began.

"It is with great sadness that we gather here today to mourn the passing of The Reverend Father Walter Green of Sipondel. Father Green was a man of dignity, worthy of all who touched his hand — and when you did, your life was touched in turn as well. As mine was. As all of ours were. Father Green was always there when we needed him most. For shelter. For advice. For friendship.

On a day like today, he would not want us to mourn his death, or think upon what we have lost, but rather to rejoice in the things that make it worth gathering here together. Things like companionship, fond memories, and a life well-spent serving the Lord and all His followers. Many people take life for granted, but not those who knew Father Green; he would never let you get away with that. He would want what's best for his flock, a flock that I now can proudly guide in his place..."

"You have all been made fools of!"

Right on cue, Issachar burst through the doors with his boot, wearing the mask I had crafted the night before along with my black cloak, introducing the phantom of my revolution-inciting persona.

"If you look inside the casket before you, you will not find the body of your beloved Father Green, but rather the ash from whence his body-double was created by the Dark Power — by the Dark King. That bear you shot dead was the Dark One's clever trick upon you, transmogrified from the body of the *real* living priest. *You killed your own priest*, citizens of Sipondel — and you have done it *exactly* as the Dark One wanted you to."

Gasps and murmuring spread throughout all in attendance. The casket was opened to reveal nothing but ash, suggesting almost irrefutably the stranger's words were true. All eyes fell back to him.

"Unless we act now, there will be no peace unless you accept it through your own enslavement. Those of you here who fled the Dark Kingdom know these words to be true. But know this! The power you have come to fear — the unequalled displays of power that leave you looking like fools as you go about killing your own people — it is no longer the Dark King's alone, but rather a twisted gift possessed by every citizen of the Dark Kingdom who has taken pledge to him. The Dark Power has consumed them; citizens' minds are now shells of what they once were, as they are no longer their own to control. As we speak, they are assembling an army that will wipe out Sipondel in a little over a month."

"Excuse me, sir, but... who are you?" I asked Issachar, going along with the plan.

"Call me by any name and the truth of my words shall remain

unchanged. You hope to label me? To Hell with your labels! You can only label what you know, and you most certainly do not know me. But you will. Much sooner than you think."

"But why do you interrupt the assembly before you, overshadowing the words meant to honour the life of a good man?"

"My presence is not an overshadowing of such deserved honour, but the amplification thereof. You want to honour this man? Then cripple the Dark Ones by joining together under my command. The Dark King has made you all into the poor, hapless souls you are today — remember that. He has robbed you of your confidence: a critical absence that has doomed you to an entire life of wasted potential. You have become inured to second-rateness. All of you have the potential to prevent the Dark One's attack, but instead you cower in fear. Why? You all waste your lives looking to people like your dead priest for help. What can he give you, but words? Words give inspiration, nothing more. You want redemption? The very thing you seek inspiration for? Fight for it like your life depended on it, because it always does."

He then fell silent in perfect confidence, looked at the crowd, and walked quietly toward the door with well-planted, authoritative footsteps. Most of the people followed him outside to the street, curious to see if he'd say anything else. As he mounted his coal-coloured horse and took its reins in hand, he turned to the crowd, and said succinctly, "Join together. Stop envying and you will soon find yourselves worthy of being envied."

And with that, he rode off with such speed that he left a cloud of dust in his wake and the ears of the crowd wanting more.

As everyone filtered back inside, they asked what I thought of the man's words.

"They are certainly words worth discussing; however, instead of telling you what I think, *your* thoughts matter just as much. I would like to hear what you think by meeting with you all in small groups. Please write your names on a piece of paper with your preferred time for tomorrow, placing it in the box at the back before you leave. I will arrange the groups tonight, so that we may start as early as tomorrow."

In the following hours, we resumed Father Green's service with respect, despite the distractions that filled our minds, and held a comforting after-sermon for those who sought further help in their

time of mourning. The people in attendance also left their names as requested, even others who didn't attend the church regularly.

Sipondel's church was ours to command. When everyone left much later that night, The Silence gathered in Father Green's old office to finally explore his mysterious painting up close. The colours of the painting masked all its elements well, but there was no doubt that was the entrance that lead down into the catacombs and connected to our base. Issachar's eyes looking through the slit on the other side gave it away a little bit as well.

"I hope you can open this, because it's a long jaunt back," he joked with a dash of seriousness from the other side of the painting.

Fumbling through Father Green's key ring, we found the only four-pointed key on there — cross-shaped with thick wiring at the top bent into what looked like the letters "HP" at the top — and slid it into the keyhole. Exactly like the one in my father's puzzle box, though I kept that knowledge from the others. More importantly, having access to that door meant that we could run our operations more efficiently and covertly than ever before; we could use the passage as much as we pleased.

"Issachar! That was spectacular! You could not have performed better," I applauded. "And now that they have seen both you and me in the same room, no one will suspect my role as either."

"Of course you liked the speech — you wrote the damn thing!" he smacked me on the shoulder, laughing.

"Did you like the mask?"

"Fearsome and haunting, yet deep and understanding. I think it carried just enough mystery to have them hang on our every word, but just enough trust to make them believe every one too."

The mask was truly beautiful, symbolic of my inner self in a way. Its dark, hard wood was crafted to resemble the face of a fiercely mysterious elephant; small, menacing eye holes with thin, wine-coloured tribal markings upon its face and trunk. The markings weren't so thick as to be distracting, but just enough to accent what its features showed of the spirit within: immensely powerful, truly confident, and eternally secured by its natural glory and might. With the mask framed under a cloak black as night, it showed itself as the dark force you couldn't help but fear, yet oddly felt as if you didn't need to... unless provoked. It represented an ancient royalty, a deep wisdom — the kinds of things that gain the respect of everyone who laid eyes upon it before words are even spoken. And no matter how latent its abilities, you knew immense forces resided somewhere inside it at all times, just waiting to be unleashed upon the world when the time was right. That was my mask, constructed in part with wood to represent myself, and in part with metal, to honour my father.

"And hang on every word they did; after you left as dramatically as you came, it got the people talking and looking to me for answers and direction exactly as predicted."

"Which means..."

"Which means now we can invoke Benjamin's categorization test, revealing on a basic level how we should use our subjects to their greatest potential."

"Precisely," Benjamin cut in. "Essentially how it works is we get each member of the congregation alone among a staged group of peers — that is, *you* guys. Then Morningstar will ask the group a few questions, and you will all deliberately give the same answer by a show of hands, the dependent variable being how the subject chooses to respond. For all intents and purposes, their responses will show us if they are free-thinkers, or easily cave to peer pressure and how frequently."

Issachar looked pensive but accepting of the notion.

"Interesting. But how does that let us categorize them? What are we categorizing them into?"

"Groups and roles of similar thought," I took over. "The ones who are influenced some-to-most of the time will take on soldier roles: able to take orders, but can remain capable of thinking in group-minded contexts, adapting on-the-fly in combat whether a superior is present or not. The ones who refuse to be swayed by the others are the strong thinkers — not that the others aren't, but these you could say are more... rebelliously independent. They are the type to go with their own opinion regardless of what they have been instructed; their presence is best removed from the group as a whole, then given 'special tasks' such as setting up our outposts outside the Dark Kingdom. These outposts can be run however they wish while they report happenings-of-interest back to us. It will give them a sense of independence and

power while keeping them from meddling in our affairs. And finally, the others who are swayed by their peers every single time will be our enforcers: the ones who will execute our commands without question. They will be our messengers and punishment-dealers for the rest of our followers."

"Statistically," Benjamin spoke up, "half will give the same answer as the others, while a quarter of subjects will not be influenced. Then of course, we're left with a very small fraction who will always say what the others say. The findings of past experimentations show that overall, a third of subjects will completely forget what they believe is true just to go with what the group insists on. If we can categorize them using this technique, it could iron out a lot of issues for us down the road."

"I see. Sounds deceptive; I'm in. Anything you need me to do, just say the word," Issachar said as he slid past us and left the room.

It was getting late, so we called it a night. Everyone filed out of the room in unison, but I hung back to look upon my mask briefly one more time, and turned out the lights ready to head to my room. But I had no sooner closed the door when I heard the sound of crying coming from the upper pews. I feared Arkade was taking things pretty hard, and headed up the stairs to tend to him. When I got there, however, it turned out it wasn't him at all, but Elektra.

She was sitting there with her head resting on the pew. I'd never seen her cry before that day; she was always strong and perceptive the way Naphtali had trained her to be, but I suppose one can never truly be free of overwhelming emotions if a strong enough situation arises. I sat down and put my arm around her, not saying a word. Emeline taught me that, saying, "The best way to comfort a broken heart is to be silent and to remain close-by, letting them start the conversation when they're ready — if and when they want to."

"Arkade said he doesn't want to hang out with me anymore," she mumbled quietly from behind her tears. "He said there are more important things to do than waste time with me."

"Why would he say that?"

"I have no idea… he used to be really nice and sweet. We used to talk all the time because we had so much in common. But now he wants nothing to do with me. He doesn't want to run down the street together anymore, or drop things on people's heads from the rooftops and hide like we used to... he was having fun too! But then all of the sudden..." she wiped her nose, "he just stopped, and when I asked him why tonight, that's what he said."

"That doesn't seem like him... I wonder what changed..."

"He started hanging out with *you!*" she yelled. "All he ever talks about now is you, and what you think, and what you talk about, and this whole Dark Kingdom thing. And if I wanna talk about something else, he'll insult me and treat me like I'm below him! I don't even *want* to be around him anymore!"

"Elektra, Arkade is going through a very tough time in his life right now; he's going through a lot of changes trying to fit in with us, because no one's ever wanted him around before. With us, he is starting to feel like he belongs to something bigger than him that accepts him for who he is — and he's scared to lose it, so he compensates by acting tough like that."

"He told me about the priest."

I let out a sigh and tried to pacify her by tightening my arm around her shoulder, but she seemed even angrier and more miserable than before, leaning away, but still allowing my arm to be around her. I knew by his actions with the priest he was becoming more servile, but I didn't want Elektra feeling like it was by my request that that happened.

"And I take it you feel that for him to do something so extreme only means he is growing closer to *me* and further away from *you*," I said, realizing after I said it that it had more bite than I wanted it to.

"And *I* take it that *you* feel like this is all a part of some *phase* he's going through, but he's NOT! He's a completely different person now thanks to you!" she yelled as she pushed my arm off her completely.

"Elektra, he's never felt like a part of anything. You've always had The Silence and have never truly known what it's like to feel alone or like you don't belong."

"I don't even know who my parents are, or where my family is, and *you're* telling *me* I don't know what it's like? Where are all the other kids I've been able to talk to my whole life? All *my* friends? All these privileges I *apparently* have had showered upon *me*? Don't act like you know me, okay?! Just leave me alone!" she shrieked as she ran out of the church with more tears streaming down her face than when I got there.

I sat there alone with my thoughts, considering her words. Maybe she was right; maybe in wanting to do good, I'd actually become the person I was trying to stop. But at the same time, I knew evil didn't have the capacity for self-reflection, nor did evil people re-examine the morality of their actions. If I was still able to do that, I must have still been on the right side. Maybe I was just looking at things from the wrong angle. I did feel immeasurable remorse when Arkade murdered the priest, so that had to count for something... but then again, in the grand scheme of life, nobody grows old keeping their soul unblemished. For all I knew, Arkade's rejection by everyone as a boy may have led to an appetite for pickpocketing and cruelly murdering people simply for *entertainment* all because of the acceptance he never felt and the ridicule he faced in his past. Maybe I saved him from that. The way I see it, every choice in life sets us on a different path and carries its own set of "what ifs" and consequences that we *could* worry about, but what's the use? Rather than plaguing our thoughts with the unknown, we should focus on and accept only what we do know — and all we know is the path we're currently on. That was his new path. Any other paths he *could* have taken, he simply did *not* — and in turn, that makes the "what ifs" irrelevant. What mattered was I was there for him when he performed his first grey-area act — an act he did for noble and honourable reasons. Sure, some moral lines were blurred, but at least I could oversee him and protect him from a life of meaningless murders and countless other sins that would only increase if he wandered about life with a continued lack of purpose. Above all, nothing was more true than that, because I knew first hand that without purpose and meaning in our lives, we banish ourselves to wander this plane of existence with self-destructive tendencies until the bell tolls and our breath capsizes in our lungs, snatching our chance to redeem ourselves forever. Without me, he was nothing, and by the gods, through me, he would know a purpose like no other before...

CHAPTER THIRTY-SIX

Aggressive Negotiations

The next day our meetings with the congregation went exactly as planned. I was able to use the line of questioning to wormtongue opinions, while The Silence influenced the majority of the people toward their staged opinions as well. It was a successful day for us all.

To the religious ones I met with, I explained that I trusted the masked Morningstar, and had made my decision to follow him into battle. By association, if they trusted me, and I trusted him, the transfer would be a smooth one, thus encouraging "loyalty to the mask" quicker than leaving things up to chance. That's the beauty and ugliness of lionization — to make ourselves celebrities on our own takes a lot of hard work, dedication, and luck, but for a celebrity to create another celebrity, it's so easy that it almost detracts from the blood, sweat, and tears of those who came up from nothing. In any case, as a religious celebrity, it was now within my power to make new ones, and with the masked Morningstar leading the way, the pawns were lining up perfectly.

After meeting with them all, everyone came back to the church the next day as requested, to start a rally that would get the attention of King Valenvy. People created signs, effigies, carried torches; all the theatrical things that would be hard for you to ignore if they assembled on your doorstep.

When we were ready, I went into the back room, slipped on my mask and cloak, and took to horseback along with Blackheart and Naphtali. Our three horses led the crowd of 500 to the steps of the castle where we met a blockade of guards behind a cast-iron gate that would be tough to penetrate, even with the rushing force of a much larger crowd.

"We are here with peaceful intent. We wish no harm to you or your king, but it is imperative that you let us speak to him immediately," I informed the guards through the fence.

"King Valenvy is not taking any visitors, and certainly not any masked ones. Turn around and go home — all of you!"

"I admire your sense of duty soldier, so I will make you an offer: allow me and only my two most trusted advisors here to meet with your king — just the three of us — and everyone else you see before you shall wait patiently at these gates for our return."

"This is not a negotiation! Turn around and *leave*! Now!"

So much for negotiation. Lucky for us, we had Zebulun and Ephraim. Ephraim's special bombs lowered the molecular integrity of the bars and walls while Zebulun's massive explosion blew everything to pieces so small, you could blow them through a straw. The crowd waited behind me, ready to charge if we charged.

The guards drew their spears and pointed them at us, looking nervously at each other, but ready to defend their king while more reinforcements fell in line behind them. Fear seemed to fill their eyes and hold them in place; any confident guard would have rushed us by now.

"One last time: I wish to speak to King Valenvy. Though it may look like we are here with destructive or malicious intent, we have information that will *save* the life of your king, and the lives of all of you who take up your sword in his name. Deny us, and we will surely take every last one from you now. Make your decision wisely, Captain."

"Alright! Alright; there is no need for bloodshed. Just the three of you then. No more."

"I don't believe you are in a position to make *demands*, considering the size of the mob before you and the lack of defense you have, Captain... but be that as it may, I am *willing* to keep it just the three of us — as I originally suggested. Take us to your king, and the others shall wait here for my return. Do you accept these terms, Captain?"

"Yes, sir. Sorry, sir. Please follow me."

The three of us dismounted our horses and followed the Captain along with what I can only assume were ten of his best guards up the steps to the entrance of the castle. The castle was nowhere near as majestic and awe-inspiring as the Dark King's, but for man-made architecture, it was still respectable. The size of its ceilings gave it a feeling of greatness while the lack of upkeep and cracking stones quickly took that feeling away. The corridor we passed through was lined with wooden-framed paintings of all the past rulers of Sipondel. In theory, that corridor should have made all who walked down it feel smaller, like all those kings were watching you, so great in number that you felt as if an entire army lurked nearby, ready to correct your every misspoken word or foolish action. But not there. There were so many portraits that if you plotted them along a timeline, it would be so cluttered that you'd be left to infer only one thing: that each king's rule was greatly shortened by whatever quality he lacked most. Philosophers overthrown by militaristic men; militaristic men killed in battles far too ambitious for them, leaving the throne to be filled by a charismatic commoner, who then has his charisma cut short by a close disloyal friend who helped him get there. Of course, that would lead to more rebellion until tyrants and dictators brought stability back to the kingdom through the inevitable suppression and oppression that managing those who can never be satisfied demands. Sipondel's greatness lay in its distant past, but like any object gone uncared for or unappreciated, it stood before us no more impressive than the church we came from.

As we approached the throne room, King Valenvy appeared calm and collected, a demeanour that would've been useful in a typical negotiation — that is, if he had turned out to be that way. He had well-armoured guards on each side of his throne, and two more upon every second step, fanning outward from his throne like bridesmaids and groomsmen at a wedding. There were twelve guards in total in that throne room, none of whom seemed to pose a threat to assassins who cut their own keys to the doors of the afterlife.

"My lord," I kneeled in false allegiance, Naphtali and Blackheart falling in behind me.

"I am no lord, I am a king, and you would be wise to hold your tongue until I have asked you to use it. So... Morningstar, is it? My guards tell me you have blown up my gates and damaged my walls."

"Your Captain's *fear* blew your gates and damaged your walls, sire."

"You speak outside my request for you to, and in a lie, no less! Tell me, fool, what is it you seek that you kneel before me with false humility like an imbecile taunting death?"

"I seek use of your army, sire."

"My army, you say?" he chuckled condescendingly, looking toward his guards with a cocky look on his face. "Well if it's my army you seek, then you shall have them. Guards! Bring me their heads."

From her kneeling position, Naphtali quickly pulled two concealed daggers from her lower-back and plunged them into the guard's knees behind her, using her bladed leverage to pull him to the ground and stabbed him in the neck. Then, dropping to her back, she thrust her legs up, spinning like a windmill to clear a small space around us. That's when even more guards started charging in from the doors in each corner of the room. With lightning-fast reflexes, Naphtali grabbed handfuls of glass delirium canisters from her belt, scattering them in arcs to the sides of the room where they shattered on the breastplates of all who were foolish enough to enter. Every guard who was showered in her gaseous poisons began to lose control of their senses. First sight, then touch, until they were banished to a void where they knew not where they were, nor could feel the ground beneath them or even feel the swords in their hands. But that was fortunate compared to the poor souls in our immediate area. Blood spilled and bones snapped as I watched her throw blade after blade into the eye sockets of any and all reinforcements who poured into the room. Next to me, I watched as Blackheart drove his elbow into the groin of the guard behind him without even looking, forcing the guard to drop his sword, which Blackheart snatched from the air and spun to tear across the tiny exposed area of the guard's midsection, disembowelling him while his heavy blade carried on to two more guards whom he soon decapitated with the same swing. Faster than their heads could fall, Blackheart had already recoiled his blade to jam into the stomach of a fourth.

With numerous guards already disposed of and the rest struggling to keep their wits as they witnessed the true Hell of delirium flooding their lungs, I took advantage of the Captain's shock and tackled him to the ground, where I removed his helmet and beat him over the head with it until two more guards came at me from my left and right. I dodged the swings of their blade, reaching out to take hold of the neck of their breastplates, and pulled them into each other, smashing their noses together with a loud crunch as Naphtali flew over me, plunging a dagger deep into each of their stomachs before meeting a third one whose chest she skewered with both, lifting and pinning him against the stone pillar while his breath hissed out of his lungs.

Just then, the two largest guards from either side of the throne came charging toward us. Valenvy's personal guards. Punching them in the face or stomach did nothing; either they were made of solid muscle, or they had some beneficial nerve damage from the scars of past battles. But that was no matter to us, because pain is not a necessity for death. As they ran in unison, side-by-side straight for me, I ran straight for them as well, parkouring off the breastplate of one, to the breastplate of the other, and back to the first's helmet where I took hold of his neck and brought it with me along my trajectory. I'd never heard a spine grind that gritty, hollow grind before, but the way his legs dropped to the floor, I'd say it was effective.

That left just one more. As he rushed at me, Blackheart grabbed Naphtali like a battering ram and threw her straight toward his face; when she struck, she wrapped around him, constricting his right and left arms until they popped from their sockets. The guard wriggled around frantically trying to break free, but before he could, Blackheart lunged between his legs, kicking out the backs of his knees, dropping him to the floor where Naphtali rolled off so my knife could drive up through his chin and into his skull. The blood in his throat gurgled as his eyes came to a close.

Realizing the major threats were all neutralized, Naphtali casually walked around to each of the choking, blinded guards, and slit their throats considerately, one by one, until not a guard was left standing in the scarlet-coloured throne room. As she made her rounds, there, hiding behind the nearest pillar, was the Captain of The Guard.

"Please! Please don—" was all he could say before his throat spilled with the crimson incarnation of regret freed by her blade.

King Valenvy's eyes were wide as the moon that night.

"What... what do you want? Tell me anything and it's yours," he trembled, feeling the effects of his pig-headedness, and cowering behind his throne like the leader he wasn't.

"I told you, sire. I want your army. Your *whole* army."

"Okay, it's yours. What do you need it for?"

"To save your life, ironically. And the lives of those in your kingdom and others. The Dark King is preparing an army of his own as we speak. With yours under my command, and the compliance of the other kings and queens, we can meet him on his own ground before his plans have fully developed. A surprise attack is our best chance, but a surprise attack without numbers would surely result in our slaughter."

"If you would have said that in the first place, I would have given you the army you asked for!" the ignorant king exclaimed with distorted retrospection.

"No, you wouldn't have. But take this as a lesson to remain open-minded, even when you believe yourself to be a king among peasants. You never know what blessings can be gained or crises averted just by listening."

"Forgive me, Morningstar; you are wiser than I."

"Well thank you for your kind words, O King of Hindsight," I mocked with a patronizing, masked bow. "There is one more thing I expect, before I go — something you have that will expedite the development of a certain... mental aspect that I need our loyal followers to have in a time of war."

"Anything you ask is yours."

"I require the freeing of your prisoners, and the use of your prison."

"Of course; I shall give the command immediately. Do you require my guards for however you intend to use it?"

"That won't be necessary. Have the cells and prison area clear by the time I visit you next. It's been a pleasure to meet your acquaintance... Valenvy."

CHAPTER THIRTY-SEVEN

Strategic Expansion

We walked back to the gates with confident eyes locked straight ahead. Hands steady. Auras fearsome. The guards parted before us with puzzled faces, unsure if they should seize us by the amount of blood that soaked our clothes. But the command to seize us never came. Before us, a stunned crowd awaited words I would never speak, and a story they would never know the details of. We simply got on our horses, and rode back to the church cloaked in a renewed sense of accomplishment. It was a new page in The Silence's history — a new chapter in the history of the kingdoms.

Though we made no commands, the crowd followed close behind, their curiousity burning within them to hear what had happened. Before the masses piled in, Issachar followed me into the back room and took my cloak and mask while I washed the blood off my hands and face to don the bishop's robes once more.

"Valenvy wasn't very cooperative at first," I told him. "He commanded his guards to kill us almost immediately. The sharp blades and hulking strength of thirty of his best men were all he was willing to negotiate with, and our lives the only risks he was willing to take. But in moments, all that turned around as their corpses convinced him to hear our requests. In the end, however, we achieved possession of his army and use of his prison to use as we see fit. The prison we will put to use in due time for Operation War-mind, but no one is to know about that, except us. The only thing the people out there are to know is that they are pawns to a king that sees them as expendable, and that their trust and protection is best kept with us, under our cause. But don't linger too long — the less people see you, the more important, intriguing, and effective your presence will remain."

"As you wish, Morningstar," Issachar agreed and walked out to address the crowd. I followed close behind.

He began with a booming voice, using a rag to wipe the blood from his hands, as if to let its symbolism sink in.

"Your king is most stubborn. His ignorance and overconfident pride senselessly led to the bloodshed of thirty of his men. He put their lives in danger and sacrificed them without a second thought, ignoring our peaceful attempt at negotiation that would have kept them alive. Valenvy does not think with such consideration and concern, so *you* are to do the thinking in his place: citizens — if he would sacrifice *their* lives so thoughtlessly, the ones who protect him and keep him upon his throne, do you really think he wouldn't treat *your* lives with the same expendability? War is upon us! Be silent no more! Follow me, Citizens of Sipondel, and I will show you a world where your lives carry meaning and your destiny is not made fragile because of kings who care nothing for your existence. Tomorrow I depart from Sipondel, but I shall come to call upon you before long. If you stand with me — if you choose life and shun helplessness — then mark your doors with the sign of the elephant so I may know who the loyal among you are. As for those who do not... pray to your gods and pray to them well, for the giants you will soon face are not the kind that disappear just because you keep your eyes shut."

And with that, he threw some of Ephraim's smokeflash bombs to the ground, vanishing into thin air. Issachar was definitely getting a sense for the theatrical.

The citizens that filled the pews spoke among themselves, growing agitated by his words. They knew their time was coming; that they were being called to order. A time to put their envious ways aside, no longer seeing themselves as lesser people just because they didn't have what others had. They were faced with the hard, but redeeming truth: Fate, War, and Death hold the keys to mass equalization; at any point in every life lived, it doesn't matter who has what, what a person has done, or what their bloodline is, because no one can escape them when they come to stake their claim. As such, time spent worrying — about anything — provides no emotional or physical benefit to us; such things only weaken us for the fights we must endure in our lives; fights that we must never stop fighting, no matter how many "gifts" of misfortune we are forced to open when they are brought before us. Every day we must fight. Always. Even if our last breath must be given to do so. For when all seems hopeless and all has gone silent, that's Destiny turning down the music so that all may hear our response to life's great storms, giving our response the chance to echo throughout eternity with the level of greatness it deserves. When your time is done, what will you be known as? "The Great"? "The Fearless"?

..."The Squanderer"?

"Fellow believers," I took over, "the Masked One is right. We can no longer idly sit by and allow ourselves to be conquered through inaction. We must join together under him, even if our principles and methods don't align perfectly with his, because we are united by something greater and more valuable than our beliefs alone: the freedom to *have* those beliefs, and believe what we want without persecution — we must protect that at all costs. We each want to preserve this freedom for ourselves and all generations that follow, so why allow ourselves to get hung up on our disagreements when our energy can be more effectively put towards fighting *alongside* each other instead of against? It is because of this realization that I have decided to go with The Masked One when he departs tomorrow."

Scattered murmurs of scandalized disbelief broke out among the people again.

"I know some of you disagree with my decision, but I hope, in time, you will see by my example that by joining with him, our unity will always be a greater force with *mixed* ideals than if we demand that others change for *us*, to what *we* believe. The former teaches us patience, tolerance, and helps us work towards a harmonious coexistence in light of our differences... but if we allow our philosophies to be consumed by the latter, then we sentence ourselves to a lifetime of battles that will not relent until nothing is left but the aftermath of all that was once good. This rings true in war, in peace, in marriage, and in friendship. With that said, I will return to you soon with word of our progress, and hope that in that time, the pursuit of the greater good overcomes your fears of letting go of past mindsets forged in steel. In my absence, I leave my duties to my most trusted advisor, Judah, whose words have brought light when times seemed darkest. Hear his words and ponder them, as you would mine, until I return. Until that time, may the Lord bless you and be with you all, through all your struggles in these trying times.

Judah?"

Judah took the stage while I was there so the people would associate and transfer part of my authority to him. He had a way with words; from my first time in camp, he went out of his way to make me feel at home before I even realized I *was* home. Since that day, he was nothing but kind, warm, and accommodating through good times and bad. He was the perfect replacement to look after things while I was away, and I had every bit of confidence in him. There is a peace that comes with that kind of trust — a peace I never thought I'd know through a trust I never thought I'd be capable of feeling. Undoubtedly, trust is always a risk, but when placed in the right people after a trial period where they prove themselves worthy of it, it is a reward transcendent of all the emotional mire that bogs down a person's potential. With that peace of mind, I was ready to depart.

Though I wished every member of The Silence could have accompanied me to Excarpathia, I limited my choices to Naphtali, Blackheart, Simeon, Ephraim and Elektra, who waited in the tunnels for me as Issachar handed over the Masked One's guise to me once more. The others stayed behind to maintain the hard work that had gone into that kingdom, ensuring that in our absence, the people wouldn't revert to their old ways of thinking, making our efforts for naught. I hand-picked each of them for a reason, because I had alternative plans in Excarpathia, "The Golden Kingdom" — plans I would keep secret until the exact moment they needed to be shared. Those members were my ticket to seeing them through.

Just as I was entering the tunnels through the painting's entrance, Arkade came running into the office.

"Sir, I know I let you down with Father Green, and I'm sorry. I wasn't ready when I killed him, and I know you probably think I'm weak the way I hid, and I know you probably think I'm not worth the time and can't help you, but I know I'm ready now. I just know it. I've been thinki—"

Got to give the kid credit for persevering.

"Arkade," I interrupted.

"Yes sir?"

"I want you to come with me."

"You do?"

"Yes. It's not about being ready or feeling prepared all the time; sometimes you just have to do what you know you have to do. And when you do — you will always see that you're more ready and more prepared than you realize. Never doubt yourself or you may never do anything of significance."

"Okay," he nodded acceptingly, as if anything I said would be good enough for him to hear and act upon.

"C'mon; the others are waiting."

And so our party became seven.

CHAPTER THIRTY-EIGHT

Excarpathia Bound

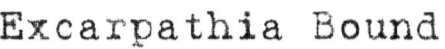

"Everyone, Arkade here is going to be joining us on our trip," I said, placing my hands upon his shoulders the way a father would of his son.

"Ugh, noooo!" Elektra tantrumed with disapproval. "Whyyyyy?"

"Shut up, Elektra!" he shouted back immaturely. "I'm not here for you; I'm here for them."

His words hit her like a frigid wind on a cold winter day. She fell silent. Tears started to well up in her eyes.

"Enough you two," Naphtali cut in. "This will be the last time I ever hear you speak that way to each other again. There is enough discord in the world; we don't need you adding to it."

"Naphtali's right," I reinforced. "Remember the Code: we teach each other to grow stronger, learn from each other, seek unity... these things share a common bond of togetherness for a reason, and you *will* abide by them until that bond forms between you as well."

"There is one more thing I think you both need to learn before we go any further," Napthali added, stopping us all as she turned to them and placed a hand on each of their cheeks, looking them deep in the eyes. "The older you get, the faster time passes in your mind, so use your time according to what is most important. Love is one of the most motivating and self-defining forces in our lives, whether we turn from it or allow ourselves to be drawn to it. If you allow romantic possibilities with others to consume all your time and energy, they will distract you from the things of interest that fill your life with passion and purpose. Know that love is not a purpose, it's a paradox; it's not an end-goal, it's an auxiliary fuel source to help get there. The most inefficient and self-harming thing a person can do is go out looking for love. Let it find you when the time is right and you're out doing what you love to do. Only then will you find it in its truest form. You both can already see and feel how it's pulling you apart. That is because it's not time, or it's not meant to be — and the sooner you let it go, even if things were once perfect, the better off you both will be."

We all stood there, allowing the words to sink in. At first it was for the kids, but as we all stood there, you could tell by our faces that they had transported us back in time to those feelings of love in our own lives. Memories we could not escape, and just had to accept and move forward with as we stashed them away somewhere inside us. Memories and feelings that never really go away. Like that of Emeline; I missed Emeline. I'd *always* miss Emeline.

Blackheart broke the silence.

"Well, we should probably get moving. The longer we are separated from the group, the less effective we become."

"I'm with you," I said, joining him at the front.

"Ever been to Excarpathia?" Blackheart asked me as we started to walk the tunnels, hoping they led where we wanted them to.

"Not yet, but considering it's known as the 'Golden Kingdom', I have no doubt that the trip could be my favourite stop yet."

"That may be," he laughed, "but it's not as sublime as you might think. As abundant as the kingdom is, the people do not share that same abundance when it comes to their kindness. Especially when it comes to visitors… they're not exactly held in disregard, but foreigners are definitely treated much differently. Simply put, it is a kingdom of very materialistic and covetous people — get between a person and their riches, or their acquisition of riches, or even their *thought* of riches, and you will find yourself at the mercilessness of their greed. It is not a place you or I would easily call home, you know. There are dens of iniquity spread through the streets where thieves await the unsuspecting."

"We're assassins; we can handle petty bandits with ease."

"I wouldn't be so confident; an animal backed into a corner can be more vicious and unpredictable than they were before you arrived. We will be on *their* ground, and as such, they have the advantage and the numbers. The reason why it's so dangerous for visitors, as you'd expect from a greedy population, is because their laws regarding the protection of one's possessions are most severe; no one wants to lose what they have gained, and are free to protect what they have

by any and all means — enter the credulous visitor, however, and the kingdom as a whole gains more wealth with no detriment to one another's horde."

"And King Congreed — where does he fit in?"

"He is by far the wealthiest cheapskate in the kingdom, descendant from a long line of hot-tempered warriors who are worthy of their terrifying reputations. Since the War of the Kingdoms, however, these plains have not known battle quite as profoundly as his ancestors did. The blood of greatness still courses through his veins despite his lack of experience, however, so we should remain ever-wary, for one never knows when another's latent abilities may shine through and take charge. For a man like Congreed, it would certainly not be to our benefit.

Though he's known to be somewhat of an alcoholic pleasure-seeker, he is extremely intelligent with his wealth, and definitely no Prodigal Son. Rather than just acquiring and amassing great wealth, he puts it to use to gain himself more. After all, wealth under a mattress or buried in a hole is no more effective and grows no quicker than a seed planted among bricks. Because of this, Excarpathia is the only kingdom to have their own lapidary and alchemy school, where its students are so successful that they can create gold faster than the fabled King Midas' touch ever could. But gold is not all they can create. Known elements are merely a stepping stone for their alchemistsmiths. In the past, they have fashioned impenetrable, indestructible armour that is lighter than air itself, blades that never dull, and horseshoes that make crossing water or canyons no different than land... be careful, Morningstar. This would be the army the world would fear, if not for the Dark Power keeping Congreed's ambitions in check."

Blackheart's words struck a chord of deep thought within me. Even ridding the Dark King of his power still wouldn't rid the world of theirs. There will always be tyrants-in-the-making. Sometimes so many that they keep *each other* in check by fearing the other's potential display of power, knowing the repercussions it could have. But either way, with power gained comes a more fragile responsibility. Like Naphtali once told me: if we are to be truly free, that freedom will come through cooperation and tolerance with one another, not by fighting the endless supply of tyrants, hoping we'll be rid of them all one day. If we continue along the path we currently follow, we will keep ourselves captive within an age-old cycle of war, conflict, and rebalance. Granted, we grow more powerful technologically with time, but we remain prisoners in a wheel spinning without progress the same way unhappy lives repeat the same actions day-in and day-out, as if doing the same thing over and over will yield different results. But it won't.

I can't believe I didn't see it before; everything I wanted to help people change back home was the same problem the rest of the world had. I needed to help people escape the meaningless, mundane cycles of life, but how could I expect that to change when the bigger picture is no different? People learn by seeing and observing living examples, but such things only exist — if only rarely — within enlightened individuals. Perhaps that's why religion exists: to help us escape the world temporarily and find transcendental peace, so when we leave our holy place with the teachings, we can take what we've learned and share it with the world. But then why doesn't the world change? The teachings are sound; the religious texts carry many truths. Perhaps we don't progress, because there are so many views — so many paths to peace and happiness — that we get hung up on each path's differences. Trying to sort out right from wrong when the rights mean so much to us that we can't look at them objectively. We want to believe that everything we've been taught is right, lest we discover that we've been living a lie. So, of *course* we don't change! To change would be like performing a major surgery on ourselves with only a rusty knife and some alcohol. Instead, we stay the same as we've always been, keeping to the path we've walked our whole lives. Paths that carry so much importance and perceived stability that we are utterly convinced it is the only one to walk — that anyone not walking it with us is being misled, despite not having walked theirs before so we can know it for ourselves. So then what is the real issue? Conflicts in compassion? Moral tour guides with too much pride? Would tolerance really solve everything?

I didn't think it would; it would be a better alternative, but it would only lead us down separate, uninhibited individual paths to truth. The thing is, when people arrive at the end of their journey and find their truth, how do we unite them again? At some point, we must see that we are all a single species who needs to develop as a whole, rather than a group of individuals in pursuit of individual truths, individual happiness, and individual power. The Code of Silence was right: we must act to unite the world, not divide it... but like any significant end-goal, if I was going to achieve it, I had to break it down into

smaller, more easily-conquerable steps first.

As we continued walking, I began to identify and organize the parts of the whole that needed to be conquered. Unity was the primary objective, but to get there, I had to identify the means to achieve it — the power structures I had to break and commandeer before unity could truly be brought to the world. The first had already been secured — Sipondel's population: the largest of all the kingdoms... though also the least trained and prepared for action. The second was the Dark Power: it held the potential to develop a utopian future limited only to my imagination. Once the Dark Power was mine, the only remaining threat, as Blackheart directed my attention to, was Congreed's technology. If Congreed was to see the Dark Power eliminated, or shown to be *imperfect* enough that even a mortal could steal it, there would be no stopping him from trying to take it for himself. As such, the Excarpathian technology would need to be commandeered while Congreed and his kingdom's greed would need to be neutralized.

Though I only had three kingdoms to base the pattern on, it seemed as if the kingdoms were each sustained by a key characteristic that defined them — something they'd spent generations upon generations perfecting to use as a weapon instead of as a tool. Each and every one, condemned by their own actions and fears to psychological prisons that no warden needed to oversee, nor guards maintain, simply because they threw away their keys of awareness long ago. Rather than spend the last few centuries putting aside their differences and sharing their main assets with one another to create one unconquerable, unified, master force, they distrusted one another and allowed their skepticism to conquer, divide and enslave them all within their own kingdoms, making my revolution necessary.

The more I thought, the more I found that trust was the main obstacle we all face. Can't say I blamed them either; when people let you down, take you for granted, steal from you, discredit you, betray you... all these things build up within the mind and are never forgotten. Our minds easily forget the good and hold tight to the bad by default. But that is not a genetic flaw; we are born with potential beyond what we can even comprehend. What seems like a flaw is merely our higher consciousness telling us we're not looking at it in the right light yet. By forgetting the good and holding tight to the bad, we learn what doesn't work. But just because we learn from it, doesn't mean we know how to handle the power of self-preservation without it damaging us

and limiting the fullness of life we are entitled to experience. I admit, I didn't know how to handle it while still keeping an ability to trust, but after having lived with The Silence, I was learning that trust is not a gasoline-soaked blanket that succumbs to the matches of betrayal, never able to be used for its warmth again; it's a tapestry that wears thin in places, but can be patched over if you have the right materials, circumstances, and patience to repair it. If you don't, you're always the one who feels the coldest when winter comes.

There was still much more to learn, but travelling with capable people I trusted made all the difference. We had similar enough perspectives that made moving in the same direction easy, and our objectives seem attainable. They shared my view of unity. They were willing to break what needed to be broken so we could construct what needed to be constructed. And for that reason alone, I knew I was exactly where I was supposed to be at that moment, even if I didn't have all the upcoming details worked out yet...

CHAPTER THIRTY-NINE

Lies and Deceit

When we arrived at the next juncture in the tunnel, it looked similar to the first: skulls to the left, smoky deathtrap to the right. We took the obvious path and found ourselves in the same column-like observation point as Sipondel, only the column was in the sanctuary itself, near the back of the church.

"How are we supposed to get out of here when a packed-out sermon is being delivered?" Simeon asked with a whisper.

"I still have the skeleton key from Sipondel; I assume it's the same for this one," I whispered back.

"If not, I have a metal-melter with me," Ephraim mentioned. "Just stick 'er to the side, light 'er up, and she'll sear a hole big enough for us to crawl through and out the back."

"Is this metal-melter completely silent too?" Blackheart asked.

"...Good point. I could always dampen the sound by packing some thick cloth or something around it."

"Let's just give it a few minutes," I suggested. "They might just be wrapping up."

Two hours later, the prosperity sermon about needing more, deserving more, and not being ashamed to want more came to a close. I remember Father Gregory doing a couple of those in the past, saying the more gold you had, the better position you had to fund and finance the Kingdom of God — which was logical — but something told me that was the *only* topic they preached about in that kingdom, and that it wasn't so much to further the "Kingdom of God", but rather themselves. According to Father Gregory, the amount of gold someone has is never the issue, but rather the love of it and the want of more for personal gain that consumes the hearts of many good people. From Blackheart's description, those were wise words long gone unheard in that place.

When the sanctuary cleared out and all that remained was their priest, I slipped on my mask as Ephraim lit the fuse and stuck his metal-melter to the inside wall. In seconds, it burned through the column's thick walls and we crawled out to conceal ourselves in the shadows.

"The only thing we need here is the skeleton key to the column," I said in a hushed tone to Simeon. "I'm guessing the priest has it on him, as Gregory did — you know what to do."

"Why do we need the key to open a column that we just burned a man-sized hole through?" he asked.

"Simeon, in the field, we *do*, we don't *ask* — our opportunity could be blown or we could be killed in the time we spend talking about things."

It was an understandable question to ask, and perhaps a cold response, but a necessary one. Truth is, I had a sneaking suspicion that if that priest also had a key similar to Father Green's — and the one in my father's puzzle box — then there had to be much more to their significance and purpose than merely opening columns and misleading paintings.

"You're right. I'm on it."

With that, Simeon crept stealthily across the floor with his cloth-wrapped boots, quiet as ghost. There were moments he was only a hair's breadth away from his target, searching his pockets, between the folds of his robe, and everywhere else he could, but the priest remained unaware of his presence. When he finally spotted it on a chain around his neck, Simeon picked up an empty collection plate and threw it at the wall, clanging loud enough for him to clip the chain and have the key fall to the floor as the priest went to investigate the sound. Brilliant.

"Okay, let's go," I whispered, leading the way out the front doors.

Outside we were met by a dirty mendicant sitting on the church steps, with his hands out, hoping for a display of our generousity.

"Be gone, you filthy mongrel," Blackheart dismissed.

Simeon gave Blackheart a dirty look, then walked over and sat next to the man.

"Oh, gracious me!" the man replied. "Who are you that you humble yourself enough to sit next to a beggar like myself, sir? It's difficult trying to get anyone 'round these parts to share their gold, let alone with one such as myself. Even those who exit these doors, but it's unheard of for anyone to sit and talk with me."

"Let's just say I know where you're coming from. I was poor myself once, not through choices of my own."

"Oh? Well then surely you will share your gold with me, won't you?"

Simeon reached into his pocket and handed the man two gold coins and smiled.

"Thank you! Thank you! You know, I gave up everything to rely on others' generousity, so that they too might learn to give."

"That's admirable of you, sir. Take another two coins," he said as he stood to his feet. "Just remember, sometimes it feels like you have nothing, or aren't going anywhere, but while you're waiting for fortune to deliver you, there is always something you can do to help yourself, or teach yourself to better your situation. I turned to pickpocketing and knife-throwing because I was good at both, and kept working on my skills until my friends here found me and asked me to join them — I haven't looked back since. I hope one day you fall upon the same luck yourself, sir."

"Thank you! Yes, of course! Thank you for your kindness! God bless you!" the man ecstatically expressed with gratitude, rocking back and forth in half-worshipping bows toward Simeon's feet as we walked away.

"That was kind of you, Simeon," Naphtali affirmed.

"I figure in a place like this, there's bound to be a division of wealth between the rich and the poor. Sometimes, you just got to help another out."

"Where excess lies, usually someone had to give something up for the other to get it," I added. "You did a good thing, Simeon."

"Thanks Morningstar. So I guess we're on our way to the castle?"

"We are."

"I'm right behind you."

Our journey to the castle was lined with dirty looks and unwelcoming glances that roamed our bodies for loot with every step we took. Those were definitely not the kind of people I expected to find in a kingdom of such affluence. Had I not brought the others with me, I probably would've ended up face-down, naked in a gutter somewhere while onlookers danced in my clothes and threw my coins into the air in celebration of their new found riches — even for just a few coins. If that was what greed did to people...

It wasn't hard to find the castle. High upon the mountainside it sparkled, reaching up to the sky with abundance. The outer wall that housed the gate was thick, made up of a conglomerate of massive chunks of precious metals and gemstones; the gates themselves, made of a metallic, crystalline gemstone I'd never seen before. Probably the same stuff their armour was made of that Blackheart told me about earlier. It was beautiful in every connotation of the word; to be even a beggar outside those gates seemed to carry a prestige that would make kings and entire kingdoms jealous. Except for Congreed of course, but who knows: maybe he had so much that he even coveted what he *already* had, simply because he forgot he had it.

"Who are you? Why do you stand at the gates of the Great King Congreed's Castle, uninvited?" asked one of the guards, secure in his tower.

"My name is Morningstar, and I seek to offer your king a once-in-a-lifetime opportunity to overthrow the Dark One, his mortal enemy, who has a new-found weakness that only I know of."

"What is this weakness, you speak of?"

"That is for your king's ears only. If he knew you were holding me up now, he would not be too impressed, for an unfathomable amount of riches is at stake, if he will hear us out."

"Tell me then," another guard interrogated, "why do you wear a mask to visit our king if all you wish to do is speak to him peacefully?"

"My boy, we all wear masks. The reason I wear mine is of no concern to you; perhaps I would simply like to remain anonymous, as anyone betraying his home kingdom for personal gain would. Do the right thing and open these gates, so that we may not keep your king's ears from hearing the good news any longer, nor his hands from

holding more riches than he could even imagine."

"Very well; stand back — these gates do not open as they do in other kingdoms."

We took a couple steps back and watched the gates tilt forward, and slide down diagonally into the ground. I'd never seen castle gates move like cards shuffled into a deck, but after seeing it, I'm amazed more don't do the same. But there it was, exposing a secret underground pathway leading to the real doors of the castle. If the extravagance of the exterior walls didn't convince you of the city's greatness, the hidden passage below the sparkling gates would have easily made you a believer.

We entered into the torch-lit tunnel accompanied by only two guards. I wasn't sure what to make of it: they had impenetrable gates, a strategically-hidden entrance, but only a mere two guards to accompany a masked man with seven strangers to their king, each fully clad with weaponry and explosives? Either their greed was overriding their survival instinct, or we were about to walk into a trap...

But as we walked on, no trap was sprung, nor ambush encountered. The two guards led us straight to King Congreed as promised through all the proper pathways of the castle — or "palace" I suppose I should call it, after seeing the excessively-showy style that lined every inch of its interior and exterior.

Congreed seemed to be a jolly kind of man with the body of a wartime Santa Claus. When we entered the golden throne room, he walked over and gave me a giant bear hug, despite the fact that we'd never met before. Going by the faded red stains on his white beard and that wine-barrel breath of his, there was a good chance he was drunk, but that only made his mind more pliable for our upcoming mind-tinkerings. Nonetheless, his friendly demeanour was an unexpected delight as he welcomed us into the luxurious lounge room.

"Please, please come in! Sit down! Would you like some wine?" he asked us, but before we could answer he continued. "I sure would! Har har."

Yeah, he was definitely drunk.

"No thank you, Your Majesty. But kudos to your selection," I flattered, pretending to know the first thing about wine.

"Only the best FOR the best! Har har!" he shouted, raising his goblet and sloshing wine all over the place. "To ME! Everybody now!"

"*Lord, here we go,*" I thought to myself before speaking. "There is no better king than you, sire. But if I may get right to the point: I, Morningstar, have come before you today with a proposal. It seems—"

"A proposal? I accept! I've never had a wild night with an elephant before... but you don't know unless you try, right fellas? Har har har."

I slowly looked at Blackheart who just shrugged subtly with confusion at his crude brand of humour.

"You see sire—"

Out of the blue, his facial expression dropped to straight-faced seriousness, and his eyes took to staring at the floor intensely. But no more than a few seconds later, he started laughing an uncontrollable laugh — but at *what* was anyone's guess. I continued on, despite his half-closed eyes and inebriated mind-wanderings.

"Sire, the Dark King has recently decided to call off the truce established when the War of the Kingdoms came to an end. He has infused all the people of his kingdom with the Dark Power, and plans to use his army to go after *your* kingdom, among others, conquering you one by one before you even know he is upon you."

That sobered him up.

"That news is most distressing for the other kingdoms no doubt, but the glorious Excarpathia is *more* than equipped to handle the Dark King! He may have some kind of magic on his side, but his magic is no match for my alchemistsmiths! He may have driven us into submission two hundred years ago, but those two hundred years have been spent perfecting our craft to such magnitude that he would be a fool to challenge us now!"

"What if I told you that the Dark King also used his power in that time to fill a silo full of precious metals and jewels so tall and so deep that it would take you an eternity to relieve him of his possessions and bring them back here?"

"...Go on..."

"I know you are the most luxurious king of all the kingdoms — well, only second to the Dark One, that is, but—"

"I am second to *no* one!"

"With all due respect, my good king," I persuaded, "those two hundred years have not been wasted by the Dark King either. While you spent many of those years *learning* how to create the abundance you have today, the Dark One has always had incredible power, as you know. He has amassed so much wealth for himself, that if you only had it..."

"Enough! You insult me by discrediting all I have! I created all of this! Myself! Look around you — all this is mine!" he shouted with pretentious self-glorification.

"My apologies, Highness. I merely wanted to mention it so that you, the true and rightful king, could know of its existence and add it to your own, not to mention the Dark One's sacred artifact that can... oh, never mind. We will be on our way then, and I shall make the pitch to King Repride in your place," I bluffed as we stood up to leave. We made it only a few steps before he called us back.

"Wait... what artifact?"

"It's just an ancient artifact the Dark King has that puts all riches and wealth in the world to shame."

"What does it do?"

"You're sure you want to know?"

"Yes! Of course! Tell me of it."

"Well," I leaned in with a whisper, playing on his curiousity and embellishing the non-existent artifact's secrecy, "during my inquests into the Dark Kingdom — you know how your alchemists need to mix metals and compounds to make new ones?"

"I do."

"And you've heard the story of King Midas?"

"I have."

"Well the same way King Midas could turn any object to gold, this artifact — a magical glass ring — can give *life* to those same objects. What your alchemistsmiths create, can become your new army without ever risking another life or even your own. These golden statues around you can become your new servants — servants that will hang on your every word, never tire, never betray you, or even ask for payment. They can build any structure you can dream of, working all day and night without the need to take breaks, or even *sleep* for that matter. But most of all, you will never have to share your abundance with them nor worry about them stealing it."

"Such an item exists?"

"Such an item exists. And you know, King of Abounding Wisdom," I manipulated him further, "if you were to lend me your army — to join me in this fight against the Dark One — not only would your technology be a beacon of light and the envy of all the other kingdoms who join, but when we win the battle, even if it's with only one soldier left, you can replace your population with these creatures and have all of your kingdom's wealth, food, and all you can imagine to yourself. With such loyal subjects who ask and require nothing in return, you can still ensure they can — and will — protect all you have gained. No one from that glorious day onwards would ever question your place as the supreme ruler of these lands."

"I would very much like this artifact. What do you need from me?"

"I need you to join me and the other kingdoms when I send for your forces. We will battle the Dark One on his own ground before he even has time to prepare. The element of surprise shall ensure that you and the Dark King's artifact shall be kept apart no longer."

"You have my full support. We will join you when you send word requesting our assistance."

"I look forward to it. It has been most pleasurable to meet your acquaintance," I flattered with a bow, as the others with me followed my lead. "Good day… 'Emperor' Congreed."

"Ooh! I like the sound of that! More wine for everybody!" he yelled, spilling more of the drink upon himself than what ended up in the gemmed goblets.

"Oh no, that'll be quite alright, but thank you, Generous King. We should be on our way."

"Guards! Show my friends here back to the gates. And see to it no one gives them trouble," he commanded then raised his goblet to me. "Until we meet again, Morningstar."

CHAPTER FORTY

Stuck in a Rut

"Well, that went smoother than expected," Blackheart spoke with a hint of doubt in his voice. "You really think that worked? We need to be able to count on him when the time comes…"

"He *was* pretty drunk; we'd be lucky if he still remembers us by morning," Simeon added.

"He'll remember — we weren't exactly parasitic bootlickers like most kings are forced to meet with; we offered *him* something instead. You saw from his responses how strongly his greed, success, and never-ending desire to have more drives him. Drunk or sober, his greed won't let him forget what he has heard today. We can count on him," I reassured.

We arrived back at the jewelled wall, where the guards left us to ourselves once again.

"Is there anything more we have to do here?" Simeon asked.

"I don't think so; we got what we needed from Congreed, not to mention the second skeleton key from the priest… I think that's it. Let's join back up with the others in Sipondel."

"I would *kill* to have a position like Congreed," Simeon commented.

"But instead, you kill people who *have* positions like Congreed," Ephraim laughed.

"Um… guys?"

"What is it, Simeon?"

"Do you remember all these barrels here lining this path when we arrived?"

As if that was their cue, the tops popped off each one, and from within sprung more blades pointed at our throats than we could dispatch while still guaranteeing our survival — especially Elektra's and Arkade's. You didn't need to be a linguist to understand the many dialects of knife-point.

"You know, I was hoping we'd be ambushed by some fearsome warriors before we left, but looks like we'll have to settle for the bottom-of-the-barrel ones instead," I added, wishing Gad was there to appreciate the pun.

"Quiet! We didn't come for your words, we came for your things. Throw everything you have over here in front of me," their leader shouted.

"Everything?" Ephraim ran past them again.

"Everything. Packs, weapons, clothes... everything but your foreigner skin. And you," he turned to me, "the mask. Make it quick, we don't have all day."

"And now you know why our services are required here so often..." Blackheart muttered.

With about fifty blades to our necks, there wasn't much room for negotiation. I'd always believed peace and persuasion were the best approaches to resolving any conflicts — but that day I wanted nothing more than to let my blade do the persuading for me — for the cold metal of my knife to be warmed by the justice found only in the separation of their skin. I'd never found myself thinking like that before that day, but it was oddly satisfying. The more I tried to suppress it, the more the bloodlust began to grow inside me. What are you supposed to do when words fail and others take control of your life? Or worse — place the ones you love at risk, making you a helpless victim to the evil deeds of unremorseful transgressors?

I was at their mercy, but what made it worse was knowing Arkade was watching me, learning from me as I did nothing but accept my powerlessness. Though my blood boiled at my forced submission, I let them take our things and leave us naked in the streets without a fight. I wanted to fight — to kill — to slit every throat in vengeance — but there on the ground, my knees chalky with dust, I realized sometimes you just need to know when a fight is best saved for another day when the odds are more in your favour. Our knees will inevitably get dusty from time to time, but when they touch the ground, we must never allow the dust to convince us that our submission in that moment is the acceptance of our defeat for an entire lifetime. Sometimes to

submit is to know you have a life worth living for a higher purpose, worth seeing through to another day.

They spit on the ground in front of us as they picked up our things and left.

"Looks like these barrels are all we have to wear for now... unless you want to walk through the streets like this," Blackheart suggested.

"Absolutely not," Naphtali spoke firmly, walking over to a barrel, kicking out its bottom, and passing it to Elektra before doing the same for herself.

I can't say the barrels were our top choice for back-up clothing, but it was a kind gesture, albeit unintentional, of our muggers to leave us old wine barrels instead of ones that smelled like fish.

"So what now?" Simeon asked.

"Well, we could head back to Sipondel where we can replace much of what was taken from us," I thought aloud, "or, we can find the ones who did this, take back what's ours, and show these Excarpathians why greed robs you of more value than the price of what you've gained. Any ideas?"

"We should go get some weapons from a shop in town before going after them," Arkade naïvely suggested.

"And buy them with what exactly?" Elektra snapped back, keeping just within the line of acceptable behaviour when responding to Arkade.

"We could just steal them."

"Wearing our barrels?"

"Or without them."

"Ew. No! Morningstar??!"

"She's right, Arkade," I cut in. "We're not in the position where we want to make more enemies here — at least not until we're better equipped. We'll have to find another way."

"We must always be careful never to make more enemies than we could handle if they were all to attack at once," Naphtali added, taking Arkade's chin between her thumb and forefinger.

"Too late for that," Simeon mumbled.

"All that is beside the point. This is Excarpathia — a land where only fools come to borrow, simply because of the unregulated moneylending that goes on," Blackheart mentioned. "There are no places here that would lend us any sum on our word alone, even if we gave our word to pay it back ten-fold."

"How bad is it?" I asked.

"In most places, you only owe a small percentage on what you borrow, but here? Greed and shame go hand-in-hand. It's not uncommon to owe triple or quadruple what you borrowed, but if that's not enough, they brand you a borrower for life."

"Brand you? Like with a branding iron?" I asked.

"That would be a fate much more fortunate than most receive," Blackheart answered. "While thieves here have their hands cut off, and adulterers have their eyes cut out, borrowers... are shamed in ways far worse; not only are you considered a leech for taking from another Excarpathian, you're showing you're not wealthy enough — good enough — to be among them, and don't deserve an identity. That's when they do horrible things to your face until you can no longer be identified as someone worthy of their own identity. And if you are caught associating with a faceless one, your entire living bloodline is either killed or forced to leave Excarpathia forever. It's a kingdom of standards set by those without them."

"Now I see why stealing from foreigners is so appealing to them..."

"For now, we should probably just head into town and start asking questions," Blackheart recommended.

"I suppose you're right," I confirmed.

We made our way into town along the road that came from the castle. The eyes that wanted to strip us of our belongings as we passed the first time, now looked upon us like punch-lines of a cruel joke. But it was no matter; it was probably better to be seen as a pitiful joke than to walk those back roads fearful of being murdered for the shiny piece of lint that you didn't know was stuck to your coat. As soon as we got to the marketplace, we started looking around for any leads. Shortly thereafter, Simeon smacked me on the arm, taking a harder look down one of the lanes.

"That's not... who I think it is," he said.

"I can't tell for sure with the golden, fur-lined robes, but I think it just might be."

"Son of a *bug*! Hey!" he shouted, running after the man as he tried to hold up his barrel before growing tired of it, throwing the hindrance off his body. "Hey you! C'mere!"

The man froze in his steps as he did a double-take at the enraged naked man running towards him and took off running the other way as fast as he could.

"What was that all about?" Blackheart asked.

"Remember the beggar we met outside the church? Turns out he's just as self-serving as the rest of the people here," I explained as we all burst out laughing. After our earlier misfortune, the mirth was nice to have back in the group. "Should've known; honesty isn't a common trait among beggars."

As we looked about, asking around for any leads, Arkade came to my side. He just walked quietly at first, but kept looking up at me and then back to the ground. I figured he had a question, so I broke the silence.

"Something on your mind?"

"I've just been thinking, you know, like about you being a bishop and all, but the masked guy too, like at the same time..."

"Mmhmm?"

"Well, it's just... they're so different, but neither one is you... and I was always taught you should be yourself."

"Precisely; we *should* be ourselves. And within ourselves, we all have the good fighting the bad — the light at war with the darkness. But why do we put them at odds? Our mind and body are most healthy when we have found balance inside and out — when we have embraced all that is truly ourselves. Many think they have to choose one side or the other, and end up focusing only on the light because they are told to, or because they fear social consequence, but everyone has a dark side in them, whether it's acted upon, thought about, or repressed inside. It is the call of our primal selves — the other half of our natural being — and both sides need proper outlets for expression if we are to keep ourselves in balance."

"I'm not supposed to be good all the time?"

"I'm saying you must always focus on and pursue the good, but when that darkness surges up from within, you need to know how to handle it, use it, and release it wisely, not just deny its presence or appropriateness as you suppress it within you. Let me put this in terms you'd clearly understand: Suppressing one's inner darkness is like swallowing a burp or holding in a fart: it's socially unacceptable to release, but the more you keep it in, the bigger it grows inside and the more discomfort is caused until one day you simply lose control and *it* decides when it's time to release — usually all at once — and that's when you, and everyone else, are at its mercy."

He giggled. "So I should try to be good, but when I need to fart, I should do it."

"Only if I'm far enough away," I chuckled back as I put him in a headlock and released him again. "Just remember, you need to always stay open-minded and seek to understand both sides; allow their presence within you and express them both without worrying what everyone else will think. Those people are your limits. Ignore them."

"Why do you go through the trouble of playing both sides at once though, like as the bishop and the masked one instead of just being one person and embracing both sides like you say to?"

Leave it to children to be the most observant.

"Because the ignorance of the world often makes people believe that life should be black and white — that you must choose sides — and so the world of colourful gradients goes unadmired. It is for the unfortunate souls who haven't learned this, that I must play both sides without their knowing, because some only follow the holy man while others only follow the warlord. But the truth is, both sides are within all of us, and if people could only see that, they wouldn't have to wear masks, or pretend to be holy like a holy man, or pretend that nothing can hurt them like a warlord. They could just be themselves, unjudged, and focus on reaching their potential both as individuals and collectively. This is my dream. This is my idea. And there is immense power in an idea, because it unites people. It motivates them toward change. But the real power lies in their unity, in coming together — if enough can be rallied to a cause, no matter how ridiculous, it *will* be

seen and heard. I'm just trying to bring them all together the best way I know how."

"Oh..." he muttered, deep in thought.

Before he could say anything more, Simeon rounded the corner, dragging the man by his coat, who then tried to slip out of it and make a run for it again. Simeon was too quick for him though. He sprinted after the man and tackled him to the ground, placing his knee upon his back as he laid face-down in the dirt.

"I think I found some information that may be of use," Simeon informed. "Go on scum; tell them what you told me, or you'll never live to swindle another soul out of a single coin again."

"I — please! I'm sorry. You're all very nice people. You wouldn't hurt me, would you?"

"Enough of your prattle, vagrant!" Simeon shouted, putting more pressure on the man's back.

"I... I don't know much," he said in a panic, "but there is someone I know who might be able to help you."

"Who? Give me a name," I commanded.

"Her name is Mercedes Green. She's very kind. She will help you."

"Where do I find her?"

"Not far from here. Just around the corner, really..."

"Forgive my distrust, but you have misled us more times than we care to accept. So let me tell you what will be happening now: you will be taking us there — *all* the way there — and if you even *think* of making a run for it, we will spill your blood and make you drink every last drop until your veins run dry. Do I make myself clear?" I threatened, placing my foot upon the side of his face.

"Yes, of course. I ain't gonna run! Please! Just help me up and I will take you there," the beggar said. His pathetic pleas and doubtful assurances made me want to follow through with my threats sooner.

"Help *yourself* up, degenerate," Simeon spat as he removed his knee from his back. "And give me your robe too. I've been in the public eye long enough," he demanded, snatching the flashy robe to cover himself.

"Here. Come. Follow me," the man gestured as he led us to a hole-in-the-wall that otherwise would have gone unnoticed.

"This is it? If you're trying to pull a fast one on us, so help me…"

"No! I promise! Here — I'll even go in first. You'll see!"

We looked at each other, skeptical of the man, but followed him into the hole anyway. Our barrels just barely fit the opening.

Inside looked like an abandoned tea shop, with canisters of herbs and crushed leaves of all kinds and colours lining broken shelves that had grown thick with dust. A pleasant lady, about in her early-thirties, rounded the corner with a dish rag and looked at us as if expecting our company.

"Come in," she gestured to the benches. "Take a seat; I'll be with you shortly."

Take a seat: an ability you take for granted when not wearing a barrel that has a hard time covering your nether-regions satisfactorily. We tried our best, but decided to stand after looking like apples bobbing in a tub full of water as we kept shifting to reach an unattainable level of comfort that covered… everything.

"There, you see? She will help you. Now I'll be on my wa—" the beggar said as he tried to leave, but found his hair firmly in Simeon's grasp.

"Sit. You'll be staying with us until we have no further need for you," Simeon enwisened.

"So," the woman said entering the room with a tray of hot tea, "I take it by your choice of clothing that you're here because you've had something stolen from you."

"By some bandits, Miss Green. We were told by this man that you might know something about them," I motioned to the beggar.

"I might… what's it worth to you?"

"Would you settle for six bottomless wine barrels?" Ephraim joked, making her laugh.

"I'm just kidding. I don't need anything from you."

"You're… not from around here, are you?" Naphtali asked.

"What makes you say that?"

"The others. The greed. I would never have thought I'd hear someone say something like that in a place like this."

"I'm not... I came here for those reasons with my mother years ago, but while the greed consumed her, it only opened my eyes to a path that I realized was one I didn't want to take."

"Where did you come here from originally?" Naphtali asked politely.

"Where you just came from: Sipondel. I actually saw all of you from the back row at my father's funeral."

I put two and two together. "You're Father Green's daughter?"

"The one and only."

We looked at each other confusedly.

"I know what you're thinking: a priest with a daughter — so much for the vow of celibacy right? But the truth is, he took his vows after my mother and I left him. Around when I was just about her age," she reminisced, looking at Elektra and smiling. "He wanted a life of meaning and she wanted a life of possessions; as I'm sure you all know, my father wasn't the easiest to get along with — always so preachy and corrective all the time — so I chose to go with my mother over him."

"I see," I nodded. I didn't really feel like listening to her life story, but I assumed it was going somewhere. Then again, a lonely woman in an old tea shop could potentially ramble on for hours about nothing in particular, but I hoped that wasn't the case.

"When we came here, we didn't really have much to our name. So my mother sought after others who felt the same as she did about riches, and they joined with her to make a name for themselves stealing wealth from anyone and everyone they could. I tried heading back to Sipondel, but my father wouldn't take me back. He said I was corrupted and wanted nothing to do with me. So I came back here, dug this hole, and have been living here ever since. Before long, this kingdom's greed grew to levels not even Congreed's soldiers could control. Her band of misfits grew quickly and became very wealthy in just a short time, calling themselves *The Neutralizers*, like a group of Robin Hoods who decided to steal from the rich, but keep the money instead of giving it away to the poor. They are now the kingdom's most feared group, mainly because of their numbers. There's a home base and everything, though the grounds are so rigged with traps and explosives that anyone unaware of their placing would be a fool to try and enter."

"So Father Green's ex-wife is actually the leader of a gang of street thieves... hmm. Go figure," Simeon said without tact.

"Why doesn't Congreed do anything to stop them?" I asked her after looking at him disapprovingly, hoping to distract her from Simeon's comment.

"He can't! Well, he probably could, but ever since he began to pour all his time and energy into his alchemistsmiths, I guess he figured he could make his own riches and would just let the people decide how they were going to share rest of the wealth among themselves — as long as no one ever took from him," she shrugged.

"Mercedes, will you help us find your mother's base? She has things of ours that cannot be replaced, and we can't head back to Sipondel until we get them," Blackheart asked diplomatically.

"I could show you where it is, but I do not want to see that ill-tempered mother of mine or what she has become. Too many years have passed already and I'd rather just let things be."

"I understand. Your help is appreciated more than we could ever repay to you," he said.

"I hate to rush you, but time is of the essence..." I added.

"I apologize; I'll take you there shortly. But first, let me get you something better to wear."

She went around the corner again and grabbed some burlap sacks.

"I hope you don't mind smelling like potatoes, but they should be much more manoeuvrable than what you have on now."

"Thank you so much. Again, we are filled with gratitude for everything you're doing for us," I mentioned to her. "Do you mind if we leave our barrels here?"

"Not in the least; I'll find a use for them somewhere. Now follow me. I'll take you to their hideout."

Friends in Low Places

"Well... here we are," Mercedes pointed out with a heavy sigh.

"Mercedes, why don't you come with us inside," I tried to convince her. "I know first-hand how hard it can be dealing with a parent when you don't see eye-to-eye on things. My father died before I could make peace with him, and I regret it to this day. But I know how that disconnection sticks with a person. Let me help you come to terms with it, to heal from it, before it consumes you with regret, as it did with me. The longer you wait, the more your mind will suffer. And you never know when your last chance to make amends might be..."

"You're probably right," she sighed again. "As much as I don't want to accept it, I do need to move on."

"It's for the best. You can fall in behind me so if anything unexpected comes our way, you'll still be safe, okay?" I comforted with well-planned subterfuge. If her mother really was the leader of those thieves, having her with us could give us the strategic edge we needed, if we needed it. Not to mention, walking into a place without our usual weapons left me feeling a little unprepared in case the situation called for aggressive negotiations — and I wasn't going to leave up to Fate what I didn't have to.

"Since we don't know where the mines or other explosives and traps are placed in here, and we don't have Gad or Zebulun with us to disarm them, and Ephraim's tactical bombs were taken, we don't have much choice but to keep our eyes open... unless you have any other suggestions, Ephraim?" Blackheart led.

"Most of our typical options aren't possible right now. We could collect and send in a mass of rats and hope they set some of them off, but if there are ground mines, their weight alone won't do the trick," Ephraim added.

"That's your cue, Rat," Simeon said, forcefully pushing the shoulder of the beggar toward the door. "I'm gonna tie this rope to you. You're gonna walk and keep a distance between us of about fifty paces — and you'll do it slowly so we can trace your steps accurately, understand? Now get going."

"Please don't make me do this!"

"Go," he replied sternly.

We all trailed cautiously behind, watching as the shifty beggar took his first steps safely. Then his next. And then a few more. But on his forty-seventh step, he set off a clustermine that blew his limbs clean off his body, scattering his insides in all directions with such force that even his organs set off chain-reactions of their own.

"Well, there goes that option," Simeon commented.

"That confirms the mine-presence in here. With luck that's the last of them, but with all likeliness, we don't know *what* to expect in here, so keep your eyes peeled," Ephraim mentioned.

"We're just going to have to proceed carefully. Single-file. We need to be as alert as possible, so I'll be looking straight-ahead, Mercedes to the ground, Blackheart left, Naphtali right, Ephraim above, and Simeon behind us. Elektra and Arkade, you fill in the gaps — keep your eyes sweeping all our areas in case one of us misses something."

The explosion that dirty con artist set off didn't even collapse any part of the building's structure — probably because the gold had a much higher melting point and molecular integrity than the ceramic bricks used to make most buildings. I guess there was more to Excarpathia's choice of materials than just looking good...

We proceeded with caution as carefully as possible through the winding hallways, following a path that seemed to sink lower and lower into the ground. You could feel the temperature get cooler too. But the strangest thing to me was the fact that we were the only people there; there wasn't a thug or bandit in sight. If that was their hideout, they definitely hid out.

We carefully followed the dark corridors until in the distance we noticed a faint light and even fainter voices. As we got closer, we could see that the small room contained three Neutralizers, just sitting there, playing cards, and drinking by candlelight. If Asher and her bow were with us in that moment, their heads would be triple-shish-kebabed.

I quietly gave the signal to the more capable members of the group to storm in suddenly to take them by surprise. We rushed that room in less than a second — so quick that they didn't even have a chance to take their swords out. Within seconds, their bodies laid on the table with their bets, symbolic of the dangers of going all-in. We stripped them of their uniforms and weapons, but since there were only three of them, I figured their equipment was best given to the ones who could do the most damage with them: Naphtali, Blackheart, and our throwing knives expert, Simeon. The three of them suited up in the guards' leather armour, ready to carry on better equipped than we arrived.

That left us with one man in a gold, silken, fur-lined robe, three slightly-armoured soldiers with swords, and some unarmed burlap sackineers. More pitiful than fearsome, if you saw us.

From that hallway branched three more. Each filled with treasure so abundant you couldn't see the floor.

"Better take some of this to barter with in the market later," Blackheart suggested, "but not too much that you're weighed down or that it jingles in your pockets when you walk. Only take what's of highest value."

We placed a few precious gems in our pockets and phantom-stepped toward the next group of voices. Peering around the corner, there were only two bandits waiting there, drinking and exchanging thug-gossip. Quiet as the dead, Naphtali and Simeon snuck up behind them, thrust their blades into their mouths, and made them taste cold steel where their tongues had tasted fine wine just moments before; a punishment suitable for gossiping tongues everywhere. I took their clothes and put the first bandit's gear on, passing the other set to Ephraim.

We looked more capable with our new found gear too. It's amazing how just dressing differently can affect your influence; dress like a beggar and your assumed poverty gains you looks of contempt; dress in gold-lined robes and people are more willing to accommodate you; sport armour and you look strong, dutiful, and prepared — but mix all those together and throw in two naked kids wearing burlap sacks and you have us looking like a bunch of... well it did not look good, that's for sure, but we worked with what we had.

The room we had found ourselves in had only one other exit: a large, round, golden door with jewels encrusting it similar to the wall outside Congreed's gates — and without a handle to open it. The tongueless bandits were all we saw nearby who would've had knowledge of how to open it, so we searched their pockets for anything of use: keys, wedges... anything. Simeon figured maybe it was one of those "secret knock" doors.

I approached it to see if I could decipher how it opened, but before I could even touch it, it rolled to the side, into the wall, and there before us stood about twenty of the fifty who had taken everything from us along the road.

"Come with us," the first one instructed, clearly expecting us to be there when it opened.

I looked at the others, who I hoped were prepared for whatever happened next.

The guards led us through some deceiving passages, some whose paths you wouldn't have even realized were there as they camouflaged perfectly into the rock face around them. But at the end of those paths was a room larger than any room I'd ever seen — palaces and castles included — with mountains of gold and stolen wealth as high as the ceiling in some places. In the middle of the room, sitting upon her makeshift throne, was Father Green's wife.

"Hello dear," the gang mother said to Mercedes.

"Hello mother," she replied with slight contempt.

"I see you've finally decided to come see me after all these years... and with a small army carrying weapons! I don't know if this is your way of apologizing for wanting nothing to do with me, or if you've come for my head!"

"Mom, you know I'd never want anything bad to happen to you. I love you. Just as much as I always did... obviously there's some resentment, but you can't blame me for that; I left dad to be with *you* and when we got here, you acted like I barely existed... all you wanted was to be rich."

"I never treated you like you didn't exist!"

"Mom... mom... I didn't come to fight. I came to tell you I love you, and I'm sorry for walking out. It was what I needed to do at the time and I don't regret it for a minute, because it brought me here now with a better understanding of the world, and of our relationship. After dad's funeral, it just made me realize how quickly someone you love, even a disciplinarian like him, can be gone forever without letting you say goodbye or spend any more time with them."

"Your father's... dead? Since when?"

"Since a few days ago. If it wasn't for my friends here and Morningstar's help, I might've locked myself away in my home and never come here today. Or ever. But he convinced me to come make amends with you, and made me realize my happiness with the future and the present depends on my ability to let the past go and make peace with it," she expressed with her hand on my forearm.

"Is this true? I take it you're this 'Morningstar' my daughter speaks of?"

"I am."

"I see... are you two sleeping together?"

"Even if we were, what does it matter?" Mercedes defended questionably well.

"Mrs. Green, I assure you that my concern for Mercedes' circumstances with respect to your relationship was — and is — good and pure and noble. She was actually helping us find you so that we might ask for our things back that your men stole from us."

"What things?"

"Our clothes, our packs... but most notably so, my mask."

"A mask? And just what purpose do you have for a mask? Those things bring more bad than good."

"My mask represents everyone who has ever wanted to fight back, but didn't; who wanted to stand up and say something, but held their tongue. It is the voice of a generation gone silent, and with that mask, masses shall be rallied to take back what they deserve, bringing our oppressors to their knees in acknowledgement of the power we can have through uniting together. A unity that, perhaps, I might convince you to join — that is, if you care to share in the unfathomable spoils of war that shall be left in our wake."

"An eloquent young man, from the sound of it... As you may already know, I, too, share in the ideal of unity and the use of it to oppose established beliefs, customs, and traditions. Look around you. All my efforts have led up to this. Only this. Some may find this impressive, but it's barely a fraction of what it could be. I've been fighting for the upper-hand against that tight-fisted twit Congreed for decades, using all the tactics and resources at my disposal. But things didn't work the first time and they still don't work now. I've exhausted all my options. But you... you know," she thought aloud, "you may be exactly what I've been waiting for. I'll make you a deal — how about I give you your equipment back in exchange for your help in overthrowing Congreed once and for all."

"You want to take Congreed's place on the throne?"

"If it's too difficult a task for you—"

"No, no, it's entirely possible, Madam Green. As a matter of fact, Congreed has agreed to help us as we go up against the Dark King. If you will lead The Neutralizers into battle alongside us, I can arrange for a 'private' meeting between you and Congreed — one that you have the choice to let him never return from. You see, I've promised him something there that will surely lure him away from his guards long enough to acquire it on his own — so while he is enamoured by his new relic and without his usual protection, that will be your moment to strike and seize his crown."

"And how do I know I can trust you?"

"Because he's been caring and is protective of *me*, mother," Mercedes added. "More than *you* have been all these years."

Her guilty low-blow of emotion became the timely redemptive strike I needed to seal the deal.

"Mind your tongue, Mercedes," Madam Green said using her authority to try and mask her convictions. "We will join you in your war, Morningstar. You align the timing with Congreed, and I'll return wearing his crown."

"Thank you, Madam Green. It is a much more comforting thought to know your forces will be fighting with us."

"You will find your equipment to the left of my throne, through the tunnel marked by the sapphire. You'll find it once you've crossed through there — just be sure to only tread upon the floor tiles that have a shadow cast upon them, or else we may not be fighting together on the battlefield as planned," she warned.

"Thank you again. Until the battlefield... Your Highness," I forebodingly flattered.

"Morn," Ephraim whispered with concern as we walked toward the sapphire, "how do you know she's not walking us through that tunnel to our deaths?"

"She's not," Mercedes cut in. "I know she doesn't have a reputation for integrity, but she wants that crown too much. She wouldn't dare risk her opportunity at finally getting it for herself. She's wanted it for as long as I can remember."

"Just remain on your guard at all times — be ready for anything," I advised. "That goes for everyone."

As we walked through the entrance and out the other side, we found ourselves in a cave no larger than Sipondel's sanctuary — only from the looks of things, it was an area that had much fewer entrances and exits — one, to be exact — which was same way we came in. There was nothing inside that claustrophobe's nightmare, except for a giant, unsocialized, cross-eyed mutant of a bandit waiting for us. He looked a lot like Manasseh actually, the way his body was basically stacks upon stacks of solid muscle. Didn't seem nearly as bright, however. He just sat there looking at us with his head cocked, blinking slowly, from atop a massive boulder that no ordinary man could lift — a boulder from which one long metal shaft protruded, with oddly-shaped, thick spines protruding from that. If ever a room could double as the perfect torture chamber, it was that one.

Unsure of how to go about communicating with the mammoth that sat before us, I spoke slowly, hoping he would understand.

"Morningstar," I said, pointing to myself. "Friends," I drew out syllabically and gestured toward the others. "Mask?" I asked simply, placing my hand over my face with a downward smearing motion.

"MAAASK? UNNGGHH! NO MASK AGAIN! MORAM BE GOOD!" he bellowed as he crawled into a corner and began to suck his thumb.

"*What*, the *Hell*, just happened...?" Simeon said looking around confused.

"I... don't have the slightest idea," Blackheart responded.

"Aww, you guys scared him," Mercedes revealed as she walked over to comfort the beast. "Moram okay? Moram safe with Mercedes. Safe. Moram remember Mercedes?"

He looked up at her, staring blankly for a moment.

"Moram know Mercedes," she smiled, gently touching his face. "Moram played with little Mercedes. Mercedes friend. Me Mercedes. Big Mercedes."

"You Big Mercedes?" he squeaked in a way that was anything but cute.

"That's right! Me Mercedes," she reinforced.

"MERCEDES!" he roared, picking her up onto his shoulder as he started running around the room. I inched slowly back toward the doorway in case his excitement brought the whole roof down on our heads.

"Okay! Okay!" she said laughing. "Mercedes down!"

He placed her gently on the ground. At least he understood *some*body.

"Mercedes need mask. Moram find mask for Mercedes?"

"Moram open door for Mercedes," he self-narrated as he walked over to the giant boulder he was sitting on when we entered, and picked it up like a pebble. With both hands wrapped tight around the giant rock, he marched over to the back wall and inserted the boulder's metal rod deep into a barely-noticeable hole, the way shadows covered it. As he cranked the boulder around and around, the wall separated, revealing some of the most amazing things ever stolen or created. If ever there was an uprising in Excarpathia, Congreed's guards would've easily met their match by the unexpected forces that would've awaited him behind that wall.

All seven of us seemed to gravitate towards it, lured into its material glory by the awe it commanded. We almost entirely forgot about our equipment the way every inch of treasure gleamed and technology pulsed: weapons so sharp it practically cut the air that brushed against it, modes of transport centuries ahead of current technology. There was a plethora of things I would've stolen from there, if only I could've slipped them past Madam Green unnoticed — but that was unlikely, seeing how there was only one way out, and *that* way crossed in front of her throne. However, where there is desire, the means to fulfill it are endless; if one way didn't work, I was determined to find another.

"Mercedes, do you think your mom would mind if we took a couple of hoverboots with us?" I asked.

"I wish I could say no, but just because she's helping you, doesn't mean she's any less greedy. Don't forget, this is all to benefit herself. She wouldn't even be helping you if there was any chance you'd get the better end of the deal."

"Hmm... then we'll just have to find another way."

"Good luck with that," she said with little assurance.

It's true what they say, that words are the true weapons. Those who fight with steel are limited to the strength of their arm, the reach of their blade, and the timing of their strike; but those who fight with persuasion know no limits — not time, nor status, nor chance. They plant the seed of doubt or inspiration, and from there the target's mind falls victim to itself. It is the magic of the magicless, and the most effective way to scale the walls of limitation.

Lucky for us, all our equipment was tossed in a pile together, so when Simeon found the first pack, the rest was there along with it. Well, almost everything; after exhaustibly looking through our belongings and all around the hidden cavern, the most important piece of equipment — my mask — was nowhere to be found.

"Can't you just make another one?" Elektra asked.

"Our recent alliances were formed by that mask. Without it, we have no allies; no revolution," I expressed with frustration.

"Let's keep calm — we'll just ask my mother about it. She knows absolutely everything that happens within her organization, the big-picture and the intricate details alike. She's bound to know where your mask is," Mercedes assured.

"I hope you're right, Mercedes — that mask is everything and time is of the essence. Alright, let's go find her; there is something I wanted to speak to her about anyway," I said, thinking of getting my hands on some of the technology we saw in that horde of stolen goods.

As we made it back to the luxuriously cluttered throne room, I knelt before Madam Green and the others followed my lead. Presenting a humble façade gains trust; flattery appeals to ego; combine the two to gain an ego-based trust within someone, and you will find in your hands a discernment-clouding tool second only to love.

"Your Highness, it appears as if the mask we came here for is missing. We could spend copious amounts of valuable time looking for it, but everyone in this kingdom knows if they want something found, you are the one with the all-seeing eye. Might you point us in the direction of its whereabouts?" I inquired.

"If you're referring to that ugly wooden thing, I had my men throw it away. Do you really think in a palace of gold and rubies we'd keep a piece of garbage made of wood and junkyard metal?"

"There's the antagonistic mother I remember..." Mercedes whispered.

Her insolence and disrespect toward my most-valued handiwork only amplified the anger that grew within me; the fact she willingly exploited my trust, however... that wasn't something I was about to let go of so easily. I'd have acted upon it right then and there, too, if she wasn't my only lead to its whereabouts; but she was lending her forces to my aid, and I needed those forces to see my bigger plans through, so her pile of treasures would have to go unadorned by her head just a little longer.

"Of course not, Your Highness; how foolish of me. Even still, is there any chance you could tell me where it was last seen? What was done with it? The influence commanded by that mask is indispensable — so indispensable, in fact, that without it, the crown shall never know its rightful place upon your head. Help me find that mask, and you will surely find yourself upon Congreed's throne as queen."

"And just how do you expect me to help you find what I don't know the whereabouts of?"

Simeon whispered to me, "You'd think she'd be an expert at that..."

"My father used to say that 'though finding is a Boolean, searching is a spectrum'. I always thought of that saying in terms of an adventure: that our destinations are Booleans — we reach them or we don't — but our journeys are spectrums, because there are so many paths we can take to our destination that make getting there that much better.

That is to say that while we don't know where the mask currently is, nor do we have control over its whereabouts, we *do* have control over how fast and efficiently we search, how equipped we are to deal with opposition — which of course influences how quickly we find the mask and how quickly the crown is placed upon *your* head, my queen."

"And I suppose this is your way of leading up to asking me for the treasures you just saw in that chamber when looking for your precious mask. Well you can forget about that. Those treasures are mine and mine alone," she snapped as the eyes of her fellow thieves looked to one another, too scared to move their heads, lest she see them. "You can prove yourself to us by showing what you're capable of *without* our help. If you can succeed without it, then you are worthy of us to lend it."

She was really testing my patience.

"An understandable request, Your Highness. We have both worked very hard to get ourselves to where we are today. Though there is much we still want, there is much we already have, and that means we have much to lose as well. It's that potential loss that can keep us bound so tightly that we never reach our biggest dreams, because the biggest dreams require the most risk. But I guarantee you: your biggest dreams can become reality, not by brute-forcing the end-goal, but breaking it down into smaller, more manageable parts. If your goal takes years, breaking it down into months and days will let you improve your lot little bits at a time. Before you know it, anything you dream of will be yours simply because you've focused on the steps you could take instead of the distance to get there."

One of the thieves from behind her throne walked up to her side and spoke up. "Madam Green, he raises a good point: it would be more beneficial to all of us if we let him borrow some of our technology, even if we make him bring it back with your crown when they are finished."

She pretended to scratch behind her head as if she was thinking, but pulled a dagger instead that deeply slit his throat faster than the man could pull away. His body fell only a few steps before his head came loose, rolling the rest of the way down the stairs, and stopping at Elektra's feet. A replacement underling stepped in to take his place like that was a common occurrence.

"Let's get one thing straight," she said emotionlessly, "*you* are asking for *my* help. I know nothing about you, other than the fact you were able to get this far, past armed men and deadly traps with what looks like little more than your wits. That may be enough for me to hear you speak a few words, but you still have much to prove to me — and begging for my treasure because you're too weak and unprepared to do things on your own is not going to get you very far. If you want my support, you sure-as-Hell better not ask me for one more thing until you show yourself worthy of it. Do I make myself clear?"

My emotional control was starting to loosen its grip on my inner volatility.

"You make yourself clear," I said with much more restraint than I wanted to maintain.

"Then we will see you when you have found your mask. And if you can't find it by the time your war is set to begin, you can count us out."

I bowed in place of words that would have erupted volcanically from my inner anger, and left her to her dealings as we made our way back to the surface.

CHAPTER FORTY-TWO

The Impostor

The woman was insufferable! Had she not been so stubborn, I would have put her on the throne without so much as a second thought, taking comfort in knowing Congreed's bloodline would no longer rule. After all, with her on the throne, Excarpathia would be thrown into a state of disarray for years — disarray that would've spawned civil war lasting for decades, keeping them out of my way as I went about my plans. But she was stubborn — a vexation — and her greed was a symbiote too well-bonded to her through a lifetime of deception; if I couldn't trust her in the small things, there was certainly no way I could trust her in the more significant things later. At least with Congreed I knew what to expect: though greedier than a hungry wolverine, he was direct and upfront about what he wanted and quite observably dismissive of whatever he did not. As far as I was concerned, that made him trustworthy, because I always knew where he stood. But nonetheless, he was more of a threat on the Excarpathian throne than she. It was a choice between two evils, but which one was the lesser evil, only time would tell.

We wandered around Excarpathia in search of the mask, but it was a large kingdom and we had ultimately nothing to go on. It would have been useful to at least be able to get some information out of Madam Green's bandits — namely the ones who threw my mask to the curb-side — but instead she was making us inefficiently prove to her we could do it on our own when clearly the resources to help us and means to expedite the process were right there within her power to lend our way. It was a completely useless trial for something of utmost importance. At least we were able to wander the streets clothed and equipped again.

"I hate this place," Simeon spoke as we left the hideout. "I can't wait to get out of here."

"Why is that?" Blackheart asked him.

"Are you serious? Were you not just listening to that woman? I mean, no offense to you, Mercedes, but there's no hope for her — or *anyone* here for that matter. Even the damn beggars have gold robes and *still* lie, cheat, and steal to get more! It's sickening."

"No offense taken," Mercedes replied. "I feel the same way. That's why she and I went our separate ways so long ago. She was like that then, and she's still like that now. Worse even, having lived that lifestyle for so long."

Her kind response and self-control reminded me of Emeline.

"I don't know how you do it. How do you live in a place like this seeing *that* every day, everywhere you look, talking to people who can't even look you in the eye, because they're too captivated by anything and everything that shines or sparkles?"

"I guess you just learn that no matter where you go, there's always something to deal with; if it's not greed, it's lust, or envy, or pride, or something else. You just have to live your life so uncorrupted that it offsets the corruption as much as possible."

"Your ability to make a home among such things is admirable, Mercedes," Naphtali added, "but you don't have to keep living in a dystopia simply because you're strong and noble enough to accept it. Each of us came from the same things you speak of — we've seen terrible things and watched loved ones fall to the temptation of forces few can withstand. That's how we found each other, and realized we deserved better. Not deserved more, or deserved what others had, but simply deserved a better option than the ones we had to choose from. So we created our own."

"When I was younger," Simeon cut in, "my family didn't have a whole lot. We ate only one meal every day, because that's all we could afford. I grew up thinking that's just how it was, and that my parents tried their best for us. Then one night, when it was time to eat and my sister wasn't there to eat with us, I asked my parents where she was, but couldn't get a straight answer out of them. She wasn't there the next day, or the one after that, or even the one after that. For years, I wondered where she went that night, and why my parents wouldn't talk about it... until I was old enough to check things out for myself. I followed my parents for a few weeks, and you know what I found? My parents were just as greedy as the people here, only they weren't as lucky. They didn't have the jobs they said they did; they'd been lying to me for years... wouldn't you know, they turned out to be gambling

addicts — in debt up to their ears. And my sister," his eyes teared up, "in time, I found out they had given her over to a despicable man as payment to square off some of their debts: a sex-trade tycoon by the name of Rex Silverstone — the wealthiest, most worthless bag of scum the kingdom had ever known. I hated that man. I hated him for what he made my parents become, and I hated him for what he did to my sister. And I wasn't going to let him get away with it. Even though I was poor and didn't have the same social and political connections he held, I made it a point to do everything I could to make things right. And I did — with two throwing knives into the side of his head from a distance of 15 metres. I practiced hard for that chance, day and night, until I was good enough to get justice for what he'd done. As soon as I killed him, his entourage of dirt-bag thugs chased me deep into the forest where luckily Blackheart and The Silence came to my rescue. They took me in; they gave me purpose, and taught me that I still had a life worth living."

Blackheart put his arm around him.

"I'm so sorry Simeon; that's horrible..." Mercedes comforted.

He shrugged. "I haven't seen my family since that day, nor do I know if my sister's even still alive. But when one evil is removed, another just steps in to take its place right? I'm sure things are exactly as they were when I left them."

"We can only hope things are better for them now, Simeon. You know you're like a brother to me now — to all of us," I added, "now until death. No matter what happens, we always have each other's back."

After a few minutes of silence walking the streets, Arkade spoke up.

"I still don't get what's so bad about greed though."

Most of the group looked at him with a mix of confusion and disbelief.

"I mean, I heard what you guys were saying and how the people here are and stuff, but doesn't greed make you want things so you go after them? That's good, isn't it?" he tried to clarify.

Simeon took an explosive from Ephraim's pack and put it in a thick, brown hand-held coin-purse. He then scribbled on a piece of paper, and attached the note to it:

Gold coins and jewels for the homeless. Do not touch.

"You want to see where greed gets you? I'll show you what it does to you," Simeon snapped, emotionally-charged as he walked over and sat the bag down in the street. Then he came back and herded us behind the nearest wall where he and Arkade peeked out to watch the bag. "Now just see what happens."

"Simeon, this is—"

"Shhh!" he silenced Ephraim. "Just watch."

Just then a wealthy looking man with golden jewellery walked past and read the sign. You could tell by the way he looked around that his conscience was guilty, but the moment he thought he could supplement his greed and get away with it, he took hold of the bag and stuck his hand in only to have it explode unexpectedly, launching his body against the wall behind him with extreme force. The man sat there crumpled and twitching until he stopped moving altogether.

"And that, Arkade, is why you don't let greed get the best of you," he concluded.

"You didn't have to do that," Ephraim whispered to him aside.

"The boy needed to see for himself," he said in plain conversation. "Did you learn something?"

Arkade nodded, unsure if he should say anything at all.

"There you go. See? Sometimes the best way to learn a lesson isn't just hearing the words, but putting it into practice by experimenting with it and finding its truth for yourself instead of taking someone else's word for it."

"We should head back now," Blackheart suggested. "The mask could be anywhere and there's no guarantee we're going to find it. At this point it's a needle in a haystack."

"Zebulun tells me sometimes, 'When you're looking for a needle in a haystack, don't be afraid to burn the haystack to save yourself from spending half your life picking through strands of straw,'" Ephraim smirked.

"I know you love your explosives, Ephraim, but we're not going to burn Excarpathia to the ground just to find the mask... although that's not the worst idea..." I replied. "Not to mention, the mask is mostly made of wood, so we'd be burning a kingdom simply to find ash hidden among the ashes."

"I still wouldn't exactly be opposed to that idea," Simeon added. "Seems like a small price to wipe this place from the face of the earth."

"Blackheart's right though," I refocused. "As much as I hate to leave it behind knowing it could be just around the corner, we really should head back to Sipondel to see how things are going."

"If we leave now, we can make it there by the midnight mass — see Judah strut his stuff," Ephraim laughed.

We snuck our way back into the hollow column of the church and climbed down into the tunnels, bound for Sipondel. It was nice to leave that place, and head toward a kingdom that felt more like home than anywhere else I'd been. I had made it my own: the religious ones loved me, their king feared me, and the rest of the population had so much disbelief in themselves that they readily believed in everything I did. It's true, what they say: if you don't stand for something, you'll fall for anything. But their insecurities worked in my favour, and I would use them to every possible advantage I could, so who was I to teach them otherwise? The questions they lacked the courage and awareness to ask would become the foundation of my empire, and once I built my structures upon it, all hope for their redemption would be lost.

When we arrived at the turn-off to Sipondel, and the others went on ahead, Naphtali pulled me aside.

"I apologize for waiting until the eleventh-hour to tell you this, Morningstar, but there is something personal I must attend to. I cannot explain the details of my sudden departure, nor its reasons, but I assure you, before the battle begins, you shall find me there with you."

"But Naphtali, we—"

"I will return," she assured, placing a gentle hand on my chest.

And with that, I watched her walk the tunnels until the light of her torch no longer flickered upon the walls.

When I caught up with the others, they were all waiting at the top of the exit, listening intently to whatever was happening on the other

side while Blackheart watched through the opening.

"What is it?" I whispered.

"Well, there's good news and bad news: the good news is we found your mask. But the bad news... well... look for yourself," Blackheart instructed as he climbed back down so I could take his place.

An unordained impostor was using my mask to speak to my congregation. And boy, would I make him pay dearly...

"And that, citizens of Sipondel," spoke the man I wanted to strangle, "is the only way any of you will survive this war. Do exactly as I have spoken here tonight, and let any further instruction on the matter go unheard — be it from me or anyone else. Heed my words this night, and you will find yourselves waking up to your loved ones for many years after this war has come and gone — and with more to your name than any of you could ever ask for."

"That does it — Ephraim, hand me an explosive!" I demanded.

"No!" Blackheart quietly yelled as he grabbed my leg. "We can't kill him! As long as he wears the mask and the people think it's you, we have to treat him as if he was. Worship him even. If the people were to watch him die, or worse — be beaten by us, and shown to be weak — it would be detrimental to our cause. He needs to live. But as soon as that mask comes off and he finds himself alone... we'll make sure he's unable to wear it again."

"I have an idea; follow me as quickly and as closely as you can," Simeon instructed hastily.

He squeezed past me and exited the tunnel silently, sliding open the window in Father Green's office and slithering out like the master stealthsman he was. We followed him up to the rooftop and looked over the ledge above the entrance to the church.

"What are we doing up here?" I asked him quietly.

"Looking for his getaway plan, because he's likely not going to run away on foot," he replied looking over each side of the rooftop until he found a single black horse whose reins were tied to a post below. "There! See? Just as expected. Now we just wait up here, and when he comes out those doors and jumps on the back of his horse, we ambush him, and take him to the ground. What we do to him after that is up to you, Morningstar," Simeon schemed.

"Shhh! He's coming!" Arkade informed us as we quickly ducked behind the stone filigree.

"I want you both to stay up here until I say otherwise," I said, looking at Arkade and Elektra.

"But—"

"That wasn't a question," I reiterated. "Stay here."

The cloaked man ran from the front doors straight to the horse, but as he hopped over its back legs in a single bound to its saddle, Simeon swung down — and like a two-footed battering ram, slammed into his chest, knocking him to the ground where we all dove upon him.

But when we pulled his hood back, not only was there no mask on his face... it was Dan.

"Dan?! You sure-as-Hell better have a good explanation for this..." I threatened with a dagger to his throat.

"What the Hell are you talking about?! A good explanation for what?! You just told me two seconds ago to put on this damn cloak and go ride the horse down the back roads as a decoy!" he justified, just as angrily.

"And lucky for me, you followed your orders like the pitiful lemming you are," came a smooth, condescending voice from the alleyway behind us, mounted upon a horse of his own.

"Whoever you are, if you think yourself to be my better, come determine that answer for yourself, coward!" I tried provoking him.

"Morningstar, Morningstar," he said calmly, adjusting his black leather gloves. "I *know* myself to be your better — I don't need to prove it. This is quite an operation you have going here. I must say, the mask is a nice touch as well; you just... put it on and everyone seems to hang onto your every word. It's quite stimulating, really."

"Tell me who you are," I said walking toward him, "before I cut your tongue out and give you a taste of *real* stimulation."

"Oh, I'm sure soon after I take my leave this night, our friend Blackheart here will be able to tell you all about me. So let's skip the 'who I am' part, and go on to why I'm here. You see, Morningstar, I am here to show you what you could've been like. We're quite similar, you and I, but the difference between us, is I thrive on efficiency while you expend your energy through wasted effort. All this... fighting you do to make your name known: the people you lie to daily, the friends you mislead willingly... all this effort and time put into creating a power structure from scratch when all you need to do is simply *commandeer* one that's already in place. Much like I did in Toreth, a kingdom I rule not far from he—"

From a distant rooftop, Asher sent an arrow sailing through the night air toward him, but he caught it in mid-air, examining its craftsmanship, as if the arrow was more attention-worthy than him catching it.

"A new kind of arrow Asher? More streamlined and lightweight, I see," he said, snapping it in half and tossing it to the ground. He then lowered his hood and removed the mask. "You really don't need to try and kill me, for I am not here to kill you. If I was, you'd all be dead already. Am I here to help you in your efforts? Far from it; if you step foot on my soil, I will crush you and your friends here like the insects you are. I'm here simply to meet the man behind all the panic being stirred up that I've been hearing about for weeks now. It's admirable what you've done, really. You know, Morningstar, you might've even been the only one truly capable of appreciating all that I have made for myself over in Toreth. But unfortunately, you won't live to see it after this war of yours — for as surely as we speak this night, you will not make it home from the battlefield alive. But hey... even the grass needs new fertilizer to grow," he said as he tossed my mask over to me. "Enjoy the afterlife, Morningstar; I hope it holds better things for you than this life did."

As he rode off, I turned to Blackheart. "And that was *who*, exactly?"

"Repride... *King* Repride. He used to be one of us until that little dirtbag double-crossed us in one of the most critical missions we'd ever had. Most of us nearly died."

"What happened?"

"Our target was the then-king's right hand, whom the king suspected to be unfaithful in his duties. Toreth... was not your ordinary kingdom; each and every member of that population is an extension of the bloodlines of some of the most well-trained warriors these lands have ever known. They train day and night, man and boy,

boy and girl, sword and shield — so it was not an easy mission to plan, let alone complete. At any moment, any person there could have made things tremendously difficult for us, but we did what we could, running the plan like clockwork. But the plan was not enough. What I thought was my best and most elaborate, iron-clad plan to date, failed. And it failed for one reason, and one reason alone: I didn't account for betrayal. After an extensive investigation, we discovered the king's suspicions were correct. So, without hesitation, I set the plan in motion and we all moved into position. When the assassination was only moments away from completion, that was when Repride turned the tables on us. He killed the *king* instead of his right-hand. *Repride* was the one the right hand was scheming with. Before we even knew how to react, the room filled with so many soldiers that our hopes of survival plummeted to near-zero. They came at us harder than we were prepared for; but we made it out alive — just barely. Issachar's scars, Zebulun and Ephraim's shared wounds to the ear and face, the psychological damage and distrust born into some of the other members — Dan especially, who was particularly close to him... they are all lasting reminders of his double-crossing that night."

"And we just let him ride away? Let's get him!" Arkade exclaimed, climbing down from the rooftop without my permission.

"Not tonight, my boy, not tonight," Blackheart acknowledged, then continued his story. "From what our sources told us, that same night, Repride slit the right-hand's throat and usurped the throne for himself. We should've seen it coming; he was always complaining to the others in camp, saying his skills were being underutilized and he deserved to lead instead. Always saying that no one was more deserving than he was. But it was that exact mentality that was the reason we wouldn't allow him to. It didn't matter that he was a better strategist than I or even the fact that he held the number one rank for a brief time until he double-crossed us — he was too unstable and his pride was too much to allow into a position like that.

"He was ranked number one in camp? Above Naphtali?"

He let out a deep sigh. "Yes; though not because he was the better combatant... Repride poisoned Naphtali the night before challenging her in combat. She barely had any of her wits about her, and though it was clear to all of us she wasn't herself, there was nothing we could do; once a challenge begins, no one — of any rank or position — is allowed to interfere in any way. By the time the fight was over, he'd beaten her so bad she could barely walk... barely speak. She looked nothing like herself. It's because of that fight that most people don't challenge for rank anymore. Days later, when Benjamin was tending to her wounds, he discovered Repride's toxin in her blood — a toxin that only comes from a plant root we kept on hand for missions where discretion was key — a plant root known explicitly for its lethality... he wasn't trying to *dull* her senses so he could beat her in combat; he was trying to *kill* her, so he could take her rank and ensure she would never take it back from him. To this day, we don't know how she survived, but as if by some divine miracle, she did. It's probably for the best she wasn't here to see him tonight despite how well she maintains her discipline, even when most would throw it to the wind."

"I suppose that would be the only way anyone *could* beat Naphtali. I'm curious though: if Repride and his people are as capable in combat as you say they are, do you think there's a chance we could get them to fight with us?"

"You'd really want a man like *that* fighting with us? A *traitor*?! Even if he didn't *completely* screw us over by the end of the battle somehow, it's unlikely he'd join us. You heard him speak! He wasn't here to exchange pleasantries — he was here to evaluate you and size you up! He wanted to see who his rival was. And be not mistaken: though he flaunts his kingship and projects himself to be fully satisfied with all he has, the moment your success commands more admiration and followers than he has, is the day he will rear his ugly head again to convince the world that he is still the one most worthy of being worshipped. I wouldn't put it past him to try to take all you've made for yourself as his own either. Not because he wants it, but just to show that he can. Knowing him, he will let you do all the work, and then, when you are at your weakest, will swoop down like the vulture he is, and scavenge all you have left for his own. The man cannot be trusted!"

"Well if we can't get a force like his on our side, we better get started planning the aspects we *do* have control over to such perfection that even if we fail, our failure inspires others to complete the job for us. As it stands, we don't have nearly as much force as we need to bring down the wielders of the Dark Power, but if we can't overcome them by force alone, we'll certainly create the illusion of it and let fear conquer them for us. Come with me; we don't have much time."

Blackheart and I left the group and headed for Father Green's office

where I cleared the table with one sweep of the arm. I rummaged through our belongings, pulling out the map of the kingdoms that used to hang in our base and handed it to Blackheart to pin to the wall. I also pulled out the blueprint I'd created of the Dark Kingdom, laying it on the desk, and placing tokens on it to represent all our forces: The Silence, the Sipondelis, the Excarpathians, and The Neutralizers. It wasn't until I stepped back and looked at the table that the imminence of the war became apparent. Those were the final moments before the world as everyone knew it changed, and a whole new era began for them. An era of freedom, of inner strength. Of a time when people would wake up breathing the fresh air of lives they own for themselves, allowed to walk wherever their feet could take them, bowing before no one. The world would be theirs and their destinies and dreams their own — dreams made real by their hard work and dedication, instead of determined by the casting of dice by those more powerful than them. Their redemption was upon them; one final plan away...

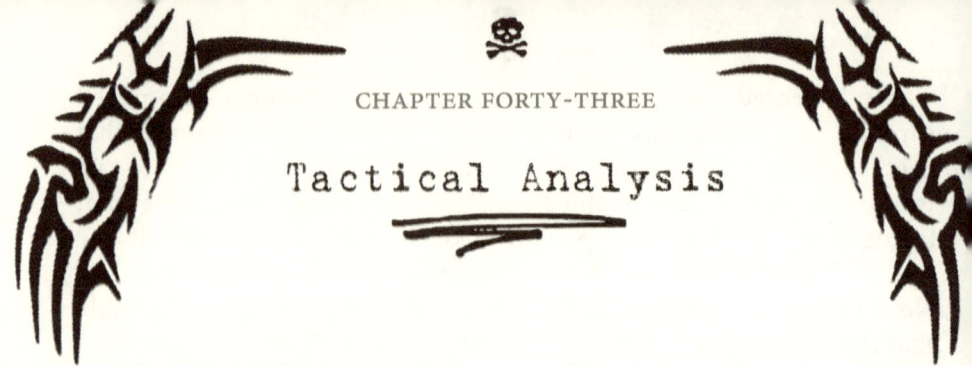

CHAPTER FORTY-THREE

Tactical Analysis

"Alright," I began, "let's start off with a quick outline of our forces."

"For numbers, we now have roughly 4000 from Sipondel, 1500 from Excarpathia, and about another 500 with the Neutralizers on our side. And, of course, The Silence's 16. What do you know about the Dark Kingdom's population?" Blackheart asked.

"They don't have many — maybe about 400 or so; we definitely have them in numbers, but I've seen what they can do since gaining the Dark Power for themselves... and without a solid battle strategy with equally-impressive contingencies, our 6000 will offer barely the oppositional force that a tissue offers a heavy sneeze."

"I hate that; then there's all that snot in-between your fingers, and—" Gad said, resting in the doorway and taking a bite of an apple.

"Gad, go get Benjamin for us and tell him to bring the data he collected when interviewing the Sipondelis," I instructed. "And Arkade as well; I want him to learn something."

"Was it something I said?" he asked jokingly as his mouth frothed with half-masticated apple chunks.

"Gad, if you please," Blackheart reinforced.

"Now who's being a wet tissue..."

"GAD!" we yelled in unison.

"Okay! Okay! I'm going!"

"Alright," Blackheart thought aloud, "so we're not going to win this by brute-force alone, then; it'll all come down to strategy."

"And lucky for us, you're the master strategist," I flattered, hoping it would incite confidence and creative thought.

"I have to be honest Morningstar: I've never planned something this large-scale before. Sure, I've come up with strategies for countless missions, but those focused on a single target or task or outcome. An entire war is a whole other story."

"No war has ever been won by trying to win a war. Wars have been won by winning battles; battles won by killing individual soldiers; individual soldiers killed by a well-crafted enemy strategy — something you excel at more than anyone. You have more potential to develop a war-winning strategy in the tip of your dagger than almost any king in history who ate, breathed, and slept war his whole life. Don't let the fact you haven't done something before convince you that you can't do it, or that it cannot be done perfectly the first time you try your hand at it. I know you *can*... and I know you *will*."

The confidence trickled back into him as we took hold of each other's wrists in solidarity.

"Now," I continued, "think back to all the types of assassinations you've planned in the past: making the most closely-guarded marks disappear without a trace, firing arrows from so far away that no one knows where it came from, poisonings made to look like an accident..."

"Okay, let me think... we have 6000 troops... so what if we send 5000 into the tunnels quietly, while the remaining 1000 surround the kingdom on the hilltops? Then the 5000 sneak into the kingdom, blend-in among the citizens already there, and when we make our attack known from the hilltops outside their walls, our enemies will be too preoccupied with us on the outside that they won't expect the strike from within..."

"That could work if our 5000 could instantly appear beside each person in there; that way, we could kill them all and this whole war could be over in five minutes. However, in the time it would take for our 5000 to charge into the kingdom, they would already be on to us, and as such, we couldn't kill them all before they took notice. Even if we infiltrated the kingdom quietly and slowly, hoping to get more of our people in position before they took notice, they only have a population of about 400 or so. A population that small is going to notice an infiltration of 5000 faces they haven't seen before. The Dark Kingdom is extremely close-knit as well: if they see even *one* unfamiliar face, red flags will be raised," I informed.

"True... alright, what about the tavern owner you told me about before? He needs to restock his supply from time-to-time, correct? What if we tampered with the incoming alcohol shipment, got Benjamin and Elektra to concoct a poison of some kind, mixed it into the bottles and barrels, and let their social interactions solve our problem for us?"

"Subtlety has always been my favourite approach; however, poisons will not work on these people due to the healing factor they possess. Remember the little boy I told you about who healed my leg when I fled? If he can heal *that* large of a wound in *that* short of time, poisons would burn up and be neutralized in their body before it even had a chance to take effect."

"Hmm… if that's the case," he posited, "then the weapons we currently have will be of no use; the lacerations and stab-wounds we inflict will be healing before our blade even leaves their skin. And without poisons and hallucinogenics, we will have to adapt our strategy to focus strictly on instant-kill techniques, assuming they can't be brought back from the dead to resume the healing process."

"A good point, but they could still heal *each other*. And with all the fighting that would be going on, another is more-than-likely to come to his rescue."

"So we would have to lure them out to their deaths one-by-one somehow, without the others seeing them leave the kingdom."

"Ideally yes, which is much easier said than done: I was the first person to leave the Dark Kingdom in all my years living there. Perhaps the *only* one ever to leave, with the exception of the War of the Kingdoms — something we know very little about due to the lack of records kept at the time. I don't know how we would get them on their own… although… that *could* be all the convincing they need…"

"Very well could be; think of the allurement! They've never been outside the Dark Kingdom's walls, but I bet they've *thought* about it and wondered what it would be like to experience it in person. Maybe we just need to provide them with the opportunity to explore their curiousities…" Blackheart spoke, as if he and I shared the same mind.

"Do you think that's really possible?" I asked as doubt sluggishly wandered through my mind.

"Boy, *all* things are possible; if something seems like it's not, it's only because enough people aren't being deceived into the possibilities yet."

I'd never heard Blackheart speak like that before; he planned for deception many times in the past, mostly for success and the safety of his fellow assassins. But the way he spoke that time, it was as if his duties had become him; what he'd been doing for other reasons for years was no longer something only his hands did, but what his mind thought and tongue spoke. It reminded me of my father's words: beliefs forming from repetitive actions and not the other way around.

"Then let's get deceiving," I deviously agreed.

With perfect timing, Benjamin and Arkade entered the room.

"You guys called for me?" Benjamin asked.

"Yeah, come on in; Arkade, I want you to sit here, watch, and listen while we discuss our strategies. But what you hear in here, stays in here. Every word is meant for our ears only — understand?"

"Yessir," he nodded.

"Good boy. Benjamin, thanks for coming; Blackheart and I were just discussing strategies to take the Dark Kingdom."

"Count me in — where'd you leave off?" Benjamin asked as he sat his books down on the table corner and leaned over the blueprint with both hands.

"From the looks of things, our best chance of victory will come from luring each of our enemies outside the safety of the kingdom walls. Possibly into the forest, or even into our tunnels."

"If you do it one-by-one, I'm sure that will only work for a couple of citizens before the others start realizing that no one's coming back; they won't keep letting people leave if no one's returning. And once they become suspicious, we've lost our element of surprise, which is the best thing we have going for us. No one has defeated the Dark Kingdom in history — not even once — even when it was just the Dark King defending it alone," Benjamin reminded us.

"But he's not the same as he was — he's much weaker which makes him much less of a threat to us now that his magical potency is divided among 400 people. Not to mention the Dark One is the only one among them whose life has never truly been limited by the fear of human mortality. Or restricted by the limits of time and space and the pitfalls of the human mind. As for the others... that's *all* they know. Even with their power, they don't have the imagination, mental acuity, and experience to make themselves truly deadly — they are just as likely to injure themselves or their friends while attacking us," I contributed.

"Even still, more enemies mean more unpredictabilities and more factors to consider. Even with a fraction of the Dark Power, we're dealing with 400 enemies wielding incredible power — more than we have," Benjamin justified.

"They wield incredible power, yes — but though each has the power of a whole army, they do not fight as an army. They fight as individuals. The power that fuels their confidence is the same power that fuels their over-confidence. Don't forget: these people have never known war in their lifetime either — never been in battle, and as such are unprepared for it. There is no cause to unite them, nor inspire them; no experience to help them adapt to dire situations quickly. When we attack, they won't even see it coming, and when you mix a lack of experience with the element of surprise, the mind cannot help but feel threatened, releasing its grip on logic to enter self-preservation mode. Once in self-preservation mode, people take bigger risks, making them act based on the fear of loss and impending harm that consumes them," I reasoned.

"He's right," Blackheart added. "They won't be thinking clearly, and when they do, it'll only be about themselves wanting to stay alive. But I'm sure those thoughts will only last for a few minutes; once they see just how powerful they are compared to us and they start dispatching our soldiers like tossed-about rag dolls, they'll quickly regain their confidence—"

"—Which will then quickly grow back into over-confidence," I said, finishing his sentence. "And once they become over-confident again, they'll only be thinking about what they can do to *us* instead of what we can do to *them*. That's when we'll strike for the second time."

"So we'll need two strategies," Blackheart anticipated. "First, a surprise attack, where we appear much stronger than we are, then, when they regain composure, we pretend to retreat and appear weak; their egos will inflate, they'll think they have us, and then we'll supply the coup de grâce."

"Precisely. The biggest threat we can exhibit at this point is probably

through a visual display of our numbers," I expanded. "If we want to appear strong we should have all 6000 soldiers on display at once... although," I reconsidered, "perhaps it wouldn't be wise to show them everything we have, since mystery is the key to keeping the odds of success in one's favour; the more mystery, the more options we allow ourselves. So if we use 5000 of our soldiers for intimidation while the other 1000 are sent in through the tunnels — still more than double their population — then we can create the instant chaos that makes them realize the threat before them is not merely visual, but real, menacing, and worth fearing."

Benjamin cut in. "If we take this route, the 5000 cannot remain outside the kingdom walls for long; the 1000 we have inside will need all the help they can get — and quickly. If they cannot provide assistance to the 1000 fast enough, we will have sacrificed one-sixth of our forces in just the first few minutes of battle before we have even killed one of theirs."

"A good point," Blackheart conceded. "With that in mind, we have two options for the 5000 gaining entry afterwards: digging an access point to the tunnels from the road for all to use, or storming the kingdom gates. The way I see it, the first shouldn't be considered an option for more reasons than I can count, so we'll need those gates open as soon as they can be; that should be the priority of the 1000 who get inside first, because our enemy is certainly not going to do it for us."

"That may lead to our demise, however, Blackheart," Benjamin rebutted. "If we're sending 5000 soldiers into the heat of battle through a single access point, we'd be creating a bottleneck where our troops will be concentrated in too small of an area, making their execution not only guaranteed, but achieved with utmost ease."

"So let's turn it around," I said with a sly grin. "If the gates would be a bottleneck for us, let's make *them* come through it instead."

"How do you propose we make them leave their kingdom gates and fight outside where 5000 enemy soldiers await them?" Benjamin asked.

I thought for a moment, then began speaking my thought process aloud. "Well we can't burn their buildings and use fire to herd them out like sheep, because they have semi-mastery over the elements. Same goes for flooding them out. We can't take some of them hostage to make the others come out to save them, because we don't know how to restrict their power to actually hold any one of them captive. We can't play dead to exploit their religious morality and ethics so they feel obligated to come out and give us proper burials, nor do we have the power to upset the ground and let gravity force them to tumble out toward us the way the Dark King could have in his prime... Blackheart, any ideas?"

"Hmm... well such an approach would greatly restrict their offensive power and turn the odds more in our favour... but as for bringing them out, sometimes it's best to trade an ideal for something more practical that you can guarantee: instead of waiting for a bottleneck and relying on chance to lead them out to us, I think we should use ladders and ramps to scale the walls from multiple access points. Even if they see us doing it, their only solution will be to divide their forces anyway. The more access points we have, the thinner their forces will be spread."

"Levi's going to love that approach," I commented. "Okay, let's recap: we'll have 1000 troops enter the kingdom in small groups through the tunnel until it's clear. Once inside, they all spread out so as to not draw any attention to themselves. The kingdom gates get unlatched, and someone from inside signals us from a rooftop so we can initiate our intimidation from outside the walls. We'll sound the horn to get our enemies' attention, and when all are looking our way, and panic sets in, our troops on the inside can unleash Hell upon them. Then we'll storm the walls from all sides while they're occupied, and soon have our 6000 soldiers fighting together as one against a divided and confused enemy force. Anything we should change or add so far?"

Blackheart expanded upon the idea. "We could even play up the theatrics a bit to amplify their fear if we pour a slick of oil in front of our 5000 troops and light it on fire as the horn sounds. Not only will the fire all around them appear more menacing, but if we give our 5000 troops longbows to launch flaming arrows over the kingdom walls, it would help raise the panic and threat level."

"And what about our 1000 already inside? You'd launch arrows at *them*?" Benjamin questioned.

"We wouldn't want them out in the open, clearly; they can stay safe and hidden until the arrows have been fired," Blackheart justified. "With their kingdom on fire, they will be surprised enough, but when our 1000 run out of every nook and cranny right after that, they won't have a clue what's happening."

"Not to play devil's advocate," Benjamin added, "but didn't Morningstar say they have mastery over the elements? What good will fire be as a threat, if only *our* troops can be burned?"

"Oh, our enemies can be burned as well, the only difference is they can heal from it," I enlightened. "But for every second of discomforting heat, for every flame that lashes out against their skin, the pain they feel is very much human. Come to think of it, we are much luckier than the wielders of the Dark Power in that sense, because Death can offer us mercy after prolonged exposure, but for them? They would burn and heal, and burn and heal, over and over, never knowing the mercy we take for granted. Perhaps fire *could* be a good offensive weapon for us, after all..."

"That's much too cruel, Morningstar," Benjamin expressed. "We're not tyrants; we're enlighteners in a time of revolution. You said so yourself!"

"You're right, Benjamin. Nonetheless, I'm with Blackheart; adding fire strictly for theatrics and fear can very much work to our advantage, because we have to remember: they are still minds stuck in their past inabilities, much like a fully-grown elephant who remembers being chained to a wooden peg as a youngling."

"Fine, we'll add fire then," Benjamin reluctantly conceded, "but I have a feeling it'll come back to haunt us..."

"It won't; the victory belongs to us," I tried comforting him. "Besides, we need to form our strategy around the exploitation of their weakness instead of spending the entire battle trying to compensate for their strengths. No matter the cost, even to ourselves, we must win this."

Benjamin shrugged, but nodded to show he was still with us.

"Now, we have another war-time item of political interest to us: the predicament between Madam Green and King Congreed," I placed on the table for discussion. "We need to arrange a meeting between the two — alone — somewhere on the battlefield. I've given it a lot of thought, and I think we should put Madam Green on the throne of Excarpathia."

"Madam Green?!" Blackheart yelled. "Boy, you can't be serious..."

"Like I said, I've given it a lot of thought, wavering back and forth between them for hours, and believe me, I questioned myself with those same words, Blackheart. But in the end, I realized that although she's unpredictable and wildly greedy, she will be forever in debt to us. Congreed never will — even if we give him something he wants very badly. But most notably, we have to always think at least two steps ahead, and by doing so, we realize that when the Dark King is no more, Congreed will likely take his place as master of the lands. We've seen his technology; we've sensed his military capability, and we know that his greed has no limits. If he stays on the throne, when this war is over, we're going to have another war on our hands, perhaps even worse than this. Madam Green must take his place, or all we have done thus far will be compromised in the near-future."

Blackheart sighed. "Oh, how I wish that wasn't true..."

"You and me both. In any case, I know of a way to get into the church's basement, leading to a place that would make for an ideal rendezvous between them. It's full of old relics and dusty treasures of no real use to us, though it will keep Congreed busy looking for the 'artifact' I promised him. If we can have Madam Green get there before he does, and hide until the opportune moment, she can kill Congreed while his back is turned and have his crown for herself."

"Something like that is best left for the middle of the battle, or even towards the end when it looks like things are winding down; we wouldn't want the Excarpathians to see someone else wearing their king's crown, or they're likely to pull their support from us — or worse yet, turn on our own forces," Benjamin advised.

"Speaking of the end of battle," Blackheart followed-up, "we still need to plan for an exit strategy if all goes to Hell."

"Planning for failure?" I asked. "Blackheart, if you plan for failure, then you are expecting to fail. If you plan for success, you'll be successful. Once you start making a 'Plan B', you distract from 'Plan A', and the moment you start believing there are other options, you start settling for less."

"Morningstar, with all due respect, you can't plan another's death without thinking of how to avoid your own, no matter how sure you are of succeeding," Blackheart persuaded. "I've *always* planned for

exit strategies, and though they have rarely been *employed*, they have always been *necessary*. It's that one time in one-hundred that you need to plan for, because when you find yourself in an unexpected predicament, you'll be glad you have it. Trust me... I insist."

"If you really want an exit strategy, then let's say we make for the church and take the tunnel back to base. The wielders of the Dark Power don't know about that path as it is, so we can rely on that if we need to."

"That exit strategy should probably be our *secondary* exit strategy," Benjamin added. "We don't want to be followed down there and risk others knowing about our base and travel system. The fewer who know about it, the better... which gets me thinking, what of the 1000 troops we introduce to our tunnels? That's a lot of people knowing about something so essential to our operations."

"They... won't be coming back with us," I said with an emotionless expression.

The two just stared at me.

"Look," I justified, "a friend of mine once helped me realize that you do what you need to do to keep unfavourable outcomes from interfering with your dreams. We have a dream of unity, do we not? Our base and those tunnels still play an important role in helping us achieve that," I persuaded. "Besides, war is never without casualties — why not theirs?"

"Morningstar, I—"

"I know, I know; we need a primary exit strategy still."

"No, I—"

"Well there's always exiting through the front gates," I charged through his protests, not giving him a chance to speak. "If the church has collapsed or something to that effect, we'll meet back at Sipondel by taking the long way back, through the forest, which should conceal our escape. That should be sufficient for an exit strategy, shouldn't it Blackheart?"

Benjamin sighed and hung his head low for a moment before looking back up at me.

"I suppose it would," Blackheart responded as he looked to

Benjamin, likely thinking about the sacrifice I was all-too-willing to make of our troops.

"Perfect. Then that just leaves us with one more consideration we must make: how to assign roles based on the personalities of our soldiers as per Benjamin's interviews. Benjamin, what did you find and what do you suggest?"

He took a long breath, but decided to answer me professionally, despite the fact that the moral convictions within him had their torches lit like an angry mob ready to burn me at the stake.

"Mostly what was expected, really. But that only involves the Sipondeli population, not the Excarpathians, or The Neutralizers."

"Congreed will lead his own men to join with our 5000 along the perimeter, so we can leave that to him. The Neutralizers can fall in behind us as well, seeing that they're there for two reasons: to help Madam Green obtain Congreed's crown, and to pick up the golden scraps like the thieving scavengers they are. Also, I want The Silence to remain primarily as overseers... meaning far from the thick of battle, because you will be my most valuable resources on the battlefield. As for the rest of our forces, based on your information, what kind of roles should we consider for them?"

"Well according to the data I received, it turns out about 1000 Sipondelis of the 4000 are the individualist thinkers — the ones best suited to the outposts and special task units. And," he took a reluctant breath, "knowing how you plan on using the 1000 troops that will be inside the kingdom walls first, you'll probably want 200 or so of the individualists in the outposts and the remaining 800 to take up space in your 'first-inside-the-walls' unit with some soldier types."

"We'll refer to our insiders as Strike Force Alpha," I suggested.

"As you wish," Benjamin said awkwardly, and continued on. "The rest don't even have to be divided up into special teams, given our battle strategy — just make them a part of the line and when the horn sounds, send them in. Oh, except for the ones who fit into the 'enforcement roles' you spoke of. Here's a list of the people who fit that description," Benjamin informed as he handed me a piece of paper.

"Benjamin, see to it that the people on this list stay as safe as possible throughout the battle. I will be calling upon their services when the War is over."

"I'll see what I can do."

"And Blackheart, round up our spies and instruct them to set up their outposts just inside the tree line surrounding the Dark Kingdom. They can spy on our enemies for the days leading up to the event, be it from a distance or by sneaking inside from time to time. As they continue to live there, they can report their findings to us in the months to follow, so we can see how their remaining forces spend their time after we are gone. If they start planning a counterattack, I want to know about it."

"I will."

"Gentlemen, it's been a pleasure," I thanked them with a slight bow and motioned for Arkade to follow me.

CHAPTER FORTY-FOUR

Trust in Puppets

Back at my desk, I began drafting the letters I'd be sending to the other leaders as Arkade sat there watching me, listening to the words being crafted for each one. The first was addressed:

To the rightful ruler of Excarpathia, Her Highness, Madam Green,

The time for your ascension has come. Have your forces meet my own at Nightshade's Crossing in the Valley of the Dark Hills in two days' time. You will know my face by the mask I wear.

When the walls have been breached, in the basement of the church you will find the crown unsuspecting. The trapdoor leading to your destiny can be found in the sanctuary, next to the fourth column on the right. Make haste, for this will be your only opportunity.

In strength and blood,

— Morningstar

The second:

To His Royal Highness Emperor Congreed, the one whose rule the gods shall ever favour,

The time to show the other kingdoms the true strength of Excarpathia has come. Have your forces meet my own at Nightshade's Crossing in the Valley of the Dark Hills in two days' time. I shall be awaiting the honour of your presence.

When the walls have been breached, in the basement of the church you will find the coveted Glass Ring of Life. The trapdoor leading to your prize can be found in the sanctuary, next to the fourth column on the right. May you find it suitable payment for your assistance in this historical coup d'état.

In strength and power,

— Morningstar

And lastly, the final letter addressed:

Valenvy,

Have your forces ready for my command in two days' time. I will lead them to the rendezvous point at Nightshade's crossing. Equip them well, lest you find yourself without an army to defend your kingship upon our return.

In strength and dominance,

— Morningstar

"And that, my boy," I said to Arkade, "is how commoners come to rule."

"Why are all the letters different?"

"Because no letter should ever be written the same. When you write, you write to different people, for different purposes. Know your recipient as you would know yourself, and craft your words as if you were their eyes reading it. Be the voice they want to read — or fear to read; stroke the egos that want to be stroked, or crush the ego that needs subduing. When you do, you will find letters are not simply a collection of words, but a means of influence not to be taken lightly. Let your recipient's emotions be the gondola, and your words, its gondolier."

"I wouldn't know where to begin," he replied.

"Wherever you feel like. Sometimes you don't even need to know *what* to write, just as long as you do. It shows you're thinking of them — that they mean something to you. Think of it like this: every man walks his own path, and every path has its fair share of locked doors. You never know who holds the key to a door you'll need to open one day, so you best treat people as if they are all keyholders."

"If everyone is a keyholder though, doesn't that make the people we're going to war with keyholders too?"

"You're very perceptive, young one," I said, as I put my hand on his shoulder. "To answer your question: yes, they are keyholders. But just because someone is a keyholder, does not mean they will always help you unlock the door you *want* to go through — no matter how much you think you deserve to go through it. Sometimes you just have to reach out and take it."

"So we're gonna take their keys instead of asking for them?"

"Arkade, some people are born to hold keys, while others are born to use them; you and I, we're the latter — we don't spend our lives letting others tell us which doors we can and cannot access. We just walk right on through, obtaining whatever keys need to be obtained through whatever means necessary. Life's too short to ask for permission all the time. Our destinies are too great and too important to humankind to be slowed down by keyholders who stand in the way of the doors through which we need to pass."

"But what if there's a door that's just as good somewhere else — how do we know it's not there unless we've tried? Maybe we could use that one..."

"If you're okay with spending your life that way, sure. But then you're wasting what little time you have on this earth searching — settling. Once you start settling, and letting others control your life, it can quickly become a habit, so it's best to avoid such things altogether. Right from the get-go. Remember Father Green? You did something you didn't want to do because you had to do it. It wasn't easy, but without you, Arkade, all this would not be possible. Because you killed that priest, I was able to meet with the other leaders — the ones who will be joining forces with us in a few days' time. Don't you see? By killing one person, you created unity among so many more! He was the keyholder to all of this. And if the death of one keyholder can bring about the unity of multiple kingdoms, imagine what the death of many more can do! We'll have more keys than can fit on any key ring ever fashioned. When our enemies fall before us, there will be no one to tell us 'no' any longer. The land will be ours, and you and I will have made it all possible. You're destined for great things, boy... and that greatness will continue to follow you as you follow me."

He stared for a moment thinking.

"Take these," I said, handing him the letters. "Make sure Simeon gets them right away so he can make the delivery as soon as possible."

"Okay," he said, taking the three from my hand and passing by Mercedes who had been eavesdropping at the door.

"Forgive my intrusion, Morningstar, but you know my mother's not going to believe you on your word alone. She'll need to see that you have the mask before she risks any of her men or trusts you further."

"Though I wish I could secure the unfailing trust of your mother through such a simple action, trust will never be a commodity exchanged between us. But for now, we have an understanding of mutual benefit — she needs a reason to see the mask on me as much as she needs a reason to get out of bed in the morning. But every morning she rises anyway, because her greed will not allow excuses to stand in the way of who she is and what she wants. She wants that crown, and she will have it, no matter what. I don't need to be her pawn and jump through her hoops to know how bad she wants it."

"You're probably right. Even still, it wouldn't be wise to disregard what she's asked. Bow to her every chance you get, and when your dealings together are over, *then* you can pick up your pride and walk out the door a better man for it. But please, don't call for any more bloodshed than you have to. It won't solve anything."

"I will shed no more blood than I have to. But by the second moon, there will flow a river so thick with our enemies' blood that we will sail straight to good fortune without the need for paddles."

She nodded silently, and walked toward the door, but when she got to the doorway she stopped for a moment, and turned to me one more time.

"Forgive my brashness, Morningstar, but... as for the things you teach that boy... he's much too young to hear such things, and you're much too kind a man to speak them. I can't pretend that I know why you're doing all this, but what I do know is the same look I see in my mother's eyes when it comes to greed, I see in yours with power. Please... be careful; don't let your powerlust kill you," she advised, her eyes straddling the line between compassion and pity as she turned into the hallway.

"It won't kill *me*," I muttered to myself as she left the room.

Later that night, when my bedside candle had melted to little more than a flickering nub, Mercedes' words came back to me with the comfort of a bed of nails. If what she said was true about her mother and I being similar in our ambitions, then Madam Green probably saw me the same way I saw her: expendable — a means to an end. If that was the case, then refusing to abide by her requests, no matter how pointless they were, would only jeopardize my victory on the battlefield. I didn't like that she had that kind of power over me, especially considering the level of respect I should have earned by that point, but until I conquered the Dark Kingdom, my entitlements had to wait, and Madam Green would need to see my mask.

Though my letter carriers had a few hours' lead on me, I threw off my covers, slipped on my cloak, mask, and blades, and made my way to my horse hastily.

When I arrived at the entrance of The Neutralizers' Hideout, I saw Dan's horse tied to a post. An unexpected sight, considering Simeon was supposed to be the one with the letter — why Dan was there

was anyone's guess. However, knowing how much Simeon loathed Excarpathia's greed and Madam Green even more, I figured he just asked Dan to go in his place.

Making my way through The Neutralizers' tunnels that time was much easier. The bandits were not friendlier by any means, but they tolerated my presence as per my agreement with Madam Green. When I arrived at the one-way door, I ran into two more bandits who were standing guard as the others did before. Not the same two as last time, of course... though the faded red stains of their loyalty still smeared the ground in remembrance of their service. Living guards were a good security upgrade on their part, nonetheless. I used to enjoy days like that: the ones where you didn't need to stab someone just to say you came in peace.

"Open the door, gentlemen."

"Madam Green is busy at the moment," the uglier one replied.

"She's not too busy to see me, considering she's in there with my messenger as we speak."

"We cannot let you in, sir," the shorter one reinforced.

It wasn't looking like it was going to be one of those days after all.

In a blink, I took the uglier one by the throat and slammed him against the wall, his feet dangling inches off the ground. Then, I unsheathed my blade, pointing it at the shorter one.

"Are we going to have a problem?" I asked them.

The short one looked with fear in his eyes to the other whose face was getting redder by the second. When I didn't receive an answer, I slit the ugly one's throat and took the short one by the neck in his place.

"You'll have to speak up; I don't think I heard you," I said with a patronizing tone, leaning my ear in closer.

He stared at me with wide eyes, but said nothing. I put the blade to his throat next.

"Alright! I'll open it for you. Just please don't kill me," he panicked as he knocked in coded sequence on the door.

"I appreciate your understanding," I smiled, wiping the blood of his friend off my knife against his shirt, then gave him a light, playful slap to the face.

The door rolled open, but Dan was nowhere to be seen.

"Your Highness, it's a pleasure to see you again," I lied charismatically.

"Morningstar — that's you under that horrendous mask, I assume? I see you found it. Congratulations, child. That's great news."

I leaned with a slight bow, wishing the blood on my knife was hers.

"Your visit is rather unexpected; when I received your note, I understood you weren't coming."

Maybe it was my natural skepticism, but it seemed like she was being nicer than usual.

"I persevered, my queen. I apologize for any inconvenience caused by coming to visit unannounced, but as my most valued ally, I wanted to make sure any questions you had about our little 'arrangement' went answered to your complete satisfaction. Were the details in my note to your liking?"

"Very much so. I will wait for Congreed in the basement, and when he arrives, he shall meet his end. You know, Morningstar... I've been thinking, and perhaps I *should* give you something in return for the opportunity you are giving me."

That level of kindness was not natural. Something was off with her, but I had no way of finding out what. I could only hope I didn't just walk into an ambush.

"Something in return, Your Highness?"

"Well, you *are* offering me the crown which leads to a lifetime of ruling, but all I'm doing for you is offering a few men to go out and play for a few hours before returning home to me."

I wasn't one to turn down a gift, but I felt like I was better off that time just leaving with as much as I came in with.

"Oh that's very kind of you, but I don't require anything more than your help. Your help alone is more than I could ask for and everything I need."

"Oh nonsense, I insist — I know how you were eyeballing just about every item in our special wares back there. Please, take these hoverboots as an expression of gratitude. They're our most cutting-edge technology yet! You'll never wear another boot as long as you live. You deserve them, Morningstar," she praised as she passed them to me with a smile.

"I... am incredibly grateful, my queen."

"Well go ahead — put them on!" she insisted.

I slipped the boots on. They were the most comfortable boots I'd ever slipped my feet into; black leather with golden metal bracing, slightly heavier than your average pair... but then again, there was nothing average about those boots. I didn't feel their effect as I walked around, but when I lifted my leg to step down into the air, it felt like I was walking on invisible steps made of quicksand — firm at first step, but gradually dissipating until my foot had reached solid ground again. I was still curious as to why the greediest woman to ever exist actually gave me something — but with those on my feet, I stopped asking questions.

"It's like my foot is floating in a dream."

She smiled again. "I'm glad they are to your liking. So tell me, what more must we do before meeting you at Nightshade's Crossing?"

"If your men are fully assembled, equipped, and ready now, then it's only the journey that awaits. Follow me to Sipondel to meet with the 4000 there. If we head to Nightshade's Crossing together, there's not a threat in the land that would dare oppose us along the way."

"Thank you for your offer of Sipondeli hospitality, but there are just a few more items of particular interest to me that I have to take care of here first."

"I understand, Your Highness," I said, wondering what she was referring to.

"We will meet you at Sipondel's gates before nightfall tomorrow evening. See you then, Morningstar."

"Until then," I said with a bow as I took my leave and went to meet my horse out front.

As I was untying the reins, I noticed Dan's horse was still tied up off to the side. A curious sight, considering he had already dropped off the letter to Madam Green hours before I arrived — and if he wasn't with her concluding my business, that meant he was somewhere else conducting his own. Not the wisest choice, because in times of war, skepticism can be just cause for execution. If he was anywhere other than lying in a back alley in a pool of his own blood, he was going to have a lot of explaining to do.

I had a quick look around the surrounding area, but no familiar corpses belonged to him. There were no signs of struggle, nor items left behind that shouldn't be; wherever he was, he was there because of his choices — whether he was reaping the benefits or facing the consequences of them was entirely on him. I didn't have time to search around for someone who could be perfectly fine, doing perfectly legitimate things, however, so I mounted my horse and made my way back to Sipondel. If any of the other letter-carriers were aware of Dan's shadow-dealings, I was going to find out before it came back to bite me.

When I got back to the church, I went straight to Simeon's room.

"Simeon, wake up and come with me; there's something we need to discuss," I ordered the moment I walked in, finding him fast asleep.

"What is it?" he asked, still in a state of dreality.

"We mustn't speak here. Not with the others within earshot. Follow me."

We made our way into the tunnels, figuring it was the safest place to speak in Sipondel.

"Tell me what happened after Arkade handed you the letters yesterday. Leave no detail to be assumed."

"Well," he began, "Arkade walked into the kitchen where we were just sitting there, helping ourselves to the communion wine supply. Me, Dan, and Zebulun. He walked up to me, and handed me the three letters, and said 'Morningstar wants you to deliver these.' So I looked through them, and thought to myself, 'Hey, there's three of us at the table and three letters; why not each take one and go deliver them to save ourselves time.' So I took Valenvy's, because I didn't feel like travelling far, then passed that vile woman Madam Green's to Zebulun, then slid the last one over to Dan. Why? Is something wrong?"

"You passed Madam Green's to Zebulun?"

"Right."

"And not Dan..."

"Right... why? What happened?"

"I found Dan's horse tied to a post just outside The Neutralizers' Hideout."

"Why did you go to Madam Green's alone without telling anyone? I know you can hold your own, but you saw how completely unhinged she can be. My last conversation with you could have been between me and your head in a bag! That's *if* we ever saw it again!"

"I had a revelation, and seeing her in person was a necessity. But when I saw Dan's horse, knowing I told Arkade to hand *you* the letters, I wasn't sure what to make of it."

"I'm sorry Morningstar, next time I'll deliver each myself."

"Not at all — I commend your use of efficiency. It's just... there's something about Dan that's becoming unsettling. First, when my mask was missing and he went to ride away, then again at the Hideout. You can be in the wrong place at the wrong time *once* and naturally raise eyebrows that eventually fall back into position with time, but have it happen again, and you start walking the tight-rope of trust. I want you to watch him from now on. Closely. Every move he makes — every conversation he has — I want to know about it."

"Alright... if that is your wish, I'll keep an eye on him. The mask thing was just a misunderstanding though; it was Repride dressed as you that gave the order he followed."

"Like I said: wrong place at the wrong time. If it happens once, it may be overlooked, but twice in a time of war is not something my cautious mind can ignore so easily."

"I understand. I'll look into it. But right now, you need to get some rest — you're going to need it before we march out to meet with the others tomorrow."

"I appreciate it, Simeon. Your loyalty will not go unrewarded."

"No reward is necessary. A man shouldn't bite the hand that feeds him, even if another holds out a golden spoon to him as reward after his betrayal. I owe my life to The Silence and my loyalties will remain with them always."

"A philosophy all should live by, if not genuinely, then at least out of fear of the repercussions. Strength and unity."

"Strength and unity."

CHAPTER FORTY-FIVE

Fragile Alliances

And then the Day of War arrived. My first waking breaths were unlike any I'd breathed before, as if every inhalation was a warrior's breath: strong and capable, ambitious and destined. But there in that moment, time stood still. I didn't move; I just kept my eyes closed and let the air gracefully dive into my lungs, refreshing me from within while my thoughts became still. It was peaceful. Serene. A gentle calm before the storm. I knew the moment my feet touched the ground, that sanctuary would dissipate like a cloud agitated by the wind, but at the same time, knowing it would fade made it that much more beautiful... because it could never be around long enough to be taken for granted. Every second of it was more valuable than the last until it was gone forever.

When that moment came and I sat up in my bed, it was as if every good memory from the past visited me, reminding me of why I had to bring war to the doorstep of a place I once called home. Reminding me of the reason I had to fight, and what I stood to lose. And not just me, but everyone around me who deserved the same freedom I was ready to give my life for... or at least the lives I was ready to give in my place. I was much too valuable to die and even more irreplaceable to sacrifice. Fate had created a dream for the world that was meant to reshape it forever, and entrusted the task to me, and me alone; I was its rightful vessel to be used as the catalyst for even greater things to come. The one chosen over every other.

I slipped on my pants, my new boots over top. Strapped on my knives and concealed them with my cloak. And when my body had been consumed almost entirely by black, I slipped on my mask, and was lost in its persona once more.

The moment I left my room that morning, it was as if the universe made time itself run slower, allowing every moment to linger for me, every intricate detail to be embraced. As if the realms of gods and men overlapped just long enough for me to see and feel what it was like to live behind the Great Curtain that separates humanity's cluelessness from the universe's omniscience — a place where everything made sense and everything seemed right. There's security in that kind of confidence. And on a day when so much was riding on so little, to be free of Fear's chokehold, free of all worry and doubt... it was an emotional armour no arrow could pierce. I was called to lead when I had no followers; misfortune had always been my catalyst to opportunity. But that day, no valley would precede my ascension as it always had in the past; I no longer felt like the mountain climber, but the mountain itself — the one that *others* had to climb over. I felt invincible.

I took that feeling with me as I searched the halls for the other members of The Silence to rally. I checked Simeon's room first, but he wasn't there; Zebulun's room was empty; every room, nook and cranny carried little more than a shattered expectation. Not even the faintest whisper echoed through the halls for me to track — when The Silence went silent, they really knew how to play with a man's thoughts.

As I went to leave the final room, however, the door slammed shut, the bedside candle blew out, and the floor began to fill with smoke. It was pitch black. I drew my knives and started feeling around for a way out, but there was nothing. It was only after my survival instinct kicked in that fifteen candles began to light around the room in rapid succession, one-by-one, until I found myself in the middle of a shadowy Stonehenge, surrounded by black cloaks.

Found them.

"My lord," Dan said as he knelt down before me and offered up a sword with both hands.

"What's this?" I asked.

"A token of our appreciation," Blackheart said.

"Appreciation for what?"

"For leading us, of course!" Judah answered.

"For being a good friend," Ephraim added.

"For being cute," Asher flirted.

"For not killing us when you could have," Zebulun joked.

"I don't know what to say," I said as I took hold of the sword from Dan's hands. "Thank you."

"I stole it from Madam Green's vault," Dan expanded, proclaiming his thievery with a look in his eye that didn't sit right with me, "which is why my horse was there when you arrived last time. I didn't know you'd be showing up there to spoil the surprise."

"*Maybe*," I thought to myself, still cautious of falling prey to his underhandedness, "*unless this is just your cover for something much more cloak-and-dagger.*"

"This was from Madam Green's vault? How'd you get it without getting caught?" I asked.

"The details aren't important. What's more worth talking about is what the sword you hold in your hands can do," Dan replied, walking toward me, ready to demonstrate.

"Just extend the hilt here..." he twisted the bottom, pulling it out a little further.

Every flame on the candles around the room left its wick and attached itself to my blade, swirling upon its surface.

"You've got... to be kidding me."

"Whatever element is closest to the blade at the time of activation," Dan explained, "is drawn from a five-metre radius and is held upon its blade until you release it. Water, fire, wind... even earth and rock, though I wouldn't advise it, unless you're Manasseh here."

"This is unbelievable," I said, staring at the blade in amazement.

"You deserve it," Blackheart added. "From all of us."

"Now let's go win us a war!" Gad cheered, throwing his fist into the air to rally us up as he ran to the door with overflowing enthusiasm... only to find it was still locked. At first, I thought we'd accidentally locked ourselves in, caught up in the moment, but when I heard Issachar chuckle quietly and saw the key in his hand, watching Gad try to keep the fervour of the moment alive while trying to open the door became that much more entertaining.

"Heh... going to war... yeah!" he awkwardly reinforced while he jiggled the handle a few more times, trying to cover up his attempts with some forced coughing. It didn't work, but it did turn an anti-climactic attempt at opening the door into a much more amusing one. When the line between amusement and cruelty started to blur, however, Issachar decided to step in and save what was left of Gad's dignity.

"Do you need some help there, Gad?" Issachar asked, smiling.

"Help? Heh, heh... with what? Everything's fine here..."

"Here, let me get that for you," Issachar leaned in, not even trying to conceal his laughter anymore.

Gad let out a sigh and reluctantly walked over to us.

"The uhh," he pointed behind him with his thumb, "door's locked."

"Your perseverance was still commendable," I said with a smirk and a hand on his shoulder. "There's always next time."

Issachar opened the door with a hollow click and held out his arm, motioning for us to pass through. "Gad's unbeatable adversary has been conquered, everyone. You may now pass through with ease."

We filed out of the room laughing, sympathetically patting Gad on the back as we passed by him.

"First an escaped pig, now a locked door?" Issachar teased Gad as he was the last to leave. "We're going to have to start holding try-outs."

"It's gonna happen to you one day, and when it does, I won't let you forget it," Gad warned.

With our new-found freedom, we made our way to the church doors, opening them only to find ourselves looking upon a sea of faces. The Sipondelis had gathered in the streets, filling every corridor, every pathway, awaiting my next instruction. Almost every eye looking back at me reflected a fear that churned deep inside them — but their fears were of little concern to me. What *was* of concern to me was their lack of armour, their dull, dagger-length swords, and wooden shields warped by time as if they'd been torn from the bark of trees that lost their will to live centuries ago. Valenvy's guards were the exception of course, but even so, to look upon that gathering as a whole was to feel the inspiration of a three-legged dog who did little more than lie in the shade all day under the weight of his own depression. They were *there*, but not ready; *equipped*, but unprepared.

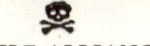

It was that pitiful, undeveloped group of push-overs that would make up the vast majority of my army... but they would have to do. After all, every victory requires some sacrifice — they just made knowing what and who to sacrifice when the time came that much easier.

"Follow me into battle this day, People of Sipondel," I bellowed. "Leave behind the pathetic lives you live and become something more. You have fear? Good! Embrace it; let your fear drive you to evolve into greatness. But mistake this day as being like any other, and your deaths one day will go as unmourned as the insects of the field — your lives as uncelebrated as the existence you now lead. Come with me now, *seize* this day in history as your own, and you will live on forever in story and song, mourned for all eternity by those who never even knew you."

"And if we choose to stay behind?" a man's voice in the crowd called out as I was mounting my horse.

"What's the use in prolonging life if you don't do anything with it? Would death really be that different from the life you now lead? Fate has given you this day as a gift — an opportunity to not only honour the hard work of all those before you, but to continue it, correct their mistakes, and pave a path for future generations that each and every one of you here today can only dream about. Your life is not a countdown to your death, but a stepping stone for the lives that will live after you. Squander today, and you will find yourself useless tomorrow."

And with that, I snapped the reins and took off into the crowd, barely giving them time to part before me. I knew they were relying on me to put their hearts and minds at ease, but I was not there to coddle them; I was there to call them to something greater. Emotional states change like the wind, and to indulge them only gives them more power over a person. I was there to free them, not captivate them, least of all to themselves.

For the next few hours, we walked the land, through over-grown forest and wide open plain, bound for Nightshade's Crossing. I led the way with Blackheart to my right, while the rest of The Silence fell in behind us on horseback. The Sipondeli people trailed behind them, on foot, of course — not an easy journey to make, considering how far we had to go, but as long as they made it to the battlefield, the condition of their feet didn't matter. Hunger, on the other hand, was an unavoidable annoyance; I didn't want them getting to the battle and passing out before their duties could be completed, but at the same time, having to feed people who would be dying in just a few more hours seemed like a waste of our rations. Nonetheless, they were fed anyway — in part to boost their energy, in part to keep their morale up. Not that it was very high to begin with, but every bit counts. Most physical battles begin once mental ones have been lost, anyway. Conquer the mind, conquer the body.

We stopped to set up camp briefly when we were about halfway there, close to where the road splits toward the Dark Kingdom — the place where The Silence and I emerged from the forest for the first time as we headed for Sipondel all those years ago. As food and drink were passed around the camp, I gathered The Silence around me to discuss their specific roles.

"I have here the list of Sipondeli names Benjamin categorized for us after Father Green's funeral. You've all been mingling with these people for a couple of years now, so I suspect you will all know these people when you hear their names. According to the list, there are roughly 1000 'individualist thinker' types; Blackheart and Simeon, I want you to take this group when we're done here; Blackheart will take 200 of those and set up four strategically-placed outposts of 50 people around the Dark Kingdom for present and future surveillance — the rest will follow you, Simeon. Take them into the tunnels through our base in the forest. The church should be empty when you get there, but if it's not, wait until it is before leading them into the streets of the Dark Kingdom. Pace it out as long as you like, so one-by-one our troops can blend into the population. Your stealth here is imperative to our success."

"You got it," Simeon confirmed.

"Your main objectives are to unlock and open the main gate as stealthily as possible, then signal us from a rooftop once all your people have doused the kingdom in oil and are safely out of the way for when our fire arrows rain from above. We'll launch them upon your signal."

"You bet," he confirmed again.

"Blackheart, I'll need you to establish a leader — some sort of hierarchy — in each of the outposts so the people have a clear idea of how to resolve their disagreements."

"Keep in mind," Benjamin added, "these are individualist thinkers, so if you establish a hierarchy, make sure it's no deeper than one or two levels at most. These people are empowered and most effective when they see themselves at the top of a chain, and start to become troublesome when there are too many above them with differing views."

"I will," Blackheart verified.

"Then, join back up with us in the outer-perimeter," I instructed him. "That brings us to the people you have listed here as my future 'enforcers', Benjamin. I'll need these people kept as safe as possible for the duration of the fighting, because once the Dark Kingdom is ours, I'll need them to establish and keep order."

"They'll be kept close. I'll use them as part of a flanking strategy — you'll lead the forces in first, and we'll follow later once the fighting has died down a bit."

"Perfect. If you see we need the assistance, however, don't hesitate to bring them into the thick of things early — because if we don't win the war, there'll be nothing for them to enforce anyway."

"Of course."

"The rest of us will line up shoulder-to-shoulder as discussed around the Dark Kingdom itself. When the fire arrows have been launched and the horn has sounded, let Congreed and Madam Green charge the kingdom first. If anyone is going to die first among us, let it be our allies. Keep that in mind at all times as you're fighting. Instruct the units you take command of in this manner, so their actions may reflect the same approach; we don't want them being aware of it, nor having to struggle with it morally. Their minds should be clear at all times and focused on one thing only — winning this war so they can spend the rest of their days in peace with their families."

"A curious approach..." Naphtali's voice was heard from a branch of the tree above us.

We were all overjoyed to see her. She couldn't have returned at a better time.

"Naphtali... I'm so glad you decided to come back," Blackheart said as he stood to his feet, kissing her on the cheek and she climbed down the tree with ease.

"It was never a question in my mind, Blackheart," she tenderly replied.

"Same here; the girl power around here was starting to take a beating," Asher joked as Elektra got up and ran to hug Naphtali. She smiled.

"Where did you go, anyway?" Ephraim asked.

"I went to seek truth and advice from an old friend... someone I was once very close with that I thought could give me counsel regarding something that had been plaguing my mind," she responded generally with an odd glance in my direction.

"Did you find what you were looking for?" I asked, wondering why her eyes were focused on me.

"I did; something I'd like to talk to you about in private, if I may..."

I nodded as we walked off into the woods away from prying ears and sat on a fallen tree trunk together. "What is it?"

"Morningstar... I went to the Dark Kingdom."

"I see..." I said, standing up, starting to pace slowly.

"The situation you told us about — the killings, the tyranny of the Dark One, his oppression of everyone in his kingdom — none of it was true."

"Look, Naphtali, I don't know what you—"

"Wait," she spoke calmly, placing an understanding hand gently on my forearm in an attempt to soften my sensitivity to her words. "Before you jump to conclusions, come sit with me. Hear me out. There's something I need to say."

I stood there looking at her, hoping she wasn't about to use her legacy and undeniable reputation with The Silence to undo all I'd been working so hard towards — exposing the lies I'd built everything upon.

"Please," she reinforced, hoping to still the churning volcano within me.

I sat back down, slightly further away on the log than my original spot.

"Morningstar, when I was in the Dark Kingdom, and I saw the truth of what was going on, my first thought wasn't one of anger, nor was I displeased that you didn't tell us the truth. Far too many people allow broken egos and wounded prides to convince them to seek justice before they seek understanding. So I asked myself instead what might have caused you to go through all that trouble to construct a lie when you were already accepted for who you were among us, fully in the comfort of our company, with all your needs taken care of. I thought back to all our training sessions, our talks, remembered your speeches, recalled your interactions with the others... and I realized something I never noticed in you before."

"And what's that?" I snapped semi-defensively. I hated when people acted like they knew me.

"You're a Voltairib."

"A Voltairib?"

"A world-changer; someone whose destiny calls them to fix things far beyond the typical throes of ordinary life. They are born with dispositions unlike most of the people you meet; often you can see it in them as children, but it's usually not until they mature, soul-search, and begin to question the established order that the world begins to take notice. They are the universe's way of bringing balance back to a world that our naturally chaotic, human energy slowly tears apart.

However, Voltairibs are rarely born with the inherent, unshakable good inside them needed to bring about such a rebalance; they must be shaped and sculpted as human beings the same way everyone else is: through nature and nurture instead of divine intervention. In turn, they are equally susceptible as everyone else is to the allurement of the dark side of our humanity — especially when they start to become aware of the potential they possess within themselves. It's that potential that drives them to accomplish that which will gain them power, recognition, and status — things that are not inherently dark, but can easily persuade the mind to focus on the things of the self, instead of the good of others.

I believe that you have the spirit of a Voltairib within you, Morningstar, incessantly driving you to accomplish everything you can until you feel you've lived a life of not just meaning, but of significance. For a time, it may seem like these accomplishments will bring you happiness and satisfaction in the end, but they won't — no matter what the dark desires of your heart promise to deliver with your success. Gaining satisfaction through accomplishments is and will always be a slippery slope, because there will come a time when you realize you have accomplished all that is within your power to accomplish in the realm of good, and will have nowhere else to turn but to the realms of greed and powerlust to find the satisfaction you crave. The more powerful you grow, the harder it will be to avoid becoming reprehensible. Continue along that path, and you will crumble beneath the weight of the ambitions you can no longer keep up with — and on that day, will bring about the death and destruction of everyone and everything around you. A finite life cannot compete with an infinite list of things to accomplish. You need to choose wisely."

"So I should just stop accomplishing?"

"Not at all; without accomplishments, we'd have no evolution as a civilization. Just be careful of which accomplishments you pursue and know where your pursuits are taking you at all times. Never overestimate the strength of the torchbearer's arm, for even the strongest arms grow weary."

"But you're saying I need to be happy while doing it or I'll bring about the death and destruction of everyone around me..."

"I'm saying unhappiness gives birth to anarchy; it will sneak up on you, and, as Zebulun once put it, 'will rig your life with explosives and push the detonator when you least expect it, turning your whole world to dust.' Remember your training: *the path to happiness begins with possibility, and from possibility comes choice, and then direction, and then purpose before you get a chance at satisfaction.* There is more to it, however: if you think you know what your purpose is, but can never seem to gain satisfaction from it, then it's probably not the purpose you're destined for."

"I see. So all this talk about purpose and happiness and accomplishments... why tell me all this now?"

"I'm telling you now both as a warning and as a reminder to you: we are assassins, and we facilitate the flow of the greater good to all — not only to the deserving, because that is not for us to distinguish. At times, we are required to intervene, but only do so when it becomes necessary — after all other peaceful options have been exhausted. This

is one of those peaceful options," she leaned in, taking a firm grasp of the cloth on my chest as her other hand fell upon the sheathed dagger at her side. "Now I'm going to talk, and you are going to listen without interruption. Understand?"

I nodded.

"I know that what you're doing is not based in truth. Yet, I have also seen you, heard you, and know you are capable of great things. As a kind gesture of faith, I will keep what I know between you and I alone, and continue to follow you as long as you don't cross the line. But know that what you plan to do — going through with this war — it isn't assassination, or conquest... it's genocide. And I will never condone that, even in the name — or under the façade — of the unity of all others who remain." She released her grip, but kept her deadly glare. "I saw this coming and should have spoken sooner, but I held my tongue because I thought that maybe you would create a warpath so disastrous, that both the good and the bad ahead of you would be cleared away, wiped out, leaving the possibility of a fresh start behind you for all of humankind — a chance for unity to bloom in a time of need and reconstruction. But then I realized to believe that, I would be compromising myself. Peace does not exist because there is nothing left — it exists because everything is *right*, and learned to tolerate everything else. So mark my words and mark them well, apprentice: serenade Lady Death and court Disaster, and soon your enemy will be your master."

And with that, she stood up and walked away without even a glance back at me. I'd never seen that side of her before... and it wasn't one I wanted to see again.

CHAPTER FORTY-SIX

More Than Meets the Eye

"What did Naphtali want?" Blackheart asked me when I'd finally emerged from the trees.

I did a quick scan of the crowd for her, but she was nowhere to be seen. "Just to talk about some of the concerns she had with the war; it's fine."

"Careful, handsome; you know what it means when a *girl* says 'it's fine'..." Asher insightfully teased.

"Let's just pack up camp and head for Nightshade's Crossing. Congreed and Green are probably getting close by now, if they aren't there already," I commented, ignoring the questions about Naphtali.

As everyone dispersed and began to take down camp, I pulled Zebulun aside.

"Do you happen to know where Naphtali went?"

"Not the slightest. She took Elektra with her though. Didn't look too pleased either. Like something was on her mind. I didn't ask though."

"She didn't say when, or *if* she'd be back?"

"Couldn't tell ya. Everything alright?"

"Yeah...yeah, things are uhh... thanks for the info. Let me know if you hear anything about her, alright?"

"You got it."

I didn't have the slightest idea where she went, nor why she took Elektra with her, but knowing how much she meant to her, I feared her verbal warnings to me could develop into something much less abstract and less contained. Naphtali was the smoothest strategist and speaker I knew — even more so than Judah; when she spoke, she spoke with poise, and depth, with a wisdom that carried logic so sound that even the most advanced thinkers' minds would become putty in her hands. Taking Elektra aside like that was a strategic move — but to what end, I didn't know. All that was certain was Elektra would be in Naphtali's hands, being fed words that seemed as sweet as honey, until one day her stomach would turn — and in her sickness, somehow blame me for it. For all I knew, she was priming her for a time of revolt, striking when I'd be least prepared or when I'd be counting on her in a critical moment. If I was going to stay on top of her schemes, I needed to take the offensive and form some contingencies of my own...

Two could play that game.

My eyes connected with Arkade's from a distance. With the brief motion of rolling fingers signalling him to come see me, he was at my side in a flash.

"Sir?"

"Arkade, over the time that I've known you, you and I have been through a lot together. We've talked about life and its many complexities, debated morality and philosophy, encountered and removed obstacles of inconvenience together — no matter how great and no matter the cost... we've truly been there for one another in our greatest joys and deepest regrets — and all the while you have proved yourself to be the greatest student I have ever taken on as my own. I've watched you grow up from a distraught child who allowed people to influence how you felt about yourself, into a boy who now questions everything around him while remaining secure in himself and his abilities, no matter what others tell him. It prides me to see you growing up into a respectable and fearsome man before my eyes. Arkade, you are like a son to me and there's nothing I wouldn't do for you. I hope you feel the same as well."

A tear began to form in his eye. "You've been a better father to me than anyone who's ever tried to be in my life. And my friend too. My only friend... and you understand me. I'd do anything for you."

"I'm glad. I'm always looking out for *you* as well... which is why I need to tell you something about Naphtali and Elektra. But you have to keep it a secret between us — you and me. Do you promise?"

"I promise."

"Naphtali is no longer happy among us; she has stopped believing in our ideals and methods and has let her fears and insecurities take her mind to a place where our trust can no longer follow. But what's more: she is molding Elektra's mind to mirror her own.

You and I both know the kingdoms need us now more than they ever have before. They're crying out for our help — *your* help, my help — and if we don't stand together and work as one, everything we've been working so hard to achieve will crumble. Naphtali and Elektra must not become the cause of our failure. Though they do not pose any direct threat to us yet, their minds are wading in a pool of distrust which can only lead to one outcome — and when they inevitably turn on us, we need to be ready for them."

"But… Elektra's nice. She'd never wish anything bad upon anyone. She'd never do anything bad to us," Arkade replied.

"Not yet, but she will — mark my words, boy. I know this may be difficult for you, considering your attraction to her, Arkade, but—"

"It's more than that," he interrupted. "I know she's beautiful, but it's beyond just how she looks; she's smart, and kind, and was a really good friend to me when I needed her."

"And that's precisely why I need your help in saving her now — to *preserve* that in her before Naphtali taints the purity that you've grown to love in Elektra. Arkade, I know how you felt about her only a short time ago — and I know you still feel that. I need you to remind her of those feelings."

"What do you mean?"

"I need you to show her you love her again. Make her smile. Give her flowers when she least expects it. Bring her a blanket when she's cold. Carry her pack when you see she's tired. Whatever it takes, let her know you're there for her, still interested in her, and wish it to be something more. If you care about her, that is."

"I do care about her, but—"

"Then make her fall in love with you again. You have my full permission. Whatever you have to do, do it, so that every moment she spends away from you is one spent wishing you were at her side. Do you think you can do that?"

"I can try, but she doesn't want anything to do with me anymore. I screwed it up," he said, hanging his head.

"You didn't screw it up. Love is a road unkempt: there are bumps, holes, detours, and sudden forks without signposts to guide you. It is a road of valleys and mountains — of turbulence and promise. We take it hoping it will be smoother than the one we're already travelling, but Love's road is no more than a lane on the same highway we're already on. It requires the same endurance, the same attention and care, and we make just as many mistakes along the way as when we travel it on our own. Since both lanes hold similar obstacles, to what benefit is enduring it alone? *Tell her* you're sorry; *show her* you see things differently now than you did back then — and when all is said and done, Naphtali's words will hold little power over her compared to her desire for you."

"Well, I do miss her..."

"Then this is an opportunity you would be foolish to pass up. As you work to repair the relationship between you two, I need you to watch and listen, and report to me everything you hear regarding either one of them. Arkade..." I said, placing my hand upon his shoulder, "I am promoting you to be my personal apprentice. Everywhere I go, you will go as well. I will train you to be the best, most deadly, and most intelligent assassin this world has ever seen. You will become invincible as I am invincible, and we will work together until every kingdom has the freedom our hands have brought them. But I can only do this if you are ready to do all I have asked of you, and you accept your position at my side."

"I do; I mean yessir... I accept."

"Good," I smiled as I climbed on my horse and offered him my hand. "Ride with me, apprentice. Let all who follow us see that you are no longer one of them, fated to walk the same ground any longer."

I hoisted him up proudly to sit behind me when he offered his hand in acceptance. We still had a couple hours' journey left before we reached Nightshade's Crossing, so having him there made the time pass even more quickly. But the longer we rode toward our destination, the more unnerved I felt. Every time I looked behind us, the end of our caravan of liabilities was nowhere in sight; it stretched farther than the naked eye could clearly define, winding and bending with the road like a stream that flowed without end. For your average warlord, that would be a comforting sight, but no matter how many times I looked back, I couldn't help but wish Naphtali was there, following me and offering her wisdom and guidance — even if my own had grown superior to hers. And yet, no matter what I thought I knew, there was always something about the way she explained the Black and White that made pursuing the Grey so much more fulfilling — like there were no rights and wrongs, only cause and effect as guided by Fate's hand: you pursue the greater good through whatever means possible, and everything else falls into balance. It wasn't until we'd reached the rendezvous point that I finally saw her again. Judging by the cold stare she cast in my direction, I'd say the only reason she was still there was to see if the greater good really could come from such a grand, lie-driven coup d'état. I knew the outcome would be a favourable one that would change the course of history, but until *she* believed that as well, there was no telling what she might do if she felt her intervention was necessary.

The trailing end of the caravan filed in, clustering the area like a thick fog as we waited for Congreed and Green to arrive. Part of me felt remorse for keeping all those people in the dark, knowing most of them would not live to see another day, but deep down, I knew it had to be done. Significant change requires significant sacrifice. I needed to lie and they needed to believe that lie, for it is the crimson tongue that paints the world others think they see — the world people think they live in. And the only ones who see it for what it truly is are the ones who don't use their eyes at all, but search for truth where there exists only illusion conjured by the clever.

Just then, a faint golden light baptized the hillside as Congreed's forces sped toward us from out of the darkness on their hoverbikes. The closer they got, the more fearsome the steel-plated warriors appeared: black-and-gold armour as fierce as it was beautiful, long obsidian staffs laced with gold and crowned with sharpened jewels that they carried like lances as they raced towards us, covering as much ground in seconds as the fastest horse could do in several minutes. When they reached us, they dismounted with near-perfect synchronicity, and each standing a uniform seven-feet-tall as compensated by their highly-customized, mechanical armour, crafted with excellence to each soldiers specifications. Some people spend a lifetime trying to earn respect, but they wore it — with ease.

"Oh, how I have long-awaited this day," Congreed spoke with a confident stance, as a servant removed his crown-bearing helmet and disconnected the crown quickly, placing it back upon Congreed's head.

"As have I, Emperor Congreed," I said, shaking his hand.

"And Emperor I will *be* in a matter of hours," he acknowledged with misplaced assurance.

"Morningstar," Blackheart whispered as he took me aside, "I think our other guests have arrived." He pointed into the distance at what looked like a large pile of grass and dirt slowly and quietly approaching us.

It was Madam Green and her band of camouflaged bandits, barely noticeable to the untrained eye. If they were able to sneak up on us like that for the second time — in that great of numbers, no less — they were certainly a welcome addition to my ranks. Blackheart and I watched as the dark mass continued to move toward us like a bad nightshade trip, with the crowd of Sipondelis none-the-wiser until they were within stabbing distance. Lucky for them, their blades remained sheathed.

"Madam Green, at last we meet," Congreed commented sarcastically. "Pardon my stare, but I did not expect you to be so... prehistoric, given your reputation."

"Come a little closer and I'll show you this dagger's reputation, as well," she threatened, stepping toward him. A few of Congreed's soldiers took an offensive stance, ready for Congreed's signal.

"Hmf — petty words from a petty thief," he responded. "Your empty threats don't scare anyone. You will have to try harder than that if you wish to make me sweat, woman; you're playing with the big boys now."

"Cherish that crown while you still have it..." she mumbled audibly to Congreed as she cast a subtle glance in my direction. A little too brash for my liking.

"Enough," I interrupted calmly. "You may not *like* each other, but in my presence, you *will* respect each other. Both of you stand to gain much here today, as well as your followers, and the followers after them. If this squabbling continues, or either of you become a wartime liability to me, jeopardizing our chance at victory, then as the gods are my witnesses, I will not hesitate to strike down either one of you to keep that from happening. Work it out, or I will take you out. Understand?"

"Remember who you're talking to…" Congreed warned through gritted, wine-stained teeth.

"Gather your men around," I redirected after a defiant and fearless stare back at him. "We've wasted enough time. Now, we bring our plans to action."

I took to horseback again to raise myself above the others, maintaining the same visual authority as the day I first stood before the Sipondeli congregation. Only I was no longer the same as I was back then. Something had changed in me. I had evolved. I was no longer *pretending* to be their leader — I *was* their leader. Looking out over all 6000 warriors instilled a feeling of satisfaction in me I never thought I'd feel again, especially after having everything I'd ever known and loved ripped from my grasp. I couldn't take back what was stolen from me, but I'd found a way to give back what was stolen from others — even if they didn't know it was gone. The soldiers congregated before me that day were the authentic display of what is possible for those who believe the world *can* be theirs, and do not stop until it has been made so. They were the single idea that met perseverance and became greatness somewhere along the way. What was once a dormant potential asleep in people too scared to wake it, had become a unified effort whose insurrection would be so loud, it would never sleep again.

"Makers of history," I bellowed with sword in hand, "today we find ourselves standing before Fate's throne, staring defiantly into his eyes, and refusing to bow before him. For too many years we have been the nail while Fate has been the hammer. For too many ages, our bloodlines have bruised their knees on the cold, hard ground, picking up and living off the scraps of what the gods have thrown away. What they spill, we drink; what they spit out, we feed upon.

Is this the kind of life we deserve?!"

"NO!"

"Is this the kind of life we are destined to live?!"

"NO!"

"Then fight — and fight hard this day. Refuse to be subjugated and History will not forget you. Take your rightful place among its pages, and your enemies will be denied theirs.

For years, you have walked alone in tunnels that had no light at the end of them; for years, your fears have made you slave to anyone willing to be your master. But look around you: you are no longer just a man; you are an army. You are no longer just a woman; you are a storm of Valkyries, here to choose who will live and who will die. What do you have to fear? To fear anyone is to banish yourselves to a labyrinth with no doors, wandering forever, only to die in the same room you began. Remove yourself from those walls! Fear is for the powerless! Fear is for the alone! But as you stand together now, you are neither of those. Together, you amplify each other's strengths; you nullify each other's weaknesses. This day, you are free, because you have *chosen* to be free — and because of your choice, your days of insignificance are over.

But be not mistaken! This will be no easy fight — nothing worth fighting for ever is. If you value your lives, you must be willing to give them — for what you withhold in this life will be withheld from you in the next. The enemy we are about to face is not like you: they do not have souls; they do not have emotion. They are abominations twisted by the Dark Power that flows through their veins to keep you from your freedom. Though they may look human, they are the farthest things from it, so you must not let your blades treat them as such. Today is the day we take back what the Dark King stole from us long ago: the keys to our own destinies. We have done nothing for *far* too long. We deserve far more!

Greatness is not a gift that one can give to another, but rather is a thief's relic that we must take for ourselves. It is for those who refuse to allow *others* to decide what was *theirs* to decide all along. It is for the ones who refuse to accept their fates, and choose to make their own. Brothers and sisters, though our feet are calloused and our brows are weather-beaten by the sands of time, we cannot stop now — Greatness is within reach! It waits for us, just over those mountains, behind the thick walls of the Dark Kingdom. Breach those walls, and as surely as you stand here today, Greatness and Freedom will be yours.

The Reaper stands idly by with scythe in hand. Watching. Waiting. Longing to be loosed by the spilling of blood. Why keep him waiting?! If it's blood he wants, let us quench his thirst with the blood of our enemies until he can drink no more!"

A roaring cheer burst forth from the horde like rolling thunder. With a subtle nod to Simeon and Blackheart, they took their 1000

Sipondelis and made their way to the outposts and tunnels while the rest followed me into the mountains without hesitation. Moments later, Congreed's hoverbike was at my side.

"Quite the speech, boy. But where do *my* men fit in?"

"Have them follow me and my troops to set up a single-file perimeter around the kingdom. When it's time to storm the gates, you'll know."

He let his bike drift back into formation with his own soldiers.

"Are you sure we'll be able to do this?" Arkade chimed in. "I mean, we have lots of people, but most of them barely know how to use a sword. There's even kids younger than me here…"

"It doesn't seem realistic, does it… I'll tell you what," I said as I reached into my satchel and pulled out the Horn of Order, "take this. Hold onto it for me. And when the battle starts to become too much, and I give you the signal, I want you to be the one to sound it if things start to look bleak."

"How do I use it?" he asked.

"One long, continuous blow implements the next phase of battle. A quick blow followed by a long one lets the soldiers know I am in danger, so they may redirect their efforts to save me at all costs. And lastly, if we need to retreat, keep sounding a series of short bursts, and they'll know exactly what to do. Keep the Horn safe at all times — but only sound it when I give you the signal."

"I will."

He still looked unsure about something.

"I know you're a realist, Arkade; most people are. But don't let realism keep you from doing what you feel you need to do, even if you think it's hopeless. Never give up on the possibilities or accept what *is* when you can see it for what it *could* be. If something needs to be done, do it. If something needs to be said, say it. No matter what, don't live a life where you're too scared to die for what you believe in; always go at it with everything you've got, even if it doesn't seem to be enough. And remember: even the tallest trees were once a seed."

"I know; it's just… I almost lost you once. And I don't want to lose you again," he expressed, subtly wiping a silent tear from his eye, trying to present a strong front.

"You won't lose me. We have work to do. Kingdoms to conquer. People to lead. No matter how this battle turns out, this is not the end. We *will* live to see another day. This is only the beginning."

CHAPTER FORTY-SEVEN

The Puppet Show

As we were setting up our perimeter, an unnatural chill began to weave through the air until we could barely feel our fingertips. It took every bit of willpower not to light the oil slick that had been poured in front of us, if even just for a few minutes of warmth, but we managed to resist, considering that a fire's light may have been the catalyst to a death more brutal than merely seeing your breath when you exhaled. The frosty air helped keep my mind tied to the present, anyway — a time when there were no sentimental memories that could be constructed around what was meant to be destroyed. I didn't need to be reminded of old friends, first businesses, first homes, or family; all I needed to see was the towering, black-iron gate of the Dark Kingdom in place one last time before it fell to the ground forever.

Waiting for Simeon's team to complete their tasks inside those walls felt like an eternity in the icy conditions. The longer we waited, the more the crisp, night air crept to a hollowing chill — the kind that not only numbs your sense of touch, but your ability to feel as well. I didn't remember passing through that kind of cold when I first left the comfort of its walls, but perhaps I was too focused on escaping alive to notice. It certainly wasn't natural by any standards, but when it came to the Dark King's power, very little ever was — if it was cold, he *meant* for it to be cold. Every creation of his always had a purpose. I still admired that about him... but even admiration provides no saving grace for the inconvenient.

My thoughts were interrupted by the flag-waving of one of Simeon's agents crouched on the nearest rooftop. There, with arm stretched high, was all the warmth I needed.

"The gate is open. Ready?" I asked Arkade, alluding to the sounding of the Horn he held in his hands.

His chattering teeth and shivering body almost made his nod unnoticeable. He touched it to his lips and took a deep breath.

"Wait…" I said, staring at the rooftop as my hand gently pushed the horn from his lips.

The agent responsible for signalling us was hovering in mid-air. His limbs, pulled to their limit in every direction. I could tell he tried to remain quiet, but whatever unseen forces held him there, soon took his wits to places his silence could no longer follow. Screams tore out from his innermost fibres as bone and muscle were ripped from their sockets and sinews, showering the rooftop with his blood. His limbs were then cast to the ground with complete and utter irreverence as the commanders of the Dark Power made their way to the open gate. Within moments, multiple sets of glowing blue eyes were looking out to see what the corpse was waving to earlier.

And that's when things got worse. Much worse.

"Light the oil!" I bellowed. But before my archers could set their arrows, our enemies had thrust the blazing fires back upon them, splashing flames and burning oil onto their bodies. Their arms, faces, and chests became swirling infernos trapped underneath armour that couldn't be removed fast enough. In mere seconds, their skin was splitting and melting among screams too helpless to extinguish them.

"The sword, Morningstar! Use the sword!" Issachar yelled from the other side of the burning bodies, pointing wildly at the gift in my hands they had given me.

I turned the hilt, and sure enough, the nearby fire that swarmed the soldiers was pulled from their panicked bodies and onto my blade. I rode up and down the rest of the line to pull the rest from the remaining victims.

"Hey Morningstar!" Manasseh yelled as he drove his hands deep into the frozen ground, tearing out a giant boulder. "Light it up!"

He hurled the chunk of rock toward our enemies with incredible force. The flames left my blade and set fire to its surface instantly. The faster it rolled, the brighter its flames burned. Soon, the flaming boulder had gained so much momentum that not even their telekinesis could slow it down, forcing them to dive out of the way as it smashed into the wall with a ground-shaking boom. But they recovered quickly, immediately running out through the gaping hole, prepared to keep us from passing through their kingdom's new vulnerability.

"Hold your positions!" I shouted. "Do not advance until these enemies have first been dealt with!"

"No! We grow restless! This is our chance — We're going in!" Congreed yelled as he signalled for his troops to follow him to the gates at full speed.

"Right behind you, Crowned One," Madam Green called out with a wink to me as she and her men snuck onto the backs of Congreed's hoverbikes, conserving their energy.

"Does he think he's invincible, charging them like that? The impatient idiot will lead them to their deaths!" Issachar commented, readying his sword for the incoming attack.

Congreed's men sped off in single file toward the enemy at breakneck speed, their lances pointed straight ahead with unwavering confidence. The enemy stood their ground, determined to knock them about and prove themselves superior, but by the time they realized that Congreed's men were locked together with an incredible magnetic force that could not be broken or slowed, it was too late for them. The hoverbikes split into "V" formation, meeting the wielders of the Dark Power like a spiked-iron fence, and impaling them all like inhuman meat-skewers.

"I stand corrected," Issachar recanted.

They swiftly dismounted their machines and ran inside the walls to gain as much ground as they could. But the inner walls held an even greater surprise — a fierce opposition met them head-on, thrusting them forcefully into the walls and tossing their seven-foot, mechanical, hulking bodies about like ragdolls. Even those that Congreed's men had impaled on the way in didn't stay out of the fight for long. They pulled the spikes from their bodies and began healing each other as they made their way inside, bent on exacting their revenge. And that was barely a taste of what our enemy was about to unleash upon us.

"Levi — the path is clear. You're up!" I instructed him.

Levi and his ladder-jockeys ran for the walls as Blackheart met up with us again from the woods.

"How's it looking?" he asked.

"We'll find out soon enough; help Levi with the ladders. We need to bring the fight inside their walls where the roads and backstreets give us better cover."

"Done."

The soldiers ran in droves for the outer wall, every tenth one carrying a ladder in hand.

"I need as many soldiers as possible to get on these ladders. Let's move! Let's move!" Levi shouted as he laid the ladders out on the ground. "Manasseh — do your thing."

Manasseh took hold of the soldier-heavy ladders and propped them up against the walls.

"When you are inside," Levi yelled up the ladder, "swarm! Don't spread! The more you swarm a target, the better our chances of victory will be!"

When I reached the collapse in the wall, I saw more pandemonium in the first ten metres — more blood and dismemberment in the first five — than I'd ever seen in my life. Impaled bodies hung lifelessly from broken wooden awnings. Torsos were scattered across the road in such volume that the road beneath could not be seen. To the left, I saw a spineless soldier cowering in fear behind some barrels, tears streaming down his face while only a few paces away his comrades frantically begged for their life as they were crushed beneath massive boulders or slammed against jagged stone walls without mercy. But worst of all were the slow deaths that no one could stop; the ones dealt by the twisted, power hungry ones of the kingdom who would freeze a soldier's body until his organs ceased to function and shattered — or even more demented: the ones who set fire to soldiers only to hold them in place telekinetically so they had no choice but to feel the slow burn of their flesh being consumed with no hope of relief until Death hand-delivered it to them.

As I looked out over the dead, my worst fears were confirmed: not a corpse among them belonged to a commander of the Dark Power. Not even an arm or a finger. The torn and bloodied Sipondeli garbs barely hanging on their backs made that quite obvious. As for the Excarpathians, not even their wartime technology could save them. Every single body was one of my own — killed without even a glimmer of hope, or a chance at victory. My dominion over that kingdom was being hindered by people who had never fought a war in their lives... and my chances for correcting that inconvenience were quickly coming to a close.

Out of the corner of my eye, I caught a glimpse of a shadow quickly moving down the back lane. I followed it curiously down one road and then the next, only to find myself in front of the Church of the Dark Kingdom. It was then I realized the shadow was none other than Madam Green, in all her greedy splendour. Carefully, I peeked through one of the missing shards of stained glass to see her there, crouched in place behind a pew watching, waiting, while Congreed scanned the area with his wrist-mounted searchlights, looking around for the basement opening I wrote him about. It wasn't long before he spotted the iron ring that opened the hatch, but finding it was only half the battle — the true struggle was trying to fit his well-fed, armoured body down the hatch. Like a very round peg in a tiny square hole, there was no chance he was going to fit down there, but lucky for him, his suit carried the pneumatics necessary to pummel the floor until it caved in. Pews fell inward and wood splinters flew everywhere, but when the dust cleared, the king was unscathed and his armour still intact. I snuck inside, phantom-stepping through what was left of the upper level to get a better view, hoping to see where Madam Green had fallen among the destruction, but all I could see was Congreed, searching through the planks delicately — undoubtedly hoping he didn't shatter the glass ring trying to fit himself down the hole. As long as I had Congreed in my sights, I knew Madam Green wouldn't be too far away.

He searched long and hard for the ring with a devotion to his greed that would put most people's perseverance to shame. Though his destruction of the floor made his search exponentially more difficult, he pressed on, moving every little piece of furniture and debris he could, until he grew tired. I saw him rest only once — and briefly at that. It was the only time he'd taken his helmet off, setting it down on the table so he could breathe fresh air and wipe the sweat from his forehead. But even tired, he did not quit. He continued rummaging through the wreckage and antiques until he had overturned every last plank of wood and blew every speck of dust from his path. That's when it set in: I'd tricked him, and tricked him well. He stopped and stood there with disbelief, muttering quietly, "So that's how he wants to play it..."

Before his grudge could take root, Madam Green sprung from the shadows onto his back and plunged her dagger deep into his clavicle.

"Never judge a woman by her age," I heard her say in his ear, before she leapt off his body and let him collapse to the ground.

She walked over to the table where she took his crown and placed it on her head. Realizing there was nowhere to see her reflection, she looked for a large piece of unbroken glass — a surface she hastily found and propped up in the path of Congreed's wrist-mounted light beam. She stood in front of it proudly.

"Well hello, my queen," she said, admiring herself with a smile.

Had she not been so captivated by her own image, she might've seen the reflection of the large brick that Congreed hurled at her from afar. Gashed upside the head that modelled a newly-dented crown, she stumbled to regain her footing, but fell to her knees in a daze. Doing everything she could to reject her body's response to the brick, she fought for control of her fumbling hands in desperation, trying to grab the dagger from her belt, but Congreed was upon her too quickly — his mechanical grip took hold of her wrist, twisting it like a screwdriver until her wrist bones popped and split through her skin. In a display of superiority, he shoved her to the floor where she writhed and screamed in pain.

"You bas—" was all she got out before his metal arm backhanded her across the face.

"You want to sit on a throne, old woman?" he asked, gripping her throat tightly. "I'll give you a throne..."

He squeezed harder and harder as her fearful eyes filled with blood and glazed over; so tightly, her body went limp. Then, dragging her body by her collapsed throat, he sat her corpse on an old, broken chamber pot.

"There. This one suits you much better, anyway," he said, spitting on the ground.

I tried creeping away as quickly and stealthily as I could, but the creaky floors betrayed my position.

"Morningstar! Just the lad I want to see!" he yelled threateningly as he reattached his helmet and mounted the bent crown back in place. I broke into a full run, but his mechanical legs were closing the gap quickly. I bent and wove down every corridor I could to lose him. I climbed rooftops, obstructed his path with every obstacle available to me, but he kept coming for me. Lucky for me, Arkade was hiding in a thicket nearby, so I called out to him with desperation to sound the horn for my protection.

The Silence ambushed him with everything they had — knocking him to the ground, pouring thick, translucent oil all over his visor and cutting the hoses at his joints so his suit could no longer operate. But no matter how hard they tried to open his safety hatch, Congreed stayed well-protected in his metal casing, emitting a deafening alarm of his own from his shoulders, until a handful of his mecha-soldiers came to his aid. Their arms swung violently, smashing bricks and wood alike, but what abundant strength they possessed in their suits, The Silence more than countered with their dexterity. Seeing that the skirmish would not be settled any time soon, Congreed's mecha-soldiers stood around him, forming a protective barrier so he could be helped out of his suit and into another — one that functioned — that had been given up for him. The suit instantly adjusted itself to conform to his body.

From his replacement suit, a new alarm reverberated through the air. Little was left to wonder what it meant the way his soldiers stopped what they were doing and started leaving the battlefield without so much as a look back. My clever trick had backfired — and I was left to face the consequences. Their abandonment meant the Sipondeli people were left to face the wielders of the Dark Power alone... and they were no match for them to begin with.

Congreed gave me a long glare before he followed his men outside the gates to their hoverbikes. I re-joined the battle, fighting my way through enemies that just wouldn't die, but it was no use — I knew if we didn't retreat soon, every last one of us would end up as another charred corpse on the pile of bodies that were already spread thick across the ground.

"MORNINGSTAR, LOOK OUT!" Mercedes yelled as a massive javelin was sent torpedoing toward my back.

I barely had time to turn around, let alone react. Mercedes lunged for me, thrusting her chest into mine to knock me off-balance. All I felt was the breeze of the javelin catching the cape beneath my arm. It yanked me with it as it continued along its designated path... plunging straight into her ribcage only centimetres away from my own. She was pinned to the wall — dead before I'd even hit the ground from her life-saving shove. I looked to the gates only to see Congreed hovering

at a distance with an evil, prolonged look of disappointment in his own accuracy before he sped off, as if to let me know it would not be his last attempt on my life. There would be no redressing the injury our alliance took — it could only be made right one other way...

Not long after Congreed took his men and left, the Sipondeli soldiers' hope hit rock-bottom and took their concentration with it. Not that they stood a chance on their own, but once they began to panic and allow their belief in themselves to reach an all-time low, the transient confidence they started with evaporated to nothingness. They became a lost cause. Walking corpses without a casket. Unworthy of even hearing the sound of the Horn's retreat.

CHAPTER FORTY-EIGHT

Sacrifice and Saviours

It was a massacre. The bodies of our soldiers lay everywhere — their lives wrenched away when they had just begun to see what they were capable of. But to the wielders of the Dark Power? They were worthless. Inconveniences capable of no more than littering the ground. Skin melted by flame. Bones numbed and shattered by cold. Internal organs constricted to unfathomable levels of pain through telekinetic cruelty. My soldiers experienced the worst kinds of death imaginable — and their sacrifice couldn't even be justified by the killing of even a single enemy. Even The Silence — who were true masters of the art and beauty of death — were rarely given the opportunity to lay blade or arrow against our enemies. And when they did, their supernatural healing quickly repaired the transgressions against them, as if reversing time itself.

My army was no match for their abilities, even with the numbers that would make any other kingdom tremble with fear. I had greatly underestimated the power of my enemies. Disorganized as they were, the mystic forces they commanded, though a fraction of what the Dark King once had, was still more than enough to overpower us. We were ants trying to defend ourselves against a soldier's boot. When I realized that, I knew I had to make an executive decision, because a good leader must have the wisdom to know when a pursuit is no longer worthy of being pursued — a time when the losses of the present must be accepted — and cut — to preserve the gains and providence of the future. Something had to be done... before it was too late.

I looked through the chaos for a clear path back to the church.

"Do you want me to sound the retreat?" Arkade asked.

I looked at the soldiers dropping like flies and then to The Silence, who were already gathered around me. I shook my head.

"That won't be necessary, Arkade. Come — let's get out of here while our enemies are still distracted with what's left of the Sipondelis.

There's a shortcut just down this corridor here," I instructed.

Zebulun and Ephraim continued to stare as the soldiers were killed one after the other with little resistance.

"All one can hope is that the gods have mercy on them as they are laid to rest. But we must go now, or we will share the same fate. Hurry — there isn't much time," I convinced them.

We made our way to the corner adjacent to the church that was left barely standing after Congreed had ploughed through it the way a child ploughs through a sandcastle. The fight was still heavy near the entrance, but it was our only way in.

"Asher, I need those enemies distracted," I told her.

She pulled some arrows from her quiver and launched them at a stack of crates and barrels, knocking them over. As they crashed to the ground, a few more of our enemies wandered over to investigate.

"There's still four more," Blackheart commented.

"I've got this one, Ephraim," Zebulun assured, as he reached into his pack for a bomb the size of Manasseh's hand. "You guys get ready to make a break for it. When this bomb goes off, run like your life depended on it."

Zebulun weaved through the shadows until he was in place to cause the most distraction. With the bomb armed, he hurriedly retraced his steps, but only made it about half way before the bomb went off.

We ran for the dilapidated church door and waited for Zebulun to close the gap.

"You guys go on ahead into the column, I'll join you once Zebulun gets here," Ephraim said.

"I'll stay with you," I added. "The rest of you make haste. Go! Go!"

The smoke from Zebulun's bomb was already clearing by the time he got to the last street corner across from the church. Even if he ran at the speed of the hoverbikes, there was a very narrow window between being seen and a retreat we would live to tell about.

When his chance came, he made the best of it — running faster than I'd ever seen a human run. He was only a few metres away when I saw one of the wielders of the Dark Power take notice.

"Quick Zeb! Quick! I think it saw you!" Ephraim exclaimed.

But as Zebulun got to the door, his pursuer's telekinesis swept his legs out from under him. Zebulun sailed through the air straight into Ephraim's arms who took hold of him tightly.

"That was close. Now come on!" he yelled at his brother, but his legs had been taken hold of again.

Zebulun let out a painful roar as he fought for his life, taking hold of Ephraim with all he had. I grabbed hold of his robe and planted my feet against the door frame, pulling with all the strength I had left. His painful wail got louder.

"Ephraim — Ephraim! Listen to me — no matter what, you stand by Morningstar. Always. Promise me. Don't you—"

"I'm not letting you go!" Ephraim yelled back.

"Promise me! You stand by him til the end, you hear me?"

"Zeb! Don't do this! Don't give u—" Ephraim shouted again, but was interrupted by his brother once more.

"Morningstar... I never thanked you for saving me that day. I thought I hated you, but I was only hating a brother — you showed me that."

"Ze—"

It was all I could get out before his legs were torn from his body, and his torso dragged out with them.

"ZEB!" Ephraim screamed with outstretched arm.

"Ephraim, we have to go! Now!"

"ZEB!" he yelled with tears streaming down his face.

"NOW EPHRAIM!" I bellowed as I took hold of his jacket, dragging him over to the column so we didn't have to face the same fate.

It was a struggle trying to get him down the tunnel, but if I left him there, he'd have senselessly gone after what was left of Zebulun, and been killed in the process. And I needed a bomb-maker.

As I entered the tunnel, I saw a tiny crimson light in the distance. It was too far ahead of me to see exactly what it was at first — gone just as quickly as it appeared — but the way adrenaline rushed through my body, I knew my higher consciousness was unraveling mysteries quicker than my conscious thoughts could keep up. Then I remembered the entry in my father's memoirs speaking of a "Crimson-Eyed One" — an enigma of sorts whose existence kept my father baffled until his death. Though Duty called me back to our base, the sirenesque charm of Curiousity and Intrigue were much too strong to resist; those muffled, hasty footsteps that fled along the dirt path contained secrets long withheld from humankind, and they were getting farther from me with every passing moment. The next thing I knew, I was running after it and yelling to the others to meet me back at the base.

Like a dry mouth realizing its thirst at the sight of water, my thoughts became overpowered by the unfathomable curiousity to know what no one in history had ever known — an arcane knowledge that was only a few paces away if I could only force my legs to run faster and endure the burning sensation that seduced them to stop and rest with every step. But I persevered, giving it everything I had until I'd tapped into every last energy reserve my muscles tried to hide from me. My efforts began to close the gap between us, but when I reached out to take hold of him, he just... vanished.

My running slowed to a stop as I looked all around for a sign of where he'd gone. But as I stood there analyzing my surroundings, not a trail or shadow of a clue was left behind. When I turned around, the slightest blue glow could be seen coming down the corridor behind me, intensifying by the second. The brighter it got, the louder the footsteps grew that accompanied it, even on that muffled cave floor. The steps weren't soft and swift like that of the Crimson-Eyed Shadow, but heavy and echoing with a vengeance. Zebulun's devourer. Safe to say, I wasn't going to stick around to see what he wanted: I could tell by the footsteps that that abomination wasn't there on any kind of peacemaking mission *I* wanted to be a part of. There was no doubting how it found that tunnel, but it was too late to stop and analyse the obvious; I needed to start running and fast — not only to see where that shadow-figure went, but to distance myself from the predator who surely wanted to add my body to the pile of corpses that layered the streets above. If I was thinking clearly, I would've left my curiousities alone, and lead my pursuer back to our base where my deadly alliance could've possibly neutralized the threat, but with the crimson glow so close only moments ago — right within my grasp — I couldn't bring myself to do it in case I lost my chance forever.

When I arrived at the skull-embedded walls, I stared hopelessly into the dark smokiness — in part looking for the eye to reveal itself again, and in part wondering where I could hide to escape certain death; it was hard to tell which was closer at any given moment. The smoky pathway was probably the safest bet — to hide first and then keep looking for the crimson-eye once the blue had passed — yet that smoke had nearly killed me twice, and I wasn't about to risk a third. But then I figured if I could crouch down just enough for the smoke to conceal me, I'd at least have a small chance of still escaping alive. It wasn't the most ideal scenario, but definitely the option with the highest odds of survival. Typically, my large, black cloak would've concealed me in darkened areas such as that, rendering me invisible to the naked eye, but the wielders of the Dark Power... they had a vision that was beyond inhuman. Godlike even. Complete darkness was no obstacle to them; I would be identified with ease. In that thick, unnatural smoke, however, there was evolutionary equilibrium — a salvation and safe haven for the less-evolved.

My feet had barely begun their transition into the corridor to seek refuge when the large crimson eye opened suddenly from within the darkness and burst out of the smoke, lunging straight for me. I had come face-to-face with impending doom and had nowhere to go, no place to hide from either side. The answers to the crimson-eyed mystery were finally within my reach — answers, it seemed, that I would be buried with in mere moments. I reached for my pendant, hoping for a moment of luck and glory to deliver me from the clutches of Death, but before I could even touch it, its crimson eye began to swirl hypnotically, summoning some paralytic force within me that restrained my movements until my body had succumbed to the paralysis completely. I fell limp to the ground, helpless. My eyelids, the only part of my body still under my control. Fearing the worst as it walked over to me, I expected it to administer the killing blow, ensuring its secrets were kept the way Illyana or any other assassin would have. But to my confusion, it simply dragged me until half of my body laid there inside the corridor with it, and my other half baited my tracker from the main tunnel — letting it know exactly where I was. There was nothing I could do about it either; my potential was disintegrating from "ruler of future empires" to "sacrificial lamb" in just a few mere seconds. Even with all my ambitions, efforts, and accomplishments, my ultimate fate still resided in the grasp of another.

When the approaching footsteps reached their loudest and the blue glow from his eyes radiated their most fearsome light, my executioner slowed his steps to an overconfident stride, staring me down as he approached.

"Now, who is this masked lad we have here, causing all this trouble in our kingdom?" he asked rhetorically, taking a knee beside me as he tossed off my hood and pulled off my mask.

It was Moorden.

"Great gods! ...Morningstar?! It's been *you* raising all this ruckus?! Well, look at you... I didn't think I'd ever see ya again, but lo and behold here ya are. Ooo, I'm gonna en-*joy* this. Don't ya worry, lad. I know *juuuust* how ta welcome ya home..." he sneered with a dastardly smile.

In his hand, I saw him start to muster all the preliminary power-charge he was soon to unleash upon my defenseless body. When he raised his palm to me, I just closed my eyes, and accepted that my time had come. I'd failed.

Laying there, waiting to die.

And then some more.

But surprisingly, my death never came.

His magic-infused body succumbed to the crimson paralysis just as easily as mine had: his arms went flaccid, his knees gave out, and his body collapsed to the ground like a sack of potatoes. There upon the ground, motionless, robbed of free-will and any chance of redemption, the light in his palms quickly faded to nothingness and his overconfidence along with it. Against all odds, the Crimson-Eyed One had bested a commander of the Dark Power, suppressing his power to complete dysfunction — and doing in a single, effortless act what I had failed to do with all the time, planning, and soldiers any war in those lands had ever experienced. I'd seen first-hand the awe-inspiring capabilities of the Dark Power, but in its fragmented state, it was nothing compared to the Crimson-Eyed One's magic I witnessed in those tunnels that day. And that wasn't the end of its impressive displays of power either.

I watched as it walked toward Moorden and leaned over him, unsheathing what looked like a ruby-bladed dagger from under his cloak. It knelt down and stared deep into his eyes for a few moments...

and then his crimson eye began to pulsate. The pulse was slow at first, but as it picked up speed, the tunnel grew darker and the air grew heavier, thickening like the smoke. He placed his hand on Moorden's paralysed neck and drove his dagger straight into my would-be killer's throat with the other. The dagger's blade — like a blood-coloured crystal, hollow to its core — began to light up from within, faintly illuminating every surface in the immediate area with a spectrum of refracted red light that made time stand still. The glowing blue once imprisoned in his eyes faded with life-relinquishing breathlessness the more his body began to rapidly decay until all that remained was a withered corpse that looked like it had been mummified for centuries — the bottomless blue in his eyes, stamped out forever. Upon his death, the remnants of the power in his body seeped through the cracks of his brittle remains and joined back together into a tiny sphere of pulsating cerulean light, hovering above him like a spirit preparing its journey for the heavens. Then, in a blink, the sphere rushed back through the tunnel as it did in the Dark King's chambers once upon a time, bound for a destination as unbeknownst to me as the true identity of the hooved godsend. After his work was complete, just as mysteriously as the tiny-hooved cyclops appeared, there its body faded into the shadows, dissipating into the vast expanse of smoke, and all my paralyzed body could do was watch him leave.

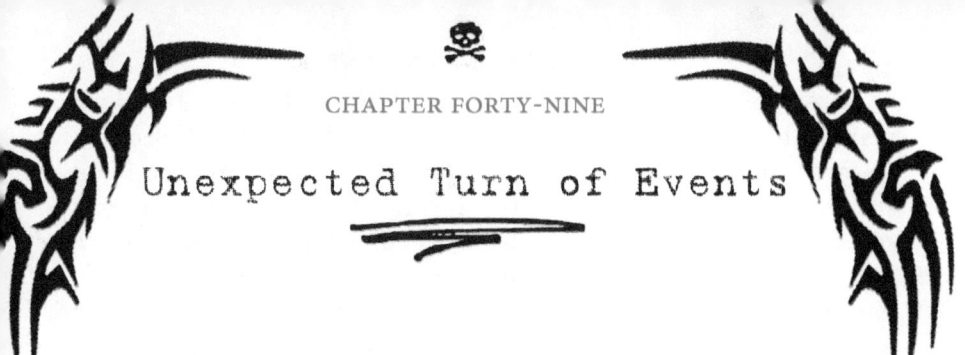

CHAPTER FORTY-NINE

Unexpected Turn of Events

In a few hours, when the paralysis wore off, I made my way back to our old base to meet with the others. Arkade came running to me, beaming with ecstasy at the fact I was still alive, but I quickly sent him away to call the others into The Core for a meeting.

"By seeking knowledge, I have freed myself; by freeing myself, I have freed the world.

Honoured soldiers of the Great Cause, what happened today was beyond what any of us could have predicted. The losses we sustained shall forever torment my heart. Let us remind ourselves that each and every life that did not make it back, was not a life lost, but a life honoured. A life that served a greater purpose, that died believing in an idea greater than ourselves. My friends, our enemies can kill a soldier, but they can never kill an idea. To do so only creates a martyr, and martyrs incite revolutions aspiring to right the wrongs caused by injustice, spreading that idea sometimes quicker through death, than life alone.

Nonetheless, we will honour the ones who died today — Zebulun most of all. Sometimes we exist long enough to lead the next generation; other times, only to plant a seed and let its resonations of our time here on earth ripple into new waves. But we can honour them in ways that go far beyond burying their bodies, or making shrines, or allowing their memories to live on: we can honour them by showing them that they did not die for nothing. That we will not back down from our purpose, afraid of meeting the same fate. No. We will overcome our obstacles, and prove ourselves to be worthy of their sacrifice — a sacrifice made pursuing the same ideals that we must never stop fighting for.

I know our collective morale is burdened with the images of war we all saw today in one form or another, but I assure you, I have seen the light. *You* have seen the light. That burden does not need to weigh upon us any longer.

After we retreated, I went to investigate the one I believe is responsible for creating the tunnels we now use today. Not only did I search, brothers and sisters — I *found*! Although its true identity still evades me, I know that to fear it is to be mistaken. Whatever it is, saved my life. It fully paralyzed and killed one of the wielders of Dark Power that followed us into the tunnels. I cannot be certain if the paralysis I experienced was due to the smoke that fills that corridor, or if it was through the deliberate use of a new Dark Power we have yet to research. But what I *do* know without question, is that paralysis is the one true weakness of our blue-eyed enemies. It makes the power they command no more dangerous than the air we breathe now. We *must* find a means to paralyze our enemies! Perhaps by finding ways to contain the smoke in that corridor and release it into the Dark Kingdom. Once they have succumbed to the paralysis, we need only separate their heads from their bodies before our victory confirms our places in history, as it was originally intended."

"Elixir Orange could be just the thing we're looking for, then," Benjamin contributed. "Elektra, remember when we were trying those dosages on our test subjects? A couple drops worked miracles, but in large quantities... if we smeared it over our blades..."

"Where do you keep your stock? Please — bring me a sample of it quickly," I ordered. "Quickly now. We must hurry. We might actually still have a fighting chance if this works..."

I had just finished speaking when one of the outpost members came barging in. He must have found out about our tunnel system when they watched us retreat.

"Your Holiness, we've..." he stood there looking at my unmasked face, confused why his priest was wearing the black robes of the warlord.

"Go on; I haven't got all day."

"We've been looking all over for you! The people of the Dark Kingdom — they're turning on themselves!"

"What do you mean, 'they're turning on themselves'?"

"They're killing one another! We were watching them after the aftermath of battle. They were wandering the streets, I think in search of any survivors, and then all of a sudden, there was this kind of... glowing blue sphere or something that came out of the church and just shattered in mid-air! The shards flew into each of the blue-eyed people — one into each — and suddenly... I don't know! They just started turning on each other!"

"When the sphere shattered, and 'flew into the people', what exactly did you see?"

"I'm not sure. It's like all of the pieces absorbed into each individual's chest, and they... well the more they killed each other, the more spheres we saw — coming out of the bodies, shattering — basically redistributing itself into whoever was still alive! The more they killed, the brighter their eyes got too!"

"They must've developed a powerlust..." I thought aloud. "Thank you for your prompt delivery of this information, soldier. And if I may ask... how many of you saw us retreat using the tunnel you used to get here?" I questioned, masking the true intent behind my curiousity.

"As far as I know, just me, Your Holiness. We each took it upon ourselves to watch over one area of the kingdom, and one area only — so that nothing would be missed."

"You're certain of this?"

"...Fairly certain, yes."

"Thank you for your loyalty," I said as I drew my dagger and plunged it into his stomach. The man collapsed to his knees as I walked past him, slipping the mask over my face once more. "Blackheart, Asher — if this news is true, I'll need you to pay our outposts a little visit. With Congreed looking to have my head, I can't afford to have any loose ends. Leave no witnesses."

Benjamin returned with a small vial of the Elixir Orange and tossed it to me.

With that, I ran into the tunnels, making it back to the Dark Kingdom with haste while the others stayed behind. As soon as I got to the broken door of the Dark Kingdom's church, I stretched my head out slowly, cautiously, to see what was happening. I needed to see the truth for myself.

The outpostman was right; they *had* turned on themselves. Their bodies laid motionless, lifeless on the ground without as much as a glimmer of blue left in their eyes — just your average corpses, indistinguishable from the remains of the army I had left behind earlier. Venturing out a little farther through the doorway, I saw the remains of all who were left scattered in the streets the way grass covers an open field. Every step squished below my boots and sunk just a little lower into the ground than it should have.

"Psssst — Morningstar, sir," a voice whispered to me from a darkened alley.

I looked harder into the darkness, but couldn't see anything until the figure walked out from the shadows to present itself.

"Who are you?" I asked, drawing my blade.

"I'm Ksathra," she said. "leader of the Neutralizers, now that Madam Green has been killed."

She gave a hand signal that made the others come out of hiding. It seemed about thirty of them had camouflaged themselves well-enough to escape the aftermath.

"We heard your words and saw you and your assassins fight. We'd like to pledge ourselves to your service."

I thought about Congreed's threat and the army I no longer had to help me slay the Dark King. With all the commanders of the Dark Power dead, their power was certainly redistributed back to the Dark One as well — an unsettling thought, since I'd brought war to his doorstep, barely cheating my *own* death in the process. With two kings wanting to see me as dead as the army I'd left behind, I decided to accept their pledge.

"On one condition," I clarified. "I want you to transfer the full contents of The Neutralizers' treasure room to a place I will designate upon my return. After today, Excarpathia will not be a safe-haven for me, and it would be a pity for all that to go to waste."

"It shall be done as you wish, sir. In the mean time, we would wait at your base, but... you'll have to forgive us, but we don't know where that is, exactly."

I looked down at the outpostman's blood still fresh upon my blade. It was Sipondeli blood — the blood of the weak and envious. Blood I did not want diluting the greatness that roamed the subterranean tunnels below, even by association. But the group of Excarpathians before me were unlike their neighbours. They were strong. Capable. They went after what they wanted, much like I did, but were still able to serve an ambitious leader — even one who treated them as poorly and expendably as Madam Green. And the fact that they followed her visions as dedicated rebels against Congreed, I felt their loyalties could be trusted. With that trust, I decided to embrace them as my own, and reveal the location of our base where the others awaited my return.

"Enter the church, climb down into the rubble, and look for the underground tunnel. Follow it, keeping your hand along the left wall at all times. The first inconsistency you feel in the wall is the path you'll follow back to our base."

"With all due respect, sir, won't your men try to kill us if we go without you?"

"Take this," I said, handing them my mask, "and recite these words: 'By seeking knowledge, I have freed myself; by freeing myself, I have freed the world.' Memorize those words — every last one of you — keep them close, for they will be the maxim by which your lives will now be guided."

One of them whispered to Ksathra something inaudible.

"Do you take issue with this maxim?" I asked with direct authority.

"No, my lord. He was making reference to the hoverboots Madam Green gave you — the ones you still wear on your feet. They're not what you think. They're booby-traps. We were supposed to activate the trap upon seeing her leave the church with Congreed's crown... leaving you and your men on the battlefield unassisted and to die, but she never came back out."

"I see... and just how are these boots booby-trapped, exactly?"

"There are collapsible spikes and blades hidden in the lining, hence why they're so heavy. When they deployed, they would've amputated your legs from the knees-down."

"Can the traps be removed?" I asked, hoping my fondness for the boots could continue with the use of my legs.

"Of course, sir. The traps have not been activated yet anyway — if you remove them now, you can wear these leather ones instead. They may be a little small, but they'll do until we can safety those for you."

"Thank you."

"Will there be anything else, my lord?"

"Not as of yet. Join with the others back at base. They will show you to your chambers."

Minutes after they left, I heard voices coming from where the kingdom gate used to be. They must have been all that was left of the Dark Kingdom's population after the powerlust consumed them — a relieving thought, knowing the Dark King's power wasn't fully restored to its original limitless glory after all. I phantom-stepped closer, only to see a twisted version of my old priest, drunk with power, blocking the exit from a family of three who were trying to leave the kingdom without conflict. I overheard him telling the man, woman, and child no older than ten, that he could not allow them to leave without giving up their power to him first — and seeing that the only way to do that was through their death, well… let's just say his vows were probably just "guidelines" at that point. The priest attacked, but the mother was clever, strategically dividing the priest's attention until he had no choice but to fight the father in front of him while trying to keep an eye on her from behind. They outsmarted him in the end, with her delivering the deathblow as his back was turned to her. It was the brilliant action of a woman I would've been proud to have been married to.

The dead priest lay at their feet as his power transfused into them.

"C'mon honey; let's go find somewhere safe, okay?" the woman instructed the younger boy in a familiar voice as they left the kingdom for the Forest of Dreamlock.

My curiousity was piqued. So without hesitation, I began to follow them, applying Elixir Orange to my blade generously. It was time to start testing my theory on some test subjects of my own…

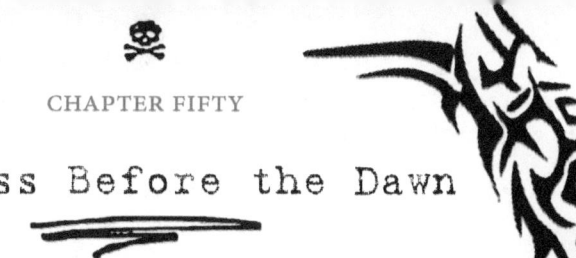

CHAPTER FIFTY

Darkness Before the Dawn

Though most would have considered me a fool for pursuing the family alone, it was a risk I needed to take. After all, emperors are not made from cowards; they are made from those who take great risk where there stands to be even greater gain. I knew I stood no chance trying to win them over by showcasing my physical strength; the battle that took place only hours before was a testament to that. But where arms and blades fell short, there you'd find my words, gracefully slithering into minds of the vulnerable. Be not mistaken: everyone *is* vulnerable — even the immensely powerful family heading for the woods before me. Perhaps they couldn't be won by the allure of greed or power, but by their protectiveness of each other. You could tell, even from a distance, that their love and togetherness were quite clearly of great importance to them. And the values most important to us are always the most easily exploitable...

I trailed behind at a distance, moving swiftly and silently, with a level of stealth that would have made Naphtali proud. They were smart — keeping off the beaten path and away from streams and anything else that might otherwise attract curious travellers. Soon thereafter, they arrived at a small, unassuming hut deep in the heart of the forest. I concealed myself in the trees, careful to approach, waiting for the right moment to make my presence known. As luck would have it, no more than an hour later, the little boy and the man set off into the forest — to hunt for their evening meal, I assumed, by the pointy sticks and netting they carried off into the bushes with them. That was my opportunity. The woman was alone, vulnerable — a grey-matter tailor's dream stage just waiting for the curtain to rise. Every step I watched them take, I took a step of my own, creeping closer and closer to the door until they were out of audible range. Then — when all seemed safe enough — I knocked.

And when the door opened... I couldn't believe my eyes.

I stood there with a blank stare as apparitions of memory

resurrected from beyond the grave. Apparitions of what had been laid to rest for nearly eleven years.

I was at the mercy of the moment, flooded with every heartbroken and soul-fulfilling emotion known to man. The emotional dam I'd created within myself to deal with the past all those years began to crack and rupture, until it gave way completely and I could hold them back no more. When it burst, every forgotten tear, every ocean of pain and loss, flowed — their salty wetness, a mere puddle compared to the typhoons of confusion, joy, anger, and relief that raged with them. There were not enough words or names in existence for every emotion I felt.

It was her.

My Emeline.

Alive.

"Morningstar..." she whispered, shocked to see me there.

"...Emeline..."

"Please... come in..." she said, inviting me through the door after looking around outside to see if the man and boy were within sight. "There's... a lot you're probably wondering right now."

"I'm not sure if 'a lot' quite captures the magnitude of it..." I miffed.

"I know," she hung her head. "No matter what I say, I can't make my words mean what I wish they could; but despite knowing what I did — what I had to do — my love... all I ask is that you *hear* my words, but *listen* to your heart as I speak them. Sometimes the heart can hear what the ears do not."

"Believe me when I say you have my *full* attention," I retorted.

"Thank you, darling," she said, exhaling deeply. "Morningstar... I just want you to know that I loved you so very much. So much that I took something of the apothecary's that no human should ever take... but *please* know it was my only choice. I'm *so*, so sorry I had to put you through that; it tore my heart to pieces watching every tear roll down your cheek. But having you think I had died was the only way I could give you the closure you needed to accept what I had to do."

The tears made everything blurry as they welled up without the courage to fall. "But why? We had a love that people only *wished* they had. Emeline, I *loved* you... I've never *stopped* loving you."

"I know, darling. I felt the same then — and I feel the same still. Seeing you in that doorway when I opened it was all I ever hoped for every time a door opened these past eleven years."

"Then why did you do it?"

She exhaled deeply again. "I was pregnant."

My eyes ceased to blink.

"Darling, I loved you more than anything, which is why it was so painful to do what I did; I debated it every minute of every day for *weeks*. But when it came down to it, I know we would've both wanted the best for our children, and... financially we never could have given them what they deserved. So to offer them a better life, I..." she trailed off.

"You...?"

"I found someone who could give them what we'd want them to have. I found Armand."

"You keep saying 'them' and 'children'..."

"We had twins: Paradox and Kade. Oh Morningstar, throughout my entire pregnancy, all I could think about was you. Wishing you could be there to touch and kiss my belly, and talk to them like I know you would have. At first, we thought Paradox was the only one, but when the pain didn't stop, I knew another was right behind him. While I waited for him to descend, however, something unbelievable happened. No one really knows exactly what, but there was this blue substance that came through the walls, and before we knew what had happened, our eyes began to glow and we had these abilities we never had before. Paradox received the gifts too, but because Kade wasn't born yet... he was just a normal child."

"When I had followed you here, I saw you and... *him*, but why was there only one child? Did the other...?"

"They're both fine. Safe and healthy and smart. Kade was such a beautiful baby, Morningstar," she smiled. "You would have loved him. But... he looked so much like you that I couldn't keep him without Armand realizing neither one was his one day. So... since Kade didn't have the glowing eyes I figured he would be the easiest to hide. I took some of Armand's money and gave it to my midwife, who then met with her sister, Mary. She took Kade and is raising him well in a nearby kingdom from what she tells me. That way, even though I can't see him, I always know he's close by and well-cared for."

She began to cry.

"I didn't want to give him up... I wanted to give them both a life we couldn't give them," she sobbed. "But then one lie had to be covered up by another, until..."

"Shhh," I took her and held her close, comforting her as best as I could. "You won't need to lie anymore. I can fix this. We can make this work again. I'm not who I once was — we can provide for them, live together, happy, with both our children — far from the burden of everyone else's expectations."

"But Arkade..."

"Arkade? And Mary... Emeline — you're not going to believe this, but I think Arkade and I have been travelling together already for quite some time. Through some... fate-induced serendipity, I've already found him. And the connection I felt with him then is only starting to make sense now..."

"You found him? He's been with you all this time?"

"For a couple years now. Emeline... we can make this work again. If you want us to, that is..."

She smiled that same heart-melting smile I'd missed with every cell in my body.

"I wouldn't have it any other way, my love."

I smiled back and gently placed both hands on her cheeks, pulling her in for an intimate kiss of exoneration. Her breath was life-bringing magic; her lips like crawling into the softest, most comfortable, warm bed after sleeping on the cold, unforgiving cobblestones of the street. Her kiss, an embrace that wraps you in loving arms so all-encompassingly that to let go would be to deny yourself every desire you've ever longed for and deserved. I loved her — every part of her — with the same burning passion I always had, and every part of me was hers in turn to reignite any way she wished. And yet, no matter how much I loved her, no feeling brought me more fulfillment and true, soul-kissed completion than knowing she still loved me too with the same burning passion after all that time. Saving her heart for me, even when the arms of another tried to reach out and take it for himself.

I looked into her eyes and knew in that moment we were thinking the same thing.

Like a groom carrying his wife over the threshold, I picked her up and took her to the bedroom. Our hands couldn't undress each other fast enough as the raw emotion surged within and consumed our minds until all that was left was our two naked bodies, intertwined with destiny once more.

But the path of destiny is not always paved smooth with gold.

We had been so wrapped up in the moment that we completely lost track of time. The wooden panels of the door suddenly burst into splinters, disintegrating before they could even hit the ground. Even the hinges that once held the door in place melted almost instantly with the vengeance that boiled in Armand's fiery-blue eyes as he walked in with murderous intent. The entire room bent and formed around him as he passed through the doorway, the way the Dark King's castle shape-shifted, instilling a level of fear in me that I didn't even know I had; I knew I was no match for the punishment he was about to unleash.

Realizing she was my only chance at escaping alive, Emeline used all her strength to create a protective shield around us trying to delay Armand's rage, but she could not hold him off long. With telekinetic exertion, the furniture began to fly around the room, spontaneously combusting, and smashing upon her shield, one after the other, until Emeline had grown too weak to maintain its protective barrier around us. I knew my time was quickly nearing its end, so in desperation, I rolled to the ground and struck my pendant to the floor where the thick smoke of the Crimson-Eyed One's corridor instantly filled the room, clouding all of our sights. Armand channeled winds of gale-force strength, hoping to clear it as any other smoke or fog would have, but not even his power could clear whatever it was made of. Sight, however, was not a prerequisite for Armand's pursuit of mortal justice — the smoke only made him angrier. He summoned columns of fire all over the room, crumbled the walls, and brought down the ceiling upon us, but still the smoke did not move — it merely held the broken wooden beams in place, refusing to ignite. It was much too thick to do little more than conceal our positions, but that's all I needed.

I rolled under the bed to the other side of the room where Emeline was, hoping I could help her escape through the window, but the creaking of the floorboards betrayed my confidence. With inhuman speed, Armand reached out into the smoke, his hands coursing with deadly voltage, and took hold with a most unforgiving grip. He intensified his electric current to levels that made the whole house flicker a merciless blue, as if enjoying the screams of pain that tore from lungs ready to burst. The screams, however, only made him take hold even tighter, squeeze even more cruelly, until the whole room fell silent.

As the smoke faded, there, in his angry hands, was the limp body of my Emeline.

He stood there, completely paralyzed by what he'd done. He dropped to his knees, overwhelmed with shock and confusion while the rest of his emotions fought hard for representation on his face. It was as if he forgot about me altogether while he held her there in his arms, staring in disbelief, trying so hard to use his power to heal her and bring her back to life. But while my heart shattered into more pieces than the room was in and hoped with every facet of my being that he could bring her back, that was not my time to mourn; his remorse was the only opportunity I had to still get out of that room alive. With a tormented heart, I accepted Fate's cruel, yet bittersweet offering, and used the last of the fading smoke to my advantage. Crawling over to our pile of clothes on the floor, I quietly unsheathed my elixir-coated dagger, slipped behind Armand as stealthily as I could, and plunged its razor-sharp tip deep into his back.

He didn't even move or struggle as my blade slipped deep in-between his shoulder blades, once, and then over and over again. He was too focused on trying to bring her back: touching his hand to her face, trying to use his electric surges to jumpstart her heart, guiding the air into her lungs — anything to try to give her life back to her. But his efforts did nothing. Soon after, he just... stopped, as if overcome by the paralysis of regretful transcendence. No matter how many times I plunged the blade into his back, he just continued kneeling there, as if accepting the pain as his punishment for what he did to Emeline, succumbing to the paralysis more completely with every passing moment.

As his breaths became laboured and the cobalt glow in his eyes momentarily weakened, I began to feel the same shock and remorse that Armand was feeling — only deeper — suddenly overcoming every part of my being. My legs could barely move; my feet were frozen in place. No matter how much I willed them to move, Emeline's lifeless body was a destination I couldn't bring myself to reach from where I stood. I couldn't look at her like that. Not again. Losing the love of my life once was unbearable, but twice? It was a sentence passed by a judge more cruel and sadistic than all the dark forces of evil incarnate combined.

Just then, the boy appeared in the doorway, trying to make sense of what he was seeing.

"Dad?" he asked with confused tears welling up in his eyes.

Armand reached out to him from the floor with a groan, and, like a faithful son, Paradox ran to him. But before his hand could touch the one he believed was his real father, healing him, I took him by the arms, and looked deep in the boy's radiant blue eyes. They were nearly as bright as the Dark King's used to be.

"Paradox, I need you to understand something; I know it might not make sense right now, but your father has just murdered your mother. She di—"

"What?! No! Dad, it's not true! You didn't! Say it's not true!"

Armand gurgled with struggling breath. You could tell he wanted to say more, but I turned Paradox away from him, and back to me.

"Paradox, look at me. Your mother died trying to save me, but more importantly, she died trying to save *you*. Whatever you think you know about your father is not true. She told me so with her final breaths."

"Dad—" he yelled, struggling to run over to him, but I held him tighter.

"Listen to me, Paradox. Your mother wanted you to know something. This man you've called father all these years, is not who you think he is. Your father is, in fact..."

I reconsidered what I was about to tell him.

"...An evil, evil man. He is a criminal — wanted for the murder of many others. Victims just like your mother. He has been known to play the family man and father figure for years, earning the trust of the innocent just like you and your mother, until opportunity strikes and it's time for him to move on. That's when he..." I covered my mouth and looked back at Emeline. "Your mother didn't deserve this," I turned away, muttering deceptively, "...and all because he just wanted more power..."

Confusion and anger quivered in his lip.

"Paradox, if you don't kill him now, this instant, then there's no telling how many other mothers and children will fall victim to his misdeeds. I would do it myself, but you are the only one left who is powerful enough to stop him. He's much too powerful for me now. He... injured me badly," I started to lay the act on thicker, "as I tried to save your mother when I heard her screams. He is much too dangerous to keep alive. Do it for your mother, and all the others he killed, and don't look back. From this day on, if you choose to heal me, I will take care of you, just as your mother wanted me to in the event of her death."

"Par... heal... don't lis—" Armand struggled to get out, his eyes begging for the boy's healing. The elixir was keeping his words right where I needed them.

With tears in his eyes and teeth clenched tight, he raised his hand to Armand. Armand shook his head with panic in his eyes, but before he could make one final plea, Paradox, in an unequivocal display of raw power, tore open a temporary void in the space-time continuum, and slowly pushed Armand's body screeching across the floor toward it. Trying to hold onto anything he could, using limbs of limited movement, Armand fought hard to resist banishment, but Paradox grew more and more fierce. I watched as the light in his eyes glowed brighter and brighter as more and more of Armand's flesh and bone tore away, piece-by-piece, and sailed into the void to be sealed up forever.

I was overcome by awe.

"You did the right thing," I said, trying to comfort the crying boy. "I'm sorry you had to witness that. Your mother was... the most incredible woman these lands have ever known. A mother so warm that no family could ever feel quite so much like home."

I looked him straight in the eye.

"She wanted you to know," I continued, "that if ever you had nowhere else to go, you could always take refuge with me. To live with me, and train with me. To become the highest form of man she wanted you to become someday. It's a shame she won't be here to see it… but I will not let her down — either of you. You *will* become the man you were born to be. Now go; gather your belongings while I get dressed, and meet me outside; you will be *most* welcome where we're going."

As a father, I should've felt something more as we walked side-by-side back to the Dark Kingdom — a pride, a love, a void being filled — but as I glanced down at him, I realized I felt none of those things. It seemed he was no more than a broken souvenir from a past I couldn't remember. Yet, when I looked into his eyes, there she was. Looking back at me. Underneath that supernatural blue glow was her inconcealable, ever-present radiance kept close at all times — and as long as that boy lived, Emeline would never die; if for no other reason than that, I wanted him with me. But I had much greater plans in store for him than mere reminiscence alone. With him at my side, I wouldn't need an army, or enforcers, or even The Silence to bring the freedom and unity to the lands I dreamt. As long as I controlled *him*, I controlled half of the Dark Power for myself — and as long as I controlled the Dark Power… nothing — *no one* — could stand in the way of fulfilling my dream. Some believe the only path to freedom is first found through peace. Well, I have five words for those people: *sic vis pacem para bellum* — if you want peace, prepare for war.

WEB DESIGN | TECH REPAIR | GRAPHIC DESIGN
SPEECH-WRITING | POETRY | BOOKS | PUBLISHING

Mistero is your one-stop shop to help you through life's most common speed-bumps. No matter our career path, there are certain skills we all need to succeed:

Writing/speaking well: to persuade, influence & engage our followers.
Computer/internet skills: to be more prepared, effective & efficient.
Intrapersonal (self): to improve knowledge, awareness & confidence.
Interpersonal (others): interactions are everything. Make them count!

We can't always excel in all these areas, but no worries — you have Mistero! Whether you are a local individual or international business, check us out at:

www.mistero.co

WANT TO GET EXCLUSIVE OFFERS?
FIRST-HAND NEWS? CONTEST INVITES?
RARE A. J. DARKHOLME GIVEAWAYS?

BECOME A PART OF THE DARKHOLME ELITE TODAY!

- ☑ subscribe to A. J. Darkholme's newsletter at ajdarkholme.com

- ☑ write a five-star review for Rise of the Morningstar on Amazon.com

- ☑ join the discussion at: ajdarkholme.com/riseofthemorningstar

And you can also...

FOLLOW A. J. DARKHOLME AT:

facebook.com/ajdarkholme
plus.google.com/+Ajdarkholme
@AJDarkholme

A. J. Darkholme is a Canadian author and
poet kickstarting his writing career with the
highly-anticipated "self-help fantasy" series,
The Morningstar Chronicles. He lives in
Winnipeg, Manitoba, where he works in
IT for the federal government, runs his
own creative and technology business, and
spends a lot of time thinking up new ways
to keep life interesting, one day at a time.

For more about A. J. Darkholme,
please visit www.ajdarkholme.com.